# Raines in the Day

## Gene Lee

ALL THINGS
THAT MATTER
PRESS

Raines in the Day

Copyright © 2021 by Gene Lee

ISBN 13: 9781734685596

Library of Congress Control Number: 2021934081

Cover Photos: james-wheeler-HJhGcU_IbsQ-unsplash

Cover design © by All Things That Matter Press
Published in 2021 by All Things That Matter Press

This book is dedicated to my grandfather,
Christopher Lafayette Chancey

# Acknowledgments

Many thanks to Phil and Deb Harris at All Things That Matter Press for taking me on in the first place.

And much appreciation to Lucinda Merritt for her excellent eyes and ability to correct my poor usage of the English language at times.

And a never ending gratitude to Suzanne Fox who showed me how to find the true arc in the stories.

And finally, but never least, and in fact always first, love and thanks to the two women in my life who mean the most, my wife, Donna, and my daughter, Allison.

# Prologue

Besides the boy and his grandparents, a ghost lived in that old house on the edge of the pine and saw palmetto scrub. It was true the boy had never seen the ghost. He only heard his grandmother—never his grandfather—talking to it. This usually happened late at night, often right before dawn was about to break. John Raines didn't see the ghost either or judging by his groggy comments those nights when the ghost came calling, didn't believe it to be any such thing.

Thomas Morgan hadn't thought about that ghost in a long time. Close to fifty years he figured one night on his back porch overlooking the river. The poor fishing of that day led to the realization as he was heading back to the slip of how nothing was as it once had been. The third whiskey before dinner—these things perhaps, were what had brought back that time when he lived with his grandparents on the edge of the scrub. Brought back the very first time the ghost came calling to his grandmother.

"Wake up Sadie, dammit," he'd faintly heard his grandfather one night when everyone in the house should have been asleep. "It's a dream for God's sake."

Tom had been there on his grandparents' ranch for perhaps a month, no more than two. Spring in Florida was gone, the days—and the nights—hot and humid. Now, when instead of his grandfather he heard his grandmother calling out in the night, "Please, son, don't go," he came awake fully, hot and sweating, on top of the sheets and not sure of where he was.

"Please son," Sadie Raines said again, this time much louder and carrying easily from the other side of the bathroom connecting the house's two bedrooms. "Stay with me."

"Now that's enough, hon," John Raines voice was firm, yet strangely gentle, too, it seemed to the boy. "You've got to wake up, now."

And then the boy's grandmother was sobbing. Painful racking sounds, the same as the boy had heard from his mother that day her husband was leaving. When the boy, sitting on the floor by the kitchen table, watched as she held onto his father's legs with both arms, begging him not to go.

"Oh God, John," Sadie Raines cried out through her sobs. "I wasn't sleeping, I swear. He was here. Hilton. Right here, I'm telling you."

"Our boy's gone, Sadie." And then a little harsher, "Dead and gone and you know it. Now stop this foolishness. It's killing you, hon. Killing me."

"I know, John, I know. I'm sorry, so sorry." Though she had stopped crying she still sounded weak and strained. "But he *was* here. It was no dream."

"Okay, Sadie, it's okay now. Just go back to sleep. Please. I've got a long day tomorrow and need my sleep, too."

But what scared the boy right then—more than the thought that a ghost had been in the house just on the other side of the bathroom—was that his grandfather, always so strong and in charge, sounded like the one begging now. Then it was quiet in the other room, quiet all through the house except for the calling of a whippoorwill, somewhere out in the pines, coming in the open window of the boy's room until suddenly it was morning, the day's light flooding in, so that despite himself the boy must have fallen asleep.

Over breakfast in the morning the only allusion to the disturbance of the night before was a sheepish apology from his grandmother.

"I hope you didn't hear me last night, Tom. That I didn't wake you up?"

The boy was surprised by the shy look in his grandmother's eyes, the haggard appearance of her face. Her green eyes usually flashed with a certain determination when she spoke. Sometimes that determination, when she was amused by the behavior of her husband or the boy, was replaced by a different light—one that lifted the boy's spirits when it shone on him. Now, and still unsure of his place in this new life his mother had dropped him into, the boy said nothing.

"He's a boy, Sadie," John Raines snorted behind his newspaper at the other end of the table. "They can sleep through a damn hurricane."

"Is that true, Tom?" Sadie asked again. "I wasn't a bother last night?"

"No ma'am," the boy lied. He didn't like being untruthful, but by the worried look on her face he figured it to be best he did. "Not a bit."

All the rest of that summer the ghost stayed away. When he returned, though in the fall, the night before Tom was to start the fourth grade at his new school, the ghost came back. This time with a vengeance.

The whippoorwill out in the pines had awakened the boy and he lay in the dark awhile listening to both the sad cry of the unseen bird and the lowing of cattle in the big pasture behind the house. He knew morning was a way off yet, and though nervous about his new school and what awaited him there, he still managed to fall back to sleep. He didn't stay sleeping long.

This time, instead of the sobbing pleas of his grandmother begging the ghost of her son not to go, it was the loud insistent banging of something against the wall of his grandparents' bedroom that awoke him—a loud hard banging that in the boy's half-conscious state seemed as if it would tear the house down.

"Jesus Christ, Sadie," his grandfather yelled out above the banging. "Stop it! Stop it right now."

Suddenly it was very quiet in the house—the boy wondering, if his grandfather managed to scare the ghost away. But it was only quiet for a moment, and then the boy heard his grandmother crying in the other room

"Oh God, John, he was so angry. So angry."

"It's okay now, honey. You're awake—the dream's over. We'll all be okay in the morning. I promise."

As he drifted back to sleep to the sound of his grandmother softly crying in the other room, the boy hoped what his grandfather had just said would be true. His last conscious thought before sleep came to him fully was a comforting one—even if he felt a little guilty about it. Yet the fact of the matter was that he wasn't the only one afraid, in what sometimes could be at a very lonely place for him

\*\*\*

Had the boy ever been asked he would have said his grandmother's ghost. Besides that, he led a normal life. He went to school, did his homework at night, had chores to do when he came home from school. The chores involved keeping his room straight, bed made, clothes put away, feed the two dogs in their kennels, and whatever yard work his grandfather or grandmother asked him to do. His grandfather got him atop a horse almost from the time he arrived at the ranch so when he was older the boy helped with Pop, Cecil, the ranch foreman, and the other cowhands, mending fence line and bringing in the beeves when it was dipping time.

During the school year he had friends there, though not ones he could play with afterwards, other than at recess or while waiting on the bus in the afternoon that took them to their respective homes. These homes, for the most part, were farms and other ranches west of Jupiter. His grandmother kept his reddish-blond hair cut short and neat, the same pretty much as the other boys at school. Like them, he wore blue jeans, a white, button down short sleeved shirt and Keds sneakers. They played and talked sports at recess, mainly baseball and basketball, games they could play on the rough diamond and basketball court behind the school. The boy enjoyed playing these games, even if he wasn't as good at them as some of the boys. That being the case, he *was* good enough to avoid being picked last for teams, a situation he felt counted for something.

All in all Tom Morgan never felt different, or out of place, with the other kids at school. After a while, though, how long a while he couldn't pinpoint, he quit feeling out of place at his new home. It was only later, when he was much older with a family and life of his own, when he had finally managed to put away the hurt and anger he felt towards his parents who he never saw again after that May night in 1951, that he was able to see how he had had a great childhood. Something, at the time he was living it, he couldn't see.

For the boy had questions. Many of them, in fact, and all of them concerning who he really was. Who his family really was—both his absent mom and dad, and these grandparents, who through no choice of his own, he had come to live with.

A glimpse of an answer to all of this came the night when he first heard his grandmother talking to her ghost. When she told her husband that Hilton had been there. John and Sadie Raines' son. His uncle. Dead and gone. Killed in a war, that like his uncle, the boy knew nothing about.

So, if that night a window into all that the boy knew nothing about had been cracked open, it wasn't until seven years later this window was cracked open again. No, instead of being cracked, that window was thrown wide open.

***

The visitations in the night to Sadie Raines by her dead son tapered off over the years. By the spring of 1958, when the boy was pushing fifteen and a sophomore in high school, it had been two years, if not longer, since his last appearance. But in early March of that year the ghost came back. By the end of the month these visits totaled five—five more times than John Raines would have liked, as the boy heard him say to his wife one morning after yet another episode.

"This has got to stop, Sadie. No good comes from these dreams of yours."

"Jesus. John, you act as if they were something I could control."

The boy had just come out of his bedroom, dressed for school, wanting only to eat his breakfast and be on his way—away from the crying, screaming and headboard banging against the wall the night before. A ruckus even John Raines's soothing voice hadn't been able to put an end to.

Now the boy could see the toll this recent visitation had taken on his grandmother. She was sitting with her husband at the big table in the dining room, her face worn and red from crying, the gray hair she usually wore in a neat bun atop her head, hanging down around her cheeks and shoulders. This was bad enough—but even more shocking to the boy was the fact she had used the word, "Jesus" in a context that had nothing to do with the bible she kept on the nightstand by her bed.

"Maybe once the day's come and gone," John Raines was saying as the boy sat down at the table. He stopped for a second, looking at the boy as if he were wondering he should continue, then went on. "Maybe then these crazy dreams will stop, and you can get some sleep at night." And with that tight grin on his face, said next, "Maybe we can all get some sleep."

"I hope so, John," Sadie said, managing a tight smile of her own as she turned to the boy. "You don't mind do you Tom, if your grandfather runs you up to the bus stop this morning? I didn't sleep well last night—as I'm sure you know." The strained laugh she followed this with had nothing of fun in it that the boy could hear.

"No ma'am," he said. "I don't mind at all."

"Then get your breakfast, son, and let's get a move on here." John Raines pushed back from the table, stood up, and adjusted the brim of his hat. "You've got school and I've got work to do."

"Yes indeed," Sadie agreed. "God knows I've plenty around here to keep me busy. You men get on now."

It wasn't mentioned by any of them at the breakfast table that morning, but the boy could see it was so. The three of them just wanted to be out of there. Out into the light of the day and away from the house. Away from the ghost—or perhaps just a bad dream as John Raines insisted that had rattled them so in the night.

Two weeks to the day, April 14th on a Wednesday morning, John Raines left to go down to Fort Lauderdale.

"Damn, but I don't want to go, hon," Raines said to his wife at the front door. The boy was on the porch putting on his shoes, getting ready so his grandfather could drop him at the bus stop on his way out. "I'd rather stay here with you and the boy. Let us remember in our way. With none of that grave site visitation and talking about how it might have been." The old man's voice rose then. "Damn, but I don't go in for that—just wasn't raised that way. We left our dead where they were and tried to get on with it. Goddamn it all."

"She asked you to come, John. It must mean a lot to her," Sadie said in that soothing tone she used the boy was familiar with from when something wasn't going the way her husband—or for that matter, the boy—wished it to. "She *is* your daughter-in-law. The boy, our grandson. God knows I'd go but someone's got to be here with Tom"

The boy didn't think so and felt that at fifteen he was quite able to manage on his own. Judging by the way she'd said it, he thought as well that she really didn't want to go with her husband anyway. But seeing the look on his grandmother's face he knew better than to say so.

"Just damn it all." Raines picked up the little duffel bag he put down by the door before saying his goodbyes to his wife. "One year—ten years—what's it matter? He's dead. Can't we just leave it at that?"

He didn't wait for an answer—was down the front steps and in his car, cranking the engine over and about to back out of the driveway.

"Wait, John," Sadie called out. And to the boy, "Hurry up, Tom The mood he's in he's forgotten you're going with him."

Come that Friday afternoon, just as dusk was falling, John Raines wheeled his Plymouth back into the dirt drive in front of the house and came to a stop. The boy was sitting out on the porch with a soda and the latest issue of the *Saturday Evening Post* when his grandfather returned. He didn't know much about drunken men, having seen only two in his life up to then. The first had been his father, that day seven years back when he had walked out of the boy's life. The other one had been three years ago, a cowhand that worked for John Raines. He showed up at the house one night when they had just finished dinner. The cowhand was a younger man, probably in his mid-twenties who the boy recognized from the fall round-up just concluded.

That night, though, this cowhand pulled up in his beat-up pickup and standing half in and half out of the truck called out to the house in a loud voice for his, "Hard-earned goddamn you old man back pay."

John Raines stood up from the table and taking the old double-barreled shotgun from the rack on the wall, went out on the front steps. The boy stood up from the table as well and followed his grandfather, despite his grandmother's pleas not to.

"You might have earned those wages, Luke, it's true," John Raines said once he was out of the house. He held the shotgun loosely in one hand by his waist, the boy just behind him and hoping to see a good old-fashioned shootout right there in his own front yard. "But you owe them to me, now. After running my cattle truck, all drunk up and fool of foolishness, into the ditch and tearing up the front end the way you did. Yes sir, I'd say it was you who owed me. Now here you are, drunk again by the looks of it."

"I *am* drunk," the cowhand said as he stepped away from his truck and staggered up towards the steps. "And Goddamn I guess I'll just have to take it out of your hide."

The roar of the 12 gauge in the night stopped the man, who, suddenly didn't seem so drunk to the boy, in his tracks.

"There's your warning, Luke," John Raines said. "The only one you get. I don't see how I can hardly miss at this range. But you're welcome to keep coming and find out for your own self."

That was the end of it. The cowhand backed up to his truck, managed to get inside, and once the engine was running, roared out of the drive. They could hear him cursing out the window as he drove away, "Goddamn you Raines! I'll get my money one way or the other. You Goddamned old man."

John Raines fired the second barrel of the shotgun after the truck, then turned to go back inside the house. "Empty threats," the boy heard his grandfather say softly. "Nothing but empty threats." He stopped, one hand resting on the open door, that tight grin cracking his lips as he looked at the boy—looked as if he had just realized his grandson was there. That he had been there the whole time. "Well now, Tom," Raines said. "That was some fun for a Saturday night, wasn't it?"

"Yes sir, it was."

"I'm glad I didn't have to shoot him" He broke the barrel of the gun and pulled the two empty shells out, cradling them in the palm of his hand for a minute; looking at them as if they held some mystery that he needed to know. "If I'd had to, it would have been one of his knees. Ol' Luke there, is going to have a hard enough time finding work around here as it is. After tonight he will. With a ruined knee, it'd be damn near impossible, wouldn't you say?"

"I imagine you're right, Pop," he answered as he caught the spent shells his grandfather tossed to him

That had been the last drunken man Tom had witnessed. Until now, when his grandfather slowly got out of the Plymouth, made an attempt to arrange the Stetson on his head just the way he liked it, and then walked slowly and carefully up toward the house. John Raines certainly looked drunk to the boy—especially when he came up the front steps, opened the screen door, and came into the soft light of the porch. The Western cut suit, so clean and sharply pressed when his grandfather had left, hung disheveled on his lean frame, jacket un-buttoned and tilted to one side, the gray pants wrinkled and bunched up as if he might have slept in them. He'd been wearing a black string tie when he left for Lauderdale, but it was nowhere in sight now, and the white-pearl shirt visible with the jacket open like that, was stained with faint brown streaks. Worse, this shirt was spotted with what looked like burn holes from the Pall Malls his grandfather smoked.

The boy's suspicions were made real when his grandfather leaned over to shake his hand. "Evening, Tom," he said, the sour smell of recently consumed bourbon wafting out of his mouth to envelop the boy where he sat. "You ahright?" But before the boy could answer, he pushed on through the open front door.

"How'd it go, John?" his grandmother was asking then from inside—followed quickly enough by, "Good lord, John, look at you."

"I plead the fifth," John Raines said, his voice thick and unsteady in a way the boy had never heard before. "Just the fifth, Your Honor. Several of them in fact."

His grandfather's cackling laugh at that moment, like the whiskey heavy voice, was another thing the boy couldn't place in connection with the man. The slamming of the door into his grandparents' bedroom put an end to the drunken cackling.

When the boy finally went inside, he found his grandmother in front of the bedroom door, faded apron on, a spatula in one hand, and staring at the closed door as if she could see right through it. There was a thud inside the bedroom of what must have been John Raines's boots hitting the floor, silence, then the sound of heavy snoring.

His grandmother turned away from the door, saw the boy standing in the doorway. "Dinner's ready, Tom," she told him "We'd better sit down and eat it before it gets cold."

The boy would not have been surprised if the ghost had shown up that night. What he heard instead, coming from his grandparents' bedroom in the small hours of the morning, was scarier than any ghost, though. It was the sound of crying. And not from his grandmother, either.

***

Goddamn but he didn't like dwelling on the past. But the evening, the whiskey and, his last doctor's visit two days ago, had made him maudlin. With his evening's allotment of whiskey done—an allotment Thomas Morgan reminded himself he had exceeded—he sat now at the dining table with a cup of coffee. Beyond the big bay window, he could see how the day had gone completely dark, the lights of houses on the far shore of the river just little blips in the night.

Why bring up all that past now, he wondered. It had been only a simple thought on the quality of the fishing lately that had brought it on. Maybe it was true—what Faulkner had said once. That the past wasn't even past. And try as he might to forget, it was with him now. And in spades.

How long ago had that night been when his grandfather came home drunk, went to bed, and then woke the boy up with the sound of his lonely crying? Morgan was sixty-two now—had been fifteen then, best he could recall. Forty-five years? No, his math was off. Forty-seven years. Both his grandparents were dead now. Long dead. John Raines four years after that night, a fluke accident the cause and that Morgan had been witness to. Sadie Raines followed him to the grave but took her time about it. Twenty years later? That seemed right to him, now. It had been not long after she had called to tell him that his mother had passed. Her words, not his. His mother had died. An accident, too, on a lonely road in Mississippi. One that only she and a drunk redneck in a pickup truck were driving on. How long had Sadie lasted after that? A month. She had called him again, this time from a hospital bed in Jupiter, giving him just enough time to make the trip down from Quay Dock and be at her side when she slipped away.

And then they were all gone. His mother, his father, dead three years before his ex-wife died of a heart attack. With both his parents and grandparents gone that left just Thomas. And a cousin, Emmitt, his Uncle Hilton's son who Thomas knew from occasional visits to the ranch when they both were boys. A cousin Morgan had lost track of over the years. Who on the few occasions he had thought that, Hey, maybe I should try to look him up, had decided instead, Why bother? He had nothing to say to him It was for the best this way.

This had been his family. At least the small one he'd been a part of until he went off as a young man and started one of his own. A family, the Raines, and that even living with them as he had—growing up with them, growing up *because* of them—he'd known so very little about until the morning after his grandfather had come home drunk. On that morning, when Tom came out of his bedroom, he found his grandmother sitting alone at the dining table, the rest of the house empty—very empty of John Raines's presence, Sadie Raines had looked up at the boy and waved him over.

"Sit with me awhile, Tom," she said. Her voice was weary and uncertain, like it was on those mornings after her ghost came to visit. "There are some things I'd like to talk to you about. About your grandfather. And about me." Perhaps because of the look he knew was on his face, her voice grew stronger—grew more like what he was accustomed to hearing from her. "Nothing to be worried about, Tom, nothing like that at all. Just some of what I know, from being there. And some of what I was told. This is what I would like to talk about."

He had sat. And listened. And could still remember, after all these years.

# PART ONE

War was coming. In agreement with the president and outraged as well by the lurid tales of fresh German barbarities revealed almost daily in the *Fort Myers Press*, John Raines decided he had to do what was right. Not only right but demanded of every red-blooded American male of fighting age. His law career, working beside his brother in the tiny office on Second Street, could wait. It would still be there for him when he returned from Saving the World for Democracy—as return Raines was certain he would.

Differences, both physical and in outlook on life, existed between the two brothers. At five-feet eight, John was an inch or so taller than RL. He was leaner, too, with a serious face and stark, grey eyes. His head of dark black hair was just beginning to recede a little from his forehead. Eventually—a fact he had come to accept—chances were good he would be like his father: bald on top with lines of thin hair running along both sides. As for life and what it had to offer, John was more than willing to work for what he needed, a successful career, a family, and all the comforts this family would require. Even if sometimes, usually at night as he lay in bed, he wondered if there might be more to living than just that.

RL, on the other hand, was five years older and considerably stouter than his brother. His face was round and florid, the black hair, once like his brother's, gone except for a few long strands on the side that he combed over the top and held in place with hair oil. Years of city living, and drink had made him soft, the tough farmer's frame of his youth already gone by the time John arrived in Fort Myers seven years back. As far as John could tell, what RL wanted out of life was more. More money, more power, more of the status these two things would bring. Had he learned this from his association with Judge Landry over the years? John Raines believed that to be the case.

It was because of this wanting John was certain, that RL didn't see his decision about joining the Army in the same light as he did

"For God's sake, John," he blurted out when informed of his brother's plan to go to Jacksonville and enlist. "Why the hell would you do such a damn fool thing?" RL's normally florid face seemed to turn an even brighter shade of red. "Have you lost your mind? You can't leave now. Not when your future holds such promise for you here. Don't you remember what the judge told us? About all the money to be made?"

These were hard questions for John to answer. It was true his future in Fort Myers was looking up. With his new status as a bona fide attorney at law, RL was talking of making his practice a partnership. RL was to be head partner with John the junior. Making this proposition even more enticing than it already was, Judge Landry—RL's friend and mentor—had assured the two brothers of sending a lot of work their way. "Lucrative work," as the judge had put it. Not only that, but a certain young lady had caught John Raines's eye. Vera Robinson, daughter, and granddaughter of two of the most leading citizens of the community. So yes, there was much for him to be leaving behind if he did go off to war. And he told his brother as much.

"But even looking at all that, I can't help it. I have to do my part."

"Then all I'll ask of you, John," RL replied. "Is that you think about it for a bit. And don't go rushing off like some dumb farm kid who doesn't know any life better than the lower forty and thinks war will be a grand adventure. Just think about it."

"I will." And after a long minute, "If only because you ask me to and I respect you, RL. I don't know that it will change anything. But I *will* think about it. I promise you I won't go off half-cocked."

"Thank you." RL took another sip of the bourbon they'd been enjoying in the office after a good day of work. The red in his face had receded some and he looked to be more himself—looked to be contemplating something. As it turned out was the case. "Maybe I'll have a little talk with the judge tomorrow. Get his opinion on this foolishness my eager younger brother is considering."

The judge—Judge Horace Landry—was a force to be reckoned with, one that one took lightly at their own risk. John Raines knew this well enough. Landry had come to Florida, law degree in hand, from New York when he was thirty-six years old. A quarter of a century later not only was Horace Landry a judge, but the owner of twenty thousand acres of prime pine woods, good grazing land, and a herd of cattle that numbered in the thousands.

It was this land, and head of cattle, that RL Raines wound up riding herd on after answering an ad in the *Fort Myers Press* seeking a sturdy young man, not afraid of hard work, and looking to make a future for himself. RL was indeed sturdy and looking to make a future for himself. He hadn't worked for the judge and his wife for more than two years when the judge recognized there was more to RL than appeared at first. Landry took him under his wing, tutoring him at night with the same Blackstone John Raines ended up studying, and helped him to pass the bar. It didn't hurt RL's prospects that the judge and his wife had a daughter. If the judge never said as much in words, it was more than evident after a while that Horace Landry looked at RL as more than just a fellow who worked for him

By the time John Raines left his father's farm in Georgia and came to Fort Myers the judge was retired, and RL no longer worked the judge's cattle. Instead, he was the leading attorney in Fort Myers. Not only that, but he was also engaged to the judge's daughter, Ellen. Beyond his upcoming marriage, it seemed that the next step in RL's bright future was to occupy the office of Mayor of Fort Myers—a position the judge assured him was RL's for the taking.

"But it's time we got started," the judge said to RL and John Raines one night. It was a few weeks after John had passed the bar, the President hadn't declared war yet, and the three of them were relaxing in the law office in the front room of RL's house with a bottle of well aged Scotch the judge had brought. The local elections in 1918 were right around the corner, the judge continued. "Now I don't see you winning the first time you run. No sir, I don't. But you won't act that way while you're campaigning."

"If you don't see me winning, sir," RL said as he poured them all another shot. "Then why invest the time and money. Why not wait until 1922?"

"We've got to get your name and face out there, son. Let the folks around here see you as more than just a good lawyer. But a man with a vision, a plan for this fine city we live in. War's coming surer than hell. And when it's over the folks running this city now will be either dead, or at the least, much older. After a war people are going to be weary. And maybe just a little afraid. They're going to want something new, something living and exciting, something they feel they can grow with. Something to make them believe life is worth living for, striving for once again. And you, RL Raines, will be the shining new face offering them just that. But we've got to start putting it out there now."

"It all sounds fine and dandy, Judge," RL said as he leaned back in his swivel chair and contemplated the musky liquor in his shot glass. "But I don't exactly have that plan, or vision, you're talking about. War coming or no."

"You don't worry about that, RL. Don't worry about that at all. When the time comes, I'll make damn sure you do!"

For his part, John Raines offered nothing to this conversation—was perfectly content to listen to, and enjoy, both the talk and the judge's Scotch. But he marveled at what was unfolding for his older brother, couldn't help but marvel at what had already unfolded in the twelve short years since the day RL left home. On that day—a hot, miserable one in the middle of August—RL, seventeen, fought their Pop to a draw in the mean tobacco field outside of Pendleton where the Raines family scratched a living out of the red Georgia clay. When the fighting was over, both man and boy blooded and weary, Pop shook RL's hand, gave him five dollars and the mule, and RL rode off. To his destiny, John thought now as he listened to his brother and the judge make plans. God, but I hope something to the like happens for me, he thought.

But what the judge had to say concerning John Raines and his plans—which pretty much echoed what RL believed—held no sway with him

"I'm sorry RL," Raines told his brother on the Monday morning a few days after promising not to go off to war half-cocked. A busy week lay ahead of them and John was in the middle of preparing a brief RL needed to give the court before noon that day. As usual for a Monday morning, RL came in late. The day before he had been drinking and playing cards with some less reputable friends of his outside of the city limits, so Raines wasn't surprised he was late. Some Mondays after cards RL didn't bother to come in all.

But this morning here he was, and without even an acknowledgment that John was buried in the brief, demanded his brother's answer regarding the war.

"Like you asked me to, I've thought long and hard on it." John continued. "But I've made up mind and I'm going. It seems the right thing to do."

"Seems like a jackass thing to do, if you ask me," RL said as he sat down behind his desk and shuffled some papers around. "But the judge's offer still stands, concerning the draft when it comes. As both he and I are certain it will. Promise me at least you'll wait until then. Maybe this whole war situation will have blown over by then."

"It looks like I'm the one making all the promises around here, lately." John meant it as a joke but to his surprise RL didn't see it that way.

"Goddammit Johnny!" He stood up suddenly from his desk, his face red and swollen. "Haven't I promised you a partnership with me? Promised you a chance to make damn good money and a life for yourself? And for Vera, if she'll have you. Though damned if I can see why she would. And what about me? Don't you think I might want my little brother here with me? Safe and sound? And not off in some foreign country getting his fool head shot off?"

"All right, all right. Settle down, RL. Before you give yourself a heart attack." This was no joke on John's part. For RL's face looked fit to burst with his anger—anger coupled with the hard shine he had consumed while playing cards the day before could kill a healthier man than his brother. "I promise I'll wait until after the draft comes. If it does. Will that make you happy?"

"Yes." As sudden as he had risen up from behind the walnut desk, RL sat down, the redness draining from his face as he did. "Though not as happy as I'll be if I can get that brief to the courthouse on time."

"You will dear brother. If you leave me to it in peace."

"Peace it is," RL said. It was quiet in the office then—except for the sound of the bottom right drawer of RL's desk. Inside the drawer was RL's silver bourbon flask. John Raines pretended to ignore that sound and busied himself with the brief he'd promised to finish.

***

The first draft lottery was to be held on July 21st of that year. This gave Raines almost three full months to get his affairs in order. He realized his promise to RL to wait until after the first draft made little sense. Called up on that day or not he was going into the army. If RL hoped that somehow between now and then he might change his mind—if this made his brother feel better—then so be it.

The good thing about waiting until then—and perhaps what RL had intended all along—was that the law office was very busy at the time. The judge and his business partners were in the middle of acquiring a large tract of land between Fort Myers and Punta Rassa. Their intention was to develop a brand-new town. Not just a town, though that would be good to do to start with, the judge said. But a shiny new city. One smack dab on the best coast in Florida. Cool Breeze was the proposed name for the new community, a name Raines thought misleading at best. Anyone familiar with the southwest coast of the state knew cool breezes were limited to a very small part of the year—that for most of it they were nothing but hot and humid. Still, Cool Breeze was a damn sight better name than the judge's first one: Landryville.

"Why not?' the judge demanded when RL raised an objection. "Ol' Brooks got a city named after himself. And Baron Collier's fixing to get his own county."

"Brooksville isn't much of a city, Judge," John jumped in. "And the state hasn't given in to Collier yet. Besides, Landryville doesn't roll off the tongue quite like those others."

"I suppose you're right," the judge reluctantly agreed. "That's what the others said when I brought it up. Galls me to admit they're right. Especially when they're just a bunch of peckerwoods with money."

In the end Cool Breeze won the day, with both Raines and RL glad they'd been able to overrule the judge, a rare feat.

So, with title searches, drafting of deeds, writing proposals, along with the normal run of briefs and court appearances concerning the various civil suits and small claims the two brothers handled, John Raines was indeed busy and glad for it. At night, with the day's work done he liked to sit on the small porch on the front of the house with a glass of bourbon and water, watching the last of the shopkeepers in town down the block close and shutter their business and begin their way home. As peaceful and satisfying as those moments were, Raines couldn't help but ponder what came next in his life. The army, a complete unknown. And war, the biggest unknown of them all. But if this pondering caused him an amount of nervousness—like when he had taken the bar exam—he was still confidant he'd succeed.

Not that it was all work. Come Friday night, weather permitting, the local band played at the pavilion at the end of Main Street. John and RL were in the habit of joining in with the rest of the town's people, both young and old alike, in strolling out after supper to take in the music. With Florida spring on the verge of summer, the nights were warm and mild; the breezes off the Gulf twenty miles away, just cool enough to offer relief. Making sure he wore his best suit, Raines on these Friday nights was most happy to be away from the office, having spent most of the week bent over at his desk poring over legal papers. While his brother sipped discretely from his flask and tapped his toes to the music, Raines kept one eye busy scanning the crowd, hoping to see Vera coming down the street.

Vera Robinson, tall, with a mass of blonde curly hair flowing down along her face and shoulders that highlighted her blue eyes, was hard to miss, no matter the crowd. Something about the way she moved, her regal bearing acquired in the school for girls she attended in what she called her "formative years," made her stand out. The fact that she was usually in the company of Ellen Landry, some four inches shorter, with blonde hair as well, though nowhere near as opulent as Vera's, and whose looks could only be considered plain at best—helped the illusion Vera created of being the only one around.

Ellen had been the one to bring Vera into Raines' life. This was on a Saturday afternoon right before Christmas of the previous year. Thanksgiving at the judge's house, when dinner was over RL had stood up from the table to announce he had asked Ellen to marry him and she'd said yes. While the others were congratulating the happy couple, John had stayed politely silent. Truth be told, he felt a little sorry for Ellen. He liked her very much and this was the problem. He was pretty sure marrying Ellen was simply a means to an end for RL. He based this belief on how RL treated her—with courtesy and kindness certainly, but always with an underlying indifference that maybe only John and perhaps her father could see, judging by the tight smile on his lips as he clapped along with the rest of those seated at his table that night.

After everyone left the table, as they made their way out to the front veranda with brandy and cigars, RL held John back, saying softly in his ear, "You're next, boy. Just wait and see."

"I seriously doubt that, brother of mine," John said and left it at that.

Yet three weeks later, while waiting for the annual Christmas parade and standing with RL on the sidewalk outside of the courthouse, Ellen came up the street, with her, another girl who John had seen before but never imagined actually talking to. Introductions were made, and though John was awkward at first, almost to embarrassment, both Ellen and Vera were able to smooth out the rough edges and finally put him at ease. Not that he could ever be fully at ease in her company—wondering as he constantly did at what a beauty such as her saw in him

As to what RL had meant at Thanksgiving? His possible part in who Ellen brought with her to the Christmas Parade? The nod and sly wink his brother exchanged with Ellen when he thought John wasn't looking, answered these questions to the full.

The next time he saw Vera was at the Pavilion on a Friday night two days after Christmas. Again, both RL and Ellen were there, the four of them acting as if this were something they had been doing for a long time. After that night, Fridays at the pavilion became a routine. On Sunday afternoons—when RL wasn't busy playing cards and getting drunk—the two couples met downtown in front of the hardware store. From there it was a short stroll to the wharf along the Caloosahatchee River, which served Fort Myers as a promenade. Depending on what clients had paid their legal fees—or how much RL may have won or lost at cards—John and RL would take the girls to lunch at the Windemere Hotel, *the* best hotel and restaurant in Fort Myers as everyone knew. If short of funds the men would arrange the afternoon stroll for later in the day, after lunchtime, and then treat the girls to a lemon ice from the little stand at the end of the wharf. Lemon ice in hand or not, RL always had one hand free to slip his flask out of his back pocket when necessary.

By the time war was declared John felt free enough with Vera to tell her his plans. After all, they had reached a stage in their relationship where they held hands at the Friday night concerts, and as they walked along the wharf on Sundays. They even took to kissing one another goodbye after these outings, the first few times chastely enough on the cheeks. Until one night after he'd walked her home, instead of her cheek she offered him her lips. The next time they kissed like this she shocked him more than a little by slipping the tip of her tongue into his mouth, laughing when he pulled back.

She surprised him again, when after explaining how he was going to join up she said immediately, "Of course you will." After squeezing his hand softly—a squeeze made even softer through the white kid gloves she wore that afternoon. She added, "I don't *want* you to go. As I know both your brother and the judge don't. And have told you so on more than one occasion, I'm sure."

Her laugh right then, soft and easy is what pushed his feelings for her over the edge and into love.

"But I would not suppose it upon myself to tell you that," she continued.

"Thank you for that, Vera. And you are very right about RL and the judge. They've expressed their opinion so many times I'm sick of hearing it."

"I just want you to come back safe." She hesitated a minute before adding, "John."

"To you?"

"Yes." And perhaps seeing what he knew was in his eyes, she said quickly, "But don't think that gives you leeway to ask me to marry you right now. I won't be a war bride for any man. Not even you, John Raines. It will be unsettling enough as it is, with you off somewhere overseas and I not knowing from one day to the next if you're alive or dead."

"When I come back then?"

"We'll have to see where we stand with another then. When that day comes."

This was good enough for him—more than good enough—enough even, that added to the fact he was in love with her, he had a very difficult time falling asleep that night.

***

If John Raines knew little about what the future held for him, he knew even less about women—he was twenty-four and Vera was the first woman he had ever kissed.

RL, on the other hand, certainly seemed to have an eye for the ladies, would embarrass John at times when they came upon a good-looking woman on the streets or elsewhere. After a polite tip of the hat, once the lady in question was safely out of ear shot, RL's comments had nothing to do with what a nice woman she was, or something along those lines. They were usually how he wouldn't mind knowing her "in the Biblical way." Having grown up on a farm John understood the rudiments of sex and the procreation act. He was aware, as well, that people didn't always engage in that act just to have children—that there were women and men, too, in the world who were known as "fallen," or of "loose morals."

Still, it bothered him to hear RL say such a thing—reminded him of that awkward afternoon under the oak trees when Leila asked if he wanted to touch her and not knowing if he did or didn't, he'd pretty much run away.

Once, after leaving the hardware store where they had encountered the young, pretty wife of a teller at the First National bank who John had to do business with every Friday, RL made his usual comments about what he would like to do with her, given the opportunity.

"Good lord, RL," John said, the blood rushing to his face. "Have you ever once given thought to just how rude it is to talk about a woman in that way?"

"Why no, Johnny," RL answered. "I haven't." And then seeing the look on his face, RL asked a question of his own. "Jesus, Johnny, are you still a virgin?"

"I'm not sure that's any of your concern, RL."

"Well now, I think it is, Johnny boy." With a rough laugh RL added, "So much so that we're going to have to do something about this sorry state of affairs. And soon." And seeing the concerned look on John's face, RL reassured him "Don't worry about a thing, brother. You just leave it to good ol' RL."

If he hadn't met Vera Robinson by the time RL got around to taking care of his "sorry state of affairs" John might have enjoyed the loss of his virginity more than he did. The two brothers had to go up to Tampa in mid-February on a legal matter. The judge had filed a complaint against a group of investors trying to buy the same parcel of land he needed for his new development. "Goddamn carpetbaggers," the judge had deemed this group. "That's all they are, goddamn their souls to the greedy hell they so richly deserve. I'm depending on you boys, now, to stop 'em in their tracks. You and the Honorable Judge Carson that is. He should smile very favorably on our little problem—'specially once he opens that envelope you'll be bringing along."

Judge Carson did exactly that, Judge Landry prevailed, and to celebrate their success in court, RL took John to dinner at a Cuban place he knew of in Ybor City.

"Good food, a little Cuban rum, and for afterwards, one of their finest cigars," RL told him in the taxi. "Just what we need after a day such as this, little brother."

John was on board for all of that—his reservations came about at the end of the meal when RL suggested they stop in at one more little place he knew of. "For a nightcap, Johnny boy," RL said. "And perhaps the pleasure of a woman's company. If we're lucky."

John was pretty certain luck would have nothing to do with it as long as they had cash with them. His assumption was proved true when the taxi let them out in front of an aging, nondescript two-story house on the outskirts of Ybor City. A red light above the door shone softly in the darkness of the winter evening. Other houses, much the same as the one the brothers were about to enter, stood on both sides of the street, most of them adorned with the same kind of welcoming red light. If he didn't know much about the ways of the world, even at that age, John Raines was aware what the red lights above the doors of these houses signified.

"I don't know about this, RL, John said as his brother rang the bell. "I don't think Vera would look kindly on this."

"Vera's not here, Johnny. Never has to know you and I are. Therefore, she won't be capable of forming an opinion one way or the other as to the merits of the adventure we are about to embark upon. Besides, the thought of the both of you being virgins on your wedding night is ludicrous, as far as I'm concerned. I only have your best interests in mind, little brother."

"We haven't discussed marriage."

"Oh, you will, little brother," RL grunted. "It's only a question of time. And as I was saying, you both can't be virgins when you retire upon the sacred marriage bed. Since we can rest assured that Miss Robinson is as virginal as the day is long, that leaves it up to you. Now c'mon."

Inside the house, a colored man in white livery opened the door and showed them in, the light wasn't much brighter than what the red light outside offered. Colored globe lamps placed on little round tables at various spots along the walls, with plump armchairs positioned on both sides of these tables provided the only illumination. This soft incandescence allowed John to see RL's face on the other side of the round table, once the doorman sat them, more as a soft shadow than anything else. If his face hadn't been so red—with the rum and the pending excitement of what was to come, John figured—he might not have even recognized his brother.

From somewhere in the room, bigger and more cavernous than the outside led him to believe possible, John could hear the tinkling sound of a player piano, the tune one of those "Dixieland Jazz" songs that were all the rage. They hadn't sat for long when a middle-aged woman in a voluminous dress of some sort, appeared in front of them. John supposed she was middle aged—the heavy rouge on her cheeks, the very black mascara, along with the bright red lipstick on her mouth, made it hard to tell. She was white, he guessed, but with the makeup and the soft light that might not have been the case at all.

"You gentlemen comfortable enough? Would you like something to drink, a cocktail perhaps, or a cold beer?"

Her voice, the polite, perfect way of speech, with no accent of any kind, told John she was indeed white. Without the gaudy dress, the heavy makeup, the place they were in, she could have been just another lady of indeterminate age found on the streets of Tampa, or Fort Myers, for that matter, at any given time of day.

"Your finest rum," RL answered her, "will be just the thing, Madam."

"Our house rum is distilled right here in Ybor City, sir. Will that be suitable?"

"More than suitable, my dear lady. Please."

"And girls?"

"We damn sure didn't come here for boys, Madam." RL's loud, guttural laugh seemed perfectly suited to the house they were in, John thought, even if for some reason he found it crude and a little disturbing.

"Then girls it is, gentlemen. Enjoy your evening with us and if you need anything at all, and I mean anything—within the law, of course," at which she winked, a tight smile just breaking those red lips of hers, "just ask."

She waved a hand behind her, and just like that, two girls appeared at their sides—out of nowhere it seemed to John. Then the Madam was gone, another colored man in similar livery, brought their drinks, bowed politely, and left them to their own devices. John almost wished he hadn't.

Young, around his age John thought, the girls were Cuban, light skinned, both of them with rich black hair and very dark eyes. They were dressed in thin, frilly, shifts, the girl with John's a pale green, the girl with RL in a bright red one. The perfume they wore was strong, a bit cloying for John, and he was glad RL lit up a cigar right then. The rich smoke helped to mask the scent.

"Yes sir, little brother," RL said as the girl sat in his lap and began running her fingers through his thinning hair. "Now this is what I call living. Wouldn't you say?" And then he kissed the girl, a long lingering one that made the girl laugh.

"It's something different, I'll give you that." Suddenly, the other girl was in *his* lap, her face close to his. He could feel her body settle into his, the softness of her plump bottom, obviously naked beneath the thin shift, getting his complete attention.

"You like Dalila, señor?" She didn't wait for John to answer, though. Instead, she ran her tongue along the bottom of his ear and down his cheek, an act—if that were possible—even lewder than the kiss his brother had bestowed on the girl sitting with him "Maybe when you finish your drink you like to take me upstairs, yes?"

"It's a very pretty name," he told her, which made her smile—a pretty smile, too, he thought, her white teeth sparkling in the soft light not what he imagined they would be. Then to be polite, "My name is John."

"She doesn't care about your name, little brother." RL laughed, one hand fondling his girl's breast while the other raised his drink to his mouth. "She's only interested in how much money's in your wallet."

"Don't listen to him, señor. Is not true." As if to prove she meant this she moved her bottom against his lap. "I like your name very much. It's distinguished. Like you a very important man. Perhaps a senator. Or president. A president who like to take Dalila upstairs, yes?"

Senator, president, distinguished name, or not, something about the way she moved in his lap decided things for John. Despite his earlier doubts about this venture of RL's he very much so wanted to take her upstairs—right then and there.

"Our new President seems to be in a hurry," RL laughed when John stood up, barely giving the girl in his lap time to adjust to his sudden move. "But that's okay, Johnny, quite okay. Just not too much of a hurry when you get up there."

RL's laughter was smothered by his girl's lips—but when John looked back as he and Dalila mounted the stairs, he could see RL on his feet, as well, holding her by the hand and following after them

Once inside Dalila's room she lay back on the bed. Other than a small dresser with mirror and chair pushed up against one wall, the bed was the only furniture in the room A small lamp on a bedside table provided light, though not any more than the ones downstairs. The green shift she wore rode up towards her waist, exposing her plump thighs, and just a hint of the dark vee between her legs.

"Take your clothes off, President Johnny," she said, patting the bed with one hand, "and come lay with me."

Her voice was thick and husky, unlike downstairs, an act he was willing to bet. Still, he hesitated, until she smiled and said, "Come, please." He hung his jacket and shirt on the chair by the dresser, turning away from her as he pulled his pants off. Out of modesty, or embarrassment, he wasn't sure. When he turned back to the bed, still in his underwear, his hardness very evident—which this time did cause him to be embarrassed—he saw that she had taken off her shift, lying naked on top of the sheets with just a smile.

"Take these off, too, señor," she laughed as he stood by the bed. Running her hand along his length hidden by the cloth, she added, "You don't need them"

When he did, still standing in front of her, she rose up on her knees and suddenly took him into her mouth.

"Too much, yes?" she laughed when he jumped back. She pulled him down on the bed beside her. "We just fuck, okay?"

Though he didn't think about Vera at all while he was thrusting into Dalila, he did afterwards. With guilt tasting strong in his mouth, he dressed and hurried down the stairs after giving Dalila the five dollars she requested when they were done. This might have been what brought on the guilt. The fact there was nothing personal at all between him and Dalila. It was a business transaction, plain and simple. One that men like his brother, and probably the judge, too—judging from some of the ribald stories he liked to tell over Scotch and cigars—engaged in on a regular basis. Men that up until that night John Raines had told himself he was not like at all.

"I guess we were both in a hurry, Johnny." RL was waiting for him at the foot of the stairs and taking him by the arm, steered him out onto the street and down to a taxi stand where, to John's surprise, the world was going on just like before. "But that's okay. To be in a hurry sometimes. Besides, those gals are just whores after all. Truth be told, they prefer you be in a hurry."

"Let's just go back to the hotel, RL." The sound of RL's rude laughter only added to the guilt John felt.

"As you wish, little brother. Though, I would think a thank you is in order."

"Thank you. Now can we go?"

"Certainly."

***

The first Draft Day came and went on July 21st and neither John's nor RL's numbers were picked. Reading the list in the Fort Myers Press the day after the ceremony, RL mentioned how he was glad that was the case. "Looks like I don't need the judge to call in that favor for me, after all," he told John as they began another busy day at the office. "For now, at any rate."

"I'm happy for you RL," John said. "As for me, it doesn't change a thing."

And it didn't. On a hot, very humid morning the first day of August, with thick thunderheads building up over the Gulf to the west, he boarded the train for Jacksonville and the enlistment office there. Sitting in the coach as the train rumbled across the flatwoods of Central Florida, he thought about what the year had brought for him thus far.

He had passed the bar and become privileged to practice law in the Great State of Florida—as the official notice of his success had so eloquently proclaimed. Met, and then fallen in love, with a most beautiful young lady. Lost his virginity—though thank God not to her. Now he was off to war. To defend hearth and the homeland and make the World Safe for Democracy.

He couldn't imagine what else possibly lay ahead for him. But despite a sudden homesickness starting to nag at him a little, and his thoughts for Vera Robinson, he was eager to find out.

***

It didn't turn out to be much of a war for John Raines. Still, when peace came in early November of the next year, he was glad it was over. He was only three days out of the hospital and still so weak and unsteady on his feet that he needed a cane to walk when the Armistice was announced. Worse yet was that instead of celebrating with his fellow soldiers in Paris, he was at Camp Jackson, South Carolina. The same army camp outside of Columbia the sleepover train out of Jacksonville had brought him, and thirty other new recruits, to in August of 1917—and where he had been ever since.

So as much as he would have liked it to be the case, it was not his gallant actions on the battlefields of France that earned him his hospital stay. The Spanish Flu had brought him down. Not the Huns. The same flu that not only decimated the ranks of the troops stationed at Camp Jackson, but the Acting Adjutant General's office as well. Raines was a head clerk in this office, a position he had held for the majority of his career thus far in the army—a position he performed so well at he earned sergeant stripes.

Major Follet was the first one to fall at the hands of the flu. "I'm feeling a bit under the weather today, gentlemen," he informed the office one morning after putting them at ease. "If anything important needing my attention comes up, I'll be in my office. Otherwise, I'd prefer you just leave me be."

Nothing very important, as the major had said, came across Raines' desk, or any of the others, that day as it turned out. But at the end of it, when the major hadn't come out of his office for lunch, or even more alarming, for cocktail hour at the Officer's Club, Corporal Wills, after knocking politely and receiving no answer, went in to check on him Finding the major slumped over his desk, unconscious, in a cold sweat. Wills backed out of the office yelling for the medics.

The corporal was the next to fall, followed by the private who stood sentry outside the office in case of German attack. Raines and Lieutenant Cramer—an eager boy three years younger than Raines, fresh out of West Point and waiting for his orders to go overseas—did their best to carry out the duties of the Acting Adjutant General's office. But it wasn't long before the lieutenant went down, dying, much like the major, and then the corporal had, a few days later. Raines figured it was just a matter of time for him.

But a week went by. And then another. And still Raines stayed healthy. While rumors of peace floated around the camp, October turned into November. The base hospital filled to overflowing and to meet the needs of the sick, white canvas tents began going up on the far end of the camp. Every morning as he left his barracks for duty, Raines couldn't help but notice those white tents shining brightly in the fall sun, looking clean and white and incapable of hosting the sick and dying inside.

The business of the Adjutant's office ground damn near to a halt with only Raines and two PFC's to handle the workload. He put in a request for more help, receiving no reply for several days. Then a terse telegram from D.C. came to his desk, informing Sergeant Raines that the deadly flu was everywhere now in the stateside camps. *Do the best you can, Sergeant. Stop. With what you have. Stop.* And there it was. In black and white, no confirmation or further requests needed.

Talk of peace, along with the flu outbreak, filled the pages of the daily newspapers. Between the two of these, as well as the dwindling war still going on overseas, it was plain to Sergeant Raines that the high command in Washington had its hands full. It was up to him in Camp Jackson to carry on. To do, as the telegram ordered, the best he could. He was a soldier after all and would do just that for as long as he stayed healthy, and on his feet.

Fortunately, by the end of the first week in November new cases of the flu had dwindled and Raines began to believe he might be spared after all. The organizing of burial details and getting letters out to the families of the dead slowed. Instead of spending his days behind the typewriter composing these letters, and when they were done forging the major's signature, he was able to leisurely read the papers and take long coffee breaks. The business of the letters had saddened Raines very much and he was grateful there weren't as many now to write. It seemed such an ignoble way for a soldier to die. The line about how so and so had served their country well in its time of need had rung hollow inside him He found it hard to believe that such words could bring comfort to any grieving family. But it had been his job that he had learned quite well and couldn't question what his superiors ordered him to do.

On his way back to barracks from the NCO club the first Saturday in November he felt a little off. Queasy in his stomach, along with a certain weakness in his legs and a watering of his eyes. The food at evening mess had tasted funny. The two beers at the club after hadn't sat well, either. He would feel better in the morning, he decided. After a good night's rest.

That Sunday morning dawned fresh and cool with the first hint of fall in the cloudless sky. Not that one could tell it by John Raines. He was burning up with a fever and a wet hacking cough that wracked his chest with pain whenever he hawked up. He tried to get out of bed but couldn't. When he lifted his head, he could feel with one hand how the pillow and sheets were soaked with sweat. He fell back against the pillow and the next time he awoke he was on a cot in one of those white canvas tents on the edge of the camp.

"It looks like you've come down with that damn flu, Sergeant." An Army doctor, tall, of indeterminate age, wearing a white coat, and with spectacles hiding his eyes, stood over Raines' cot. "We'll do our best to take care of you, son. But for now, you just need to rest."

Raines was too weak to talk. Besides, even in his feverish state he knew enough to know that the "best care" the doctor mentioned, would be precious little. He would either get better or die. No matter what the doctor, and the nurses, busy going from one sick bed to another, did to help him

He lay on that cot for several days, drifting in and out of consciousness. How many days he had no idea. The doctor stopped by every morning and evening to check on him and the others. Actual treatments were left to the nurses. This consisted of aspirin three times a day, fluids, mainly water and warm tea, and once a day a shot of something in his arm. When awake he lay on his cot trying to ignore his surroundings. The smells and the sounds could be overwhelming. Stale sweat, his own and the others, dried urine, and vomit. The moaning and cries of the sick—sometimes, also his own. Orderlies removing the dead, doing their best to be quiet and unobtrusive. If he happened to be awake at the time Raines couldn't help but notice, the solemn way in which they pulled the sheet over the dead man's head, lifted him from the cot and placed him on a stretcher, and then carried the body out through the open flaps of the entrance.

Whatever the treatments were, they seemed to work. One day he awoke to realize he wasn't burning up with the fever and that the hacking cough had eased off. A nurse stood by the side of his cot, a curious look on her face. Raines was also conscious enough to notice something else about her.

"Nurse Doom?"

"Excuse me?"

"Your name," he said, pointing at the tag on the white shirt above the grey apron the nurses all wore. "I was making a little joke."

"Oh." She looked down at the name tag. "It's Doon, not "Doom." And then she laughed—the first woman's laugh he'd heard since Vera's in Fort Myers. "That's a very good joke, soldier. Specially in a place like this."

"Yes," he said, her comment a reminder of where he was. Just that morning the ward attendants had taken two more dead soldiers out for burial. "A place like this."

"If you're able to make a joke you must be feeling better?"

"I'm feeling better. Not much, but definitely better than I have been." But when he went to sit up, to swing his legs over the side of the cot, he couldn't. "I'm still pretty weak, though," he said as he lay back against the pillow. "As you can see."

"There's no hurry, Sergeant. It will take some time, yet to be back on your feet."

In the morning light, strangely bright, and probably because of the white canvas tent he lay in, he thought, Raines took a long look for the first time at this nurse who could laugh at his feeble joke. She was pretty enough, he decided, in a buxom sort of way. Her black hair was very thick, and cut short, just below her ears and brushed back. Her eyes were dark. She was tall for a woman. Taller than Vera at any rate, his only yardstick for comparisons of the female race. The thought of Vera, sudden like that, and in this place where he lay, made him groan.

"Are you all right, Sergeant?" The curious look on her face had turned to one of concern. "Can I get you an aspirin, or a cup of tea?" She leaned over then and put her palm on his forehead to check for fever.

"No," he said. "No, I'm fine. Or as fine as to be expected. I just thought of someone."

"Oh," and she stood up again. When she did, he was surprised at how he missed her hand against his skin. "You were thinking of your wife, then? Or maybe your best girl? If you'd like I could write a letter for you. Let them know you'll be okay and that you're getting better."

Though there wasn't anything funny about what the nurse said, Raines couldn't help but laugh—a short, barking sound that sounded ugly, even to him

"What did I say?"

"It's not that." The laugh had led into a wracking spasm of coughing and it took a while for him to catch his breath. "There's no wife. Or best girl, though I was pretty sure at one time there would be. A wife, at any rate."

"Oh, I'm sorry to hear that." He could see by the look on her face that she was—which made him feel suddenly much the same as her hand on his forehead had. "It's always sad, even if I suppose I should be used to it by now."

"What's that?"

"More than one of you poor boys has told me their girls tired of waiting for them to come home. Wives, too, which I could never understand that these women wouldn't take their vows seriously."

"I wish that were the case." The rest of this was going to be hard for him—the words he hadn't said aloud since he'd received the news in a letter from RL. "It might have hurt less, somehow. But no, she died. Not long after I enlisted."

Raines talked then and then talked like he had not to another human in a very long time. He told this nurse, a woman he didn't really know but who was there to listen, of Vera's death three months after he arrived at Camp Jackson. Spinal meningitis had swept through Fort Myers, taking men, women, and children, away in its path, Vera being one of the first to go. He spoke of how RL's letter came for him. Of how excited to have mail from home he saved it for later that night to read before lights out. He couldn't believe what he read at first. He had to read it again. And then again before the truth of it sank in. He told the nurse how he had lain back in his bunk when he was finished and cried, quietly so as not to disturb the others He didn't know at the time—wasn't sure even now. But he cried—telling himself he was sorry for Vera to go like that. A lovely, bright woman who had her whole life ahead of her. And then he cried for himself. For the unfairness of it all. And when he finally slept, and then awoke the next day, it was still true. Vera was dead. He was alive. And nothing to do for it but to carry on.

The nurse said nothing—not until he was finished with his sad tale and thanked her for listening, saying as well how strangely enough he felt better for the telling of it.

"Well then, I'm glad," she said. "That I could be here to listen." Her face brightened. "Now we just have to get you all better from this flu and back on your feet again."

She turned to go but Raines reached out and took her hand in his—it felt soft and warm and alive in his.

"Will you be back?"

"Tomorrow morning I will. I work the morning shift so I will see you then."

"Good," he said, and when she was gone, he fell back against the pillow, exhausted suddenly, and he hadn't even left his cot. But he had meant what he said. It *was* good. Seemed like the only good thing, in fact, he'd known since the major took sick and died. Beyond that? The only good he'd known since coming into the army and three months later RL's letter came and there wasn't a damn thing he could do about what was in that letter. He sat behind his desk in the Acting Adjutant General's office typing out orders and memos and trying to forget that he had ever had a sweet dream of someone lovely and living waiting for him when the war was over — when his future stretched out in front of him bright and shining like it was supposed to be.

*** 

He was released from the hospital by mid-November. Though not yet cleared for active duty, he was able to return to his barracks. As far as Raines was concerned anything, short of death, beat lying on that cot, day in and day out, beneath the white canvas of the hospital tent. Just the fact of being out and away from the sick and the dying made him feel better than he actually was.

Fall settled in while he was sick and unaware, the nights cool, the days mild and pleasant beneath cloudless skies. With the sickness and the stifling wet heat of the South Carolina summer gone, Raines felt he could breathe again. If he was still weak and needed a cane to keep his balance as he walked about the camp, so be it. And weak he still was. For several days after leaving the hospital, the short stroll from his barracks to the mess hall was enough to wear him out — the short respite of sitting of sitting down and eating, necessary to fortify him for the return walk. Once back at his barracks, he liked to sit outside on the steps and watch the sun go down over the pine scrub beyond the camp. When the sun finished its descent, he would go inside and lay on his bunk reading until the bugler blew *Taps* and it was time for lights out.

He thought of the nurse a lot. The first time he was on his way back from noon mess he pondered the idea the going over to the hospital tents and see if she might be there — on break and free to chat a little bit. He didn't though, wondering as he did what they could possibly talk about other than the condition of his health and how he was feeling that day. These were not the things he wanted to talk with her about.

One evening in late November as he was headed back to the barracks after mess, dusk coming on and the night looking to be colder than they had been of late, he saw her walking in front of him, hurrying along the dirt street running between the barracks and offices toward the main entrance of the camp.

"Nurse Doon," he blurted out, half hoping she wouldn't hear him and continue on her way. "Nurse Doon!"

But she *did* hear him—not only heard him but turned to see who was calling out to her. There was a smile on her face, bright enough to see even in the falling light of the day and that made his heart lurch suddenly in his chest. Not only that, to his surprise she stopped, obviously waiting for him to catch up.

"Sergeant Raines," she said. "How nice to see you again. I've been thinking about you."

Just those simple words—that she had been thinking of him—along with the smile on her face in the fading light made his heart lurch again.

He walked with her the rest of the way to the front of the camp and the bus stop. A group of nurses and other civilians who worked on the base were at the stop already waiting for the last bus into town. As he and the nurse walked, they talked. Of little things really, the sort of conversation Raines was never very good at. Of how she was finishing up her tour of duty at Camp Jackson. The flu seemed to have run its course. There were more nurses now at the hospital than needed to attend to the normal cases of minor injuries and sickness prevalent in an army camp. No longer needed there she was set to resume her studies at the college in town. The new term began in January. When winter break was over. And how was he doing? Now that he was back on his feet again?

And though he had feared such talk, for some reason his nervousness wasn't there. He was able to tell her that he had been finally cleared for duty. His report day was the coming Monday, and he was eager to get back to work. And yes, he felt much better, now, thank you very much. The Acting Adjutant General's office was very busy now, and it was good he was returning. A new major had replaced Major Follet. Raines had met him once and he seemed to be capable of running the office as well as Major Follet had. There was no replacement as of yet for Lieutenant Cramer, but Raines took from the new major's tone of voice that he, Raines, might be promoted soon to fill the lieutenant's post—in our time of need, the new major had said. A need that was very evident, as Raines had witnessed for himself just that morning when he stopped by to check in and saw the stacks of white paper besides each typewriter waiting to be filled out with the various transfers and discharges coming down the line now that the war was over. Raines hoped that he'd have the pleasure of filling out the form for his own discharge, soon. He had left a career back home in Fort Myers and he was eager to get back to it.

All this tumbled out of him in a steady stream so that he wasn't even aware when the bus pulled in—that those waiting for the bus were getting on board.

"I've got to go now, Sergeant. It's been really nice seeing you again, though."

"I won't be getting a pass for a few weeks," he said as she went to get on the bus. "But when I do, perhaps I could call on you in town?"

The smile she turned to him with was encouraging, at least.

"That would be fine, Sergeant." She paused at the bottom of the steps; the smile replaced by a little frown that he couldn't imagine the meaning of. "Yes," she continued, to his relief. "I think I would like that. Would like that very much."

The others had taken their seats by this time and the driver at the wheel was giving her an impatient look.

"I'm at Mrs. Loames' boarding house. On Harrow Street. You can call on me there, Sergeant."

And then she was gone, aboard the bus, the doors closed behind her as the driver put the engine into gear and rumbled down the macadam road towards town, dusk gone as well, replaced by the night and that Raines was hardly aware of as he walked back the way he had just come, alone this time, but he didn't mind.

***

With the threat of the Spanish Flu diminished, and along with the Armistice, Camp Jackson seemed to have come alive again. Instead of the somber mood that had hung over the camp like some evil shroud of doom, the men fairly buzzed with their new state of being. Smiles filled their faces, and there was a more vigorous step to their carriage as they went about the daily chores necessary to the camp. *Soon,* these smiles, the vigorous step, seemed to say. Soon I'll be going home.

Just as Raines had told Nurse Doon it would be, the Acting Adjutant General's office was very busy. Swamped would be a more accurate assessment, he thought at the end of his first day back. The stack of blank request and order forms filling the *In* tray on his desk seemed no smaller when five o'clock rolled around and it was time for evening mess. The same could be said for the stack of completed forms in the *Out* tray, even though the privates had been busy picking these forms up all day. If every day from then on until he was discharged was going to go like this first one had—well, he didn't know. It was too depressing to ponder. That night as he lay in his bunk reading, he was glad when *Taps* was blown, and the day was done.

Over a period of several days, though, the office settled down. The work got done, seemingly to the rhythm of the incessant clatter of typewriters, phones ringing, and doors opening and closing as men came and went with stacks of papers in their arms. Sooner than Raines thought it would, the frenzy began to ease. By the end of the week the backlog was caught up, the office seemed back to normal, and a sense of calm replaced the sense of urgency that had driven Raines and the other clerks the last five days.

The new major—one Gerald Wahl—took notice of it.

"By God, gentlemen," he declared that Friday afternoon as he came out of his office promptly at five o'clock. "I think we've finally got a handle on this godawful mess."

He sent a private down to the canteen for beer—when he returned all those in the Acting Adjutant General's office drank a toast to what the major called, "A job well done, gentlemen!"

In Raines' viewpoint, well done or not, the tedious, steady, paperwork the men of the Acting Adjutant Generals Office had performed over the course of the war had done little towards the winning of it. This had been done on the fields of France with the blood and the heroics of his fellow soldiers who fought there. Still, he and the others in the office *had* made a contribution. A small one, perhaps, but a contribution none the less. What they were doing now, the typing of transfers and discharge papers—this was the most important work the office had done in his time there. A fact struck home to Raines as he opened another of the bottles of beer the new major has graciously provided. Yes, they were doing the good work now. This facilitating of sending the returning survivors home. Back to wherever it was they had come from to whatever life it was they had known then.

Where Major Follet had been stern and kept to himself, the new major was very outgoing, friendly to officer and enlisted man alike. He was quick to correct any mistakes made during the day, but in an easy manner that left no bad feelings between the major and the one who had committed the error. With men like Raines, who rarely made mistakes, he was complimentary but not overly so.

"What did you do before the war, Lieutenant?" the major asked one afternoon as he went over a report Raines had just finished. "For a living?"

When Raines said that he had been a lawyer the major laughed. "It shows, my man. The 'I's' and 'T's' are all dotted. You even corrected some of my spelling mistakes, I see. Damn good, soldier, damn good!"

With his sandy red hair and thick mustache of the same color framing a freckled face, Major Wahl just *looked* like an officer. While the other higher-ups at the camp dressed in the modern uniform of the U.S Army, Major Wahl stuck to his jodhpurs, riding boots, and Sam Browne belt. "Relics," he said once after a brown-nosing corporal commented on how well the major looked in his uniform that day. "Just some leftovers from my days with Pershing chasing Villa down in 'Ol' Mejico." And then, to the rest of the office who were busy being disgusted by the sucking up of the corporal who no one liked, "We had some times then, gentlemen. Chasing that damn outlaw all over hell and highwater." The major frowned for a moment. "It was a different war— hell, a different world—back then. We fought on horseback, for Christ's sake. None of that godawful trench business and wholesale slaughter of this last mess. Soldiers were looked upon as men and not just cannon fodder. Yes sir, the time of civil conduct between opposing men of arms is gone, I suppose." He brightened up suddenly. "Hells bells, I suppose it was gone then! Back when I was getting saddle sores from tramping along with Pershing. I was just too damn young and dumb to know it."

Raines and the rest of the men in the office came to like the new major very much. Hell, Raines figured, it was near impossible not to. Other than the brown-nosing corporal, Major Wahl treated them with courtesy and respect. Even the brown-nosing corporal was a recipient of this courtesy, the lack of respect in the major's voice when he spoke to him, noticed by the others in the office, if not by the corporal in question. The main result of the new major's easy manner with them, Raines realized, was that the productivity of the office had greatly increased—the success of those days of frenzy when Raines had first returned to duty, proof enough of that.

"Come along, Lieutenant," the major said as he came out of his office. It was a Friday, five o'clock, and the office was closing for the day. "Let's go over to the 'O' club and have a cocktail. We deserve one, wouldn't you say?"

Raines' new rank was courtesy of the major—just as he had hinted at when Raines was first introduced to his new commanding officer. At the end of that first crazy week when the major handed Raines an order form, and he told him to type it up ASAP. Raines did so and five minutes later Major Wahl signed it, handing it to an orderly rushing by with the order to get, "This out immediately, Private." A week later it was official. John Raines was a first lieutenant in the United States Army. Until that Friday afternoon, Raines had not availed himself of the courtesies of his new rank, but now the major was pushing him to do so.

Both the officer's and the NCO club occupied the same building, a low-slung wooden affair with a wide veranda out front where the officers entered. The NCO's went around back. For the enlisted men, there was a canteen where they could buy cigarettes, snacks, and beer, but nothing stronger. For hard liquor, these men had to go into town on pass and drink it there. A few braver of these men managed to bring hard spirits back into camp after pass, hidden on their bodies or tucked away in an overnight bag. If found with this contraband, or worse, drunk, a night or two in the camp jail was in order, depending on the severity of the offense, or the MP's mood at the time that arrested them,

Raines enjoyed a drink of whiskey on occasion, a good Scotch, or an ice-cold beer. But not to the lengths some of his fellow soldiers went to. He was a lawyer after all. A night in the camp pokey, as far as he was concerned, was too stiff a blemish on his record for a pleasure he could take or leave well enough alone.

Still, as he sat at a small table off to the side in the dimly lit club, he had to admit that the first sip of Dewar's—courtesy of the major who insisted that first round was on him—went down surprisingly well. Of a sudden it was as if Raines could just sit back and let all the weight of his army career slip away. The fact that he had been deskbound for the entire duration of the war, the Spanish Flu that took him down, the Armistice that ended the war, all of this was of no matter.

"Damn good Scotch, wouldn't you say, Lieutenant?"

The satisfied smile on the major's face as he leaned over his drink was hard to argue with.

"Yes, it is, sir. Damn good."

Four Dewar's later the two men were on first name basis—again, at the major's insistence.

"John—can I call you John? Or do you prefer Jack?" Without waiting for an answer, the major went on. "When we're away from that office just call me Jerry. What do you say?"

"I say that's just fine, sir, I mean Jerry." If Raines had a hard time referring to Major Gerald Wahl as Jerry, he was just going to have to do his best to learn how. "And no, I don't prefer Jack at all. Never been called that in my life. My pop always called us boys by just our initials. My older brother was RL, the youngest, TJ, and myself JR. But John works for me. In fact, I'd prefer it."

"Good, good. Rank and courtesy have their place in this man's army, no doubt. In fact, without it, we would be one disorderly mess. But there are times in the day when it has to be laid aside. Especially," and here he paused to take another sip of the Scotch, "especially when two men after a long day—hell, a long week—of mundane work are sitting back in a comfortable club enjoying the beauties of an excellent Scotch."

"I couldn't agree more, Jerry."

It was true, what Raines said. The Scotch was very good, and the 'O' Club was the most comfortable setting he had been in since leaving Fort Myers. The room was softly lit with a long bar running half the length of the room, draped with American flag bunting on the wall behind it that came down almost to the top row of the various liquors on hand. Like the table Raines and the major sat at, others were scattered around the room, three of these occupied while several officers stood up at the long bar drinking beer. A pool table sat in one rear corner and two men were playing billiards. The sound of the balls clanking when hit, instead of being annoying, only added to the comfortable atmosphere. It was a peaceful place he had never imagined could exist in such a bare bones place as Camp Jackson, South Carolina. He was a far piece away, no doubt, from the hectic days in the Acting Adjutant General's office and the daily hubbub found there. Not to mention his time spent with the sick and dying in that hospital tent on the furthest edge of the camp.

To remind the men of something other than their patriotism, on either end of the flag bunting hung behind the bar, were paintings of nude women hidden in shadow against a velvet backdrop. Tasteful, yet somehow tantalizing as well, he needed to ask where he could procure one of these for RL's office, a man who would surely appreciate such a painting. For the office of course. RL's wife wouldn't allow such a thing in the new house the judge had given the couple for a wedding gift.

After the fifth drink Raines knew he'd probably regret it the next day. But the major made no move to call it quits, and next day regrets beside the point, Raines didn't want to leave the secure environment of the club. He ordered another round.

They ended up staying, drinking and talking, until last round at midnight. The major told Raines of his family, waiting for him in Chillicothe, Ohio, a place Raines had never heard of until then. She was a good woman, the major said. His wife Hazel. A true-blue Army wife who had put up admirably with the different postings over the years the major had been assigned to. She would have come to South Carolina, but their oldest daughter was engaged. To a marine, thank God, the major said. There were wedding plans to be made. It was simply too much to uproot the others now, she had had told him, and he understood. With the war over and retirement looking for him, the major planned to return to Chillicothe. Take off his uniform for good and with no regrets. He was young yet, only fifty. There was a life yet for him in civilian dress. Take some of those trips Hazel had always wanted—to where? She said anywhere was fine with her. As long as there was no army base anywhere nearby.

Raines spoke of his life in Fort Myers. Practicing law with his brother RL and the judge. The major laughed and said that the judge sounded like quite the character. Said that he would like to meet him sometime. It saddened Raines to say that this would not be possible. That the judge was gone. No, not from the meningitis that had taken Vera from him. It was a heart attack that struck the judge down—sort of fitting, actually, as he bent over to take up the first shovel full of dirt at the groundbreaking for his development. "Cool Breezes," a town where no cool breeze would blow now for the judge even if RL and the other partners planned to continue on with the project complete with a plaque adorning the town hall in the judge's memory.

The evening turned only sour once when the major, frowned, grew serious over his drink.

"I'm worried about the peace, John," the major said out of nowhere, his eyes not on Raines but on the cocktail glass that he rotated slowly in his hands. "Afraid the President, the rest of those so-called 'crowned heads,' will make a mess of it. And that would be a damnable shame after all those lives expended in the pursuit of it."

"I don't see how that's possible," Raines said. "The war's over and we won it fair and square. Going to be the last one, the President tells us."

"That's a lovely sentiment and must have looked awfully good on paper when Wilson wrote it down. But there will never be a 'last war.' If those people in Versailles don't play their cards very carefully, if they don't leave the Krauts something they can hold on to, to live with, now that the fighting's done, the next war will be on us before we know it. When it comes, and it will come, mind you, this war we just finished? It will look like a cakewalk compared with what we'll be facing then."

Raines didn't know what to say to this. He was a lawyer, true, but he was certainly no diplomat or skilled in international law and had no idea what those who were skilled in these things had in mind. He was just happy it was over. He was happy as well when the bartender rang the last bell.

"Looks like we have to call it an evening," the major said as he pushed back from the table and stood up. "It's been a long day and probably another one awaits us in the morning."

"Yes sir," Raines said as he stood up, forgetting for the moment that they were to call one another by their first names—a lapse of memory the major didn't seem to notice. "I suppose you're right."

"Let's hope it's the only thing I'm right about."

Again, Raines stayed silent, saying only "goodnight," when they left the club, stepping out into the night to go their separate ways.

***

The weekend before Christmas Raines went into town. Up until then, a flurry of paperwork coming across his desk had kept him very busy. Discharge papers. Reassignment orders for those men already career soldiers. Re-enlistment form for those who had elected to become so at war's end. Daily requisitions—all of these had to be dealt with, leaving Raines and the others in the Acting Adjutant General's office with their hands full.

Finally, the barrage of paperwork settled down, and Raines—weary from the work, and if nervous about it, still, eager to see Nurse Doon—went to the major to request a pass.

"It's about time, Lieutenant, you came to your senses." The major smiled at him from behind his desk. "You've been working too hard lately. Go into town and unwind a little. We'll see you back here bright and early Monday morning."

"Thank you, Jerry," Raines said as he tucked the pass into his shirt pocket.

"Have a lady friend in town, John?"

"No," Raines answered, quickly adding, "Maybe. There *is* a girl I'd like to see. If she'll allow it."

"I can't imagine why she wouldn't." The major laughed. "Carry on soldier. What the hell you doing standing around looking at me for?" The major's booming laugh followed Raines out of the office.

The next day, a Friday, just before the office closed for the day Raines called Loames Boarding House where the nurse had told him she lived. The connection was not a good one, full of static before the operator's sterile voice broke through the crackling when she said, "Just a minute sir while I put your call through," then more static before someone picked up on the other end of the line.

"Loames Boarding House." The voice answering his call belonged to a female, that of an older woman who didn't bother to hide the suspicion in her tone. "Whom am I speaking to?"

"John Raines, ma'am," he told her. "Lt. John Raines, out at Camp Jackson."

But Nurse Doon was not available to talk right then. "Could I take a message?" The suspicion seemed to have left her, and maybe because he was an officer. "Yes," he said, and then asked Mrs. Loames—he assumed that's who he was talking to—to let Nurse Doon know he would be in town the following day. Around noon, he said. If it was okay with Nurse Doon, he'd like to call on her. If so, would she please leave word for him at the camp?

"Why, I'll be sure to tell her, Lieutenant. Good day, now."

And that was that. He had taken the first step. It was up to the nurse now. With a slight sense of relief Raines made his way to evening mess, where to his surprise he wasn't able to eat very much.

His plan was to get into town early, find his bearings, and settle himself before going to the boardinghouse. But the major sent for him first thing—a new corporal had made a mess of recent discharge forms and Raines was needed to sort the disaster out. By the time he had redone the orders, got them typed up, signed by the major and on their way, the eight a.m. bus to town was long gone. He had to hurry as it was to catch the ten o'clock bus, making it to the stop and scrambling aboard just as the driver was about to close the doors.

Busy as he'd been with the emergency at the office, Raines had forgotten about his nerves regarding meeting the nurse. But as the bus pulled away from the front gates of the camp these nerves came rushing back. For one thing, he hadn't received a reply to the message he'd left with the landlady. He could chalk that up to a variety of reasons, he supposed. The landlady had forgotten to deliver the message as promised. Nurse Doon had come off shift too late to respond. These two he could handle. But what if she hadn't responded for the simple reason she didn't want to see him? Gracious invitation for him to call, the night he walked her down to catch the bus, beside the point.

He did his best to put these thoughts aside. As the bus rattled off towards town, he let the groans of the springs, the whine of the tires, the idle chatter of the other soldiers on board, cover his nervousness about this leap of faith he was taking.

Surprisingly enough, he fell asleep, waking only when the bus came to a stop. They were at the station in the heart of downtown Columbia where Raines had arrived for the first time just the year before. His initial glimpse of the capitol of South Carolina, before boarding the shuttle to Camp Jackson with the other recruits, had been of a town in the midst of a building boom Crews of men were busy putting up storefronts that hot August morning in 1917, places of business necessary to serve the needs of the new Army camp. A livery at one end of the main street stood as counterpoint to a new filling station at the other end—that livery idle now, having been put out of use by the cars and trucks replacing its usefulness. What hadn't been replaced by modern progress, though, were the saloons erected during that building boom. They seemed to be doing a steady business, judging by the men, soldiers, and civilians alike, going in and out of their open doors. It was like it was before the Great War, just another sleepy Southern town—state capitol or not—minding the business it needed to, year end, year out.

Now, Raines saw as he stepped off the bus, Columbia was a town no longer. Instead, a city had been built to replace it. A thriving one, bustling with men in suits going about their business, in and out of the various storefronts, the banks facing each other on opposite sides of Main Street as well as women, doing their shopping and the like, cars and trucks, and still, a few horse drawn wagons going up and down the streets, country folk coming into town on Saturday to get what was needed back home and that they no longer had to grow, or make on their own, now that the war had ushered in a new era.

A city, he thought, as he stood out on the sidewalk in front of the bus station, that might well be in need of a young lawyer. One eager to make a fresh start for him and his new bride. But he was getting ahead of himself, he realized. To wash the dust coming through the open windows of the bus out of his throat, as well as to ease his nerves, Raines went into a saloon conveniently located right next to the station.

Two beers and a half hour later he took a trolley south out of town to Hanover Street. Sitting in the open trolley Raines didn't need the Christmas decorations adorning the lamp posts and storefronts as they rolled by to let him know what month it was. The fresh, cold air of the December morning did that job just fine. Moving out from the heart of town the tracks led along the river at first. On the other side of this river textile mills spewed smoke into an otherwise clear winter sky. The wind was blowing away from the trolley, Raines glad he didn't have to smell what the ugly smoke rising out of the mill's stacks carried with it.

Before long, the tracks veered away from the river and the mills, their smoke and stench left behind. Now they were in a residential part of town where white sidewalks and homes made of wood or brick with green lawns, sparkled in the morning sun.

"Hanover Street next stop," the conductor called out above the clanking of the iron wheels. When it came to a stop Raines stepped out the back of the trolley, the little bouquet of flowers—bought at the last minute from an old colored lady on the sidewalk in front of the saloon—in one hand, his cap in the other. As the trolley moved away, he put the cap on his head, made sure his jacket was buttoned correctly, and set off for the boardinghouse.

*** 

"Now that you're back, Johnny, my hope is that you're ready to take over for me. Here in town."

They were sitting in RL's office on a cold, raining, Wednesday morning in mid-February. Raines had been home for just two days, his discharge—at his request—expedited and signed by Major Wahl. RL had picked him up at the train station Monday afternoon, and on the ride to the office hinted at something serious he needed to go over with him. Now, here it was, plain and simple.

At least it didn't come as a total surprise. In his letters the last several months before Raines' discharge, RL had hinted at how busy he was and how it was almost more than one man could handle. "Not that I'm not giving it my best shot, Johnny." At how there was a business arrangement he wanted to discuss with him, when he got home. "And hurry up, for God's sake, while you're at it and get here."

What RL had to say came as no surprise. Not like Sadie's revelations had been that recent night in January—when in answer to his proposal she told him she could not say yes. That she was already engaged to another. A man who would be coming home soon from overseas. That she was sorry, but that was how it was. And yes, he was sorry, too. Now he was back in Fort Myers where it seemed, on that cold, dreary morning in February, as if he had never left.

Raines had hoped to be spared from any big decisions for a while. What with his homecoming, the fact he was out of the army—and as always, since Sadie—a little time to get used to the lay of the land seemed only fair.

And yet, in his typical hurry to get where he was going, RL roared on past whatever his brother's concerns might be at the time.

"How's that sound to you, John?"

Raines almost laughed at the suddenly serious look on his brother's face and the use of "John," as opposed to either "Johnny," or "little brother," RL usually addressed him as.

"You better tell me a little more, RL, before I answer one way or the other."

'Well, it's pretty much like what I just said." He needed to step away from the practice of law for a while. Needed to focus on the ranch and the other interests Judge Landry's death had shouldered upon him "The ranch is a handful in itself, Johnny," RL told him. "Enough to keep an honest man busy from dawn to dusk. Then there's 'Cool Breezes,' which fortunately, with the judge gone, the other partners and I have decided to rename 'Orange Heights,' a name more suitable to a town in Florida, wouldn't you say? Hell, just that simple little change has boosted lot sales ten percent."

RL went on to explain how it wasn't that he was turning over the practice completely to his brother. "I'll still be senior partner, mind you." Deserving of his share of the profits, he quickly made clear. "But who knows?" he asked, leaning back in his chair to rest his shiny new boots on the desktop—boots, Raines noticed, that didn't appear to have been exposed recently to the dirt and manure associated with cattle ranching. "In time, maybe two, three, years, you and I will take stock of the situation. If it warrants then perhaps, I'll bow out completely, turn it all over to you, and then you'll be the number one attorney in our lovely little community."

A certain little, self-satisfied, smile on his brother's face indicated there was more and Raines asked as much.

"What about the elections down the road, RL? 1922 will be here before we know it. Have you forgotten what the judge was suggesting, back before the war? Or just put it on hold?"

"You've got a good memory, John. A knack for recording the pertinent facts in that keen mind of yours—one of the many reasons you make such a good lawyer. Perhaps one day, a most able judge."

"And the mayor, RL? When I'm this judge you speak of?"

"Why that will be me, Johnny. Does that answer your question?' And there was that self-satisfied little smile again.

"It does, RL. It does indeed."

***

So that by the time April rolled in, bringing with it the first spring weather of the year, Raines was as set as he figured to be in the law office of *Raines & Raines, Robert Lee Raines, Esq., Senior Partner, John Randolph Raines, Esq., Junior Partner.*

Not only that, but he was also busy. RL had not been wrong when he said that with his new responsibilities at the judge's ranch, he had been somewhat lax with the business of law. "You might say, little brother, I somehow managed to let a few of the smaller matters escape my attention."

Poring over the stacks of briefs and motions not yet filed Raines couldn't help but wonder what the bigger "matters" were that RL *had* attended to. Deeds to the new development—*Cool Breezes*, since re-named *Orange Heights*—that should have been recorded months back, and were not, made up the bulk of the paperwork. When Raines wondered aloud why the owners of the lots in question hadn't been pounding down the door, RL shrugged and took another sip from his silver flask.

"My gift of gab, I imagine."

"Must be one hell of a gift, RL."

"Oh, it is, Johnny. It damn sure is." His red face broke out into a grin as he casually mentioned, "Did I tell you that Ellen is in the family way? Come September—God willing, and the creek don't rise—I'm going to be a daddy. And you, dear brother, an uncle."

This was indeed good news, but when Raines suggested that an expectant father should have been even more intent on carrying out his responsibilities with work, RL only laughed.

"But I have, Johnny, I have. Made you my Junior Partner, didn't I? That's the first step in my Grand Scheme."

Raines didn't answer—but instead picked up the first folder at the top of the stack on his desk and got to work.

As Raines went over the deeds, though, he came across two of them, that in his opinion it would take more than a "gift of gab," to explain away. One morning in mid-April when RL showed up at the office just before noon, he handed his brother one of those deeds he had set aside for just that occasion.

"I'm not sure I know what to do with this."

"Let's take a look-see." RL glanced at the document briefly before giving it back to his brother. "Looks fine to me, Johnny. Now c'mon. Maura Jane's got liver and onions on a Blue-Plate Special today. We need to get down there before it's all gone."

"You don't see anything wrong with this deed?"

"No sir. Not right off-hand I don't."

"That's the problem, RL. You didn't really look at it. This deed claims to be a new transfer."

"Okay."

"One with a non-authenticated signature. The deed's not binding."

"Well, I'll be damned. I told you I was up to my eyeballs with this before you got home." He gave Raines a sheepish look as he pulled his flask out of his back pocket and took a sip. "Let me have it and I'll get it straightened out pronto."

"Good," Raines said, not satisfied at all with RL's sheepish look, his explanation that the non-binding deed was just an oversight. "I've got another one here you need to attend to as well. The notary signature, the seal? They're not from any notary I know of. Not here in Collier County at any rate."

"Jesus Christ, Johnny!" RL's face went even redder than it normally was. "Not to worry my boy. Like I said, just hand it here and I'll get it taken care of. Now c'mon. I'm about to starve to death here."

"I won't be a party to fraud, RL."

"Fraud? There's no fraud going on here, Johnny. Trust me."

But Raines wasn't sure—on either statement.

Despite concerns about RL's business dealings, Raines was glad for the work. Between Orange Heights and the civil cases that came into the office, he stayed busy. If he wasn't at his desk finishing up briefs or readying new deeds to be filed, then he was down at the courthouses arguing cases for a client. Judge Sterling, as Raines discovered, seemed to be a fair and learned case decider. As for RL's disclaimer about the new judge "being pretty good, for a Jew," Raines didn't see how that diminished the man's capabilities to try a case.

Busy as he was during the day—and pretty much six days a week— Raines had no time to think of Sadie Doon. The nights though. They were a different matter altogether. Sitting on the front porch of the office at the end of the day, cocktail in hand as he watched the sun go down, he couldn't help but remember the nurse. How it was being with her. The warmth of her skin when they embraced. The sound of her voice, and the way her lustrous black hair gleamed in certain lights. How her dark eyes seemed to reflect that gleam as well. He couldn't help but remember, either, that night in January when she said no. And how all that was gone now. All but the ache she left behind.

Two, sometimes three, drinks later he was usually able to convince himself it was okay. That there would be another woman. He had been able to come to grips with Vera's death after all. A woman he had wanted to marry almost as bad as he'd wanted to marry Sadie. Then Sadie had shown up in his life. The proverbial Angel of Mercy. So yes, there would be another. The third time's the charm. Yes, that was it. That was what they liked to say.

But if the cocktails on the porch as the sun went down were able to bring him some small peace, there was more than one night when in the dark hours of the morning he jerked awake to wonder if that hole in his gut might ever go away.

RL's wife, Ellen, gave birth to a healthy baby girl the last week of August. "Jesus, son, but I thought she'd never stop caterwaulin'," was RL's first comment about the birth of his child. "It was hard on me, let me tell you."

"Imagine how she must have felt."

They were smoking cigars and drinking Scotch. "Only the very best for an occasion such as this," he said on the wide veranda of the house RL and Ellen inherited when the judge passed away.

"Now that's spoken like a true lawyer, Johnny. Bringing up the other side of the issue like that. No, now I take it back, come to think of it. Spoken like a true judge. The fine judge you'll be one of these days."

The evening was warm and humid, with no trace of wind coming through the pines surrounding the big house on the edge of the vast Landry ranch RL now owned. Both men were sweating in their suits, the only allowance to comfort being when RL loosened his necktie and suggested Raines do the same. Cattle, unseen in the pastures stretching off from the house, lowed here and there as they settled down for the night. From inside the house came the sound of the new baby crying, the gentle shushing of Ellen's friends gathered around her.

"You might as well prepare yourself for some sleepless nights ahead, RL. Remember how it was after TJ was born? And Pop had to get up and walk the floor with him?"

"Our baby brother didn't have a mama." RL splashed more Scotch into Raines' glass. "As I'm sure *you* remember. Unlike our mother, Ellen managed to survive giving birth. Though judging from how she carried on it wasn't too certain she would. She'll be the one to walk the floors at night. Not me."

They went quiet for a bit, John figuring that RL, like he, was thinking of their mother—how the birth of their brother had ended her life which began a hard time for those she left behind. A hard time that came to an end, for RL at least, on an August morning five years later when he fought their father to a draw in the tobacco rows and then left to make a new life for himself.

"Well Johnny," RL said, finally breaking the silence—apparently not thinking about their mother at all. "One of these days you'll meet a fine woman like I did. Get married and start a family of your own."

"Maybe," Raines said. "I hope you're right."

"Oh, I am, little brother. I am."

The next morning, as he was going over a brief he had to finish and get down to the clerk at the courthouse, Raines thought of his conversation with RL the night before. He knew what he had to do.

\*\*\*

"Have you married him?" Again, the connection wasn't good, the line laced with static. Bad weather upstate, sir, the operator informed Raines when he placed the call. When he didn't get a reply right away, he asked again, "Did you?"

"It's been eight months, John. Why are you calling now?"

Despite the lousy connection her voice did to him what it always had—made something inside him go upside down.

"I need to know, Sadie." And again, "I need to know."

"No," she said. "Next month. Next month we get married."

"I'm coming up there," he said. There was still time. Thank God. There was still time. "On the next train."

"If you ever loved me, John, you won't. Please. Please, don't do that."

"It's because I love you that I'm coming."

He hung up before she could say anything. Something that might change his mind. Though he didn't see how that was possible. He was alone in the office on a hot August evening, his hands shaking as he lay the phone back in its cradle. It was just him, the now quiet phone, and his thoughts. Thoughts of how, now that he had made the decision, he was going. Going to do what he should have done back in January— and instead, had walked away.

They were married in RL's backyard on the Sunday before Easter. The sky was clear and a deep blue, the light breeze coming off the Gulf just enough to keep the afternoon temperatures comfortable for the outdoor affair. The guest list wasn't long, and if RL hadn't invited people he had done business with over the years—judges, lawyers, and bankers, some from Fort Myers, others from Tampa—the wedding would have been a most quiet one. Sadie was very happy her aging mother was able to make the trip from Illinois, her mother being the only one left of her family. Not only that, RL had been able to locate TJ, RL and John's younger brother, and he showed up the day before the wedding. This surprised both RL and John completely, as TJ's whereabouts were never for certain—mainly because he liked to hop trains on a whim and go to wherever it was that suddenly seemed to him to be the place to go.

Another pleasant surprise for John was the appearance of Major Wahl and his wife. Raines had sent the major an invitation but didn't think he would come. If RL hadn't already been picked as best man, Raines would have asked the major to stand up for him. Instead, and filling a need Sadie and John had been struggling with, the major agreed to give the bride away.

The bride wore white, all flowing lace and ribbons coming off her dark hair put up above her pale neck and shoulders, the lace and ribbons flowing endlessly into a long train trailing behind her. And dressed thus, she walked down the makeshift aisle on the arm of Major Wahl. Raines felt very stiff in the tuxedo he had borrowed from his brother, his nervousness made worse by the fact that being his brother's suit it was too big for him He did his best to be mindful of RL's advice to just relax as his bride walked toward him This was hard for him to do when all he wanted was for the ceremony to be over so he could take Sadie in his arms and kiss her. Then she was standing in front of him, the somber strains of the "Wedding March" dying out, and the people gathered there quiet as the bride and groom turned to face the minister. When it was his turn to hand the rings to Raines, RL fumbled and dropped the box containing them, the small crowd tittering as RL bent over to retrieve it. Raines hoped RL's fumble would be the only mishap of the day—hoped they could get off that easy.

But before the minister could open his mouth a distraught, gaunt looking man in his officer's best, came running around the side of the house yelling, "Stop. I've not had my say. Stop!"

John Raines took his eyes off his bride long enough to see what was going on, and just as this man reached out for Sadie, Raines stopped him in mid-reach.

"There's no say here for you, sir. You need to leave now."

"I'm not going without taking what's mine. If you know what's good for you, you won't stand in my way.

When the man tried to push past Raines, it was all over. Raines didn't think of doing it, didn't know he was going to do it, but all in a moment of blind realization—the flu and almost dying, meeting Sadie, his angel in white, falling in love with her, been rejected, fled home, or where he thought home was, suffered through months of missing her, then made the decision that he loved her and wasn't going to lose her without a fight. He had never been in a fight in his life, had only witnessed them, first his brother RL and their father and some drunken brawls at Camp Jackson. Now, the fight was here, this man he didn't know, Sadie's ex-fiancé, a lieutenant, judging by the bars on his uniform, but John Raines wasn't going to have it, no he was not, and he hit this man trying to come between him and Sadie, hit him once, a long sweeping undercut that lifted the man backward off his feet. In the next instant, as the man was struggling to stand up and fight back, Raines hit him again, knocking him to the ground where this time he stayed.

"Maybe I just don't know what's good for me, then," John Raines said, turning back to his bride and the minister. A nervous laugh rippled through the small group of stunned wedding guests. Then the minister's voice rang out, "We are gathered here together ...." Two men that Raines didn't know well, RL's friends, picked the crumpled lieutenant up from the ground and took him around front of the house where the taxi that had brought him was still waiting.

A few months later Sadie came up pregnant. On a warm July evening—before the Orange Heights scandal broke and RL's troubles began—he had a snifter of brandy and a very expensive Cuban cigar, both gifts from his brother the day he and Sadie got married. While enjoying these gifts Raines had the sudden thought of how much better his life had turned out.

# PART TWO

Rumors had circulated off and on for the last couple of years about "going's on" with RL's development "Orange Heights." Nothing substantial or named, only vague suggestions that "things ain't right out there." RL's comment, whenever Raines mentioned something he had heard, either at the courthouse, or at Maura Jane's diner, was that this was just the talk of what he termed, "envious people."

In early October of 1922, when the state and local elections—RL had finally thrown his hat in the ring and was running for mayor of Fort Myers—were starting to heat up, for the first time these rumors appeared in print. In the *Fort Myer's Press,* to be exact, and according to the four-paragraph article on page four, certain "irregularities" concerning the bank funding the project were being investigated.

At a speech he gave at the Fort Myers Grange Hall in mid-October, RL denied this claim vigorously—demanded the newspaper to reveal their source, or failing that, to print a description of the so-called irregularities. RL went on to say how surprised and hurt he was that his opponent—Mr. Harding, who owned the feed lot and supply store at the far end of Main Street, as well as the *Fort Myers Press* and a man he had known for years, had done business with, broke bread with, would lower himself so far as to engage in an ugly smear campaign such as this.

In private with Raines, when John asked if any of it was true, RL said only that, "If the judge were still alive none of these vicious rumors would have ever seen the light of day. Folks 'round here knew better than that."

"Hopefully," Raines said, "it won't get any worse."

"It won't little brother." And then, as if to convince himself, he said, and more vigorously, "It won't."

Raines wanted to believe his brother. But after what he'd said about if the judge were still alive none of it would be happening, he wasn't certain that he could.

The dam broke completely for RL when the bank holding the mortgages for Orange Heights failed. Though as RL put it to Raines, "Failed is being polite." The fact of the matter was that the United Trust Bank of Tampa simply disappeared. Not the building itself, mind you, but the officers, as well as the monies held there. These monies included loan payments, funds held in escrow, as well as the building accounts held by RL and his partners who were the developers of "Orange Heights."

As more of the bank's collapse came out in the paper, it turned out that three of the five partners involved with Orange Heights, had been the ones to start the bank, made un-secured loans to themselves out of the depositor's money, then turned around and used those loans to fund their shares of the development costs. When the first reports of possible misbehavior came out, these three men vanished, leaving the remaining two partners in Orange Heights—RL, and Tom Ryan, a banker from Fort Lauderdale who had known Judge Landry—high and dry. Both RL and Ryan were able to claim innocence of all wrong-doing, and rightfully so, but the damage had been done. Certainly, to RL's political career, as with these disturbing revelations his chances of winning the mayor's office in Fort Myers were as Tom Ryan said, "Slim to none, my friend."

"Damn it all, I lost money, too," RL complained. "No one seems to care about that."

RL, John, and Tom Ryan were sitting in Raines' law office the night of the election, drinking Scotch and waiting for the returns to come in. None of the three were hopeful. Just that morning the paper had printed the news of the three developers owning the bank and their fraudulent personal loans.

"You're exactly right, RL," Ryan said as he poured the three of them another drink. Ryan was a tall, lanky, lean faced man with very bright blue eyes shining out of a high forehead where strands of sandy hair were combed back from "No one cares about you losing your shirt. All they want to believe is that you are guilty as sin. Regardless of the fact that, in the popular vernacular, both you and I got royally fucked and didn't even enjoy it."

"I heard that," RL grunted.

There was a light knocking on the door, and then one of RL's runners came in with the final returns. RL looked at the paper the runner had given him and grunted again.

"Well boys, the verdicts in. And just as Tom said, I'm guilty as sin. Guess I'll go back to the ranch and lick my wounds."

"Don't lick them too long," Ryan said as he stood up to shake RL's hand. "Your time will come around again."

"Maybe. I hope you're right. Hope I'll care enough to pay attention when it does." He reached for his jacket and hat on the rack by the door. "I just feel like I let the ol' judge down. He was good to me, too."

Raines wanted to say something, but came up empty, and instead walked out into the night with his brother and Tom Ryan. Down the street at the courthouse, a loud cheering went up as the new mayor came out to greet his supporters who had gathered there. The "hip, hip, hoorays," and "Harding's our man," drifted down to the three men in front of Raines& Raines Law offices.

"Goddamn them all to hell," RL said as he and Ryan went to get into RL's Packard.

"See there?" Ryan said. "You're near done licking all ready."

Raines didn't hear his brother's reply over the loud roar of the Packard's engine as RL gunned it, turning it on the street just before the gathering at the courthouse, and roaring off in the night.

\*\*\*

Two years after RL's defeat at the polls in Fort Myers, John Raines looked out over Andrews Avenue from the window of his fourth-floor office in the Sweet Building. At the time, the Sweet Building was the tallest structure in Fort Lauderdale. Eight stories high it was a veritable skyscraper. By South Florida standards at any rate, he thought. It might not compare to the skyscrapers in New York, known only to Raines through pictures he'd seen in various magazines—still, it was the tallest building he had ever been in. Much less, had an office in.

On that morning in November of 1924 John Raines was wondering if he shouldn't consider another line of work. A month had come and gone since hanging his shingle out, so to speak, and not a single client had come knocking. Pushing the chair away from the open window, the rusty wheels squeaking in protest, he swiveled around so he could stare at the bold lettering engraved in black on the beveled glass of the office door. Backwards as it appeared to him from his desk, he knew what the lettering proclaimed: John Raines, Attorney at Law.

He didn't feel like much of an attorney that morning, not having filed a brief or handled a case since closing his office in Fort Myers four months back, selling the house he and Sadie and young Hilton had lived in for only four years, and making the move to Fort Lauderdale. To be honest, that morning Raines didn't know what he felt. At the ripe old age of thirty-one his future appeared as uncertain as that of any newborn arriving that day at the hospital down the street.

The sudden ringing of the telephone on the otherwise empty desk startled him out of his chair, Raines just as suddenly, grateful for the intrusion on his lonely thoughts.

The party on other end of the line most likely was Tom Ryan, RL's former partner in Orange Heights. The banker and real estate broker, Raines's only friend in town, had made it a habit to call him two or three times a week to "Keep up with Fort Lauderdale's up and coming new attorney." Raines appreciated the levity, aware as he was that Tom Ryan felt a sense of duty towards him—this, more than anything, being the reason he called as often as he did.

After all, Ryan was responsible for Raines bringing his family to this town on the other side of Florida. "We could use a good lawyer in this town, John," Ryan had said over the phone in early May of that year. "Or at least I sure could use one. I'm tired of having to go down to Miami every time I need to consult with my attorney. I know you're pretty settled where you are right now, but this town is growing. There's plenty of opportunity for a young man such as you, one with a law degree and a willingness to work. I know I might be asking a lot, what with your established business there. Not to mention your young family. But would you at least consider it?"

Raines had told him that, yes, he would consider it and get back to him when he had an answer. That night when he brought up this phone call to Sadie, he was surprised at how eager she was to say yes.

"I think it's a marvelous idea," his wife told him "I'm tired of this stodgy old town. Ever since that business with RL—and nothing against your brother because I know it wasn't his fault—I have no friends here. The snobby ladies of this town will barely give me a nod when I meet them on the street. They even turned me down for that silly old women's club Renatta Watts and her friend Earline Toms are starting up. We have money saved, will make some off selling the house, and will have enough to tough it out until your new practice takes off." And with a smile and a kiss on his cheek while holding their son in her other arm, she added, "As I know it will. And in no time at all."

Raines had to admit that he felt pretty much the same—about his reception by the folks in Fort Myers who had once been not only his clients, but his friends. The next day he phoned Ryan back and told him they would be there as soon as they could wrap up their affairs. "That's splendid Raines, simply splendid," Ryan said. "I promise you that you won't regret it."

Now, as he picked up the phone and said, "Hello, how can I help you?" he wasn't so sure that Ryan's promise was holding true.

"That you, Raines?"

"Yes, it's me, Tom. My secretary had to step out of the office for a minute."

Ryan's raspy chortle over the static laced line—knowing as he did that Raines couldn't afford a secretary—made Raines smile.

"Well, I'm glad you haven't lost your sense of humor, John. But I've got some good news for you."

"I could certainly use some right about now."

There was a small mirror in a walnut frame hanging on the wall nearest his desk and Raines happened to catch his reflection in the glass as he pushed his chair in tighter. The brown hair atop his head was receding further and further away from his forehead every day, it seemed. The gray eyes staring back at him from the glass bothered him more than the vanishing hairline, though.

"I have a client for you. That is, if you're not too busy right now?"

"Yeah? Now who's cracking wise?"

"Seriously. A big one, too, John. What's even better, win or lose your career in these parts will be off on a rip-roaring start. Yes sir, John Raines's name will be a household word on every wagging tongue around."

"You've got my attention, all right. Who *is* this potential client?"

"John Ashley. Not the whole gang, mind you. Just him"

Raines wondered if it were as quiet in Tom Ryan's office around the corner on First Street, just above the Governors Club, as it suddenly seemed to be in his.

"That's a bad punch line to an even worse joke, Tom"

"It's no joke, m'boy. I'm dead serious."

"I take on John Ashley for a client I'm liable to be the dead one."

"Maybe. But that's assuming he makes it to jail, let alone a courtroom, in one piece. Considering how Sheriff Baker up there in St. Lucie County feels about the man, I'd say that's a fairly bold assumption."

John Raines knew that to be so. In his short time on the southeast coast of Florida he had heard much about the legendary feud between the Sheriff of St. Lucie County and the outlaw, John Ashley, who when not busy robbing banks, lived on a farm with his family in Gomez. Ashley's neighbors in Gomez, along with many others in those parts—the black sharecroppers, day laborers, black as well as white, and their families—considered Ashley and his gang to be modern day Robin Hoods. Sheriff George Baker had been chasing the gang for almost fourteen years, beginning back in early 1911 when John Ashley returned from a fur trapping expedition, alone. That wouldn't have been unusual if Ashley had left that way. But he'd been with his trapping partner Desoto Tiger, son of a local Seminole chief. The two of them were gone for weeks in the Everglades, after otter, nutria, panther, bobcat, and the like. Then Ashley surfaced in Miami where he sold ninety hides to a fur dealer before continuing north to Gomez and the family farm No one asked any questions until Desoto Tiger's body was found floating in the Miami River a few days later, the bullet hole in the back of his head strong evidence it wasn't a swimming accident that did the Indian in. Being common knowledge the two men were partners, Palm Beach County Sheriff Baker—whose jurisdiction the little town of Gomez lay in—had no choice but to send a couple of deputies out to bring Ashley in.

The deputies returned three days later, disheveled, unarmed, carrying with them a single .44 bullet and a message for Sheriff Baker. The slug was for him and why didn't he come up to Gomez himself and let John Ashley deliver it personally? That is, if he were man enough to do so?

A running war, often violent, one that left dead men on the streets of Palm Beach, Stuart, and elsewhere, had ensued ever since. So far it appeared that John Ashley and his band of desperados were coming out on top. Their brazen defiance of the law and daring daylight bank robberies up and down the east coast of Florida had become the stuff of local lore, not to mention a painful thorn in the side of the authorities— especially George Baker's.

"All that's fixing to come to an end, though," Tom Ryan said, chuckling. "Maybe. Ol' George Baker's got a hot tip on Ashley's whereabouts and he's setting a trap for him tonight. Which brings us to you."

"The part I'm most interested in."

"A few years back I was able to help Mr. Ashley with some financial matters pertaining to his truck farm up there in Gomez. At the time banks around here were none too eager to extend credit to a man whose son has a habit of robbing them at his leisure. But you know me, John. I'm never one to turn away from a challenge. At great personal risk to my own financial wellbeing I called some friends of mine in Palm Beach and was able to help the old man out. I have to admit it gave me no small measure of self-satisfaction to do so."

"I imagine there was more reward in it for you than just the fact of doing a good deed."

Ryan's laughter on the other end went on until it turned into a fit of coughing, the cough and raspy voice, Raines knew, courtesy of the strong Cuban cigars the banker enjoyed often during the day.

"You have me there, all right John," Ryan said when his coughing stopped. "But that's beside the point. Now it seems Old Man Ashley sees me as some kind of miracle worker. Apparently, he's heard the same rumors I have about his boy's impending arrest. 'Cause just yesterday he called and asked if I could locate a good lawyer for his son. And of course, I immediately thought of my good friend, and not only that, but good attorney, John Raines."

"I've yet to try a criminal case, so you might want to continue your search. But I'm glad you think I'm good enough to consider."

"No, I'm pretty certain you're the man for the job, John. And like I mentioned earlier, the chances of there being a trial are damn slim. But I still think it'll do wonders for your career if we can get you put down on the record as attorney for the man."

"You're probably right. But tell me, where did this information of yours concerning Sheriff Baker's plans come from? And how reliable is it?"

"Oh, I'm right, all right," Ryan said. "I can near guarantee you that. As for my information, I just happen to know a little bird down at the courthouse. I think you may know him, too. Walter Harker?"

"I do."

"Well, the good deputy has a hard time keeping a secret, as you may, or may not, have heard."

"I have," Raines said, easily picturing the loud-mouthed deputy, a man big in physical stature, even bigger in his own mind as evidenced by the cocky way he strolled the hallways of the courthouse, white Stetson perched on his head and a Colt Dragoon pistol jammed into the holster strapped low on his waist. If Deputy Harker had been the butt of jokes John Raines heard by old timers loitering on the courthouse steps, they were jokes never told when the deputy was in earshot. The lawman's propensity for quick anger, his violent expression of that emotion, reason enough for this to be so.

"Anyway," Ryan continued, "Walter couldn't contain himself and told me all about Sheriff Baker's plans for the notorious outlaw tonight. Information Walter received, by the way, from his cousin Floyd, who happens to be one of Baker's deputies up there in St. Lucie. Which goes a long way towards documenting its truthfulness. Something not always the case with Walter's secrets." Ryan started to laugh again, to cough, but was able to cut it short. "Obviously, loose lips are a family condition with that bunch."

"So it would appear."

"But like I might have said, in return for my sworn secrecy I was able to secure a slight favor from our boy Walter. He'll be by later this afternoon, to personally escort you to your first confab with your new client."

"That doesn't give me much time to prepare."

"You won't need it. Almost noon, now. Just head on home for lunch and tell that lovely wife of yours's business is taking you out of town for the evening. I'm sure Sadie won't mind. That she'll be thrilled."

"Yes. I'm sure." Just then the noon whistle rang out from the fire station on the other side of New River at the base of Andrews Avenue Bridge. "I guess that's it, then."

"It is. Good luck tonight."

Before Ryan could hang up Raines asked, "Tom?"

"Yeah?"

"Thank you."

"Don't thank me just yet."

His friend's raspy laugh lingered in John Raines's thoughts long after the abrupt click on the other end of the line.

*** 

Deputy Walter Harker's Model A had seen better days, John Raines thought more than once as the old truck rattled along up Dixie Highway north to Palm Beach and beyond. Every pothole the deputy failed to avoid sent tremors through the rusting frame and loose floorboards in the rear bed, the wooden rails thumping ominously as the truck continued on. The flooring inside the cab was none too secure either, judging by the exhaust fumes rising up through it. Raines was grateful for the mild weather of the day that allowed him to keep the passenger's window rolled down. The fresh air blowing in went a long way towards dispelling the gasoline and cigar fumes that otherwise threatened to overwhelm him in the confined space.

"Shor' wuz nice of Mr. Ryan to give me a couple o' his own smokes," the deputy said as he struck a match in the driveway of Raines's house to light the end of a hand rolled stogie. Raines recognized the brand as indeed being the same his friend enjoyed. As the deputy backed out of the drive the engine backfired, the truck bucking and lurching in the lane, a cloud of pale blue exhaust smoke belching from the rear pipe to roll out over the Raines's front lawn. John Raines turned to see his wife, and their young boy, Hilton, standing out on the front steps of the little white stucco house waving goodbye. The concerned look on Sadie's face at the mechanical sounds of the deputy's truck brought a smile to his face, his boy's arm pumping side to side tugging at his heart in the next moment. There goes Daddy, disappearing in a puff of smoke, Raines thought. Like magic, perhaps, to the little one. He wondered if he would need some sort of magic to bring him back safely that night from this reckless business Tom Ryan may have engaged him in—back to the woman and boy standing on the steps of the small cottage, that in moments like this made him realize the strength of his love for them.

"Yes indeed, Deputy, you're right," Raines said, to bring his mind back to the present. "Tom Ryan is a heck of a fellow."

"Hellfire," the lawman said around the cigar stuck in his mouth. "And Tom Ryan is a prince among men. If it warnt for him and his hep at the bank me an' Myrtice'd be living in a chickee hut, or wurse, sumwher's I shudder t'even think 'bout. Thos' high falutin' bastids at t' Governors Club and t' bank wouldn' even look at me, much less loan me any money when I furst come down from Lake Worth a few years back. No sir, believe me when I tell you they wouldn'. Ol' Tom Ryan did, tho. He shor' did. Said he'd take a chance on me. Said I looked like a man he could trust. I never let 'im down, neither. You can bet yore ass on 'at.

There was one last pothole on the ungraded road the deputy managed to find before making the turn onto the paved Dixie Highway that would take them out of town, the truck shaking so hard with the jolt that Raines thought the rear bed would surely drop off in the dirt and be left behind.

"Sorry 'bout 'at." A sheepish grin split the lawman's face as he accelerated on the smoother, two-lane road. "I wanted to take my official deputy's car. 'At ol' Buick is a damn finer ride, I'm here to tell you. But seein' as me here bringin' you on this trip is more of a personal nature 'an official business I didn' think t' Sheriff would approve. So's we gets to ride in this ol' gal." He patted the dashboard affectionately with a beefy mitt of a hand. "She'll get us ther', all right, tho. Don' you worry none 'bout 'at, Mr. Raines."

"No worry on my part, Deputy. None at all."

They rode in silence for a while after that, John Raines watching the country they went by, green pines and palmetto stands that stretched out across the region on both sides of the two-lane road once they left the city limits of Fort Lauderdale behind. The asphalt covered highway made for an easier go than the crude grades they'd been on, even within the questionable comforts of Deputy Harker's ramshackle truck. Still, John Raines thought, the area had come a long way since the days of the pioneers and the open, and covered, wagons they forced through the palmetto and mosquito infested scrub to reach their version of Paradise.

Hell, RL rode into Fort Myers in 1905 on the back of the mule Pa reluctantly spared him It had been a long haul from Pendleton for his brother, John thought, grateful he'd followed his brother as soon as he was old enough to do so. He could still feel the hotness of the summer days of his youth when he was out picking sucker plants off the tobacco Lewis Raines grew on their farm outside of the little Georgia town. Could still remember the stickiness on his hands from pulling the moist, prickly leaves away from the stalks rising up out of the red clay his father tilled so carefully every year behind that same mule he gave to RL. According to Pa, by the time RL left home that old mule had seen its better days and he was glad to have the animal off his hands. Cost him less feed, especially for a beast that wasn't earning its own way anymore.

He was still only a kid, but John Raines had seen the look in his father's eyes and didn't believe the words coming from his mouth. Maybe it was Pa's way of saying he was going to miss me, RL said later when the two brothers were older and talking about the day RL left home. I suppose, John Raines said. But I don't see it. I don't see Pa caring enough about any human being to miss them, blood or no. You're too hard on that old boy, RL said. I'm damned if I'm hard enough, John Raines said, and the brothers let it go, never to talk of it again.

It was their father who was hard, though, and bantering aside both, brothers knew it. Lewis Raines was hard on everyone. Except their mother. And TJ, the baby of the bunch, who came for Lewis and Inez Raines very late in life. This last child took a lot out of Inez. Killed her, in fact. The frailness of his wife, as she lay dying, alongside the littleness of the child trying to suckle withered breasts that held no milk, had seemed to soften Lewis Raines. But only toward his wife and the newborn. RL and John were men in his eyes, even if their ages said they were still just boys, and Lewis expected them to perform as men did. When they failed, he let them know it, with words and the strap, and though John hated him for it, he accepted it. It was all he knew.

Apparently, his father hadn't always been that way, a surprising fact of life John Raines learned one day when he was twelve and in town with his father getting supplies for the spring planting. Carrying a bag of oats out to the wagon he lost his footing and went sprawling into the dirt of Main Street. Get up, boy, is what his father had to offer. You're making a spectacle of yourself. Now put them oats in the wagon. We don't have all day.

The boy did as he was told and once back inside the store, as he was going to hoist up another fifty-pound bag of oats, he felt a hand on his shoulder. Can I talk to you a minute, Johnny? Turning he stared up into the soft eyes of the Widow Crueller, the old lady who owned and ran the general store. Your father won't mind, she said when the boy hesitated. Not if it's me whose holding you back. The boy doubted that, but Widow Crueller wouldn't take no for an answer, steering him into her office in the back of the store. At that moment, the boy's father passed by with another heavy burlap bag of seed on his shoulders. To the boy's surprise Lewis Raines said nothing, and the boy, happy for the reprieve, let the old woman steer him where she may.

"How's your father," she asked, after pouring lemonade for the two of them and setting a plate of shortbread biscuits on a small table within easy reach of the boy.

"You saw how he is," he said, regretting his rudeness immediately and covering that regret as best he could with one of the biscuits.

"Yes, you're angry with him, I see. And probably rightfully so. I just hope you won't hold that anger for too long. Your father is a good man. Even if for now you don't believe that."

She turned away from the boy to look out the window at the busy street, the starched back of the shirtwaist she wore shining whitely in the shaft of light the window allowed—when she turned back the boy was surprised at the moisture in Mrs. Crueller's eyes.

"He wasn't always the man he is now," she said. "Not in the days when I knew him better. When he first rode into Pendleton, after being away for so long, oh I guess that was in the fall of 1890, perhaps '91. Of course, when you get to be my age the time flows all together. But when he rode in that fall day on that big handsome roan of his, his hair still jet black like it was when he and his uncle went off to war, his arms strong and lean, well, he still seemed to be the man I remembered." She stopped, gave a nervous little laugh that seemed so strange to the boy, coming from an old woman such as she. "He still looked the same even though we were both much older. Yes, he did, and I couldn't help myself, couldn't help but wonder if."

She stopped again, the boy wondering what she was talking about. But the biscuits and cool lemonade were enough of a pleasant distraction that he supposed if she wanted to talk, he was willing to let her.

"Of course, when he showed up again, maybe a month later, in the wagon with your mother sitting next to him holding your brother, just a baby, in her lap, well I didn't wonder anymore."

"Yes, ma'am," the boy said, for lack of anything better.

"But that's not I wanted to tell you, Johnny." And there was that nervous laugh again, and much as he had with the biscuit and his regret at speaking rudely, she smothered this laugh with a long drink of her lemonade.

"Your father was a good man. That's what I wanted to tell you. A kind and God-fearing man. It was the war that changed him and some bad things that happened here, after. And out west. Or so I'm told."

It was silent in the office for a bit after this, the boy curious if she would tell him what those bad things were—curious as well when his father would appear and put an end to this strange, but peaceful, time in the Widow Crueller's office.

"Don't be too hard on him, is what I wanted to tell you, Johnny. Try to find forgiveness for him. I hope you can."

Lewis Raines' hard knocking came on the door then, and in another moment the boy was on the wagon seat next to his father, the words of the widow going over and over in the boy's brain as he and his father rode home in silence; words still in his mind as he said his prayers before bed. In the morning, though, hard at work with RL and their father in the fields with the mule and the plow, the sound of resisting earth being overturned and Lewis Raines' angry voice all he could hear; well then, what the widow had told him the day before seemed to disappear. Three years later RL left home, the boy wishing mightily, as he watched his brother ride off on the old mule, that he was going with him—knowing as well that his time would come and soon.

Sitting in an office during the day, even if there were no clients, wearing a clean suit and not having to wipe sweat out of his eyes every few minutes, was one hell of an improvement over that sorry lot. John Raines had no problem with hard work. Pa's regular whuppings with that worn razor strop of his had beaten the inevitability of it into him, he supposed. The endlessness of it on the tobacco farm that had seemed so useless: chores at sunup, then school, more chores after school until the sun went down. The only time away from it being when the sermon was over at the Primitive Baptist Church on Sunday, and he and RL—and later TJ—could disappear into the pine woods ringing the farm, where they chased after imaginary Yankee soldiers, bears, outlaws, and other dangers, vanquishing them all with wooden sticks for guns, their bare chests brown from the everlasting Georgia sun shining above, bare feet hardened by the days spent walking the fields, woods, and red clay roads that made up their world.

That was the part he sometimes missed. Those few hours once a week with his brothers when they could get out from under Lewis Raines's heavy thumb. It wasn't much of a thing to miss, he thought as the Model A, with Deputy Harker at the wheel rattled on up the road. He wished there were something else but there wasn't. Maybe his mother, he supposed. But she'd been dead a long time and Pa not hardly long enough.

"C'here's where I grew up," Deputy Harker said as they came up on Lake Worth. The town was like any of the other small ones they'd gone through the last forty miles, Pompano, Delray, and such, consisting of only a few buildings, a post office, feed store, barber shop, drug store and a red brick bank on the corner of Main and Dixie. Beyond it, the lake from which the town had taken its name, shimmered in the distance, the afternoon sunlight turning the water a hazy blue. "Growin' pineapples wit' my Pa, two sisters, an' my Ma."

"Looks like a nice place," John Raines said.

"Wurn't 'at nice. Pineapple growin's some Goddamn thankless work if you ask me. I flat couldn' wait to git my young ass outta there. Thank God for the War and the Army's all I gotta say. Ke-rist, this being a deputy an' all is a sight finer 'an windin' up a dum' ol' fruit farmer!"

So, he and the good deputy had something more than just being fellow officers of the court, in common. Studying the gruff looking man at the steering wheel of the Model A it was hard to imagine. He hadn't realized they were roughly the same age. The deputy's flowing black handlebar mustache and bushy dark eyebrows hid that fact, making him seem older than he probably was. The mustache, Colt Dragoon strapped to his waist, polished snake-skin boots, and white Stetson perched rakishly atop his head, gave Deputy Harker a Wild West appearance, Raines thought. Yes indeed, he laughed to himself, the deputy had gone to a lot of effort and expense to look like anything but the truck farmer's kid he'd started out in life as. Just as he, in his stark office, double-breasted suits and pressed handkerchiefs wanted to forget he'd ever worked for nothing in the dry, dusty tobacco rows of South Georgia.

***

It was almost dark when they pulled into Vero Beach, still some ten miles shy of their destination for the evening, according to Deputy Harker. St. Lucie County ended in the middle of the Sebastian River Bridge just up the road, he said. Sheriff Baker would lay his trap there before the outlaw could escape into Brevard County and out of the Sheriff's jurisdiction.

"Not likely to prevent 'im frum givin' chase, tho. If need be. Not if I know George Baker."

Fall was upon them, with its early darkness so unlike the recent days of summer, Raines thought as the deputy wheeled the truck slowly down the quiet main street of the town. Shopkeepers came out of their stores, a Rexall Drugs on one corner, Smoke Shop & Out of Town Papers on the other, the men hanging "Closed for The Day" signs up before starting down the sidewalk toward their homes. He realized as they drove past the closing shops that it was the first day of November. A new month. Soon the cool weather would be on them, a slight touch of chill already in the evening air. Along with the cooler weather would come the holidays, Thanksgiving, Christmas, and the New Year. He hoped 1925 would be a better one for him Financially, at least. Hopefully, the actions he was taking tonight were the first steps towards that.

"We got' bout an hour or so to kill," the deputy said as he pulled the truck into the dirt parking lot of a roadhouse just north of the town. "Might as well get sum grub. 'Less you want sumthin' stronger? Ol' Alma inside can hep us wit' 'at, too, I've heard."

"No," Raines said as he opened his door and stepped out onto the solid, un-moving ground of the parking lot. "Just food sounds fine."

A faded, wooden sign nailed above the screen door leading into the roadhouse proclaimed in faded, as well, red letters, "Alma's Place. Good Eats!" As they pushed through the screen door into the small room and took seats at the lunch counter up against one wall, he spied a portly black woman bustling around in the kitchen, smelled meat sizzling on a grill he couldn't see. A quick desire for some real down-home food—like his mother used to cook, and that Sadie, God bless her, even after ten years out of Illinois still hadn't quite mastered— overwhelmed him. Without even looking at the menu, he ordered chicken-fried steak with all the trimmings.

"I'll have whut the counselor's havin'," the deputy said when the tired looking white waitress in a stained blue uniform wrote down Raines's order. "Here's lookin' at you." Harker tipped his cup to Raines a minute later when the girl had returned with two for the men and filled them to the rim with hot coffee. "To a gent with good taste in grub."

The "grub" *was* good, cubed beef pounded fresh and tender, fried in a spicy milk and flour gravy, with creamed potatoes, pinto beans, and hot biscuits on the side. Raines wolfed it down, surprised at how hungry he actually was, considering he hadn't done much of anything that day other than sit at his desk and on the hard bench seat of Deputy Harker's Model A. Another surprise? The brief feeling of gladness that came over him, out of nowhere, it seemed. Glad for what, he wondered as he sopped up the last of the gravy with a crumbly biscuit. The good food? His friend Tom Ryan's thinking of him? All of it? Too many questions he decided, as he drained the last of his coffee and signaled to the waitress for a refill. Best to leave it to the fact of the good food, his sudden hunger, and that he had enjoyed the meal properly. Besides, the rest of it was far too uncertain yet to have an opinion one way or the other.

"Y'know, the way I figure it," Deputy Harker said, pushing back from the counter a little to hitch his gun belt up before taking another long pull of the fresh coffee the waitress brought them "'At Ashley feller's furst mistake wus killin' 'at Indian an' not fixin' it so's the body'd never be found. Wit'out a body he could'a said damn near anythin' an' been okay wit' it. No *corpsey delicty*, no case. Wouldn' you agree, Mr. Raines? Yo're the lawyer, after all."

"There's some valid legal precedence involved, to be sure." Night had fallen completely while they ate, and with the moon at rest the only light beyond the roadhouse were the headlights of an occasional car chugging either north or south on the highway. "But men have been convicted of murder minus a victim's corpse. Of course, the prosecution has to have a pretty compelling case, reliable eyewitnesses and the like."

"Ke-rist," the deputy snorted into his coffee cup. "Only eyewitness t' any of John Ashley's doin's are dead. Or members of his gang. An' they won' talk. No sir. Not considerin' Ashley's habit of bustin' out'a every jail cell he's been in."

"That creates a problem for the State's case then."

"Now, if it'd been a nigger he killed 'at furst time back then no one'd of given it a second thought." The lawman lit up another of Tom Ryan's cigars, his mouth smiling wide around it in a big grin. "Or even jus' a reg'lar ol' Sem'nole. But not Chief Tiger's boy. Not the way 'at ol' chief was in tight with Mr. Stranahan and 'em other traders there on the New River. No sir, 'at warn't smart a'tall. Then, once they'd arrested 'im an' all, Ashley made his second mistake."

"What was that?" Raines was eager for the deputy's views on the outlaw and any potential help it may give him in preparing a defense, if given the chance, for the man.

"Why, bustin' out'a jail down there in Miamuh 'fore he could go to trial. Hellfire, man. No white men on a jury'd of convicted 'im Even Tommy Tiger knew 'at. He'd a been happy jus' for a trial. Then all parties involved could'a gone on their merry ways. Ashley, for his part, hopefully smart enuff to stay out' a 'em Everglades where the chief and his boys could get a hold of 'im and 'minster their own brand of Indian justice. Leastways, 'at's how I see it. Yes sir, an' I prob'ly ain't the only one to say so."

The deputy stood up from the stool and laid some crumpled bills on the counter. "Now, amigo, it's time to ride."

"I imagine you're right," John Raines said, as he, too, stood up. "About Ashley's decisions back then."

"Damn straight, I'm right. 'Bout all of it, too."

The big deputy pushed the screen door open and the two men walked out of "Alma's" into the night.

\*\*\*

Things began happening faster after that, Raines told his wife later. The roadhouse was only five miles or so south of the Sebastian River, the border between the two counties, and where Sheriff Baker of St. Lucie planned to finally capture his old nemesis and the men who rode with him. Raines had been on that section of highway once before, when he'd come over from Fort Myers with RL on a business trip of his brother's to Titusville. He remembered the bridge across the river as being long and narrow, a ramshackle wooden affair he'd been glad to be on the other side of safely. A feat, given the creaking, protesting wooden rails as RL's Ford rolled over them. It wasn't like it was a deep gorge with a raging river below they had to be fearful of, but the slowly moving water beneath the bridge was likely full of alligators. Raines hadn't thought of that until RL had brought it up as they started over the bridge—along with his opinion that if the bridge happened to give out and they found themselves in the water, the best advice he could give his younger brother was to swim like hell for the nearest bank. Now, with Deputy Harker slowing the Model A down as they approached the foot of that bridge, Raines wondered if any improvements had been made to the old wooden structure since his last visit.

Before they could find out, though, two men came out of the bushes on the side of the road, one waving a kerosene lantern in his hand, both of them calling out in unison, "Hold it right there."

"Now, Floyd," Harker said through his open window as the two strangers approached, "is 'at you?" In the soft light of the storm lantern Raines could see that the men were indeed deputies, in uniform and with guns drawn. "It's a good thing I ain't Ashley, you dum'ass. Or you'd be dead shor' 'nuff!"

"Put yore piece 'way, Mel," the man not holding the lantern said as he stepped up to Harker's side of the Model A. "It's jes' my cuz'n Walter an' sum other feller."

In the lantern light Raines could see a family resemblance in the features of the man standing outside the truck, who though minus a thick, handlebar mustache, still had the same lean and hard worn look of country folk that Walter carried.

"Who's t'other feller wit' you?" Floyd pointed with his pistol through the window at Raines.

"Git 'at Goddamn gun outta my face 'fore sumone gits hurt." Harker pushed the pistol, and his cousin, back with a shove of his hand. "My companion here's Mr. John Raines. He's lookin' to be Ashley's attorney."

"Ain't thet a hoot?" Floyd turned to the other deputy holding the lantern up. "Ya hear thet, Mel? There's a man inside Walter's truck sez he's John Ashley's attorney. Whut ya think of thet?"

The man called Mel let out a loud whoop, the light from the lantern weaving to and fro for a minute with what Raines figured was the other deputy's uncontrolled laughter.

"'At's sure 'nuff a good one, Floyd. Better tell 'im, tho, ain't a lawyer alive 's gonna be able to talk Ashley's way outta this one."

"Now thet's sure 'nuff a fact." Floyd was back at Harker's window. "Go on now, Walter. And when you git t'other side pull in the bushes and shut yore lights off. Jes' sit tight till you hear the all clear. Sheriff Baker an' t'rest of us 'll be right here's waitin' on Ashley an' his boys. They's comin' down from Jacksonville tonight, back down to Gomez like I tol' you. Only reason we didn' open up on you feller's 'cause we know whut kind o' car Ashley's drivin'." He thumped the side of the Model A with the flat of his hand, a tight grin on his lips, just like the one Raines was used to seeing on Harker's face. "An' this damn sure ain't it! When you gonna git rid o' this piece o' junk anyhow?"

"When you buy me a new one, I reckon," Deputy Harker said. He wasn't smiling like his cousin, though, Raines wondering if somehow a nerve had been touched by Floyd.

"Uh huh. Well don' hol' yore breath none. Now git!" and Floyd slapped the side of the truck again.

Letting the clutch out, Deputy Harker eased the old Model A forward onto the one lane bridge, the sound of the tires thumping against the wood planks vibrating into the cab. Way across the river a few scattered lights shone in the homes of people living on the edge of the water, Raines thought. Be lots of fresh fish for eating. Game too, he bet. They had to come down and drink. Not as plentiful perhaps as in the old days. Too many people coming south anymore, crowding everything out. Because of the climate. The ads placed in the northern papers by businessmen such as Mr. Flagler. And Raines's own friend, Tom Ryan. Those men wanted that northern money. Wanted to turn their Palm Beaches, Miami, and Fort Lauderdale into real cities. Not just trading outposts on the banks of nowhere. Hell, he guessed he did, too. Country lawyers didn't make a lot of money. But with them Yankee folk coming south every day now it looked like he had a shot at it. Wasn't that why he'd come to Fort Lauderdale when asked? To grab something for himself out of that Florida swamp in one fashion or another, just like Henry Flagler and Tom Ryan?

"Well, lookie here," the deputy said. They were mid-way across the bridge, the lawman's words bringing Raines's attention back from the lights over the water and his thoughts, to the beams of a car's lights fast approaching the other end of the bridge. "Whoever it is, he's gonna have to give way. I wus' sure here furst."

The driver of the other car must have felt the same, for no sooner had Deputy Harker opened his mouth than the headlights of the stranger's vehicle began moving in reverse off the foot of the bridge. Harker gunned the Model A forward and, in another minute, they rattled off of the wooden span and onto paved highway. A dark colored Buick Roadmaster sat idling on the side of the roadway and when the headlights of the truck hit it Raines could see a smiling, nondescript appearing, man behind the wheel, cigarette dangling from his lips, a straw boater pushed back from his forehead. There may have been other men in the car with him, but the Model A rolled by too quickly and Raines didn't get a good enough look to be sure.

"Evening gents," the man behind the wheel called out as the old truck drove by. Deputy Harker had let off on the gas and was hitting the brake as he pulled over to the side of the road. But by then, as Raines turned around to see, the big Buick was already on the bridge heading south, the red ember of the man's cigarette chucked out the window, a flickering arc disappearing in the night.

"Well, I'll be Goddamned," the deputy said as he wheeled the truck back around toward the bridge. "'At was the ol' devil hisself."

"Who?"

"John Ashley, man! Whut other devil you know of in these parts?" Harker banged the dashboard with his hand, a look of wild glee on his face as he whipped the Stetson off his head and slapped the dash with that as well. "Mr. John Goddamn Ashley his own Goddamn self."

The moon had been slowly rising since they'd left "Alma's" and now, parked and with the headlights off, in the soft light of the half-moon the men in the Model A could see the dark hulk of the Buick moving slowly across the bridge, its head lights sweeping the way in front of it. Raines happened to glance toward the river flowing away from the bridge, the water visible only because of the phosphorous shining on its rippling surface. It's too pretty an evening for this, he thought. For this sort of work. Just what kind of "work" he was about to engage in he wasn't sure. All he really knew at that point in time was that he had come a long way that day to be a man's attorney. A man who, according to Deputy Harker at least, was in the hulking car heading now toward the other side of the Sebastian River, where, known or not to the man driving the Buick, men, armed and serious, waited.

Car lights came on suddenly as a four-door sedan pulled out of the bushes on the side of the road in front of the Model A, the sedan coming to a halt sideways across the foot of the bridge, effectively cutting off any potential escape route—forcing Raines's attention back to what was unfolding in front of him

Just before the Buick reached the end of the bridge a voice called out, the sound of it coming over the water to where Deputy Harker, Raines, and the men in the other sedan sat.

"Halt! Or we'll shoot!" It was quiet, other than the sound of the Roadmaster's engine as the car continued on. "This is George Baker, Ashley," the voice called out again. "You know I mean what I say. You know I'll shoot if I have to."

The big Buick stopped, but only long enough for the driver to put it in reverse and start backwards across the bridge as fast as the whining transmission screaming out in the night would allow. Two men jumped out of the sedan blocking the Buick's way in front of Raines and Deputy Harker, one of the men raising his drawn pistol toward the sky and firing off a warning shot into the air. "You better hold up now Ashley.

If you boys know whut's good for you." The Buick came to a stop one more time in the middle of the narrow bridge, sitting there for what seemed a long time, the sound of the Roadmaster's powerful engine idling in neutral a low throbbing over the water.

"What's he doing?" Raines asked. "There's no escape for him."

"I 'magine Mr. Raines 'at's 'xactly whut he's a ponderin' over." In the tiny bit of moonlight that had leaked into the cab of the truck Raines could see how the deputy's eyes were wet and shining with excitement. "Tho' a smart man wouldn' never count ol' Ashley out. An' no one I know of s'ever called George Baker dumb. Not to his face, 'leastways. Not even 'at Ashley, I reckon. 'Specially not now."

As if having made a decision, the Buick began inching backwards again, though for just a moment, the driver thinking better of it and the transmission grinding in protest as he shoved it back into first gear and headed toward the lights and voices of the men behind the roadblock. The engine of the sedan blocking his escape route on the north end of the bridge roared into life and after angling back around started on across the bridge behind Ashley's car.

"Well then," Harker said as he hit the starter button of the truck. "'At's it, I gues'. Let's go see 'em arrest the famous outlaw."

In the headlights of the Model A and the others on the bridge Raines could see the shadowy figures of men stepping out of the Buick. A commotion of some sort broke out on the bridge, he couldn't really see, and suddenly shots were fired, loud reports that jerked Raines back in his seat. There was a short pause, and then one more shot rang out, its muzzle flash visible now that they were almost there, a quick splash of fire blasting into the night. The smell of spent cordite came drifting into the cab of the truck, burning Raines's nostrils even as the loud popping of the four shots still echoed in his head.

"Now Goddamn, 'at cain't be good." Harker snorted as he rolled up to a stop behind the sedan that had blocked Ashley's escape route. "Not for sumbody. An' I think I know's who 'at sumbody might be."

Once out of the truck Raines could smell how exhaust fumes from the car engines still idling in neutral had mixed in with that of fired-off gunpowder, the blue-gray clouds of both hanging over a group of men clustered in front of the parked cars. The headlights from a St. Lucie

County sheriff's sedan illuminated the scene, lighting up the excited faces of Deputy Harker's cousin, Floyd, the other deputy with him, the two men from Raines and Harker's vantage point on the far side of the river, and another man standing in the middle of the circle of men, this man apparently in charge. All of the men were staring at something lying on the bridge, a something, that as Raines drew nearer, with Deputy Harker leading the way, he could see were the bodies of four men. They lay face down on the wooden planks, ragged holes in the back of their heads oozing blood that shone darkly in the bright lights of the sheriff's car.

"Who's that with you, Walter?"

The man in the middle of the circle gestured with the pistol still in his hand at Raines. He was much smaller than Raines thought he'd be, thin and balding, and in the frayed suit he was wearing, easily taken for a schoolteacher or store clerk. If not for the gun held loosely in his right hand, Raines thought. If not for that wild look in his eye.

"Why, Sheriff Baker, sir, c'here's Mr. John Raines." Harker's smile broke wide on his face as he stepped into the circle of living men, pulling Raines by his sleeve along with him, his eyes still wet with the excitement Raines had seen in them earlier. He's happy now, Raines thought. Happy to be a part of all this. "Mr. Raines's an attorney. John Ashley's attorney."

"Now you don't say."

The wild look had left the sheriff's eyes, sparkling now with what Raines could only figure as being amusement. He's enjoying, this, too. All of them are. Standing around these dead men like it was nothing more than a Sunday after church and they're waiting out front, jackets unbuttoned, hats pushed back, and just hoping their wives' will be done soon with jacking their jaws.

"Well sir, it's a little late for that, I reckon." The sheriff turned to John Raines, who sensing the shift in attention, had jerked his eyes away from the dead men to focus on the sheriff's hard stare. "What you looking at, Counselor?"

"Some dead outlaws, I guess."

"See anything unusual?"

When Raines hesitated, the sheriff grabbed the carbide light from the deputy standing next to him and clicked it on. In the yellow glow Raines saw for the first time that the dead men sprawled out on the bridge had their hands handcuffed behind their backs.

"Now that you can see a little better in the light, I'm going to ask you again, Counselor. Anything unusual here?"

"No. Except that they're dead."

"Got any thoughts on that, Counselor?"

There were always lines in life to cross, he figured, not liking at all the one he was being asked to cross now.

"I suppose," Raines said, his eyes never wavering from the sheriff's, "I should have requested my fee beforehand."

The laughter from the men huddled around the dead outlaws on the bridge took him all the way across that line—laughter he would hear, and regret, for a long time to come.

# PART THREE

The boat was cursed. John Raines didn't believe this the Saturday morning in August of 1936 when he set out with his son, his daughter, and his best friend, Tom Ryan, aboard. By the end of the day, though, he certainly did. Believed it beyond the shadow of a doubt.

At five o'clock the day before, he left his office to walk down to Tom Ryan's bank where he paid off the last of his debt. It had taken ten years, but he had done it. The crash of the land boom in the late 20's, followed two years later by the disaster on Wall Street had hurt an awful lot of people, John Raines included. Caught up in the land frenzy of 1925 he had bought lots upon lots on margin. When the bottom dropped out in an effort to recoup his losses, at Tom Ryan's urging, Raines had done the same on the stock exchange. This seemed like a reasonable maneuver, considering how the market was flourishing at the time. It wasn't long, either, before he had money in the bank again—sort of. After Black Tuesday that money wasn't worth the price of the paper it was printed on.

"I believe you and I, my friend, have overextended ourselves," Tom Ryan said one afternoon a couple of months after Black Tuesday, when the smoke of the crash had cleared, and the damage done visible for all to see.

Raines had spent the day behind his desk going over financial statements and other sheaves of official looking papers, all of which in one way or the other said the same thing: he owed money. Now, at the end of that day, over drinks with Tom Ryan at the Governors Club, Raines listened as his long-time friend continued with what he was saying.

"Yes sir, John, I believe we have."

"Now what?"

It was a simple enough question. One with no simple answer Raines was sure. If shell-shocked by what had happened, like some of the others who had followed Ryan's lead during those crazy times, Raines didn't blame his friend for the disaster that followed. Ryan was a victim, too. Besides, Raines and the others could have said no at any time. Could have sold out at the first sign of trouble. They'd known the risks. So that no, it was not on Tom Ryan at all.

"I suppose we just carry on," Tom Ryan said, his lean face twisted into a wry grin as he sipped his Manhattan. "File bankruptcy and see how the chips fall in a court of law." His wry grin spread a little wider. "Good thing I just happen to have one of the best lawyers in town on my side."

"I'll do what I can for you, Tom. That goes without saying." Raines took a sip of his own drink, the taste of it all wrong. This wasn't the fault of the drink, he knew, but more from what Ryan had just said. "But I won't be filing bankruptcy. I borrowed the money. It's on me to make it good."

"If I didn't like you so much, John, I'd say you were a fool. Care for one more?"

"No, and maybe I am. But it won't sit right with me if I don't do everything I can to pay that money back."

They parted ways outside the club, shaking hands in the gloom of the winter afternoon. The light was on in Ryan's office at the bank on the corner. When Raines turned away from his friend, he looked up to see the light on in his own office on the fourth floor of the building at the other end of the street. Other than those of the Governors Club, they were the only lights in all of downtown.

"Good luck to you then, John."

"The same to you."

Those were some hard times all right. He had to sell the lovely little house on New River that Sadie had cried about twice—once when they moved in, and again when they had to move out. The four of them, for by this time the girl, Marilyn, had come along, took up residence on the top floor of a three-story boardinghouse Raines bought as an investment before the troubles began. For four years the Raines family lived there, Sadie doing the work of the woman who had run the place before, while John, when not doing the various chores around the place his wife was not capable of, waited at his office for clients who were few and far between.

Hard times—but times that slowly began to improve. His law practice started to flourish, mainly with the bankruptcies other businessmen in town had to file. In 1934 Raines was able to sell the boardinghouse. He used some of the profit to pay off debts, the rest as a down payment on a house in a new development he and Tom Ryan were building on the backs of rich Northerners coming back to the Gold Coast once again.

It had taken him a long time, yes, but he had done it—paid off the majority of the debts he owed. And while doing so managed to live a life.

The boat was a part of that life. As well as a good escape from it. Not only that, but a reward he had allowed himself.

Now, on this Saturday morning toward the end of August, after a long time of not being aboard the boat, he was taking her out to sea. Close to a year had passed since the last time he had done so—a week-long trip from Fort Lauderdale down to the Florida Keys. And unknowingly, when they left the dock behind Raines' house, dead into the terrible Labor Day hurricane of 1935. A storm that took RL's life and near killed Raines, his other brother TJ, and his fourteen-year-old son, Hilton, as well.

All that was a memory. The hard times—that Sunday afternoon, down behind Matecumbe when that big storm rolled in off the Florida Straits and blew his boat, and those aboard it, all to hell.

This day, unlike then, held good signs of weather. A decent breeze out of the east, coming off the Gulf Stream five miles distant, just cool enough to spare them from the heat of the summer day. Billowy clouds floated in an otherwise clear sky, the sunlight turning the ocean just the same deep a blue as the sky overhead. Good weather indeed. Weather, along with the slight chop on the water, patches of floating debris here and there, and flying fish soaring over the tops of the little waves, that promised good fishing to be had.

The good weather, the conditions of the sea, the hope for fine fishing, drove any thoughts still left of last year's hurricane out of his head, and once clear of the jetties lining the inlet, Raines pushed the throttle forward, put the boat up on plane, and headed for the Gulf Stream.

\*\*\*

The boat—the *Mari-Lyn*—was a cabin cruiser thirty-four feet from stern to bow. With her nine and a half foot beam, she was as sturdy a boat as they came. This sturdiness had been well proved to Raines during the hurricane, accounting for the fact that other than RL, they made it through alive. The cabin had two berths just forward of a small galley. A wooden table sat in the center of the living space, flanked by wooden benches topped with soft cushions that also served as berths. With an enclosed head fitted in between the portside bench and the forward berths, two water tanks below deck that TJ had been able to connect to the little sinks in the galley and head, the boat had almost all the comforts of home.

The helm was located just aft of the cabin, throttle, big chrome steering wheel, and compass fitted into the hard wooden bridge. Two tall wooden chairs, one just behind the wheel and the other on the starboard side of the hatch, were for the captain and mate to sit in while manning the boat. Canvas flaps and a canvas roof, stretched from the cabin to mid-ship, giving shade from the sun. The side flaps could be rolled up on nice days to help toward keeping everyone cool and comfortable aboard. The deck from stern to mid-ship was wide open, allowing this area of the craft for the fishing. Outriggers, one on each side, rose up just past the cabin with rod holders, again one on each side, at the stern. Thus rigged, the boat could troll four baits at a clip and not entangle the lines.

It was a good boat all the way around, one Raines had been very happy with—until the hurricane had changed that happiness. If not for his son's insistence over dinner one night back in March, Raines would have been content to let the boat sit idle at the dock. Until, he supposed, the day came when he was able to look at the boat without thinking of the long ride back from Elliot's Key with RL's dead body lying in the forward berth. And of the train ride to Fort Myers that followed, when Raines and Hilton carried RL home, to be laid next to his wife, and her father, the judge, in the family plot.

His son didn't feel the same, and now, as they left the inlet behind, Raines was glad he hadn't.

"So, Pop," Hilton said at dinner that night in early March, "don't you think it's about time we got that ol' *Mari-Lyn* back in shape? She's just sitting there going to waste while we're missing the best sail fishing of the season."

Before Raines could say anything, Marilyn jumped in.

"Yeah, Pop. I'd like to go fishing, too. Catch one of those sailfish Hilton always goes on about. Heck, catch any stupid ol' fish I can."

Raines couldn't help but smile at his daughter. At her calling him Pop like that. She only did so around her brother. At eleven, she was clearly enamored of her older brother in that way little sisters had, or so Sadie had told him. It wasn't the sort of thing he would have figured out on his own, having had no sisters in his life to compare with. When he was alone with his daughter he was always "Daddy," the sweetness they shared so different from what he had with his son. This he *did* know, and with no help from his wife.

"Well sweetie," Raines said after a bit. "I'm not sure fish are as stupid as you think. If they were, they'd be a lot easier to catch."

He pushed his plate away, thinking to let the conversation end, thinking of the Cuban coffee Sadie had percolating in the kitchen, and the fact that he had one of Tom's good Cuban cigars to go with it.

"I know one thing, Pop," Hilton said. "If we don't get the boat up and running and out on the ocean, we won't catch anything. Easy, or not."

"A valid statement, son. Arguable in any court of law, I imagine." But Raines could see by the look on his son's face this wasn't going to end the conversation. "Tell you what, son. Let's take this boat talk out to the back porch. We can enjoy the pleasant evening while we figure out where to start."

"All right, Pop," Hilton burst out. "Now you're talkin."

"I want to come," Marilyn piped up.

"Then c'mon, the both of you," Raines said. "Ask your mother if you can be excused and then let's see what our three fine minds can come up with."

For the next couple of months, Saturdays, unless work or something else interfered, Raines and his two children spent at getting the boat back to rights. He enjoyed watching the two of them together, Hilton the oldest, taking the lead while his sister did what he asked. Watching them he was reminded again that it was a good thing they took after their mother in the looks department. They both had the same thick dark hair and eyes as Sadie's—hair and eyes that even in the delirium of his sick bed in the army hospital in Columbia all those years back he couldn't help but notice.

Looking back on those Saturdays later when they were done, Raines saw how they were some of the best days he ever spent with his son and daughter—good days when the three of them, young and old, worked together, solely focused on the task at hand.

The first thing they did was take broom, shovel and dustpan to the boat, clearing up the debris left from the storm. The deck was still covered with the sand, mangrove, and buttonwood leaves blown aboard by the powerful winds. Mixed in with the sand and leaves were broken bits of glass from the windshield, as well as shattered wood from the dock they had tied up to before the storm came in, and that didn't stand up to the weather like Raines had hoped it would. Of course, he realized now how very little made by man could have stood up to those winds, let alone the tidal surge that lifted them up at the height of the storm and carried them to the other side of the key.

With the decks cleaned and swept they turned to the canvas covering the area between the helm and mid-ship. The canvas had been torn and shredded by the hurricane, hanging now in forlorn strips off the wooden frame. Raines bought new canvas sheets from Roy's boat yard and Sadie joined in here, cutting the sturdy cloth to the proper dimensions. When this was done, Raines and Hilton, while Marilyn handed up rope and tie-downs as needed, secured the new flaps and tops in place.

Replacing the shattered windshield fronting the bridge and helm was the next step. The wooden framework was badly bent and heat, saltwater spray, and the daily humidity of South Florida, had managed to seal the glass even firmer in place. It took some doing but Raines and Hilton were able to pry the two panes out, repair the mangled frame, and install new glass. Cleaned up and with the new windshield and canvas in place, the boat was starting to look like it had before. That night Raines took the family to dinner at the Governors Club where the four of them celebrated the good work they had accomplished so far.

Addressing the old Cummins diesel inboard came next on Raines' checklist. The Cummins had been a good, reliable engine for the boat. Until saltwater and windblown sand had forced its way into the engine compartment during the storm If TJ hadn't been with them—and his almost magical mechanical skills—they would not have made it back to Lauderdale when the storm was over. So now, there was no way around it: the Cummins had to go.

Hilton was happier about this fact than his father. "That's great, Pop. We can get one of those new Chryslers I've been reading about. We'll make that ol' *Mari-Lyn* fly!"

The enthusiasm of the fifteen-year-old boy was contagious enough that Raines looked into Chrysler inboards. But the price of these engines dampened this enthusiasm After all, and he told Hilton as much, he was the one paying the freight. Roy at the boat yard had a better solution.

"Fortunately for you, Mr. Raines, I jes' happen to have the perfect engine for you."

Roy was about as grizzled as they came, somewhere in his fifties but it was hard to say for sure. He had perpetual whiskers on his face, a short and stocky build, and a record with the courthouse that was impossible to ignore. Yet, when it came to boats and what ailed them, he was the best there was on the east coast of Florida.

"I think yore gonna be very happy you come to me."

The "perfect engine" was a five-year-old eight-cylinder, 165 horsepower, gasoline fueled Lycoming inboard sitting up on two sawhorses in the rear of the boat yard's big bay. Clean and shiny it stood out in stark difference to the rest of its surroundings: greasy engine blocks, broken masts, shattered hulls from boats that due to a bad end had ended up at the boat yard, to be repaired or used for parts, however Roy saw fit.

"She comes off a beauty of a thirty-two-footer," Roy said as he led Raines over to the Lycoming. "You know Lawson, up there in Palm Beach?"

"Know him well, Roy."

Layne Lawson had made a fortune growing citrus west of Lake Worth in the early days. When a hard freeze killed his trees one year, it was lucky for him Prohibition had just come into effect. From then, until that silly law was repealed, Lawson made an even bigger fortune running rum between Miami and the Bahamas. Now, he and his two sons lived in a big house in Palm Beach just down from the Flagler Mansion. How he made his living these days Raines couldn't say. Occasionally, the *Palm Beach Post* or the *Miami News* ran an article about a dinner, or society function held at the Lawson mansion, where, more often than not, "businessmen" from Chicago and New York were listed as Lawson's guests. This served to answer any questions the locals may, or may not have, about Layne Lawson and his sons.

"Sad to say, this c'here boat wus a birthday present ol' Lawson up there in Palm Beach give his oldest boy. I s'pose you can guess the rest, Mr. Raines. If'en you cain't I'll give you a little hint: 'at boat couldn't compete with the jetties down there at Government Cut. No sir, she sho're 'nuff could not."

"I imagine not," Raines said. He didn't know much about engines and wished that TJ was there with him. Still, this engine Roy was showing him—a Lycoming something or other—looked like more than enough to do the job for the "Mari-Lyn."

"I couldn' save the boat but I did all right with this engine c'here. Lawson didn' want nuthin' to do with it. Jes' tole me to get what I could for it, and it was all mine for the salvage job." He stopped, one hand scratching his whiskered chin while he pondered a price. "Tell you whut, Mr. Raines. You can have her for 1,200. Anyone else? Heck, I wouldn' let her go for less 'an 1,500."

Raines didn't believe that for a minute and ignoring the sly wink Roy threw at him, said, "How about eight hundred?"

"Here now, but yo're one tough horse trader I see."

"Just a lawyer, Roy, that's all."

"Yessir, and a mighty good one at that." Roy chuckled and scratched his chin whiskers again before adding, "As I know from my own personal 'sperience."

"That you do, Roy," Raines said. Implied, but unnecessary to add: the fact of some still outstanding legal fees owed to Raines by one Roy. "That you do."

"Tell you whut, Mr. Raines. Seein' as how you and me go way back, 'at eight hundred—and mind you now, sech a low offer might offen' another man—sounds jes' fine to me. Shake?"

Shortly before Memorial Day weekend of that year the boat was done. New canvas, new glass in the windshield, decks swept, cleaned, and freshly stained. The last piece of the restoration puzzle, the Lycoming engine, sat in its new home below decks, fuel tanks topped off with fresh gasoline. It was time for the *Mari-Lyn's* shakedown cruise and Raines figured the holiday weekend coming was as good a time as any to do so.

Saturday started off cool in the morning, the clouds sparse in an otherwise blue sky. A slight haze hung over the deep-water canal behind the house where the boat, clean and white in the morning sun, tugged at her mooring lines with the tide. Raines, aware that the morning coolness wouldn't last—that by midday it would most likely be a scorcher—was happy for the little cool in the air as he and Hilton loaded supplies aboard the board for the family outing. They were all dressed properly for the day in the sun, though, Raines and his son in khaki pants, long sleeved khaki shirts they could roll the sleeves up on when it got too hot, and long billed fishing caps to keep the sun off their face. Marilyn had on jeans, a cotton blouse, and a large straw hat atop her head. Her mother wore a sun dress and a straw hat similar to the one she had made her daughter wear, Sadie looking beautiful, as she always did to Raines.

The Lycoming 8 started right up, a steady throb in the engine compartment as Raines idled the boat way from the dock and out toward New River. It sounded different, much different, from the Cummins. Cleaner, he thought. Powerful. And maybe because it ran on gasoline and not diesel. Again, if TJ were there, he'd be able to tell him. But TJ was in Louisiana, or so the last postcard Raines had received from his brother said. That had been at Christmas. By now, end of May? Hell, TJ could be anywhere.

The Lycoming *was* powerful. Once out in the New River Raines pushed the throttle forward and it was as if the boat jumped in the water.

"Oh boy, Pop," Hilton yelled from the stern, where he sat with his mother and sister. "This is more like it."

Raines turned from the wheel and smiled at his son—disappointed, like Hilton, when Sadie said above the roar of the engine, "Slow it down a little, John, please."

The shakedown cruise went well with no problems of any kind arising. That night after dinner, Raines and Hilton sat out on the dock, watching as the boat bobbed at its moorings, the moonlight reflecting off the fresh coat of paint. Raines had a glass of Fundador in one hand, the other holding one of Tom Ryan's good Cuban cigars. Thoughts of trips—some with his family and other times not, just Raines, a couple of his friends, and his son—to the Bahamas that summer, ran through his head. He had never been to those islands. But Hemingway's articles in Esquire about the giant tuna, sailfish, and big blue marlin he had caught in those waters certainly had piqued Raines' interest. Now that the *Mari-Lyn* was back in shape there was no reason not to.

"We can go to the Keys, too," Hilton said when his father brought up the Bahamas. He took a sip of the soda he was drinking; his request for brandy having been denied. "Give them another shot."

"We'll see," Raines said. The thought of the Keys brought him up short. "Let's do Bimini first. After that, some of the out islands. Get our feet wet on them."

"Whatever you say, Pop. I'm ready for any of it."

Yes, Raines thought, but didn't say. But they'd have to see about the Keys. After a couple of runs to the Bahamas he might be ready for that. He'd just have to see.

***

But there were no trips to Bimini, or any other island that summer. Come the middle of June the rainy season set in with a vengeance. For days on end, it rained—mainly afternoon storms rolling in from the west, typical that time of year. A tropical storm in July crossed the state from the Gulf, followed a week later by a hurricane brushing the coast on its way up to the Carolinas. No real damage was done by either, but the cleanup interfered with people's weekend plans, the Raines' included, perhaps even more so. He was swamped that summer with closings concerning Tom Ryan's new development. A sunny day, when it did come, usually found him stuck in the office, or down at the courthouse.

Finally, August brought a stretch of good weather. Not knowing how long it might last, Raines told Tom Ryan, before leaving his office that Friday afternoon, to be at his place first thing in the morning. On his way home Raines stopped at Lemon's fish shack in Colored Town for bait and a case of beer. From there it was over to Roy's boat yard for wire leaders and new hooks. Unable to think of anything else he might need, Raines crossed his fingers for good weather in the morning and went on home, telling Hilton and Marilyn, who came out to greet him when he pulled into the drive, to be up early the next day if they wanted to go to fishing.

Now, twenty minutes past the mouth of the inlet they were coming up on the edge of the Gulf Stream—the water a deep blue and moving north at around four knots. Pulling the throttle back, he yelled for Hilton and Tom to get the rods ready.

"Got the flats out, Johnny," Tom Ryan called from the stern a few minutes later.

Raines had turned the bow of the boat north to follow the Stream at trolling speed, just enough to match the current pushing them At Ryan's shout he turned from the helm to look back where he could see the two rods bucking slightly in the stern holders. Their lines stretched out maybe fifty yards behind the boat, the baits attached to the end of the lines—one a long mullet strip on a big silver spoon, the other a rigged ballyhoo—skipping in the wake of the boat. A seagull appeared out of nowhere as Raines watched, diving down out of the blue sky to investigate the spoon and mullet strip combination. Not liking what he saw the gull wheeled off, screeching as he went. Raines hoped the fish below wouldn't feel the same as the gull. They would find out, he figured. If the bait wasn't working, they'd swap it out.

"Want to put the riggers out, too, Skipper," Ryan called out again. "Or go with these two for a bit?"

Before Raines could answer Hilton was already unclipping the starboard outrigger and pulling the line down. Marilyn stood next to her brother, holding a rigged ballyhoo in both hands, a mild look of distaste on her face at having to hold the dead bait.

"Looks like we're doing the riggers, too, Tom," Raines said.

As he turned back to the helm, he could hear Ryan laughing, followed by the sound of his longtime friend unclipping the port outrigger, calling out to Marilyn to bring him one of those ballyhoos when she had the chance. The click, click, click of the big reel on the rod connected to the outrigger, the Lycoming gently humming along at the slower speed, the sounds of fishing that Raines, not having heard in some time, was fully enjoyed once again.

They ran like this for a while, the four lines strung out behind the boat, their baits skipping in the light swells rolling off the edge of the Stream, the sun reaching higher in the cloudless sky with the morning wearing on—just the four of them and the boat, on an otherwise empty sea.

"Here, Pop, you look thirsty."

Raines hadn't heard his son come up, but he was at his side now, a bottle of beer from the cooler in his hand.

"You're exactly right, son. I *am* thirsty. This fishing business is hard work."

Hilton must have liked this little joke for he smiled. "It's not too early, is it? Besides, Mom's not here, even if it is."

"No, to the first one," Raines said. "It's not too early, and yes, you're right—your mother's not here. But what about Tom? Did you offer him one?"

"It was his idea in the first place, Pop."

"I should have known that. Who's watching the lines?"

"Mr. Ryan and Marilyn. I told Marilyn if something hits to come get me."

"She might not do that. Maybe she wants to catch the first fish. You okay with that?"

"Sure. Unless it's a really big one."

"And?"

"She'll probably want me to help her."

"And you're okay with that?"

"Sure," Hilton said.

"Good,' Raines told his son, adding, "You're a good brother to her, Hilly. A good boy, too."

"Boy? I'm almost sixteen, Pop."

"My mistake then. A good man, I should have said."

"Thanks, Pop."

"Keep an eye on your sister, please. Don't let her get too much sun out there. Make her get back into the shade here and there while you and Tom stay with the rods. I bring her home sunburned your mother will never let me forget it."

"I will, Pops. Don't worry."

Hilton scrambled back to the stern, eager to be there if one of the four rods went off. One hand on the wheel to keep the boat on track, Raines watched his son go, watched as Tom Ryan handed him one of the beers from the cooler, Ryan looking first at Raines to make sure it was okay to do so. When Raines waved him off, he popped the cap off the beer, clinked bottles with Hilton, man and boy taking long swigs of the beer, before and turning to focus on the baits out behind the boat.

Not long after this they came abreast of a piece of plywood floating in the water. Where it came from or how long it had been in the water was anyone's guess. The flat line in the port holder sang out, the big reel whining with the pull of the fish on the end of the line. Tom Ryan, sitting on the bench by the rod, jumped up, snatched the rod out of the holder, and struck the fish. A hundred yards out behind the boat a green and yellow fish cleared the water, a sparkling flash of silver spray in the sunlight as it fell back down into the ocean, where undeterred by the hook in its mouth, it took off.

"Dolphin, Pop," Hilton yelled, but before Raines could say anything, the starboard flat went off, Hilton going to grab it, only to find his sister had beat him too it, and like Tom Ryan, was battling a dolphin of her own.

True to his word, Hilton was good about this, standing next to his sister with the gaff in one hand, ready to help either her, or Ryan, when they got the fish up close to the boat and could bring them in.

Raines eased the throttle back, putting the boat in idle while his daughter and Ryan worked the fish into the boat. He had learned from the past not to turn the engine off during this stage of the fight. If they had to chase one of the fish down, with the engine in idle all he had to do was push the throttle forward and go. But the rods were stout with plenty of line on the reel and the dolphins didn't look to be big enough to pose a threat of that sort.

For close to an hour, they stayed with the piece of plywood, landing five more of the hard fighting, colorful dolphin while losing three others. The part of fishing Raines liked the least came pretty quick, when Marilyn brought her dolphin into the boat. The fish lay flopping and gasping on the deck as Hilton pulled the hook out and then hit it over the head with the Judas Priest to put it out of its misery. Father and son stood over the fish watching as blood leaked from its mouth to flow out of the scuppers into the sea, the bright, almost iridescent color of the fish bleaching out as it died on the deck.

"It's sort of sad, isn't it, Pop?" Hilton said. "When we have to kill 'em"

"Very sad, son. If want to eat them, though, we have to kill them. No way around it, sad to say."

"Good thing they taste so good, isn't it, Pop?"

"It is—though for them, maybe too good of a thing."

After the first one he caught Tom Ryan let the kids handle the others, coming up to sit with Raines at the helm where the two of them drank beer and watched Hilton and Marilyn catch fish. Hilton had taken off the khaki shirt, like the ones Raines and Tom Ryan were wearing, standing now just under the edge of the canvas awning, keeping an eye on all four lines while his sister sat on the starboard bench fanning herself with the straw hat. With his shirt off like that, Raines could see how his son's chest, arms, and face were tanned a deep brown from the swimming all that summer. Sadie wasn't supposed to know, though Raines was sure she did, that Hilton and two of his pals had a rowboat stashed on the New River they used to row across to the barrier island. Once there, it was a short hike over the sand dunes to the beach, and the cooler water of the Atlantic. As far as Raines was concerned it was all good fun. The sort of fun boys of Hilton's age should be occupying their summer with.

It was a damn sight better than the hard work of the tobacco fields. Under his father's tutelage that had been John Raines summer fare when he was Hilton's age. Raines had never shared times like this — fishing out on the ocean — with his father. Hell, his father had never even taken him down to the creek to fish. Lewis Raines had left that sort of thing — fishing, learning to shoot a gun, hunting — up to RL. Fortunately for Raines, RL had been as good a brother to him as Hilton was to his little sister. In most things, at any rate.

Times had changed since then, Raines supposed. How parents raised their children. For the better, as best he could see.

"You're one lucky man, Johnny," Tom Ryan said, his lanky face beneath the bill of the fishing cap split in what could be taken for a smile — if one knew the man.

"How so, Tom?"

"Well now, I'm looking at two of the reasons, not fifteen feet from where we're sitting enjoying this cold beer."

"Yes, they're a couple of good kids all right." He thought of something, surprised then that for as long as he had known Tom Ryan he had never thought to ask. "How come you and Gladys never had children, Tom? I mean before …"

"Before she died, you mean?"

The port outrigger went off and despite Hilton's best effort, kept going off.

"Something big, Pop," Hilton yelled out as he pumped the rod back hard to strike the fish.

"Looks that way, Hilly!" The conversation with Tom would have to wait and, in a way. Raines was a little relieved at this. But fishing was fishing, and it looked like Hilton might have his hands full. "Hit him again, son."

Hilton did, and now, far out behind the boat, the fish came out of the water, all bright and shiny in the morning light, water droplets falling from its scales to glitter in that light. Another dolphin, this one bigger than the others they'd been catching, five and ten pounders. When the fish jumped again Raines saw that it was much bigger than the others, this one maybe forty- or fifty-pounds Raines thought, as he yelled for Hilton to hold on tight to the rod.

"Let him run, now, Hilly," Raines shouted when the fish hit the water and took off away from the boat. "Keep pressure on him but don't horse him Tom, get those other lines in so he doesn't get fouled, while I turn the boat and we follow that big boy."

It was all going on very fast, the big dolphin on his run, Tom and Marilyn reeling in the other lines as fast as they could, Hilton walking slowly, the rod bent toward the fish, to the center of the stern to sit in the fighting chair, as Raines, once the bow of the boat pointed towards the fish, with the engine set just above trolling speed set off after the big dolphin.

There was a lot of give and take between Hilton and the fish, startling jumps, searing runs, line peeling off the screaming reel, the rod bent damn near double at times, but fifteen, maybe twenty, minutes later—Tom Ryan leaned over the port gunwales with the gaff and brought the bull dolphin aboard.

"He's too big for the fish box, Pop," Hilton said over his shoulder as Raines came back to the stern. "Maybe too big to kill with the Judas Priest."

"This fish is too big to kill, period. We'll get the hook out of its mouth and let him go."

"Aww, Dad," Marilyn said as she stood next to her brother looking down at the big fish trying not to die on the deck of the boat. "He's so beautiful. Don't you want to bring him home to show Mom what Hilly caught."

"I don't think your mother will mind if we don't. And yes, he is beautiful. Too big and beautiful to kill. Now c'mon, Hilly. You caught him, so get that hook out of its mouth and let's put him back in the water."

Raines and Tom Ryan held onto the fish for a while in the water next to the boat, Raines at the mouth, and Ryan a hold of the tail, gently moving the fish back and forth until the dolphin began to breathe on its own and pull away from the hands holding it. Ryan looked at Raines, who nodded his head when it was time, and they both let go, the fish moving off from the boat. Slowly at first, and then in a sudden rush of tail push, the fish was gone as if it had never been there in the first place.

It was around eleven when Raines decided they had enough in the fish box to make for several meals.

"Hilly," he called out to his son. "You and Marilyn bring those lines in." Between the current and the trolling speed of the boat they were almost to the end of the city limits of Fort Lauderdale. "Let's head back south and see if we can find a tuna. Roy told me Jack Chancey and his boys got into them off Hollywood earlier in the week."

"Okay, Pop. Any sailfish?"

"Roy didn't mention sailfish. He never pays attention, though, to reports of people catching fish you can't eat. But who knows?"

"That's right, Pop. Who knows?" And then to his sister. "Put that soda pop down and give me a hand like Pop says."

***

The wind had picked up from the south during the morning, throwing salt spray over the bow as Raines headed the boat into it. Marilyn, leaning her head out over the starboard gunwale to get the wind on her face as they ran, let out a squeal when a blast of that spray soaked her. Judging by the look of pure delight on her face, Raines figured his daughter didn't mind getting wet at all. With the heat of the day coming on fully the cool water against her skin probably felt very refreshing indeed. He and Tom Ryan at the bridge as they ran south would make do with the cold beer they were drinking—which bothered Raines not at all.

When they were abreast of the Hollywood Beach Hotel, a shining speck of white reaching up from the beach five miles in the distance, Raines pulled the throttle back, turned the boat again so that the bow was facing north, and shut the engine down.

"Hilly," he called out to his son in the stern. "Put a line out with a mullet on it. With this wind, and the current, we'll get a natural drift from it while we eat lunch. Might even catch something."

"Aye, aye, Captain." Hilton saluted his father and then did as he'd been told.

"That's a fine boy, you've got there."

"For God's sake, Tom, don't let him hear you call him a boy. I've already been corrected once this morning on that issue."

Tom Ryan's lips cracked just a little on his face as he got up and went to the cooler for beers for him and Raines.

"I imagine you're right," he said when he returned. "He's at that age, now, wanting to be a man, yet wanting to be a boy and finding it difficult to be both."

"I hadn't thought of it that way before, Tom But it's a good point. You know, men like me and you, hell, we didn't have much time at just being boys. Least, I sure didn't. Not with Lewis Raines at my back every minute."

Tom Ryan was quiet for a minute, turning the bottle of beer around in his hands before finally taking a long pull.

"Knowing your background as I do, John, I'd have to say you're right. Course, I didn't come from a farming life. We were city people, as was my father's family before him So things might have been a little easier for me. Which is why I've always admired you for raising yourself up from that. Might never have told you that, but it's true. RL and you both, worked hard to make something different for yourselves. And succeeded damn well, too. You, and Sadie, have done a fine job with your children as well. Not everyone can lay claim to that."

Raines looked back at his two children behind them, Hilton with his khaki shirt off, Marilyn sitting under the shade of the canvas top, a soda pop in one hand, the other fanning herself with the big straw hat her mother insisted she wear out in the sun. It was true, he told himself. They were damn fine children.

"God knows, Tom," he blurted out. "I just want to protect the two of them from everything. Keep them safe from anything that could hurt them" He waved a hand at the white, glittering city rising up from the shore five miles away. "Even if I know that might not be possible."

Marilyn had pulled out two sandwiches from the cooler that she brought up to her father and his friend. Taking one for herself, she retreated again into the shade of the canvas top, reading a book she'd brought along while she ate. *Little Women*, Raines thought. The book she was reading. A good book for her to be reading at that age when she was turning into a little woman herself.

"You asked me a question earlier, John." Tom Ryan had finished the sandwich and was looking now at Raines. "Why Gladys and I never had children."

Raines had been watching the line out behind the boat as he ate — not that he really needed to. Hilton, sandwich in one hand, was right there, ready if needed.

"If it's something you don't want to talk about, Tom," Raines said, "I understand."

"I don't mind at all, not with you, John. I haven't thought about it in quite a while. Rarely do, really, except times like this." He pointed behind him at the two children. "You never had the chance to meet Gladys. She died before you, and I, and RL got together over in Fort Myers. The Spanish Flu took her from me, that same flu that near did you in, as you told me once."

Thinking of that time — in the Army hospital sick with the flu at the base in Columbia — reminded Raines how Tom Ryan was ten years older than him It was a fact he'd never put much thought into. Yet, looking into his friend's mottled face beneath the fishing cap he wore while the noon sunlight streamed through the windshield above the bridge, it was as if he realized that age difference for the first time.

Before Raines could say anything, Hilton left the stern and came up to them.

"I'm going to lay down in the cabin for a bit, Pop. I think the sun, and the sandwich have made me a little sleepy."

"You don't think the beer you and Tom were drinking while you thought I wasn't looking had anything to do with that?"

"Maybe a little." Hilton gave his father a sheepish grin. "But I only had the one."

"Go ahead, son. Tom and I will keep an eye on things here."

If Hilton's interruption was to give Raines a reprieve from Tom's story about why he and his wife never had children—a guilty hope, and that Raines disliked himself for having—it wasn't to be.

"You'd have liked Gladys if you'd had the chance to know her. Of course," and Tom Ryan's lean face broke with that little grin of his, "hopefully not as I came to know her."

Raines beer was empty, and he was sure Ryan's was too, but his friend didn't give him the chance to go get them fresh ones.

"We were married in 1910, so I only had her in my life for nine years. So strange when I think about it now. That day we swore to one another 'Til death do us part'. I suppose I was young enough at the time to think death would never come to us."

Raines thought then of Vera, the girl in Ft. Myer's he'd known before Sadie. The woman he thought he loved then. Not only loved but figured to marry when he came back from the war. Except she had died. Not from the flu that took Ryan's wife. But from meningitis. A different contagion but deadly just the same. He thought of his mother who had died when he was just a boy, from giving birth to TJ, and whose death changed his father. Turned him into a man no one could love. And of course, there was RL, killed in the vicious hurricane just a year back and on the very same boat he was now on. Looking back at it like this he could see how, as a boy, and as man, there hadn't been a time in his life when he didn't know about death.

"I came down from Philly in '05," Ryan continued. "To work as an accountant for Henry Flagler. My father knew Mr. Flagler and wrangled a position for me in his Florida enterprises. A position I wasn't—not at twenty-two—quite ready for. Because of his friendship with my father, Mr. Flagler put up with my initial incompetence." Ryan outright laughed then, an unusual expression for him. "And believe me, John, I *was* incompetent then. Not the skilled sharpie you know now."

"You're right, Tom," Raines said. "It's hard to imagine such a thing."

"Well, it's true."

1905. The year when as a twelve-year-old he watched his older brother, RL, fight their father to a draw in the hot August Georgia tobacco field that was all Raines, as a boy, knew of life at the time. He watched as RL rode off on the family mule; the three Raines left standing in the field had no way of knowing where he was going. And because of that leaving, he began a journey that in time led him to this man, Tom Ryan.

"I met Gladys three years later, February of '08 it was. I was stationed down in Miami, where, as you may remember, Mr. Flagler was pushing hard to get the railroad finished from Miami on down to Key West."

Of course, Raines didn't remember this—he was still stuck on the family tobacco farm outside Pendleton, unaware of events going on elsewhere.

"There were some financial reports I needed to go over with the Old Man, so I took the train out of Miami up to West Palm where he was staying at his hotel. When I got out of the cab from the station and walked up those big white steps to the lobby, there was Gladys, sitting on the veranda with her mother having their afternoon tea. Oh my God but how that red hair of hers lit up in the afternoon sun! I believe I fell in love with her right then and there. Seems silly now, when I think of it, yet—"

"Doesn't seem silly to me, Tom." Raines thought of Sadie—of seeing her for the first time from his hospital sickbed, and the rush of emotions flooding through him then, even sick as he was. "Doesn't seem silly at all."

"Perhaps," Ryan said. "Of course, I was a young man with no experience of women or love. I think Gladys was the first woman I ever took a second look at. Back then, much like now, my head was full of figures and what had to be recorded, finagled, and paid for.

"Mr. Flagler introduced me to them—Gladys and her mother—the next day, where again they were having afternoon tea outside. I had no idea what to say after the formalities were over, so it was fortunate, for me at least, that Gladys was a good talker. Hell, it might have been her who proposed to me and not the other way around.

"They were from Boston, it turned out, the Flynns, though originally from Ireland. Her grandfather and father, anyways. They came over when her father was a young boy during the potato famine. The grandmother had died, and Mr. Flynn and his son somehow arranged passage on a ship to Boston. Which was fitting, I suppose. Mr. Flynn right away got a job working on the docks there—worked his way into the shipping business and a fortune. Liked to say he would never forget being hungry and planned on his children, and their children, never having to know what that was. Gladys' father took over after the old man passed on—was in fact down in Key West looking over the waterfront in hopes of expanding his business there. Concerned with Key West's rowdy reputation Mr. Flynn decided his wife and daughter would be safer in West Palm at Flagler's hotel while he went about his business in the shipyards. He and I had crossed paths, actually, just the day before, he going south in one train, and I heading north to West Palm in the other."

Tom Ryan was looking right at him, but Raines could see his friend wasn't really seeing him.

"It helped that both of us being Irish we had something in common. She was Catholic, a staunch one at that, unlike me as you well know, John. Being Catholic she wanted children, and more than one and I was fine with that. Hell, more than fine.

"We were married in the fall of '08 and by 1913 or so we both realized children wouldn't be a part of our life together. Her fault or mine? We didn't know. The doctors told us they could find nothing wrong with either of us. Of course, medicine is not an exact science, and even less so back then. Gladys thought the Scarlett fever she'd had as a child might have had something to do with it. The doctor said maybe that was it—he just didn't know.

"She turned to the Church for solace, and me? I turned to business, which has always been a sort of church for me, I guess. Then the Spanish Flu came along in 1918 and took her a year later. Goddamn but I wished it'd been me instead.

"Friends tried to tell me there would be another woman for me down the road. They laughed when I said I wasn't interested. That I could never love another woman like I loved Gladys. But I knew. Knew I just plain didn't want to and still don't."

Tom Ryan lifted his head a little and Raines could see his friend was once again in the present.

"Not that I don't have needs, John," Ryan said, that tight little grin back on his lips. "Fortunately, the girls at Miss Celia's are available to take care of those needs when they arise. You know Miss Celia, John?"

"I've heard of her." Raines was glad that was the only way he knew the madam of the local brothel in Colored Town. Even after all these years, the remembrance of his night with RL in the whorehouse in Ybor city bothered him when the subject came up.

"Of course, at my age those needs don't need attending to quite as often. Which perhaps is a good thing. I haven't decided one way or the other on that yet. So, there it is, John." Ryan got up from the mate's chair and stretched his arms up over his head. "The long and the short of why Gladys and I never had children. Which is why my advice to you once more is to take damn good care of the two you have. Damn good care. Now, how about another of those cold beers?"

Before Raines could answer Marilyn yelled from the stern, "Dad." And then, "Daddy, I've got a fish on!"

***

As Raines looked to see what his daughter was yelling about, behind the boat, perhaps a hundred yards out, a sailfish cleared the water, jumping above the swells and shaking its head, back arched, fin up, water droplets from its body shining for just a moment in the light of the afternoon sun before it crashed back down into the sea and was gone, the only evidence it existed being the bucking of the rod in Marilyn's hands as she braced herself against the stern gunwales.

"Jesus, Pop." Hilton stood in the open hatch wiping sleep from his eyes. "What's going on?"

"Sailfish, son, a big one at that. Quick, go help your sister before he drags her overboard." And then to Tom Ryan, "Tom, see if you can find that harness for Marilyn. She's going to need it once we get her into the fighting chair. I've got to get the engine up and running."

"Yes sir, Johnny," and then Ryan was searching in the locker beneath the bridge while Raines started the engine up and the chase was on.

At first Raines thought to sweep out and around the fish, which despite Marilyn's efforts was still taking line as it ran to the south. Realizing there was a better way to keep pressure on the fish, with the throttle in low he swung the bow back to the north. He just had to be careful with the boat. Not put too much pressure on the fish. Not to force a breakoff.

Hilton slid into the mate's seat on the bridge. The wind from the south had blown his hair down over his forehead into his eyes. Pushing it back with one hand he said, "Tom found the harness, Pop. Got Mari buckled up and in the fighting chair."

"Good," John Raines said. "She'll need them, the belt and the chair."

"Anything I can get you, Pop? A beer or maybe a soda?"

"Thanks, son, but I'm good right now."

"That's a big fish, isn't it?" Hilton's face was split into a wide grin that sparkled beneath his dark eyes. "You think Mari can land it?"

"Yes, on the first count, and on the second, well, we'll have to see."

"She can, Pop. Mari's a strong little cuss. Comes from me and the guys letting her play football and baseball with us all summer. You should see her smack the ball. When we choose sides for the games, she's always picked first. After me, of course. For a little sister she can be a pain in the ass. She's just knows when it's best not to be."

"Maybe that's the inherent lawyer in her?"

"Could be. Heck, if a gal can become a lawyer and Mari wants to and sets her mind to it, she'll do it all right."

"Right now, let's hope she sets her mind to landing that sailfish."

"I'll go back and give her a pep talk, Pop."

"You do that, son. You do that."

It could be a long fight. With Hilton gone, Raines was alone on the bridge, the others with Marilyn while she struggled with the sailfish. He hadn't known Marilyn played sports with her brother and his friends. Regretted he hadn't been able to take time away from work to watch them at it. That was just life, though. But Hilton was right. For an eleven-year-old girl she was plenty strong. In body and in spirit. That last would come in handy over the next half hour, or however long it took to bring the fish to the boat. She had her brother and Tom to help her, too. And him at the wheel. The boat could be a big help, if he played it right. At the end of it, though, she'd be plenty sore and worn out. Hopefully, it would be a good soreness. A good worn out feeling.

Just then a gust of wind blew the big straw hat Marilyn's mother insisted she wear on the boat, into the water. Raines watched as his daughter tried to catch the hat with one hand and because of the rod bucking in her other hand, thought better of it. Seeing her father over her shoulder at the bridge she laughed before turning back to the rod, the fish out behind the boat, and the business at hand. Not before Raines' heart—at the look of pure joy on his daughter's face—turned over inside his chest.

They ran like this for fifteen minutes, though it could have been longer. With everything in motion like it was, it was hard for Raines to keep track of time. It wasn't important right then, anyway. The sailfish jumped twice more, in between jumps taking line as fast as Marilyn could reel it in. They were just off the edge of the Gulf Stream, the Stream itself roiled in a heavy chop, the boat chugging through the swells coming off that chop. If the fish were able to make it into the Stream and they had to follow it in, what with that heavy chop the fight would be a lot harder than it already was. Raines could only hope the fish would cooperate and not do such a thing. This was the first sailfish ever hooked aboard his boat and he wanted to see it caught properly— wanted that very much.

Above the steady throbbing of the Lycoming 8 Raines could hear snatches of the conversation in the stern. "Look what I've got, Hilly," he heard his daughter say. "A sailfish! A big one, too!" Followed by, "Bet you wish it was you catching it." From Hilton: "It's a big one all right, Mari. And yes, I wish I was in your place. But you haven't caught it yet and if you don't pay attention you won't." And from Tom Ryan: "You're doing real good, sweetheart. Real good. Just stay with it, pump when I tell you to, reel when I tell you to, and you may well catch that bastard." "Huh oh Mr. Ryan, you said a bad word." "Nothing you haven't heard before, Mari," Hilton said. "Now pay attention."

Yes indeed, Raines, thought, reassured somehow by what he heard. They might land that fish. The line on the big reel was brand new, the boat was running well, there was plenty of daylight left, the southerly breeze was keeping everyone comfortable. Marilyn's brother, and Tom Ryan, were right there to help if the going got too rough. What could go wrong? And cursed himself immediately for ever thinking such a thing at such a time like this.

It took longer than Raines thought it would to make the fish began to tire. The last of its heart-stopping leaps—those bolts of almost iridescent blue over the sea—had been more than ten minutes before. All in all, Raines figured, his daughter had been engaged with the fish for close to forty minutes. Finally, she was able to bring in more line than the fish could take out. Raines hoped the fish didn't die before they could it get it to the boat, unhooked, and released back to where it came. Or that the sharks didn't get it. It would make for a splendid mount he was sure. Yet, the thought of killing the magnificent creature held no appeal to him. Of course, the sharks wouldn't feel the same way.

"Looks like he's giving up, Pop," Hilton yelled from the stern. He was putting on the heavy glove he would need for holding the wire leader when he went to gaff the fish. "He's almost here."

"That's good news son." Raines shut the engine off. The boat was no longer needed now that the fish was swimming in tired circles just off the stern. "Give Mari a hand," he said as he stepped off the bridge and started back to the stern. "Help her lead him over to the port side. Once we get the gaff in him, we can bring him up and unhook him. Good job, sweetheart," he added, standing now behind his daughter, his hands on her shoulders.

He could feel the tension in her body starting to drain as her brother took hold of the long wire leader and began guiding the fish around the side of the boat.

"Better let me handle the gaff, son." Ryan went to take the long-handled hook from Hilton, but Hilton pulled away. "That's a mighty big fish there. You sure?"

"I've got him all right, Tom."

"Could be a good idea, Hilly," Raines said. "To let Tom handle the gaff. Not only is that fish pretty damn big, he still might have some fight in him" Raines laughed with a sudden thought. "Hell, son, we'd hate to see that fish pull you over the side, kicking and squalling on the back of Marilyn's sailfish as it dragged you into the Gulf Stream."

But Hilton didn't see the humor in this. "I can do it, Pop. Just watch me."

Before Raines could say anything or Tom Ryan could stop him, Hilton leaned over the side of the boat and jabbed downward with the gaff in his right hand. In the next moment, with a mighty heave of his whole body, Hilton jerked the fish—or at least its bill and head—halfway over the side.

"See?" Hilton said over his shoulder as he struggled to bring the fish the rest of the way in the boat." "I told you I could do it."

But Tom Ryan and Raines had been right. The sailfish was very big. And it still had some fight left in it. And why Raines at that particular moment suddenly thought of Matecumbe and the hurricane the year before—of the tombstone snatched off that island by the powerful winds and driven into RL's forehead—he would never know. It was surely a jinx. But that realization was for later.

For now, the fish gave its own mighty heave, in the process driving its bill deep into Hilton's thigh. In the next instant, with a powerful jerk back and a whack of its tail against the side of the boat that reverberated like a gunshot across the deck of *The Mari-Lyn*, the fish freed itself, both from Hilton's thigh, and the gaff in its gills—and was gone, back into the sea.

"Hilly," Marilyn yelled, dropping the rod from her hands to the deck. "What happened? Where's my fish?" She stopped for a second, before screaming "Hilly, you're bleeding."

He was bleeding, bleeding bad, Raines saw as he pulled his son back from the gunwales of the boat. Hilton let go of the gaff to look down at his leg and the blood pouring out on the deck. He seemed surprised by what he saw—a surprise that didn't last long. His face turned pale, sudden sweat beading up on his forehead as he folded to the deck of the boat before his father could catch him.

"He's gone into shock, John." Tom was next to him, leaning over Raines and his son. "Seen it many times during the war."

"What can I do, Tom?"

Behind him Raines could hear his daughter sobbing, "It's all my fault. My fault Hilly got hurt."

"No one's fault, honey. Just an accident. Now, please, go get your brother some water while Tom and I take care of him."

Ryan had stripped his shirt off and twisted it into a long tight rope. "Going to use this for a tourniquet, John. Wrap it around his leg above the wound to stop the bleeding."

"Will that work, you think?" And quickly, another question, as he held his son's head up in his hands. "It bad, Tom?"

"It's bad enough. And let's hope this works."

"Help him, Tom, Please."

With the engine off, the boat drifted in the swells coming off the Gulf Stream and the southerly wind pushed them. Except for the screeching of two sea gulls hovering overhead, the rhythmic slap of the swells against the hull, it was quiet on the boat. All of it had happened so fast. One minute Raines was watching his son pull the sailfish up over the side, a look of determination on Hilton's face as he looked over his shoulder at his father and the others in the boat. The next, the sailfish was gone, Hilton's thigh was pumping blood on the deck, both determination, and success, faded from his face—a face deathly white as Raines leaned over him, not knowing what to do and hoping that Tom Ryan did.

Ryan didn't say anything as he went to work, wrapping the balled-up shirt around Hilton's leg above the gushing wound in his thigh and pulling it tight. After tying it with a sturdy knot he took the glass of water Marilyn held out, and dribbled some into Hilton's open mouth, dabbing the rest over his forehead and cheeks. Ryan seemed satisfied with what he had done as he stepped back from where Hilton lay in the shade of the canvas awning.

"That's about the best I can do, John." Tom Ryan's face looked as pale as Hilton's. "Let's wrap him up in a blanket and get him down below."

"Okay. Then what?"

"Start the engine up and get us the hell back, that's what."

Ryan wrapped Hilton in a blanket that Marilyn—on her own initiative—had brought up from the cabin, and carrying the boy in his arms, pushed through the hatch and went below.

"Is Hilly gonna be all right, Daddy?"

"He'll be all right, sweetie." He turned the key, grateful as the powerful Lycoming started right up. "Don't you worry, sweetheart. He'll be just fine. Now come sit up here with me on the bridge and let's get him home."

"I want to go home, too," she said, her hands busy wiping tears from her eyes.

"Me, too, sweetheart." Raines pushed the throttle forward as he turned the bow of the boat to the east and shore, five miles in the distance. "Me, too."

They ran for five minutes or so, the chop pushed up by the southerly winds as they ran abreast of it, slopping water over the gunwales and into the boat. Raines hated the bumpy ride, for his son's sake, but there was nothing to be done for it. Except get back. To the Coast Guard station inside the port first of all. They'd be able to help right away. Take Hilton to the hospital in the ambulance they had for emergencies. He had to get him there, first, though.

Just as they were coming down off a larger than the others swell a loud metallic clank echoed from the engine compartment below the stern. The Lycoming 8 hissed to a shuddering stop as the boat came to rest, the southerly chop slowly pushing the bow around to the north.

"Goddammit all to fucking hell, now what?"

Raines wondered who said this, wondered who had the nerve to say such a thing, what with his little girl sitting right there next to him—even as looking into his daughter's eyes he realized it was only he who had spoken.

"What just happened?" Tom poked his head out of the hatchway. "We have a problem?"

"I think the engine's blown," Raines said. "How's Hilton doing?"

"He's sleeping for now." Ryan came out of the hatch and stood next to Raines on the bridge. "I found the first aid kit in the galley and swabbed the wound with mercurochrome. That should help a little.

Hopefully keep it from getting infected. There was some morphine in the kit, and I gave him one of the syrettes. Knocked him right out and that's good. But we've got to get him ashore to a hospital." He frowned and turned away from Raines for a moment. "If we want to save his leg."

"Jesus." Raines wiped his hand across his face. "That bad, Tom?"

"I'm sorry, John, but yes, it could get that way."

"Daddy." Marilyn had come up from the stern where she had been—without being asked, a fact that impressed Raines—washing the blood out through the scuppers. "Why aren't we moving?" Raines could see how she was trying not to cry. "I want to go home."

"I know, honey, I know, and we will as soon as we can."

The smell of burnt oil drifted up from the engine compartment and when he looked out past the stern Raines could see an oil slick seeping out behind the boat.

"My guess, Tom," Raines said, "is that we blew a rod. If TJ were here, he'd know for sure. But he isn't, and even if he were, I doubt he'd be able to do anything."

"That's not good, John."

He looked weary, Raines thought. Not concerned, just weary. Raines was doing his best to keep his own emotions in check, for his daughter's sake more than anything. God knows, he was worried enough for the both of them but showing it wouldn't help anyone.

"I'll try the engine again in a little bit," Raines said. "Maybe there's just a glitch in the starter or something. If we let it sit for a bit maybe, she'll start again. Who knows. For now, I'm going below and check on Hilton." Turning to his daughter he added, "Sweetie, you stay up here and keep an eye out for any passing boats. If you see one give a yell for me and Tom"

"Okay Daddy." Just being entrusted with something important to do was enough to stop her tears. "I won't let you down."

They hadn't seen another boat in quite a while, though. Well before the sailfish hit. But maybe, Raines thought. Maybe one would come along. This late in the afternoon there might be one or two fishing parties like theirs starting to head in. If so, they could wave one down and get a tow. There was a chance of that, what with two or so hours left of daylight. A chance. It was what they had for now. They would just have to see.

"I know you won't let me down, honey. You never have." Pushing through the hatch and into the cabin he motioned to Tom to follow him "Come on, Tom and take a look at Hilton with me. See if there's anything else we can do to help him."

*** 

An hour after dark they were off of Hillsboro and the inlet there. At least Raines hoped the flashing light on the coast was the Hillsboro lighthouse. It was either that or the light at the Jupiter inlet and he didn't think it possible they could have floated sixty some miles in the time since the engine died. Hillsboro it had to be—for whatever comfort that might bring.

No boats had shown on the horizon since he asked Marilyn to keep a lookout, no savior in sight as the disabled *Mari-Lyn* and those aboard her drifted steadily north with the ever flowing current of the Gulf Stream. The flashing light from shore, five miles in the distance, cutting through the dark as they came abreast of the inlet, was meant as a beacon of safety—as well as one of warning. Considering the situation aboard his boat, Raines felt no sense of safety whatsoever.

Hilton was still asleep in the forward berth of the cabin; the morphine Tom Ryan had found in the first aid kit keeping him mercifully so. The morphine was a small favor indeed. According to Tom there was one syrette left, if needed. Raines hoped it wouldn't be, but it was good to know they had it if it were. As the sun went down, they ate the last of the sandwiches Sadie had packed for them, gathered around the little table in the cabin, the three of them, doing their best to act as if this were the most normal thing in the world. When she finished her sandwich Marilyn yawned, asked her father if she could be excused, and stretched out in the other bunk next to Hilton.

"Wake me up when we get home, Daddy," she called through the open hatch. "Of if you need me for anything."

"You can bet on it, sweetie," Raines said as he went in and pulled the rough blanket up over her. Her eyes, dark and cloudy from tiredness, struggled—despite her best efforts—to remain open. Her hair, dark like her eyes, spread out under her head against the pillow, windblown and un-brushed, a mess of childhood curls. Above the blanket pulled up to her chin Marilyn's face was bright red from the sun she was exposed to for hours on end after her floppy hat blew into the water. Raines was glad Sadie wasn't there to see her daughter in such disarray. She was going to give him hell, Sadie was, when he got home, Raines was sure of that. For the condition of both their children.

"I mean it, Daddy."

"So do I. Now get some sleep. You've had a long day."

"Will Hilly be all right?"

"He's going to be fine. Once we get home he will be just fine."

"I hope so, Daddy. I love Hilly. Even though he's mean to me sometimes."

"Me, too. Love him, I mean. And big brothers can be like that to their little sisters on occasion. But he'll get better, don't you worry."

"It's hard not to worry, Daddy."

"I know, sweetie." And again, and maybe more to reassure himself than anything, "Hilly's going to be just fine. Now do your best to get some sleep."

He left her and went through the cabin and out to the bridge. With the sun down and the wind from the south over the water, the night air was refreshingly cool after the confines of the cabin. Tom Ryan was sitting in the mate's chair and when Raines came through the hatch, he held out a cup for him.

"Here you go, John. Something medicinal for you and considering the current situation, just what the doctor ordered."

Raines lifted the cup to his lips and drank, the hot bourbon in the cup burning its way all the way down.

"While you were tucking Marilyn in, I happened across your bottle of Jack Daniels." Ryan held a similar cup in his own hands, an expectant look on his face. "Thought you might need a sip or two."

"Just happened across it, you say? Guess that means I need to find a new hiding place for it." He took another long sip from the cup, the heat of the whiskey watering his eyes. "But Hell's bells, old friend, thank God you found it!"

The two men laughed, neither of them saying it, but certainly aware that it was the first time they had something to laugh about since right before Hilton leaned over the side of the boat with the gaff and tried to haul the sailfish into the boat.

"Thank, God," Raines said again. And then the two men were silent for a while, lost in the whiskey and their own thoughts.

"It's a hell of a note," Ryan finally said, breaking the silence. "Certainly not how I expected our outing to go."

"Now there's an understatement." Raines took the bottle of Jack Daniels, sloshing some into Ryan's cup before filling his own. "I have to imagine Sadie's called the Coast Guard by now and alerted them we're overdue."

"Hopefully, that's who she called." Raines had switched on the anchor light and in the little light from overhead he could see that wry grin stretched across his friend's face. "And not," Ryan continued, "that damn fool Sheriff Harker."

This brought another laugh from Raines. He had to admit it felt good to laugh, too, considering the circumstances.

"Let's give my lovely wife more credit than that, Tom Please."

"No, you're right. I'm sure Sadie has called the Coasties by now and it's just a matter of time before they find us."

"How much time?" Raines asked. "You think before it gets worse for Hilton?"

"Jesus, John, but I wish I knew. I really do."

They left at it that, concentrating on the bourbon as the flashing light at Hillsboro faded further and further away behind them.

\*\*\*

"Pop?"

Soft and low, still, it was enough to jerk Raines awake in the captain's chair. At first, he didn't know where he was or how long he had been sleeping. He could hear the sound of water slapping against the hull in the dark. Looking up he saw the anchor light on, and beyond that little glare, the stars, and to the west, the crescent moon halfway up. He was on his boat—and with that, all of the day came rushing back to him.

So there had been no Coast Guard to the rescue. At least not yet. Someone was snoring behind him. Swiveling in the chair, in the light of the stars and the anchor light he could make out Tom Ryan, asleep on the bench under the canvas awning. It must have been Tom's snoring that woke him.

"Pop?" And there it came again. "Pop, you out there?"

Hilton. Not Tom's snoring. But his son. Calling to him from where he lay hurt in the cabin.

"Yeah, son, I'm right here," Raines said. Struggling out of the captain's chair, he managed to knock the empty Jack Daniels bottle off the bridge when he reached out to steady himself. "Right here, son. Hold on."

It was dark in the cabin, even with the anchor light. He fumbled in the dark until he found the kerosene lantern on the galley counter and lit it. In the soft light of the lantern, he could see his son and daughter's forms on the two bunks in the forward berth. They looked like shadows, not living things. Until the one of them moved and called out, "That you, Pop?"

"It's me." Setting the lantern back on the counter Raines went and squatted down between the two berths. "Right here, Hilly."

"Jeez, Pop, but I feel like hell." Hilton's eyes fluttered in the little bit of light making it into the berth. Even in that small amount of light Raines could see how drawn and pale his son's features were. "Feel like I'm gonna be sick."

"Throw-up sick?"

"Yeah."

"Okay. Hold on then and let me get a pan from the galley."

"Make it quick, Pop." Hilton tried to smile and only barely succeeded. "Please."

Raines fumbled around again until he found one of Sadie's mixing bowls she'd stored away. Bringing it back he squatted down again by Hilton and did his best to lift his son's head up enough so he could vomit into the bowl. When Hilton was done throwing up—an awful

retching consisting mainly of dry heaves and sickly-looking bile—
Raines took the bowl out on the deck and dumped it overboard. From
the morphine, Raines figured. And the shock of what the sailfish had
done to his system.

'Better?" he asked when he was beside his son again in the narrow
little berth.

"A little," Hilton said. "Mainly weak and groggy, though. My leg
hurts something fierce."

"Tom gave you morphine to ease the pain and it knocked you right
out. You lost quite a bit of blood, too, son. Probably why you feel weak
and a little sick. Here now, you just lay back and rest, son."

Hilton had tried to sit up on the bunk, but at his father's urging he
lay back against the pillow again.

"Good idea, Pop." He smiled weakly again. "I don't think I can do
anything other than that, anyway. Not the way my leg hurts."

"I bet it does," Raines said. "The morphine's probably worn off quite
a bit by now. Besides, that sailfish stabbed you pretty good."

"I almost got him in the boat, didn't I, Pop?"

"Almost. He had other ideas, though."

Hilton tried to laugh but started retching instead, stopping Raines
with one hand when he got up to go get the bowl.

"It's okay, Pop. Nothing in me to throw up, I don't think. Damn that
fish."

"Yes, damn that fish. But it happened, Hilly, and that's it. Let me
take a look at your leg for a minute."

Hilton lay still while Raines leaned over the bunk, pulled the blanket
covering him, down, and studied the wound in his son's thigh. Ryan
had cut the pants leg off up above the wound and at some point, had
replaced the crude tourniquet he'd made with his shirt, with his belt. It
must be working because there was no fresh blood seeping from the
gash. Still, it looked bad, raw, red and puffy. The leg below the wound
was swollen as well. The redness may be from the mercurochrome Tom
had liberally applied, though. At least Raines hoped that to be the
case—hoped very much that the wound looked worse than it really was.

"What time is it, Pop?" Hilton asked when Raines had covered him
up again with the blanket.

"Midnight or so, I think."

"I read somewhere that more people die around midnight, or just before dawn, than any other time of the day. You think that's true?"

"I wouldn't know, son." Raines answered. He didn't like the question. Didn't like it at all. "I'm no expert on dying, just the law."

"You think I'm gonna die? From this? What that fish did to me?"

"God no!"

He said it so loud he surprised even himself—the violence and loudness of his denial enough to make Marilyn in the other bunk, still sound asleep, moan a little before she rolled over on her side.

"I guess we'll know for sure once we're through midnight," Hilton said. "And then the dawn."

"The hell with that, Hilly. I know it now."

"That's good then, Pop. Good to know. Hey," he went on, "what happened anyways? Why aren't we moving?"

"I think the engines blown, son. Threw a rod or something, I'm not sure. TJ's the mechanic in the family, not me."

He was glad they were getting away from that talk of midnight and dying and dawn and all.

"I wish TJ were here, then," Hilton said. "He'd have that ol' engine up and running in no time."

"Yes, he would."

"I'm surprised that Lycoming let us down like that."

"Me, too. Though, I'm thinking it might not be the Lycoming that's let us down, but Roy over at the boat yard."

"You might have something, there, Pop. You just might."

Marilyn cried out in her sleep just then, soft and low, as she rolled back over on her back. Her eye lids fluttered for a second and Raines thought she was about to wake up. But she closed her eyes again, a little smile on her face as she sighed and went all the way back into sleep. Raines pulled the blanket up around her, happy that someone on the boat, at least, was smiling and sleeping good.

"Boy, my leg is really hurting, Pop."

"You want the morphine now?"

"Yeah, I think I do. Is that okay?"

"Very okay. It will ease the pain and help you sleep. By the time you wake up it will be morning, the Coast Guard will have found us, and this sorry mess will be over."

"I sure hope so."

"Me, too, Hilly."

He went back into the cabin and found the first aid kit Ryan had left on the counter. He wished Tom were awake to give Hilton the shot. But the loud snoring still coming from outside the cabin told Raines that wasn't to be—that he would have to do it himself. And that was okay. Hilton was his son after all, and Tom had already done plenty. Good old Tom. A good man. A good friend.

He gave Hilton the shot in the thigh of his good leg. Nervous at first, while rolling up the pants he pushed Hilton against the bad leg, eliciting a moan from his son for his nervous effort. He leaned back, settled himself, then stuck the needle into Hilton's thigh and eased the plunger home.

"There," Raines said when he pulled the needle out. "That's the last of it. I didn't hurt you, did I, son?"

"Not too bad, Pop. I'm okay."

"Tom's the medic around here," he said with a little laugh. "Not me. But he's sound asleep on the deck."

"It's okay, Pop. Really."

They sat awhile in silence. With the quiet, Raines became conscious for the first time of his legs cramping under him from the squatting he was forced to do in the tight quarters. The sounds of his son's ragged breathing smoothing out some as the morphine began to take hold, Marilyn's little snores from the other bunk were enough, though— enough at least to reassure Raines that both his children were still with him.

When Hilton's breathing evened out all the way and his eyes closed, Raines got up to leave.

"Pop?"

He was just to the open hatch and about to step out on the deck when he heard Hilton call to him.

"I'm right here, Hilly. Just going to step outside for a bit."

"That's okay, Pop. But tell me again—just so I know."

"What's that?"

"I'm not gonna die, right?"

"No son, no you're not."

"Thanks, Pop. I'll see you in the morning. When the Coast Guard comes."

"Yes, you will. Good night, Hilly."

But out on the deck, sitting in the fighting chair in the stern, the boat drifting slowly north, water lapping against the hull, the stars shining as if nothing in the world at all was out of place, Tom Ryan snoring away behind him on the bench beneath the canvas awning. The beginnings of a hangover from the bourbon he drank creeped over him. Suddenly, John Raines wasn't sure at all—was not sure that his son would not be dead before morning came.

He began to cry. Tried to stop and couldn't. He began to sob. Deep, gut wrenching sobbing like he hadn't done since he was a child of seven, asleep in the bedroom he shared with RL. He heard the sounds of the new baby crying out in the main room, and above the newborn's cries, those of his Aunt Cordelia, louder, frightening in their intensity, while Lewis Raines, a look on his face like none the young John had ever seen before, stood in the doorway and said, "Boys, your mother's gone."

John didn't know at that moment whether to love his father or hate him—certain only that no matter what course he chose, nothing, nothing, would ever be the same.

# PART FOUR

For the most part John Raines shot well that day. If he missed a couple of easy shots here and there, he made up for it by making other more difficult ones. He didn't think of Hilton at all, not until toward the end, and that because of a double he should have bagged but missed. He dropped the first bird as it came up out of the palmettos, wings beating frantically as it sought escape from the panting dog lunging behind it. Raines brought the gun up quickly to his shoulder and pulled the trigger as the fleeing bird came across the barrel of the shotgun, knowing the bird would drop without having to see the effect of the shot.

The second bird was a surprise of sorts, even for the dog, who didn't know he had flushed the birds in the first place. The dog—a pup actually, maybe a year old, certainly not much more than that—was happy to be out of his kennel and in the field. The dog's goofy lope, his mouth open in a sort of permanent grin, his long pink tongue hanging out dripping sweat, in the crisp coolness of the November afternoon was evidence of this.

It wasn't a true flush, but the result of the dog losing his footing in a pothole and crashing into some palmettos where the birds were peacefully minding their own business. No matter, the birds had been flushed, and after downing the first one, John Raines swung the gun on the second. Just as he was about to pull the trigger the excitable dog came barking after the bird—the sight and sounds of the young dog suddenly there in front of him, enough for Raines to hesitate, and then watch, as the second quail flew out of range.

"Ringo," The dog's handler came up and whacked the pup lightly across the backside with the pine staff he used to prod nervous birds out of the bushes, as well as reprimanding wayward dogs. Lucas, a young black man who worked for Tom Ryan, owner of the property Raines and the dog were enjoying that day, didn't seem satisfied with the first whack of the pine staff and struck the dog again. "Damn you, dog, you know better 'an to be doin' whut you done!"

"It's okay, Lucas," Raines said, smiling at the dismay on the young man's face. "What's this? Ringo's first, or second, time out?"

"Sort of his second, Mr. Raines. The first time didn't really count, not in my book. I had to whup him right off the bat an' put him back in the truck 'cause he wouldn't stop flushin' birds 'fore I give him the go."

"He's come a long way from that time, then, I'd say. Give him some water and let one of the others have a chance."

"Yessir, Mr. Raines."

Above Lucas' soft drawl John Raines could suddenly hear his son's voice—Hilton's laughter loud and clear saying, "Dad."

The voice was as plain as if he were standing there next to him, the 16-gauge Remington Raines had given him six Christmas' past, held casually in the crook of his left elbow, a slight grin of reprimand spread across his son's face. "You'll have to do better than that, Dad, if we're going to eat tonight."

The voice, and laughter, still with Raines as he decided then he'd had enough for the day after all. That he'd done well, and it was time to pack up, head for the camp, where a shower, clean clothes, good bourbon, and the companionship of a man who was his friend awaited him.

"On second thought, Lucas," he called out. "Let's just load up and head in." Lucas, busy putting Ringo into the kennel wedged into the bed of the Jeep, turned to make sure he'd heard right. Before the young black man could say anything, Raines continued. "I've had enough for one day. You know how it is, an old man like me an all."

"You're surely no old man, Mr. Raines!"

Raines enjoyed the wide grin on the black youth's face, the easy kidding that had been established quickly between them as they crossed the fields that day with the dogs.

"If you say so, son. My body's telling a different story, though."

Again, Hilton was there, beside him and saying, "At least one of you is telling the truth."

And then all of it was back. The anger and grief of missing his son. Of having to admit once again there had been a problem he couldn't fix. With whatever dignity he had left, Raines hoped Lucas didn't hear the groan slipping from his mouth as he climbed into the front of the Jeep, dogs and gun put up, the Jeep idling in neutral, one of Luca's rough dark hands on the gear shift, the other grasping the steering wheel, everyone except for Raines, ready to go.

They headed west across the field and onto the dirt two-track traversing the length of the property north and south, the tires slipping softly at first in the soft, sugar-sand shoulder of the crude road before gaining traction on the firmer dirt and trod-down grass. As they rode John Raines thought again of how it had indeed been a good first day for him in the field.

True, he had missed some shots, true, more than he was accustomed to. He could attribute this to just being rusty. If he were to look hard at past seasons, probably he'd find a similar pattern concerning first days out. Tomorrow would be better, the shotgun more comfortable against his cheek and shoulder, the birds flying truer and easier to hit, the dogs surer of themselves.

He thought again of the birds, those fast-rising quail and how it was wrong to make the birds part of the blame for his occasional poor shooting. That was a something that could never be true. Any weakness in the hunting had been him. His rustiness and age and the sorrow he carried with him. And if it weren't entirely true? This idea of his being the weakest link in the whole scheme of things? Then it had to be partly so. Otherwise—if he had paid more attention, if he had been a stronger, surer, man—then wouldn't his son be there with him? Hunting these fall quail together, as they had done since the boy was old enough to hold a shotgun steady in his hands and learn how to use it?

He had gotten away from himself. Had forgotten how tomorrow would be different. A tomorrow already on its way, what with the sun going down, the last rays lighting up the simple lodge Tom Ryan had built over the years on his property. Tom Ryan himself, tall and lanky, dressed as usual in leggings, and laced-up Army issue boots, clothing left over from his days with General Pershing during the First World War, stepped off the front porch with a water glass of bourbon, and ice, in one hand, and a smile on his face to greet John Raines and Lucas when they pulled into the yard.

***

It had been Tom Ryan who called that early morning thirteen months before. At the time of the call Raines was dreaming, or perhaps remembering, when he was aboard the Parker one day, maybe ten, twelve years before, off the edges of the Gulf Stream. That day Marilyn was also aboard, his daughter, the sweet, mischief-making girl he had named the boat for when Sadie didn't approve of the last owner's crude—although appropriate, considering the man's line of business— *Rum Bitch*. In this dream it was the day Marilyn caught her first sailfish. Raines had other company aboard, fellow lawyers and judges, all of them drinking and talking loudly and none of them paying any attention to the baits Raines had put out behind the boat as they trolled the edges of the Gulf Stream. Marilyn was along that day only because she had insisted so, and he always had a hard time saying no to his little girl.

Now, in the dream, as she had that day, she was calling for her father to come help, that she had a big fish on. When he turned away from Judge Collier—busy telling a mildly offensive joke about the last Negro neck-tie party in the woods west of town—to see what she was yelling about a big sailfish cleared the water, Marilyn being the only one who had noticed when one of the reels began screaming as line sang off it in a hurry.

It was all so clear and real in the dream for Raines. How he leaned over his daughter and strapped her into the fighting chair on the stern of the Parker, the rod bucking and straining in the little girl's hands as the fish ran and ran, and Marilyn crying, "I can't do this, Daddy."

"You certainly can, and I will help you," even if he didn't think it truly possible for her to catch the sailfish but damned if he would tell her that, the reel screaming louder as the fish took line, jumping one more time to reveal the biggest sailfish he had ever seen, the reel continuing to scream as he jerked awake.

He realized it was the phone in the hallway outside the bedroom making all the noise and remembered that Marilyn was no longer ten. That she was in fact gone from the house, married to the Bohemian professor and living in Greenwich Village. He got out of bed, sad to see the dream go, but the phone was insistent, telling Sadie next to him as she stirred, "Don't get up, honey, it's probably a wrong number."

But when he picked the phone up, he heard a familiar voice. "John?"

"It's me, Tom"

"Sorry to call you at such a late hour."

Raines, still half asleep and thinking about the vivid dream, didn't know the time, didn't really want to know, but was coming awake fully now because of the edge, that even half asleep, he could hear in his friend's voice.

"No way, I suppose, to do what I have to other than to just do so," Tom Ryan said on the other end of the line, while everything dropped out of Raines in a rush as he understood how the call, the lateness of the hour, could only mean one thing, wondering for a moment which one of his children it was, and if he had a choice, which one would he pick?

"If you're going to go ahead and get on with it, Tom" he said curtly—immediately regretting the harshness toward the man who had done so much for him over the years— "then do so."

"You're right, John. The thing is, well, Walter called me a little bit ago."

Tom hesitated again and hoping to push him along Raines asked, "Harker?"

"Yes indeed. Our very own esteemed Sheriff, depending on which side of the moral track one is on, I suppose."

"Tom, if you can't tell me what's wrong, then hang up and let me call Sheriff Harker myself."

"You won't reach him, John. Not at his house. Or the office. Why he called me anyway. Said he thought maybe I should be the one to tell you, seeing the way you feel about him and all."

"Tom—"

"It's Hilton, John. There's been an accident. A bad accident."

"Hilton? He's hurt?"

"He's hurt. Yes. I'm sorry, John."

Fifteen minutes later Raines got out of his car at the FEC crossing on Broward Boulevard. Traffic on the way over was light. It was pushing two-thirty in the morning after all, no one out and about, other than a few vendors on their way to prepare for the routes that had them up at that time of day. An occasional slow-moving car passed him going the other way. He told his wife he had to go out and would be back as soon as possible, got in the car and made his way to the tracks where Fort Lauderdale's six police cars, and one county Sheriff's vehicle, had blocked off the traffic on both sides.

On the other side of the officer's cruisers the midnight train from Miami was at a standstill. The rotating lights of the police cars bouncing off the passenger cars of the train lit the scene in a soft, but ominous glow. Staring at the stalled train cars, the flashing lights, the uniformed men, Raines' stomach dropped again. Then he was pushing through the circle of men and bending over the crumpled form of his son on the edge of pavement at the tracks and everything that was John Raines lurched inside once more before leaving him all the way.

"Accident" was the word Tom Ryan, Sheriff Harker, and the others at the scene were using. It was repeated again in the "Miami Herald' and the "Sun-Sentinel" the next day in the articles about the unexpected death of a prominent Fort Lauderdale attorney's son. He never heard the word "suicide" spoken at all that night. Certainly not by any of the men gathered around him in the circle of reflecting police lights as he held Hilton's broken body in his arms.

The closest any of the men there came to saying anything was later as Hilton's body was being put in the ambulance and Raines stood off to the side with Tom Ryan, half listening to his friend's comforting words, his main concern being how in the world was he going to tell Sadie? And Gwen?

As he watched the ambulance pull away down Broward Boulevard with his son inside, he heard Sheriff Harker's voice rising above the din surrounding the scene, the sheriff's distinct voice telling the deputy standing next to him, "Durn it all but you know 'at damned ol' train was forty-five minutes late tonight. Leastways 'at's whut 'em boys down in Miami radioed in. The boy had plenty of time to change his mind. Hell, more 'an enough time."

Of course, it was the war. It had done terrible things to Hilton. His once sturdy frame was emaciated and scarred, his dark eyes hollow and sagging when he returned from the Philippines toward the end of 1946. A lot of this could be attributed to the malaria he contracted in the jungles of the Pacific Theater. What the military physicians and Dr. Roby, the family's long-time doctor, called "battle fatigue," though, was the cause of his haunted appearance, the way his eyes never seemed to stay focused on any one object for longer than it took to blink and look away.

It was right after Christmas when he came back for good, after being released from the army hospital at Fort Ord, California, John and Sadie Raines, and Gwen, waiting expectantly on a cool and clear December morning for the train carrying him home to roll into the depot. While others of Hilton's unit had gone on to Japan as part of MacArthur's occupation force, Hilton had been deemed unfit for service and honorably discharged. The family had been relieved at this news, wanting only for Hilton to return to them

That morning, though, as the sagging, hollow-eyed stranger made his way toward them along the platform, pushing hesitantly through the throng of other families and returning soldiers, John Raines—after taking a long, hard look, at his son—wondered whether or not what they had been relieved to hear was actually good news.

But over time Hilton grew stronger, physically at any rate. The comforts of home, clean sheets, the home-cooked meals, the sounds and smells and actions of war replaced by the humdrum of everyday life in the town where he had grown up, seemed to bring him around.

A relapse of malaria, though, in the spring of 1947 set him back, the fever, accompanying chills, and fatigue, keeping him in bed for most of April. He had the Atabrine tablets the army had issued him in case of a relapse. But when John Raines came by on his lunch hour one day to see how his son was doing, he asked if the tablets helped any. Hilton confessed that he had thrown them away, explaining that though the Atabrine *did* ease the symptoms, they caused a steady, loud ringing in his ears that confused his thoughts. John Raines left the room to call Dr. Roby and tell him what Hilton had just told him. Later that afternoon the doctor stopped in on his way home and left quinine pills with Gwen. By the end of that week Hilton was much improved, was even out of bed for short stretches.

Once back on his feet again, Hilton began working at John Raines's law office, running briefs over to the courthouse and the like. Raines was glad for the help and that he was able to do something for his son. With his daughter married and living in New York and Hilton off at war, his family had seemed fragmented. Even if Hilton wasn't near being his old self, still, having him there in the office five days a week seemed like a good start to John Raines, holding out the promise as it did, that with time his family might yet be whole again.

Still, the malaria and the battle fatigue weren't gone. Over that next year Hilton suffered a series of relapses, bouts of sickness and confusion forcing him back to bed where he lay for days sweating and shaking and staring out from the covers with that haunted look in his eyes. When the spells passed, he returned to work, a cycle that continued on through 1947 and into early '48. Fortunately enough, he was healthy and on his feet when Gwen bore him a son in January of that year.

The baby—a spitting image of his father—seemed to lift Hilton above what the war and the malaria had done to him. So that on that Monday afternoon in October of 1948 when Hilton turned to his father at the end of the day and said, "Goodbye, Dad. I guess I'll be seeing you," John Raines saw no reason to believe that everything wasn't going to be fine.

His son's broken body in his arms the following morning by the FEC tracks, the flashing police lights splitting the night, the low murmur of the voices of the unaffected men standing around him drifting in and out of his consciousness, seemed more than enough, though, to prove how wrong he had been.

\*\*\*

New guests had come in while Raines was afield, a man, his wife, and son, the Owens, and friends of Tom Ryan's from Palm Beach. Though first timers at Ryan's annual after-Thanksgiving quail and dove shoot, the man and his family were not strangers to John Raines, at least the adults, who he had met in passing over the years. The husband, Tim, had a law practice in Palm Beach and had been of help to Ryan in overcoming difficulties involving the transfer of some properties a few years back.

Owen's father had started the firm in West Palm, right around the same time as John hung out his first shingle in Lauderdale. Over the years, Earl Owens managed to cultivate more than a few friendships with a number of judges, bankers, developers, and city officials in Palm Beach. These friendships enriched not only his social circle but Earl Owen's bank account as well. By the mid-1930's, and because of these cultivations, Owens was able to move his practice from the small office on Dixie Highway to a building down the street from the Breakers, effectively leaving what some in the town of Palm Beach considered squalid beginnings behind.

Tim Owens joined the firm just before the War and shortly afterwards Earl retired, leaving the practice, and the friendships, to his son while he focused on his golf game. Tom Ryan, who had known Earl for some time, naturally retained his son when a situation arose in Palm Beach not solvable by his contacts in Fort Lauderdale. At issue was a convoluted land deal involving a widow and parcels of the old Flagler Estate. Tim Owen proved to be just as, if not more so, capable than his father. Because of Owen's efforts, parcels of land that could have eluded Ryan fell into his possession, thus enabling the success of a venture long in the works and impossible to succeed without the Flagler parcels.

John Raines knew about the land parcels and the difficulties his friend went to in acquiring them. He also knew that Tim Owens's success in the matter bordered on the unethical, if not downright illegal.

It was a nasty business, and he was glad he hadn't been a part of it. If something of that nature had ever arisen in Lauderdale—where, by virtue of being Tom Ryan's lawyer, he may have been asked to do something similar—he would have refused. Tom and he had been friends a long time, it was true. Still, there were lines John Raines no longer crossed.

But the Palm Beach deal was in the past, nothing similar so far had come in between Raines and his friend, and now, Tim Owens was rising from his seat on the front veranda of Ryan's hunting lodge to greet Raines as he came out.

"Mr. Raines," the younger man said, shaking the hand Raines offered. "It's good to see you again, and in more pleasant surroundings." He paused, obviously unsure if his reference to their last meeting, Hilton's funeral, was appropriate. In a more somber tone, he continued. "I want to tell you again how sorry my wife and I are for your loss."

"Thanks, Tim and please. Forget the 'Mister' business. John is fine."

"Yes. Of course. And you're welcome. I've been working so much lately I sometimes forget I'm not in the office, or the courthouse. I'm sure you know how that can be at times."

Owens's ruddy face—red from too many boozy lunches with clients, Raines wondered—was cracked by a genuine smile of greeting. Earl Owen's son had certainly acquired the same honest social attitudes his father had been known for. If ruddy face and genuine smile were the same, the son was huskier than his father had ever been. His frame would probably go from husky to fat as he grew older if he didn't watch it, Raines decided. For now, though, the tall, burly frame carried the weight just fine, while the stylish, well-tailored suit he wore gave him a distinguished air. An air of success, both earned, and inherited.

"Well, I do know how that can be, Tim and thank God we're here and not in the office now."

"Amen to that, John."

Raines crossed the screened-in veranda to the mahogany bar Tom Ryan had set up years back, Tim Owens mention of Hilton's funeral spurring on a sudden thirst for some of the good bourbon his friend kept on hand. Night was falling outside and with it the cool of the

November day began to turn cold in earnest. A slight wind blew from the north, rustling the palmetto stands and pine trees standing off from the yard. The sound of the wind reminded Raines of how it could be at night at his own retreat in the woods. He had spent pleasant days and nights at that ranch with his family, cool nights in the winter, and hot ones in the summer—days and nights he had thought could never end. Yet, they had. Last October, a year back and he had not returned to that place, since, knowing that everywhere he went on that land his dead son would be with him.

Hopefully, the time would come when he could go back. But it wasn't now. Certainly not now.

For cool nights such as this one, Tom Ryan had dug a circular fire pit on the far edge of the front yard and arranged comfortable wicker chairs around the circle, providing a warm place where the men could get away from the ladies inside who were cleaning up after dinner and making their own conversations. With a fire blazing to cut the chill, it was a fine place to sit back with one of Tom's cigars and a glass of brandy, or bourbon, or Scotch, and reflect on the day.

Lucas was at the fire pit now, hauling logs out of the bed of the Jeep and laying them out in a neat pile by the side. A boy was with him, helping him to stack the logs, a white youth, maybe twelve or fourteen, tall, with gangly arms and a lean, awkward gait. He must be the Owens boy, Raines realized. The boy seemed to Raines to be more of a hindrance than a help. What with the way he stumbled uncertainly around the pile of wood.

But Lucas was good with the boy—as he'd been good with the dogs, and Raines, that day—showed him how to arrange smaller pieces of kindling in the center of the pit, the dried pieces of pine twigs that would flare up fast and not last long, but with enough of them lit eventually the larger logs of oak would catch and the fire would burn. The boy appeared willing enough, though, and paid attention to what Lucas told him Even better, Raines observed, he *did* what he was told. A good helper, Raines decided. Like his boy had been, always handy to have around.

"Have you met my son, Mr. Raines?"

The voice from behind, soft, and feminine, interrupted him before his thoughts took him to a place he was tired of going to. Grateful for the small favor, Raines turned to greet the woman at his side. Tall, thin, she had very straight blonde hair that fell down along her shoulders. There was an inquisitive set to her brows, the green eyes above a hard nose, managing to shine somehow in the available light. She was dressed for something other than where she was, he thought, as evidenced by the strapless evening gown she wore. Then again, her husband had been dressed for dinner as well in his tailored suit from Palm Beach. Perhaps, Raines wondered, it was he, and not the other way around, who wasn't in the right place.

"We were introduced once, Mrs. Owens," he said. "But it's been several years. He was just a child then. Not the fine young man he's turned out to be now."

It struck him then that Owens's wife was the only woman at the gathering, something he should have realized sooner. Tom Ryan's post-Thanksgiving shoots had always been traditionally stag affairs, events focused on time afield, good sport, and the camaraderie of men. At night, a lot of hard drinking transpired, along with loud laughter accompanying the ribald stories and lies older men told of days in their youth. In years past, the hunting party had usually consisted of Tom, his younger brother Eugene, Raines and Hilton—when Hilton was old enough to attend—and one or more lawyer, or banker, from either Lauderdale or Miami, men who happened to be in Tom Ryan's good graces at the time.

This year, of course, and like a lot of things after the war, it was all different. Not only was Hilton gone, but Tom's brother, Eugene, as well, killed in the Battle of the Coral Sea. Raines thought again how it could all be traced back to the war. How everything since had gone upside down and every which way.

"He's still a child," the woman said, unaware of Raines's train of thought, perhaps for the moment unaware of him as well, he wondered, judging by the tight set of her lips as she gazed past him in the falling light at her son and Lucas, boy and man visible only as dark figures hovering above the fire pit. "My name is Marjorie, not Mrs. Owens, by the way. In case you had forgotten."

"No," Raines said, "I haven't forgotten."

"Be careful, Timmy", she called out suddenly, the hand she raised to her mouth in sudden alarm striking Raines' shoulder in its flight. Her alarm, Raines saw, apparently due to the can of white gas Lucas was sprinkling liberally over the kindling and logs. "Let Lucas do the lighting of the fire and you stand back. Please!"

In the rush of flames flaring up when the match Lucas casually threw lit fuel and dry kindling, Raines could see the look on the boy's face. He was unprepared for the hatred he saw reflected there.

"I know it bothers him," Marjorie Owens said, and Raines realized she had seen the look, too. "But what can I do?" She turned back to Raines, a sense of helplessness in the shrug of her shoulders when she spoke. "He's too eager at times and usually ends up getting hurt because of it. His father won't watch out for him. Which leaves only me. And all the rewards that brings."

The woman's hard laughter caught Raines by surprise, just as the look of hatred on her son's face had. When she moved away from him to the mahogany bar to refresh the martini glass held stiffly in one hand, he could only think again of how everything in the world had changed. Very little of it for the better, as best he could see.

*** 

He awoke at 5:30 the next morning, as he did every day, a long-held habit since his time in the army. The routine served him in good stead when it came to hunting and fishing and with work, as well. More than one brief had been completed at the last minute, come trial day, on the back porch of his house as the sun was starting to come up.

The night turned colder than he had expected it would and with the window left halfway open he had felt the cold, even through the quilt Mrs. Ryan made were available in each of the two guest rooms. He woke once in the night to use the bathroom down the hall and on his return decided to close the window. But as he went to pull the glass down a shrill scream split the darkness. If one didn't know better, it would be easy to believe a woman was in dire trouble somewhere nearby. Raines *did* know better—knew the mournful racket in the night was the screaming of a panther as it marked the boundaries of its domain.

The skin of a dead panther hung nailed to the back of the front door of the house on his ranch. Raines thought of it as he lay back down in bed, the window closed tight now on the sound of the living cat out in the scrub. His younger brother, TJ, had shot the panther one afternoon as he and Hilton were on their way in after a day of mending fence on the far western edge of the property. 1937? '38? Raines couldn't remember exactly, the years before the War sometimes seeming a distant blur to him now, when in fact they weren't that distant at all.

Hilton and TJ had been so excited, though, when they galloped into the yard and reined up before the house, hollering for Raines and Sadie to come see what they had. When Raines and his wife stepped out on the porch, TJ hopped off the roan mare and pulled something off the back of his saddle, yelling as he did so for Hilton to come help him. In another moment, the man and boy held up for the others to see the body of a big cat, one that had to weigh at least a hundred pounds or better, as best Raines could judge.

The strange thing about the panther was how its coat was a deep black, not the usual pale tan Raines knew them to be. He had heard tales of black panthers roaming the wilds of Florida from his ranch foreman. An old cow hunter long in those parts had been told similar stories by others in the area, as well. But he'd never believed those stories to be true. Now, his son and TJ held proudly aloft—the horses wild with the scent of the cat, though dead, still alive in their nostrils—proof otherwise.

Raines could still hear his brother's voice yelling out, "Now lookie here my big brother, Miss Sadie, ma'am, what your boy and I done brought home.

As he fell back to sleep in the comfort of Tom Ryan's guest room, Raines thought of how it didn't really matter. TJ, Hilton, the cat? Long dead—the hide hanging on the rear of a door, tangible evidence, at least, that one of the three had once lived.

The Owens boy was sound asleep on the big daybed in the corner as Raines came into the living room, his reddish hair tousled against the white of the pillow. He should have let the boy's parents take the room he slept in, the one with the double bed, Raines thought. Let the boy and he bunk together in the room with the twin beds. But Raines had been selfish about it, though in truth it never came up. Selfish because the bigger room was where he and Sadie always stayed when they came to visit.

It didn't appear the boy had been bothered by having to sleep in the living room of a strange house. Not judging by the rhythmic sound of his breath rising and falling as he stirred, and then rolled over. Raines thought to wake him, then decided against it and headed for the kitchen in the rear of the house and the hot coffee Lucas should have ready.

But he accidentally bumped the corner of an old roll top desk nestled against the wall, the clatter of small items atop the desk and the scraping of wood, awakening the boy.

"Sorry," he said when the boy sat up suddenly in the daybed. "I didn't mean to disturb you."

"Is it time to go, sir?"

Raines smiled, touched by the eagerness in the boy's face, the way he was already out of the bed and scrambling into his trousers left on the floor by the bed the night before.

"No, no, son. Not yet. Plenty of time before we head out. The sun's not even up."

"Oh." The boy sat back down on the bed, his eagerness deflated a little it appeared as he rubbed an eye with the back of one hand and looked at Raines with the one still open. "No one said anything last night about it, so I didn't know."

"Fortunately, son, quail hunting is still a gentleman's sport in this country, revolving around what some might consider near banker's hours." He could tell his words made little sense to the boy. "Come into the kitchen with me and over coffee I'll explain it to you."

They followed the strand of light showing around the door frame at the rear of the room into the kitchen where Lucas poured out cups of steaming coffee for them from a tarnished percolator. A slab of bacon sizzled in an iron frying pan on the stove behind Lucas while on another burner a pot of grits was bubbling away. The smell of the coffee and cooking food in the brightly lit room brought Raines all the way awake, and for the first time that he could remember in a while, eager for the day to unfold.

"Wouldn't you agree, Lucas," Raines asked as he sat down at the small table in the corner of the room and lifted the cup of coffee to his mouth. "Quail shooting's a gentleman's game in these parts?"

"Yes sir, I would." Lucas was stirring the pot of grits on the stove, a big smile stretching his dark face wide. "'Specially when you huntin' with Mr. Ryan. That gentleman's in no hurry to get out of bed come weekend." He turned back to the pot of grits and the bacon strips, saying softly over his shoulder while he worked, "Not that I was in any big hurry to get out of the blankets on this cold mornin', mind you. No sir!"

Raines looked out the window next to the back door at the tin pump house in the yard where Lucas, and the hired help preceding him, slept and kept their clothes and other personal belongings. A single bed, more a cot than bed, actually, shaky wooden bureau, a chair, about as shaky as the bureau, overhead light bulb and an electrical outlet that could power a fan in the summer and a small heater in the winter, filled the room, along with the water pump wedged up against the one wall. What with the open spaces around the metal door and the irregular seams where tin roof met tin wall, it could be uncomfortable in there, heater or no, Raines thought.

"Been on a quail shoot before?" he asked the boy, quickly, wanting to get away from thoughts of Lucas shivering in the night in the small room outside. "Or dove? Any other game?"

"No sir. Only skeet. Plenty of times skeet with my dad." The boy sipped at the hot coffee, cautiously, the way Hilton had at that age, Raines remembered, when Hilton was still trying to understand why adults enjoyed such a harsh beverage. Unlike Hilton, who put spoon after spoon of sugar into his coffee before he could drink it, the boy took his with only cream, and for no reason that he could really think of, this raised the boy a notch or so in Raines estimate. "Mom comes and shoots sometimes with us. This'll be my first time with real live birds and dogs and such."

"First time for your mom, too?"

The excited smile spreading quickly across the boy's face when he realized he was actually going to be on a hunt that day, closed.

"Yeah, her first time, too. I mean, yes sir."

Not as strong as the hatred on his face the night before, perhaps, Raines saw, but there just the same.

"More coffee, gentlemen?"

Lucas was at their side, silver percolator held up inquiringly in one hand, the yellow light bulb overhead giving his dark skin a rich, mahogany hue in the soft light.

"Please Lucas. Any for you, son?"

"Yes sir, Mr. Lucas. It sure is swell coffee."

The coffee *was* swell, and swell also, the fact of having a child around him again, even if the boy wasn't really a child anymore—was on those first steps toward the man he'd become.

"Jus' call me Lucas, Master Tim. Like the other folks do," Lucas said, as he poured coffee for the two.

"That's right," Raines jumped in. "Lucas is way too young to be a 'Mister.'"

The three laughed together in the brightness of the kitchen, the boy Raines bet, if unsure of why happy anyway to laugh along with the grown men.

"So Lucas," Raines asked when the laughter faded away, "just you, and me, and Ringo again for the day?"

"I imagine so. Mr. Tom said he'd be taking the other guests out today. Up to the north end and around that slough there. Least, that's what he told me last night."

"Usually good birds up there," Raines said, remembering other days hunting that area. "More dove, than quail, though, what with the water and all."

"Yes sir, that's usually the case, but too much water now. After 'em hurricanes we had last summer. Grains all washed away and no doves to be seen at all this year. Good quail, though, some big coveys about a half mile or so west of the slough. Mr. Tom and I scouted 'em out last weekend. Should be some fine shooting there today."

"Where to for us, then?"

"South, I'm thinking. Down by that old dirt road to Okeechobee. Be plenty of birds for you to shoot down there, sir."

"Shoot at, don't you mean?" Raines said, reviving a shared joke of the day before.

"No sir. Not what I mean at all."

And though he couldn't see it, what with his back turned to him at the time, Raines could imagine the smile on Lucas' face.

Hearing the dogs beginning to bark in their kennels as the sun rose higher in the morning sky Raines had a sudden thought, and excited at the prospect he turned to the boy.

"How about you come with Lucas and me, today, son? Let Mr. Ryan entertain your folks and the three of us do some real bird hunting?"

"You mean it?"

"I do."

"Yes sir!"

All of this? Morning in the kitchen with the boy and Lucas. The day's light coming on outside. Dogs barking to go in their kennels. The smell of good food almost ready to eat. All of this certainly seemed to be a fine way to start the day. For Raines at any rate. He hoped it would be for the boy, as well.

\*\*\*

But the day didn't go as Raines thought it might—not for him, at least. Or for the boy, either. By late morning, the gray threat of the overcast sky hanging overhead, finally came true and rain began to fall. When it did Raines was glad for a reason to call it quits.

It wasn't that there hadn't been a good number of birds—there had been plenty, in fact. Lucas had decided at the last minute against using the pup, Ringo, and put a dog he called Tuff in the dog cage instead. It turned out to be a very good decision. Tuff found covey after covey of quail, large and small, the birds rushing out from their hiding places in the palmetto, chokeberry bushes, and clumps of wiregrass when the scruffy white pointer lunged off point on command and sent them pell-mell into the sky. The cool temperature of the morning contributed to the furious speed of the fleeing quail, unlike a warmer morning, say in late March, or early April, when the birds were sluggish with the springtime heat, would've allowed.

With the quickness of the birds that morning there was little time for careful leads. It was all instinct shooting—the dog into the bushes, the birds rushing out, gun to shoulder and cheek, eyes open down the barrel, pull the trigger. Raines liked this kind of shooting very much. When instincts alone guided his shots, he seemed to do better. In the end, despite of how the morning turned out, there was a considerable number of quail in the game bag. More, perhaps, Raines wondered, as he counted them, than might have been shot on another day.

At least, this was the conclusion he came to later, as he sat out on the front porch with a glass of Tom Ryan's whiskey watching the rain move across the pines and palmettos, covering everything he saw in a steady, falling, gray.

The boy did fine. He listened carefully, followed Lucas', and Raines' suggestions to a T, and because of this—as well as a natural ability Raines couldn't help but notice—shot more than his share of rising birds. Until his mother, that is, decided it was *her* turn to join in.

Therein, as the old Bard wrote, lay the rub, Raines thought, having a last drink on the front porch before dinner. He had seen it immediately, knew how it was about to go, and kicked himself in the butt once again for not having the tact to firmly say, No, when Marjorie Owens announced over breakfast that she would rather tag along with her son and Mr. Raines, that morning. Instead of Mr. Ryan and her husband, who were only going to be talking business, and she would just be in the way. Not to mention bored, she added, with a little smile that Raines could make no sense of.

So that there had been no way around it even though Tom Ryan tried.

"It's not going to be all business, Marjorie," he said from the head of the table, done with breakfast and having a last cup of coffee.

Raines stared at his old friend, dressed for the field in a freshly pressed shooting shirt—though where Lucas had found the time to do that, on top of all the other chores before breakfast, Raines couldn't imagine—his customary leggings and military boots. How many mornings had the two friends sat across one another from the table, either here, or at Raines's place, breakfast done, dogs barking and ready in the trucks, the two of them lingering over coffee and waiting for the day to warm just a little more before setting out? A few, for sure. Hell, more than a few. This one, suddenly, promised to be a little different from the others. Raines was willing to bet good money on that.

"There's only a couple of minor items I wanted to discuss with Tim on the way out this morning," Ryan continued. "Other than that, I can assure you, my dear lady, the focus will be completely on the sport at hand."

"Well, all that besides, I know I'll just be in the way. I'm sure that's what my husband believes. Don't you, Tim?"

Her face and green eyes looked pale and clear in the light of the morning streaming through the windows of the dining room. The bright red of the ladies shooting shirt she wore set off clearly her features, highlighting her eyes and the blonde hair falling down around her cheeks. Coming into the room from the hallway, riding boots clicking on the hardwood floor, she had caught Raines attention immediately, along with the others already at the table. Riding boots and breeches weren't necessarily the clothing he would have suggested for the field that morning. Hard to walk through the rough clumps of wire grass and potholes that made up a lot of the scrub they'd be hunting in, he thought. With those boots. On the other hand, she'd be well protected from snakebite. Not to mention the fact of how well they showed off her lean and muscular thighs. A disturbing thought out of nowhere that he pushed away quickly.

"Well, I don't know, Marjorie," her husband spoke up, flashing a wan smile at the others. "Whatever you think, I suppose."

"Let's leave it up to Timmy. And Mr. Raines," she offered back, her own smile one, Raines imagined, that rarely failed her in situations such as this. "What do you two gentlemen have to say about my joining your party this morning?"

Raines sat quietly with his coffee, hoping the boy would rise to the occasion, his gut fairly certain, though, that wasn't possible.

"Timmy? Only for the morning, I promise. After lunch I'll either stay here or go with your father and Mr. Ryan. You and Mr. Raines can go together then without my getting in the way." When her son didn't answer she repeated, "I promise."

"Sure, Mom," the boy said, looking up from his breakfast after a bit. "I guess so. If it's okay with Mr. Raines."

The beaming smile she turned on him was full of many things, none of which Raines was certain he cared about. But like the boy he said, Sure, adding, "By all means join us. It'll be fun."

Now, the day was finished, dark coming on and the ice of what he'd figured to be the last drink before dinner melted completely, washing away the amber color of the bourbon. Opening the door of the porch he tossed the remains of the drink out on the grass. Deciding there was likely plenty of time before Lucas called them to table, he made another drink and returned to the comfortable wooden rocker he'd been sitting in while the wet afternoon ended, and night began.

So, she was true to her word, he recalled, the fresh bourbon raw as it smoothed down his throat, the ice not having a chance to cool it any before he drank. About not going with them after lunch. Of course, there was no way of knowing if she would have done it on her own. The weather took away her choice, really, but maybe that was for the best. He wouldn't have been pleased had it gone a different way. And neither would have the boy. Raines was fairly certain of that.

She was a fine shot, though. Another thing he had to give her. No matter how he felt about the rest of it. She'd handled herself with a natural ease as she walked alongside of Lucas and Raines, while the dog roamed ahead in the scrub working for scent, eager to do what was expected of him If the scruffy dog went on point, back arched, tail out straight, and nose held firmly forward, the woman waited for any instruction Lucas or Raines may give her, gun held loosely, but ready, in both hands at her waist as she paid attention to what she was told. When Lucas said quietly, "Bird, 'Tuff'. Flush 'em up!" the dog was on them in a lurching flash, his muscular body parting the palmettos and berry bushes as he burst in and forced the quail into the air. If the woman had a shot, she took it without hesitation, swinging the gun to her shoulder and pulling the trigger at the best possible moment to do so.

If she knew how to handle herself in the fields with a shotgun and birds on wing, inappropriate boots beside the point, the way she pressed her thigh against his as she sat between him and the boy in the back seat of the hunting buggy was another matter. Cool morning air or not, he had felt the heat of her flesh beneath the riding breeches as every bump and pothole seemed to force the rest of her body into his. Some kind of game, he decided. She could have utilized her son for support on the bumps just as easily. A game was all, one he wasn't interested in playing. Even if his body reacted otherwise, the betrayal of his body, best to ignore.

The boy's mother possessed a certain wild beauty, one enhanced mightily by the shooting she demonstrated that morning, and Raines was sorry something was taken away from it. But he couldn't ignore the fact of the boy, who had retreated when Marjorie Owens decided it was her turn at the birds, to sit sulking on the bench seat above the dog cages in the rear of the Jeep. A wealth of promise had been held out for the Owens's boy, earlier that morning, Raines thought, most of it rudely snatched back. First, at the breakfast table with his mother's announcement. Then, when she took her turn at shooting. The rest of it destroyed completely when rain began to fall as noon approached.

But for now, he reminded himself once more, all that was behind him and he could sit peacefully alone for a little while on the porch, glass of bourbon in one hand, freshly lit cigar in the other, the hard rain of the afternoon disappearing into a gray mist as dusk came on. It had been both a good and bad day, he decided. Awkward at times, filled with some truths at others, and in the long run not much more than that.

"I suppose Timmy will forgive me in time."

Marjorie Owens's voice behind him startled Raines, causing his hand to slip as he went to stand up from the chair, the bourbon splashed on his pants leg from this more an embarrassment than anything else.

"For what, now?"

Her quick laughter startled him as well and maybe because it was real, he thought, not like the pleading tone of earlier, over breakfast where she got her way.

"Oh my, but you're so right." Waving with one hand for him not to stand up on her account, she sat down in the rocking chair next to him, turning her face from his to the misty dusk beyond the screened porch. "The list grows longer by the day, it appears."

"He's young," Raines told her. "He'll survive."

"I'm sure."

Raines wondered if it were really true. Hilton had been young, and he hadn't survived. Only words, anyway, what was said between him and the woman, for the most part platitudes meant to convey social grace.

Lucas rang the dinner bell from the doorway of the kitchen, the smell of fried quail and fresh-made biscuits a welcome aroma greeting Raines as he entered the house from the porch, Marjorie Owens leading the way. His wife had asked for Lucas' recipe the first time she ever had one of his down-home southern quail dinners. Now the warm odors filling the dining area reminded Raines of home. The next day was Sunday, and as he sat down at one end of the table while his long-time friend, Tom Ryan sat down at the other. Raines decided to forego shooting in the morning. He would pack his things instead and get an early start for town.

He was weary of it all. The shooting. The Owens family. Not so much the boy, but the mother, for certain. And maybe only because she had prevented him from a chance to know the boy better. The chance to have a child around him again, if only for a little while. To what end? he wondered as he took the plate of warm biscuits from Tim Owens Sr. and put two on his plate. To fill what Hilton had taken away? It couldn't be done—was a harsh question besides, one he was tired of asking.

The following morning would bring an end to it, for a while at any rate. Once home it could be put away for good.

\*\*\*

Hours yet were left in the present day, though, before home, and a forgetting, could be reached. Dinner began as a quiet affair, the only ones interested in making small conversation being Tom Ryan and Owens. The bulk of this conversation concerned details of the housing project planned for Palm Beach. Occasionally, one of them tried to draw the others in by dropping the business talk to inquire about the day's hunting and the like. Raines did what he could but found it difficult to sustain a social role for long. The morning's hunting had been gone over pretty thoroughly at lunch as far as he was concerned. Nothing new or exciting had transpired since then. He was content to focus his efforts on the dinner Lucas had set out.

Marjorie Owens, it appeared, had no qualms about covering familiar territory one more time, launching—when there was a lull in the business chatter between Ryan and her husband—into a long monologue about the birds of the morning. Lucas' skill with the dogs. What a good shot Mr. Raines was. Patient, as well, with her and Timmy. She knew her inexperience had to be hard to contend with.

This last business, her inexperience, a bold lie, one that got his attention immediately. But when he looked up from his plate to catch her eye across the table Marjorie Owens winked. Before continuing on she took another sip of the red wine she had been drinking steadily all through the meal. And yes, she started up again, it was too bad, a shame, really, how the weather interfered the way it had. But what a lovely property Tom had here. Perfect, really, she couldn't think of a better way to describe it, or the whole day. Just simply perfect.

Her face, even in the soft light, looked flushed—the wine, Raines wondered. Perhaps simply the chance to talk—the wisp of blonde hair falling down over one of her eyes reminding him of the movie actress, Veronica Lake.

"Wouldn't you agree, Timmy?" she asked when finished and turning to her son. "That it was just perfect?"

"Can I be excused?" the boy answered. Without waiting for his request to be honored he stood up from the table. "Thank you."

"Must be his age," his mother said after the boy left the room "Puberty and all, I suppose. Boys, especially, seem to be so difficult, with the change." She leaned forward across the table a little, as if she were speaking only to Raines. "It's so different with us girls, you know. We just grow breasts and hair where we didn't expect to. Didn't seem like much of anything. To me at any rate. But boys, I guess, what with the high cracking voice, and the dreams at night and messy sheets— well it must be confusing."

"Marjorie," her husband said from the end of the table, his face flushed, like his wife's.

"Oh, don't be such a prude, Tim We're all adults here and Timmy can't possibly have heard what I said."

"Just doesn't seem to be the place," Owens began, but stopped at a look from her. The table fell silent, and when the talk turned back to the upcoming legal challenges of the Palm Beach project, Raines took the opportunity to leave the table—to be free of the chill he felt descending on the room

The boy was outside, helping Lucas again with the bonfire and Raines, happy for a chance to do something manual that required little thought, pitched in with unloading wood from the back of the Jeep. He enjoyed handling the sawn logs, the rough grains of the wood against his fingers, first the smaller pieces still sticky with sap, the pine resin that would blaze up with the match and stay afire long enough for the larger chunks of pine and oak and cypress to catch. Once the fire was on its way Lucas left, Raines well aware he had plenty of chores still to do before retiring to his cot in the pump house. With Lucas gone, and the fire blazing in the ring, Raines and the boy sat in the wicker chairs across from one another watching the flames burn away what was left of the wet mist from the day. It was quiet for a long while after that, the silence broken only when Raines, having realized something was missing, returned from the house with a cup of steaming coffee and a snifter of brandy.

"Can you believe that crap she spews out?" the boy suddenly asked, before Raines had even sat back down. "Sir?" he added a moment later, making up for his lapse in manners.

"I'm not sure, son, it's my place to say." He smiled at the boy, whose face and features seemed to glow a faint red, matching the light given off by the fire. "She can take one by surprise at times, it's true."

"That's bull shit, sir, and I'm sorry for the cursing." The boy spat into the fire. "But it's sure how I feel. She goes on and on and no one says anything. Just lets her do it and I hate her for it."

"Hate's a pretty strong feeling to have for someone, Tim You have the right to feel that way towards your mother, I guess. But it seems harsh. Sort of final. And maybe that won't always be the case."

"It will."

Raines took a sip of the hot coffee and then washed it down with brandy, the liquor tasting hot like the coffee, and with an earthy bite to it, much like the cigar he had smoked earlier. Both cigar and brandy were from Cuba, he remembered, and it struck him as logical they would share a similar flavor. Coming from the same earth like that, tilled and harvested and made by the hands of the same sort of people. Other than the birds of the morning, the similar tastes of the cigar and brandy seemed just about the only logical parts of his day.

"My dad can't do anything with her. It's disgusting."

Raines would have preferred staying with the pleasantness of the strong brandy and coffee—but had lived long enough to know he would stay where he was, preferences, or not.

"He calls himself a man," the boy continued, his face hidden, now that he had pushed his chair back from the fire ring, his voice, coming from just beyond the reaches of the firelight, seemingly held aloft by the force of the hatred inspiring it. "I don't see it and I hate him, too."

"I had a hatred for my father once."

Raines put aside the coffee and brandy to lean closer to the fire, the warmth of it comfortable against his face and hands when he held them over the flames.

"You did?"

"I did. I was right around your age, too. How old *are* you, Tim?"

"Fourteen, sir. And more a man than my dad."

"Yes. I was fourteen, as well. Thought the same way, too. About being more of a man."

"What'd you do about it?" The boy's voice was eager now—hopeful, Raines thought, for some sort of answer to be finally revealed to him "Hating your dad, I mean. Did you get over it?"

"I left," Raines told him "And yes, I got over it."

"That's what I should do," the boy said.

"It's not an easy thing," Raines said, more to himself than to the boy. "A young man your age packing up and starting out on his own. Not these days and the way the world is all different, more complicated. Bide your time, Tim. Things will change before you know it."

"Yes sir. You're probably right. 'Bide my time.' But if I see my chance, sir, I'm going to take it."

"Chance for what, Timmy?"

\*\*\*

They hadn't heard her come up and now Marjorie Owens stood next to Raines' chair, in between him and her son, brandy snifter in one hand, her features flashing shadows in the firelight.

"Nothing, mother." The boy jumped up, the sudden motion knocking his chair backwards into the grass. "Nothing you'd understand. Or want to be concerned with."

He was gone, a gray figure going up the steps into the porch, becoming, in the light of the house flooding out on the porch when he opened the door, a boy, shoulders bent as he slammed the door shut behind him Raines didn't know if he was sad, or relieved, at his sudden departure. Either way, he was left with the woman and with the uncomfortable odor of expensive perfume and her green eyes looking into his.

"I could let myself be angry about Timmy." She sighed as she sat down in the chair her son had left empty. "But it's Saturday night, I'm away from home and I just want to feel good. Not angry."

"I can understand that."

He spoke more out of politeness than anything else, bothered more than he wanted to be by the swell of her breasts beneath the dark turtleneck sweater she wore when she leaned back and drank. It hit Raines then how truly attractive the Owens woman was. Disturbed by her little touching game in the Jeep earlier he'd been too distracted to notice. There was no getting away from it, now—not with her sitting close to him by the fire, the warmth of both fire and brandy somehow focusing his senses completely on her.

"Do you, Mr. Raines?" She placed the hand not holding her brandy snifter, on his, and left it there. "Understand, I mean?"

"My wife and I raised two children," he said, after another sip of the brandy. "It wasn't always easy, and we had some difficulties. There were times when both Sadie and I, though maybe just me, I don't know—but yes, some nights when I just wanted to let it go and feel good." He paused, considered the brandy in his hands again but didn't drink. "Of course, my sense of duty didn't allow such a thing. We had the occasional evening out with friends when we could get a neighbor to watch the children. The times were tough then, what with the depression and all, and we didn't like to impose. Besides, for a while there, a long while, we didn't have the money to waste on a frivolous evening out."

He pulled up short, surprised at how he had been going on, and the woman and he were quiet before the fire for a while after that. He was aware of the others in the house behind them, wondered if Tim Jr. had gone to bed, still eaten up with the anger. In the silence between him and the woman he could hear the low murmur of Tom Ryan and Owens talking inside the house. Nothing solid, just snatches of words he couldn't quite make out drifting through the windows of the house opened onto the porch.

Business talk he was sure. The sort of talk he wanted nothing to do with on a night like this one, cool, with a slight wind sloughing across the pines and palmetto scrub, the blaze of the fire enough to keep the coolness at bay, the rain and lingering mist of the day finally gone, so that instead of hulking dark clouds in the sky stars began to appear, visible in the black reaches of the night beyond the fire, the Dog Star, Orion's Belt, and when he turned a little, the planet Venus glowing steadily. On a night like this there should always be more than business, he decided. The laws that governed it. Forgetting it was empty he raised the brandy snifter to his lips—his disappointment at what he found must have showed.

"Not to worry, Mr. Man, but I thought of that danger and made the proper preparations to avoid its occurring."

In the orange light of the fire Marjorie Owens pale features looked almost otherworldly to Raines. The crystal decanter she waved in one hand, dark amber liquid inside glinting in the orange light, was every bit of the world. Raines was glad for it, wondering, for just a moment, why that was.

"You certainly make a good wife for a successful lawyer," he said holding out his empty glass for her to refill. "Prepared for any unseen motion, change of venue, or lost brief."

"Nothing as brilliant, or diabolical, as that," she replied, after filling her own glass. "My natural born laziness decided the issue more than anything. You know? The fact I knew I'd want more. I couldn't see the sense in getting up, walking back to the porch, refilling my glass, walking back, and then before you know it, having to get up and repeat the process all over again. Nope. Just didn't make any sense that I could see."

She paused, took a long sip, and smiling at him in the pale light, continued, "Besides, Tom and my husband are so busy with their blueprints and legal documents and the like, and definitely in no need of this exquisite brandy. A brandy I might add it would almost be a sin to let go to waste on such a perfect night as this."

She took a deep breath, the swell of her breasts beneath the turtleneck a slight motion that caught his eye once more, in spite of his trying not to look. "So, I made myself forward and brought the decanter out with me."

"Thank God you did," Raines blurted out, the two of them laughing and clinking their glasses together in a celebratory toast to the woman's fortunate way of thinking. "I probably would have gone in," he said when the laughter faded out, "thinking to have one more, changed my mind and gone to bed instead, and missed out on the night turning so pleasant after all. After," he added, "the soggy weather of earlier."

"Pleasant only because of that?" she asked, green eyes looking at him as she casually blew a stray strand of blonde hair away from her forehead. "Mr. Raines?"

"I don't see why your husband would ever have to try a case," he laughed. "Just have you pay a visit to the judge's chamber and win it all with that smile of yours."

Though she said nothing he could see she was pleased with this. They were quiet again in the light of the fire that had burned down to a soft glow. The brandy tasted to him like the fire: comfortable. In another minute, he thought, he'd get up and toss another log on. But for now, it was all just right, the fire, the brandy—even the woman.

"Nothing lazy about the way you handled yourself with the birds this morning'" he said after a bit, as if her comment about "natural laziness" had just registered with him

Her quick laugh, surprisingly loud, rang out in the dark across the pines and palmetto stands in the fields beyond the house—a laugh that struck him as being the first really true sound he'd ever heard her utter.

"Why, thank you, kind sir."

She regained herself, sitting a little more erect in the wicker chair as she stared into the fire. She's making a decision of some sort, he thought. Perhaps debating how far she can let the comfortableness of the fire, the evening, the pleasant conversation, carry her. But that was absurd, he decided over a long pull of the Cuban brandy. His thinking he had any clue as to what the woman next to him could be thinking.

"My father taught me from an early age." She turned wet eyes to Raines—from the hard laughter, he wondered? Or something else? "How to handle a gun and that. With no male heir to pass on his manly skills to I was elected. And my father was a man, make no mistake of that. Unlike most males I've met since."

"And where were these so-called 'manly skills' passed down m'lady?" he asked quickly, worried that the hard edge in her voice might threaten what so far, was turning out to be a good evening after all. The smile he received from her proof enough he had taken the right track.

"Columbia, South Carolina, sir." She leaned back again in the wicker chair, brandy snifter held loosely in the one hand, her face turned to the fire. "The heart of the South, as my father liked to say. To others in those parts, it was the realm—no, not realm," she corrected herself, "but the fiefdom of Judge Ferris, who obviously believed it to be true and acted accordingly. Lord and Master of all he surveyed. Most of this surveying took place under the auspices of the state Supreme Court where he served as Chief Justice for as long as I can remember."

"I'm surprised you didn't go into law." He could have told her how familiar he was with her hometown, Camp Jackson, being sick with the flu, meeting, and then losing Sadie, only to get her back. It didn't seem the time or place, though, and said instead, "You were born into it, after all. In a manner of speaking, I suppose."

"Yes." The distant wistfulness in her tone lasted only a minute. "I'm surprised I didn't do that myself. My father, unfortunately for me, certainly, didn't consider law a possible career for a woman. To my regret, I listened to him"

"Still," Raines said, wanting to get the conversation back on course as he heard that hard edge creeping back into the woman's voice, "law or not, your father took the time to teach you a few things."

"Oh, he most certainly did. Every weekend in the good weather months my family made its escape from the confines of the city to the family farm. At least that's what Daddy called it. Plantation was more like it. But since a man of humble origins was always part of daddy's grand fiction, I suppose he thought 'Family Farm' to be less pretentious. At any rate, every weekend off, the Ferris family trooped to the country and compared to Columbia, the outskirts of Red Bank certainly were country."

"It doesn't sound so bad."

He held his empty snifter out for her again, thinking how different his history was compared to hers: hardscrabble tobacco farm under the bitter thumb of Lewis Raines for him. Easy luxury, the best the city, and country, could offer, for her with the judge. "Law" in the end, what with her marriage to Tim Owens, being the only common denominator, they shared.

"No, I suppose it wasn't," she agreed. "Daddy taught me, as best he could, his passions. The old Southern traditions of fine guns, good horses, better whiskey. And money. Not that he really stressed that part of it. He would have considered that tacky, I'm sure."

"What about the practice of law? Wasn't that a passion for your father?"

"I don't know about a passion as more just a means to an end. And a way of passing the time in a respectable manner. Not to mention the power it brought him"

"Yes," Raines said. "For some in my profession it is all for the power."

"Then you know."

"Very well."

"It's not that I fault my father," she told him, eyes glinting again in the light of the fire. "There are men I fault but he's not one of them. And he *did* share his passions with me. And encouraged me to find my own."

"And did you?"

"Did what?"

"Find your passions?"

"Oh yes!"

The door to the house opened, a broad shaft of light from inside falling out toward the fire and Raines and the woman. "Marjorie," Tim Owens called out, his voice faint, far away sounding, as if it were lost in the shaft of household light preceding it. "Timmy's gone on to bed and I'm on my way. Are you coming?"

Was it weariness? Or a faint hope, instead, that he heard in Owen's voice, Raines wondered, and then brushed aside. It was only the brandy, the firelight, and the story of the woman's early days with her father that was letting him see drama in everything.

"You go along, honey. I'll be in shortly." She turned to Raines, the smile stretching her face in the orange light, nowhere close to being as real as the sudden laughter he'd heard from her not that long ago. "Mr. Raines and I are having such a delightful conversation. I'd really hate to cut it short."

"Goodnight, then." Raines watched as the shadow figure blocking the shaft of light from the open doorway, retreated back a step. "No hurry on my account, dear. You and I have had our share of delightful chats. Just don't wear Mr. Raines out."

For a while afterwards Raines listened to the sounds of the people in the house closing things down for the night. The opening and shutting of doors, the water pump outside clicking on as someone used the toilet or brushed their teeth and washed their face. Then it was quiet again, the house, other than the one light on the porch, dark and still. Other sounds could be heard now beyond the fire: creatures starting to move about in the pines, and palmettos, and fields stretching away from the house.

"Now, where was I?" Marjorie Owens nudged his empty snifter with the decanter. He allowed her to fill the glass again, even though he knew he was well past his limit. "My passions? But it's true, you know. How a few have been revealed to me over the years."

She leaned over suddenly and kissed him, her tongue pressing against his closed lips. The intensity of her wet mouth, the probing tongue, brokered no resistance and though he tried, at first, he relented and allowed her to pull him closer, her lips never leaving his. It had been a long time for Sadie and him, since they had been intimate, Hilton's death seeming to have taken that from them along with everything else. Not to mention the fact that he had aged hard since then, the graying hair above his ears and forehead thinning out by the day it seemed. His eyes, too—that stared back at him in the bathroom mirror in the morning—were softer, less bright, than he remembered. Now both hair and eyes belonged to a much older man, one he didn't know anymore.

And yet, the woman holding him close now as the fire sparked in the ring, lips insistent against his? She didn't appear to see him as an old man past his time. Seemed, instead, to believe he was a man she could do what she was doing with. And what was that? He didn't know, but suddenly wanted very much to find out and opening his mouth he kissed her back.

He didn't know how long they were like this—lips smashed together, her hands fumbling with his belt and then the zipper—when he realized there was another sound, not the low continuous moan of the woman, but of something moving behind them

Pulling away from her to look up he saw the boy standing on the far edge of the fire ring, a shadow really, but even so, one that glared at him across the dying flames before turning around and walking back to the house.

"Jesus Christ," the woman said. "Was that Timmy?"

Raines stood up, buckling his belt, and tucking himself back into his open fly. He could almost taste the disgust flooding over him A taste bringing him back to a place, and a night, he thought he had left long ago. The bridge over the Indian River where the manacled bodies of the Ashley Gang lay dead on the wooden planks while a crowd of deputies stood around them, faces ghostly looking in the flashlights and Sheriff Baker suddenly asking Raines if there was anything he wanted to say.

In that moment, Raines stepped across what was drawn in the sand for him, his mouth tasting just like it did now, even though he had sworn then it would never be repeated, not for as long as he lived.

"I'm sorry," he told the woman as he bent to retrieve the brandy snifter he'd let drop to the ground when she first kissed him "I was out of line."

"You're out of line, now."

She hadn't moved, had done nothing to make anything different, to make it seem as if none of it had happened, her face just as excited and eager and shining palely in the faint light.

"Then I'm twice that way, I suppose."

"I'll come to your room later."

"The door will be locked, and I'll be asleep."

She sat up and began to rearrange her clothing and hair, while Raines, knowing nothing further he could say, turned for the house.

"Yes," he heard behind him as he pushed open the screen door. "I imagine the door *will* be locked. Damn but I hate you men of honor at times."

The whiskey and brandy churned in his stomach all that night. Unable to get away from the images of Marjorie Owens's pale breasts, the Ashley gang dead on the bridge, the face of the boy staring at him across the fire, filling his head he tossed and turned in the bed, the steady cry of a whippoorwill in the pines not far from the open window, adding to his confusion. When morning finally came, for a while Raines didn't know if it was real—or just a continuation of his restless sleep.

\*\*\*

The worst of it came sooner than he expected and though he wished it had been otherwise he was there to see it. Having done most of his packing before dinner, he lay in bed, drifting in and out of sleep, vaguely aware of the sounds of the others in the house as they prepared for the morning's hunt. The mild hangover from the bourbon, and after dinner brandy, coupled with the restless sleep of the night, made it easy for him to stay where he was beneath the covers. But after the hunters left in the Jeep, the barking of the dogs in the cages on the back grown fainter the further they got from the house, Raines jerked fully awake, aware it was time to get on with it, even through the nausea and sickly spinning of his head from sitting up too quickly.

You're a coward, John Raines, he told himself as he staggered to the bathroom. He had never been afraid of any man—had in fact been only gut-wrenching scared one time in his life that he could remember, that being the night when that god-awful hurricane down by Lower Matecumbe lifted his boat, with him, his two brothers, and Hilton aboard, and blew it clean across the little cay. Still, there was no way around it now, he thought, as he retched into the sink. When the dry heaves stopped, he rinsed his face and wet his thinning hair down. "You're a coward John Raines," he thought again.

It was as simple as that. And the boy would know it. Not only know it but add it to his list of grievances. A list made even longer by the events of the night before and that Raines had been a part of. A mistake Raines could have rectified, perhaps, had he gotten out of bed that morning and while there was still time, taken the boy aside to apologize. To somehow explain what he had seen.

Though, as soon as he thought it, Raines knew it wasn't possible. He could apologize, certainly. But explain? How? How to tell a boy trying to become a man, that his mother, when drunk, could act like a whore. That she was a woman that a man, when sober would not have gone along with, but when drunk would treat just like she wanted to be treated. Knowing all of what he had to do and not knowing how he had found it easier, though, to stay in bed and let it all go, like the coward he was.

But the guilt and remorse were useless he decided, and after dressing and putting the finishing touches on his packing, Remington took his bags out to the car. Done with that, he headed back into the house and the kitchen where he found Lucas doing his own preparations for departure. The black man had been up long before dawn, Raines knew, buttoning down the pump house where he slept, packing Tom Ryan's things, making breakfast for those going hunting, and now, cleaning up all non-essential items in the kitchen. Endless and sometimes un-appreciated chores, Raines thought. When Lucas returned to his home behind the "Colored Movie Theater," there was more work. His young wife and two children would see to that.

For now, there was hot coffee left in the percolator. Raines sat at the table in the corner of the kitchen letting the strong brew bring him back into the land of the living, the last vestiges of guilt, self-incrimination, and hangover almost gone when he heard the sound of the Jeep pulling into the front yard.

"Lucas, come quick," Tom Ryan yelled from outside. "Hurry, man!"

As Raines and Lucas came out on the front porch, they almost collided with Ryan stomping up the steps and into the house.

"We need hot water, clean cloths and lots of bandages," Ryan said, taking Lucas by the shoulder and turning him back into the house. "And the antiseptic out of the first aid kit."

Raines didn't know what to think as he stayed behind on the porch while the two men disappeared inside the house. The Jeep was parked at a crazy angle in the yard, engine still running, the dogs in their cages barking. He watched as Tim Owens Sr. clambered down from the hunting seat above the dog boxes to help his wife out of the front seat, the boy following behind his father at a distance—as if he wasn't really a part of it.

"Hold on a minute," Tom Ryan said, brushing past Raines and down the steps into the yard toward Owens struggling with the door of the Jeep. "Let me give you a hand there, Tim. We can fix this, my man," Ryan continued as he came around the hood of the hunting buggy. "Believe me. Lucas is boiling the water and getting bandages ready. Before you know it it'll all be fine again."

By then, though, Owens had his wife out of the Jeep and was helping her toward the house. The light of the morning was as clear and bright as it could sometimes get in late November, Raines thought. The air crisp and cool, everything the day's light shone on standing out clean and apparent and with nowhere to hide. And just as clearly, now, when Owens and his wife were free of the Jeep—as clear and bright as everything else in that morning light John Raines could see the red mass spreading out around Marjorie Owens's shoulder against the white of the cotton shirt she wore.

"It was an accident, John," Tim Owens said as they were almost to the front steps, the woman held up by the two men at her sides. Owens's face was a pasty white in the sunlight, his eyes frantic as he looked up at Raines. "An accident, really."

As if unable to see that the look on Raines's face was not one of accusation, but of confusion, Owens's voice rose. He'll be in hysterics in another minute, Raines thought when Owens said again, "An accident, I tell you. The boy never meant to shoot her." And then Owens was shouting. "He never meant to!"

And there it all was, laid out in the brightness of the clean and clear morning: the boy off to one side, watching in a non-committed way while his father and Tom Ryan helped his mother up the steps. The three of them stumbled by him and into the house where Lucas had the water, bandages, and peroxide waiting on the dining room table. The words, an accident, rang in his ears so that he couldn't help but think of that other night, at the tracks, where his son lay crumpled in his arms while the deputies stood quiet around them. The papers the next day all claimed, accident. Though not a man alive who had been there—not even John Raines—believed that to be true.

Now there was the boy, and beyond him, Raines' own thoughts of cowardice earlier and how he should have explained everything to the boy. And how it wasn't that way anymore. How, in fact, it looked like there wasn't anything to explain after all.

# PART FIVE

"Well John, "Tom Ryan was saying as the waiter brought their drinks, "I suppose you're not beholden to help Walter. If that's the way you feel."

"Damn right that's the way I feel," John replied.

He took the first sip of the Manhattan Ryan had ordered for them. As usual, it was too sweet. They always were at the Governors Club where he was sitting on this late afternoon in the waning days of June. The only time Raines drank Manhattans was with Tom, and mainly because Ryan insisted on them. A gentleman's cocktail, according to Ryan. Perfect for the end of another busy day at the office. Because of that insistence, Raines' habit was to let Ryan pick up the tab. Sweet revenge, he liked to think—always followed by the thought, Revenge for what?

"It's just that our friend Walter," Ryan continued, "is none too happy with the job Joe Whittaker's doing for him concerning the Senator, and his investigation, down there in Dade County. Walter wants him to file a change of venue. After all, he's the Sheriff of this county, where the alleged illegal activity occurred, and feels he should be judged—if there is a trial—by a jury of his peers. But Joe won't do it."

"Walter means a jury where at least one of those honorable jurors owes him a favor. That would be my guess. Besides, he's no friend of mine."

Ryan laughed, and when he did so Raines saw for an instant the younger man he had been when Raines first met him. This had been in Fort Myers, when Tom Ryan came over from Fort Lauderdale after the Armistice to help Raines' older brother, RL, get his dream development off the ground. Raines had been in his mid-twenties then, an up-and-coming lawyer in RL's law firm, recently married, and with his first child on the way. RL needed money, and connections, and he had it on good information that Tom Ryan, courtesy of his bank in Fort Lauderdale, had both. At the time, the three of them were optimistic, had their health, energy, and other than RL, full heads of hair, and none of the tragedies that awaited them in sight just yet.

"You didn't used to be so cynical." But the smile on Ryan's lips faded as soon as the words were out of his mouth. "I'm sorry, John," he added quickly. "Still no word from Marilyn?"

"No, dammit. Just long-distance phone calls at all hours from that pitiful excuse for a husband of hers wanting to know if we've heard from her. He says he's concerned about the boy. If he'd been so concerned about his family, he never would have taken up with that other woman. Now that his wife and son are off God knows where, he's calling me for help. That takes a lot of gall if you ask me. I tell you, Tom, if he was here in town, and not safe up there in New York, I'd ... well, I don't know what I'd do to the bastard. It wouldn't be pretty; I know that much."

"Yes," Ryan said. "I imagine not."

It was quiet between them for a while, other than for the muted conversations of other men at the bar, or at tables like the one Raines and Ryan were sitting at.

"Look, Tom," Raines finally said, breaking the silence. "Joe Whittaker's not a bad lawyer. In fact, he's a good one. But there's no way in hell that judge in Dade County is going to grant a change of venue. Senator Kefauver packs a lot of weight, and Walter is guilty as sin. You and I know that, and so does every judge and lawyer in South Florida."

"No," Ryan said, almost a sigh, as he signaled the waiter for another round—the last the two friends would have, as was their longstanding custom "You're right, and Walter knows that. He just thinks he would feel better if you are handling his case." Ryan paused for a minute before continuing on, "But Walter was there for you, as best he could be, back when you needed him. Now, I'm the one saying that, John. Walter never did, just so you know."

The truth of what Ryan had just said could not be disputed and Raines, for one, wouldn't deny it. Knew well, in fact, how three years before when the troubles with Hilton began, Walter was able to hold the press at bay long enough to keep the sadness of that time under wraps— even at the bitter end. Even if only for a little while.

"If it makes you feel any better, John, Walter doesn't expect you to take him on *pro bono.*"

"Good," Raines said as he took another sip of the Manhattan that was still too sweet. "I'll make sure Martha doubles my billable hours at every opportunity."

Ryan laughed long and hard, Raines laughing along with him, so much so that the others seated at the bar and the tables scattered throughout the club turned to look at them, as Ryan said, "Now there's the John Raines I've known all these years."

***

Two days later, a Thursday morning, at eight o'clock, Raines had just sat down at the kitchen table with a cup of coffee and the morning edition of the Sun Sentinel, when the phone rang in the hallway. He heard his wife pick up, say "Hello," followed soon after by, "John? It's for you."

Putting down both paper and coffee, he got up from the table and went to the hallway to take the phone from Sadie, who as she handed it to him said, "I don't know who it is, John. They just asked for you."

"This is John Raines," he said into the phone as Sadie headed back into the master bedroom where she had been busy straightening up.

"Mr. Raines?" A gruff, but sounding a little out of breath voice asked, and before Raines could answer, said, "It's Sheriff Harker."

"You and I have known one long enough, Walter, that first names will do."

"I suppose you're right," and then a pause, followed quickly by, "John it is then. So listen, I know Mr. Ryan spoke to you the other day about my troubles."

"He did. I told him I would see what I could do."

"I thank you for that. If it's all right with you I'd like to come by your office today and see if we can't get the ball rolling on this. Right now, I'm looking at a world of hurt down there in Dade County and Joe Whittaker just ain't cutting it."

"Well now, I've worked with Joe in the past on some issues regarding the port and he's a competent enough lawyer." There was no reply on the other end, so Raines continued, "But it's like anything, I guess. If you aren't comfortable with him then I'm glad to see if I can help."

Raines wondered for a moment if the good Sheriff believed that last part to be true and if he believed it.

"As for coming by the office today, Walter, that's fine. It'll have to be in the afternoon, though. I'm tied up in court this morning," and at least that part *was* true.

"I'm busy my own self this morning. How about after lunch? Say one thirty or so?"

"That will be fine. See you then, Walter."

"Yessir."

And then the line was dead. No thank you or anything like that. Just the quiet buzz of the dead line as he hung the phone back into its cradle on the little stand in the hallway. Well, that was neither nor there. He wasn't going into this Walter Harker business looking for thanks. Only to relieve himself of an obligation to the man and be done with it. That was all.

The coffee waiting for him on the kitchen table with the paper had gone cold. Fortunately, there was more in the percolator, and after refilling his cup he sat down again to pick up where he had left off when the Sheriff had called. According to the headline story on the front-page, trouble was brewing in Korea. The North Koreans had stormed across the 38th Parallel in a surprise attack. Now there was fierce fighting between them, the South Korean army, and the UN troops stationed on the border in support. Senator McCarthy had taken time from his daily diatribes about the subversives in the government, to call instead for an immediate armed response from the US to meet this new communist threat to world stability.

Another war? Raines wondered. Close to five years of peace was perhaps too much for the world to handle, he supposed. If so, at least he wouldn't have to sacrifice another child to the fray. He immediately felt selfish for thinking such a thing, knowing as he did that if war did indeed blow up in the Asian sphere, and the US joined in, then all across the country there'd be parents sending their sons off to fight, and for many of those sons, to die. Raines couldn't help but feel sorry for those parents already.

On page five of the paper, a smaller item caught his eye, this one concerning courthouse news. Mostly uninformed gossip, but the one that wasn't told of how Sheriff Walter Harker had expressed his displeasure with his current legal representative, Joseph Whittaker, Esq. Not only that, but those in the know, so the story ran, had it on good authority that the Sheriff was actively seeking new counsel.

He's found his new counsel, all right, Raines thought as he put the paper down and finished off his coffee. And so it begins.

But it wasn't worth thinking about any longer. He had to be in court by ten and Judge Frazier frowned on tardiness. The case he was arguing today was a mess enough already to have Judge Frazier mad at him. He put his coffee cup in with the breakfast dishes Sadie would wash later, tossed the newspaper into the trash can under the sink, and then headed off to get dressed for whatever the day might bring.

*** 

Court, surprisingly, ran late that morning. Raines' client, the defendant in a divorce proceeding Raines regretted from the moment he took it on, had become incensed at some allegations the wife's attorney brought up. After the third loud banging of Judge Frazier's gavel and his repeated threats of holding the man in contempt, Raines was finally able to get his client back in his seat. The wife's attorney calmly moved on to other issues—though in Raines' opinion he had already carried the day—and by the time Judge Frazier ordered the noon recess, it was close to one o'clock. Noticing the lateness of the hour and citing some personal matters he had to attend to, the judge adjourned the court until the next morning, ten a.m. sharp, and that was that.

Raines was just finishing the sandwich he had bought at Joe's Diner across from the courthouse—the sandwich a far cry from the martini and fried chicken at the Governors Club he had originally planned on—when Martha knocked lightly on his office door, cracked it open, and leaning in said, "Sir? Sheriff Harker is here. Should I let him in?"

Wiping his face and hands with a napkin Raines waved in agreement, Martha nodded her head, retreated, and was followed immediately after by the sheriff.

"Sit down, Walter, please," Raines said, "and tell me what's on your mind."

"You know what's on my mind, Mr. Raines," the sheriff replied as he pulled up one of the two chairs in the room and sat down across from Raines. 'That damn Kefauver's breathing hard down my neck."

"I thought we agreed on first names, Walter."

"Yessir, we did. I guess I forgot."

It was quiet, then, for a bit, the reprieve from getting right to business allowing Raines a chance to get over his shock at seeing Walter Harker again. He couldn't place exactly the last time he had run into the sheriff, but it had been a while, most likely in the courthouse. When Raines had run into him then, Harker had been his usual burly, barrel-chested self, his head of thick, black hair hidden under the white Stetson Raines had never seen him without. Not thin and frail like the man sitting in Raines' office, now, dressed in a simple, dark gray business suit, the Stetson replaced by a fedora that matched the color of his suit. The white, pearl buttoned shirt, gold sheriff's badge on one chest, Colt.45 in the holster strapped around his waist, the cowboy boots that could be heard a mile away stomping down the halls of the courthouse—none of these were in evidence.

"Yeah, I know," Walter said suddenly, as if reading Raines' mind. "I've been sick. Something to do with my blood. Leukemia the doc says."

"I'm really sorry to hear this, Walter."

"Thanks, John, but you don't have to worry. Walter Harker ain't going to let no leukemia lick him. And no damn senator, either."

"That's the spirit, Walter, and I have no doubt that you're exactly right. Now," and Raines picked up the folder Harker had laid on his desk before he sat down, "let's see what we're up against."

And here was the real surprise—as Raines flipped through the folder, he found not much of anything. Other than a formal notice from the Senator's temporary office in Miami stating, in so much legalese, that the Kevauver Commission on Organized Crime had held a closed hearing in Dade County beginning on May 15th, and concluding on May 17th, of that year. During the course of this three-day hearing, whereby evidence of widespread illegal activities in both Dade and Broward counties having been presented to the Commission, the Commission, because of this evidence, had no choice but to schedule an open hearing to discuss this evidence further, this open hearing to be held, again in Dade County, on July 25th, 1950. This hearing would concern illegal gambling, i.e., the placement of slot machines in various establishments throughout both Dade and Broward counties, as well as other games of chance, along with offsite betting on both horse and dog racing, either abetted by, or under, the direct knowledge of elected officials in both Dade and Broward counties. The two-page long document was dated May 31st, 1950.

"This is it, Walter?"

"Yessir."

"Then I'm a little confused. Have they subpoenaed you for this proposed hearing?"

"They're going to. And soon."

"But not yet?"

"No sir, not yet. But they will. Sure as I'm sitting here."

"Then it was out of Joe Whittaker's hands—filing a change of venue request. Without an indictment, or trial date, he couldn't do it."

"I knew that John. But when I mentioned it would be the thing to do when a trial date was set, he said no. Said it would be a waste of his, and the court's, time to file such a request, if, or even when, such a date was set. Sounded to me like he didn't really have my best interests in mind. If you catch my drift."

"I suppose one could see it like that."

Raines picked up the documents and sifted through them again. This was more of a pretense than anything else—thinking that what he had told Tom Ryan at the Governors Club the other day was true. About why the sheriff wanted the trial moved to Broward County. Harker was worried. Judging by the look on his face across the desk from him. Very worried. And probably with good cause. Especially now, sick as he was. The thought of spending whatever time he had left on this earth in the penitentiary had to be a troubling one.

"Well, Walter," Raines said, "it looks like all I can do right now—seeing as there are no charges yet against you—is to post a legal notice stating that I'm now your legal representative. And to promise you, as we sit here, that I will do my best to provide you effective legal counsel, if and when that time comes."

"That time's coming," Harker said as he stood up and put his fedora back on. "Coming soon is my bet. But I feel a lot better now, knowing you're in my corner."

"Good. See Martha on your way out if you would. She'll draw up an agreement for you to sign and take a retainer. Now, and this is important," and Raines stood up then and reached his hand across the desk to shake Harker's. "As soon you as you hear anything let me be the first to know. And not one of those reporters hanging around the courthouse. You hear me?"

"Loud and clear."

"One more thing—let Joe Whittaker know what has transpired here. I don't want him reading about it in the paper. And pay him whatever you owe him"

"I'll tell him, all right. And I don't owe him a damn thing."

With a defiant tip of his hat, and a slight grin that was very reminiscent of the sheriff in his younger days, Harker left Raines' office. Through the closed-door Raines could hear the muted conversation between Harker and Martha at her desk. Not long after Raines heard the outer door of his office open, and then shut. And then he was alone, again, all quiet, except for the sound of traffic on Andrews Avenue below.

Picking up the folder Harker had brought him Raines took a last look at the papers inside. Satisfied they had revealed everything they could to him, he put them in the top drawer of his desk. He wondered suddenly if Tom Ryan felt like joining him for an early drink down at the Governors Club. Wondered as well—as he picked up the phone and dialed Ryan's number—what he was about to get himself into. And if it would be worth the trouble it most certainly would bring.

***

"I just don't see why it bothers you so much," Sadie Raines asked that night over dinner. "Neither you nor Walter even knows if anything related to him came out of the hearings in May."

"That's very true. But Walter sure seems convinced it has. And personally, knowing Walter's track record, my darling wife, I would be shocked if nothing did come of that hearing."

It was just the two of them in the house, now, and had been that way for longer than Raines liked to think of. Just being the two of them, they had taken to having their dinner in the Florida room on the rear of the house, instead of the dining room, where the spaciousness and the settings for four still on the table reminded him—and he was willing to bet Sadie, as well—of when the family had all been together.

But sitting out on the Florida room, where the screen and jalousie windows kept the mosquitoes and no-see ums at bay as they ate, seemed to comfort Raines after the long days at the office. With the evening breezes from the ocean circulated throughout the room by the large paddle fan hanging overhead, Raines felt as if the workaday worries of his life in Fort Lauderdale were far, far away. His mind focused on the sport fishing boats coming into dock behind his neighbor's homes, either on his side of the deep-water canal, or across from him, after a day of fishing off the Gulf Stream. The screaming pelicans and seagulls following these boats, hoping for scraps of offal tossed overboard after the day's catch was cleaned. The sound of the whistle buoy in the Intracoastal plainly heard when the easterly winds blew through it, sending out a warning to the boats and ships plying the New River north and south. The lights coming on inside the houses across the canal from him as the summer day came to an end and evening, and soon, night, settled in. All of this was usually more than enough to let Raines let go of yet another day at his work—but not tonight.

"You know how I feel about that man," Raines said after a bit.

"Maybe if you allowed yourself to forget about what Walter's done in the past and remembered instead how he helped us that time ..." Sadie's voice wavered a moment, before adding, "well, anyways, it might serve you better in this present situation."

"Funny, but that's pretty much what Tom told me."

"Tom knows you pretty well, John. He's always had your best interests at heart."

"He does. On both counts. But I don't think he knows me better than you do."

"I wonder."

Raines supposed she had room to wonder. Besides, how well did anyone know another human being? He had no idea, really. Sadie and he had been together thirty years, and if there were any surprises left between them, he couldn't imagine what they might be.

Not that it mattered. Not to him at any rate. He still loved her as much as he had from the start. Other than that brief moment of madness with the lawyer's wife that night by the fire pit at Tom Ryan's ranch, he had never desired another woman since being with Sadie. Even then he hadn't really desired the lawyer's wife. She was there, was willing, it was a bad time in his life, and Raines had been truly grateful for her son's interruption that put an end to the spell he had fallen under.

No, Sadie was the one, all right. Raines had known that from the first moment he opened his eyes on the hospital ward that long ago day after the war and saw her standing by his bed. A vision of unexpected loveliness that afterwards, and more than once, he told himself made coming down with the flu worth it. And then some. If the years since then had changed her—and he was certain they had, but hell, they had changed him, too—he couldn't see it. Sitting across from him at the little table on the Florida room as the summer day turned dark with night, even if her once thick, lustrous black hair had thinned, and was streaked here and there with gray, he still saw the beautiful woman he had that day on the ward. The woman he had moved heaven and earth afterwards to make his own. And in the doing so had not regretted a day since.

He didn't tell her this, now, though but said instead, "Damn it all, Sadie, you would think that fool had learned his lesson. For Christ's sake the governor suspended him in '43 for doing the same thing he's accused of doing now. He was lucky to get re-elected afterwards, which isn't saying much for the voters of this county. Still, one would think that would have been enough to steer him on the straight and narrow."

"Some people just don't learn from their past mistakes, John," and Sadie laughed a little, a dry chuckle, that faded quickly when she added, "Like our own daughter, for one."

"Don't remind me. Please."

It was certainly true, as far as his daughter, Marilyn, went. Not learning from her mistake in marrying Tom Morgan. Now she was playing the fool over him and refusing him a divorce. Disappearing with their son. Suffering under the delusion that time away from one another would change Morgan's mind and he'd come back to her. Between the two of them, his daughter and Tom Morgan, Raines didn't know who the bigger fool was. The fact that he loved Marilyn very much and had detested Tom Morgan from the moment he met him, leaned heavily in his daughter's favor, though.

"Let's not talk about either of them anymore tonight, Hon," Raines said as he got up from the table. "It was a fine dinner, and I don't want to spoil it."

"Let me put these dishes away." Sadie rose, too, picking up her plate and Raines'. "I'll straighten up in the kitchen and then meet you on the dock for a brandy?"

"Make it two brandies and I'm on your boy. And who knows? Maybe tomorrow, when I go into the office, I'll find out all of it has just been a bad dream. Perhaps brought on by something I ate."

"Not at my table, I hope."

He carried Sadie's laughter with him all the way out to the dock, thinking that it had been the best thing he'd heard all that long day.

\*\*\*

The sheriff's subpoena to appear before the Kefauver Committee on Organized Crime came on the first Monday in July. A man approached Harker just as he was about to enter his office across the street from the courthouse and asked politely if he were Walter Francis Harker. When the sheriff—knowing full well what was about to happen, as he told Raines later—answered just as politely, "Why yessir, I am, what can I do for you?" the man thrust the summons into Harker's hand, said, "You've been served," and was on his way.

At ten o'clock on the Wednesday morning immediately following, John Raines left his office and went into Tom Ryan's office.

"Why, good morning, John," Ryan said from behind his mahogany desk. "Elise told me you had called, that you were on your way. How can I help you this fine morning?"

Mere politeness, as befitted old friends, since the slight grin on Ryan's weathered face indicated clearly that he was more than aware of what he could do for Raines. Raines expected as much, said nothing as he sat down in one of the two plush chairs fronting the desk.

"Good lord, Tom, but it's going to be a hot one today. Damp, too. I would've taken the car, but Sadie tells me I need more exercise. So I walked. And can't say that I feel the better for it."

"The perils of success, eh John? Soft living?"

"Something like that, I suppose."

The perils of that success surrounded Ryan in his office, as Raines never failed to notice when he came to visit. The big mahogany desk, the wet bar trimmed in gilt against the wall behind him, the ornately carved wooden gun rack on one wall with two of the three Italian shotguns Ryan owned hanging there. Photographs on the walls of Ryan with personages such as Henry Flagler, President Warren G. Harding, surprisingly even FDR, along with others important to the growth of the town and that Ryan had helped one way or another in the past. To add a more personal touch, there was a photograph of Ryan on his ranch with a brace of quail shot with one of those Italian shotguns. Quietly, and sad as well, a photograph on the wall directly behind Ryan's desk, of Ryan and his wife, taken on the steps of the front porch of Flagler's hotel in West Palm, back when the two of them were considerably younger, and both of them still alive.

"But listen here, Tom, I need you to tell me what you know about Walter's connections with this gambling business Kefauver's looking into. I have an idea, based on what he did in the past, but I'm not sure if I know the full scope of where he stands today."

"Why don't you ask Walter?"

"I did. He wasn't as forthcoming as I'd have liked."

"I'm not surprised," Ryan said with a dry chuckle. "Not in the least. The good Sheriff likes to hold his cards tight to his chest. Especially after his last go-round with the governor. Not that you, and I, and a big part of the local community, don't have a pretty good idea of what he's up to these days." Ryan chuckled again as he reached into the top drawer in his desk, pulled out two cigars, and handed one to Raines. "I have to admit even I was surprised back then. When the governor only suspended him from office, instead of calling for a trial."

Ryan clipped, lit his cigar, and when he was done passed clipper and matches across the desk to Raines, the room filling soon with the rich aroma of Cuban tobacco.

"He would have been tried?" Raines asked after a long pull on the good cigar. "Possibly convicted?"

"I think so, and yes, I believe he would've been convicted. His public acts of contrition back then saved him. If you can imagine Walter Harker ever being contrite about anything."

"I cannot."

"Apparently the voters did two years later."

"He didn't get my vote."

"Nor mine."

Ryan leaned back in his plush office chair, a look of contentment on his face. From the fine Havana cigar, Raines wondered. Or the conversation he was having with his longtime friend? Both, Raines guessed. Ryan, as Raines well knew, thrived on these confidential chats with his pals about the goings on in the city, and what could be done about them, if possible. Especially now, in this stage of his life, when most of what was going on in community affairs usually didn't concern him, but instead, simply provided entertainment. And perhaps, Raines thought, a sense of still being vital to the world around him which struck Raines as sad. If that were true, he didn't see how Ryan could feel that way. The man had done more than anyone else to make the city what it was today.

"Sadly enough," Ryan said, cutting Raines' thoughts short. "Walter didn't learn from that little peccadillo of his. No, he did not. And now, if anything, he is even more involved than he was back then."

They sat in silence for a bit after this, Raines thinking how much he disliked the fact that once again he was entangled with Sheriff Walter Harker, a man he didn't like or trust. Raines could still hear the gunshots ringing out over the water, the smell of gunpowder drifting off with the sound of those gunshots, that night on the lonely bridge over the Sebastian River. He didn't figure to ever forget that night, a quarter of a century ago, when the man sitting across from him, now in that comfortable office high above the streets of the town, had suggested a way in which Raines could get his struggling law career off the ground.

Had he known what awaited him when he left Fort Lauderdale in Harker's rickety Model T, he would not have gone.

But he had not known. Had been there on the bridge and had resented the deputy ever since. A resentment that only grew in stature some ten years later when the deputy—now the Sheriff—allowed an angry mob to lynch an innocent colored boy on the edge of Pompano. Harker claimed he had been unable to get there in time to stop it. This may have been true; Raines did not know. Yet despite his failure in carrying out his duties to protect and serve all the citizens of Broward County, the sheriff had no qualms posing for a photograph with two of his deputies by the lynched man. And when this photograph appeared on the cover of Life magazine the following month, Harker took delight in handing out copies of the magazine to all of his friends at the courthouse.

"Now listen here, John," Ryan said, breaking the silence. "If during the upcoming hearing the Senator brings up the Progresso Novelty &

Game Company, or Jake Meyers, stop Walter before he opens his mouth."

"I've heard of the Progresso outfit, but who is Jake Meyers?"

"A businessman from Chicago."

The look on Ryan's face told Raines all he needed to know about Jake Meyers and the kind of business he attended to in Chicago.

"Jesus," Raines sighed.

"Well," Ryan said again with that chuckle. "Jesus might save the sheriff's mortal soul. But our boy Walter's going to need you, my friend, to save him from the Senator."

***

The morning of July 25th, a Monday, was hot and muggy, courtesy of a tropical depression that had blown up in the Gulf several days before and crossed across the state to the north, leaving behind gray, heavy clouds that filled the air with moisture. The hot winds coming from the west, along with the thick clouds overhead, offered little cooling relief on the ride to Miami from Fort Lauderdale, even with all the windows of Raines' Buick rolled down. "Wrung out and hung up to dry before this shebang even gets under way," was how the Sheriff described it as Raines pulled up in front of the Dade County courthouse and let his client out.

"Just go inside to the men's room, Walter," Raines told him through the open front passenger window. "Splash some cold water on your face and try to cool off a little while I go park the car. Then wait for me in front of the hearing room"

"I'd rather go into that watering hole down the street and have a cold beer. Even better would be a shot of whiskey." Harker wiped his forehead with a handkerchief already soaked from use on the ride. "Make me feel better than some ol' tepid tap water splashed on my face."

"Let's see how the day goes. Hopefully, we'll have a shot or two to celebrate with when it's over."

"One way or the other, Counselor, we're going to have those shots."

"I'll see you inside," Raines said as he pulled away from the curb.

Being a Monday morning, the courthouse was busy, and it took longer than Raines expected to find an empty spot. By the time he made it to the hearing room on the second floor, the Sheriff was pacing back and forth in front of the closed doors, looking no more composed than he had when he got out of the Buick. Making matters worse was a gaggle of reporters surrounding him, shouting out questions which Harker was doing his best to ignore.

"That'll be enough, boys," Raines said as he pushed through the crowd of newsmen and took his client by the arm "Neither the Sheriff, nor I, know any more than you do right now as to what's going to take place inside today. My client is an innocent man and that's the most important thing."

"What if he isn't," a reporter called from the back of the crowd.

"He is," Raines said. "If he wasn't, I wouldn't be here."

Leaving it at that, he ushered Harker inside, the reporters trailing after them

The hearing was to take place in Courtroom B. Raines rarely had business at the Dade County courthouse and had never been in this particular courtroom. He was pleasantly surprised to find it had a row of windows that opened to the outside. All of these windows were open, while three large paddle fans hanging from the ceiling, circulated the air throughout. It was still warm in the courtroom but not downright suffocating hot like it was outside.

Though Harker had complained about the heat during the car ride, and again out on the curb in front of the courthouse when they arrived, at least he looked better than he had that first day in Raines' office. He didn't seem as pale — as thin. And maybe it was because he had come to the proceedings that morning in his official Broward County Sheriff's uniform, the white Stetson, Colt. 45 strapped to his waist, and polished snakeskin boots that were his trademark. This was the way Raines was accustomed to seeing the sheriff. Not in the bland business suit he had been wearing that afternoon in Raines office, and that had made Harker look like just another of the worried men who had come to him for help over the years.

While the Senator's aides set out folders and loose paperwork on the prosecutor's table, Raines and his client sat silent. Raines had a legal pad and a pencil in front of him and that was it. This was a hearing, not a trial. A judge would be present to rule on evidence and to, along with the bailiffs, keep order. But there would be no witnesses called—other than the sheriff—and no jury. Raines had no motions to offer, or any evidence of his own. For now, at any rate. He imagined that was going to change.

A door opened on the side of the courtroom and two bailiffs came in carrying a large, cloth covered, presentation board. This they set up on an easel to the left of the judge's bench. Between the papers on his desk, and this mysterious presentation board, it was apparent Senator Kefauver had been doing his homework.

This activity on the Senator's side must have caught the sheriff's attention as well, for he leaned over suddenly to whisper in Raines' ear, "Are you nervous, Counselor?"

"Not particularly." And this was true. Raines was curious. But not nervous. "Are you?"

"Hell yes, I am! It's my ass on the line here."

Before Raines could say anything to reassure his client, a door on the other side of the room opened, the judge walked in, a bailiff called out, "All rise," introduced the judge, and the hearing began.

"Well now," the judge said when he was seated behind the bench. "As our bailiff informed you, my name is Judge Wilbur Hatch." Judge Hatch appeared to be a few years older than Raines—early sixties, Raines guessed—medium in build, bald, and with a thick pair of black glasses perched on his nose. "As to how honorable I am I suppose depends on the opinion of those who have come before me."

A ripple of polite laughter ran through the courtroom and when it died out the judge continued. "Today is not a trial, as I am sure most of you understand. But a hearing, wherein information will be sought, hopefully confirmed, and in the case of error, denied. I see the good sheriff of Broward County is with us today. I also see he has come well-heeled into my courtroom," and the judge pointed at the Colt.45 strapped to Harker's waist.

"Your Honor," Harker replied, though he didn't stand, as might have been required, Raines thought, under different circumstances,

"Being a sheriff my job is a dangerous one." Harker looked around the room before adding, "In, and out of, the courtroom"

And there was more of that polite laughter, the newsmen in the back of the room, Raines noticed, scribbling away on their note pads.

"Yes, I'm sure," Judge Hatch gestured at Raines sitting next to Harker. "I know you, Sheriff Harker, from some cases I tried up in Broward, but have not had the pleasure of meeting your attorney."

"Your Honor, this here is John Raines, the best attorney in these parts if you ask me."

"Good to see you are being ably represented then. But enough of this pleasant banter. It's time to turn these proceedings over to the senator from Tennessee and get on with the business before us today."

A tall man, wearing a light-colored suit similar to the one Raines was wearing, stood up from the senator's table, approached the bench, nodded to the judge, and then turned to face the room

"Good morning," he said, nodding to those in attendance. "For those of you who don't know me, I'd like to introduce myself. As Judge Hatch mentioned, I am a senator, Estes Kefauver by name, and I the have honor of representing the great state of Tennessee. Now before you all get too riled up, let me add that I consider the state of Florida to be a great one as well."

The senator paused, expecting some of that polite laughter, but it didn't come. This was Raines first look at the senator. He was tall, probably a little over six feet, and thin—lanky would be the correct way to describe him, Raines thought. Receding black hair was combed back from his forehead where sharp, black as well eyes stared out at the people in the room. These eyes seemed quick and focused. Despite the senator's easy going southern manner, Raines quickly decided he was not a man who missed much. It would be wise, Raines also decided, to pay attention to this man and what he was about to offer up that morning in Judge Hatch's courtroom

"But as great a state as Florida is," the Senator said, his long arms hanging loosely at his sides, "it has a problem A very big problem, in fact, and one that threatens the safety and wellbeing of every citizen who resides here. This problem, my friends, is organized crime, robbing the residents of this great state of their security, while robbing as well, their wallets. I feel comfortable in saying that the activities of organized crime in this state is similar to a terrible disease. A disease whose symptoms are prostitution, narcotics, and gambling. A disease that left unchecked, endangers every man, woman, and child who calls Florida their home. Even worse, though, is the fact that there are those in this state who are acutely aware of this festering disease and they do not care. Not only that, but they also abet it, and profit by it. Who are these mysterious 'They' I'm referring to, you might ask? Well, I'll tell you. They are your elected officials, beginning at the lowest rungs in this state and all the way to the very top."

The Senator paused here, walked the few steps to his table where he took a glass of water one of his aides handed him, drank deeply, set the glass down on the table and returned to where he had been standing — all of it in that easy, but dramatic way he had of carrying himself.

Raines was curious about the senator's reference to, 'the very top.' The governor? He had heard the rumors about Harker — hell, they weren't rumors but fact. Hence his suspension from office back in 1943, and by the same governor the senator seemed to be referring to now. If the governor was indeed corrupt, and if Harker knew about this corruption, then, if needed, a way might open for Harker to extricate himself from this mess. A big 'if." But one Raines might pursue down the road if the situation warranted such a thing.

"It's true," the senator continued, "that there are those who claim that prostitution and gambling, and to some extent, narcotics, I suppose, are just harmless vices. Ones that hurt no one but those who indulge in them. But I am not one of those. No sir, I am not! They are crimes. And by the very nature of being so, harmful indeed. To those who partake of them, as well as to the innocent who do not.

"This, my friends, is why myself," and here he pointed to the table where his aides sat poring over the folders in front of them, "and my men are here today. Not only to discuss these illegal activities, but to bring them out of the darkness where they hide, and into the light of day, where all the honest people of this great state can take a hard look at them, and in the doing so make their own informed opinions of whether or not these activities are indeed harmless. No, my friends, it is our intention to get to the bottom of them and when we are done with our investigations, hold those responsible for the flourishing of these illegal activities, accountable."

The senator paused again, looked around the room, and then walked over to his table where he picked up one of the folders before returning to his position in front of the bench. Raines wondered if the senator had been expecting a round of applause after his opening speech. If so, he had to be disappointed. For none came. The only sound in the courtroom was some muffled coughing and the rustling of papers on the senator's table. In the sudden quiet Raines became aware of the sheriff next to him fidgeting in his seat. When he turned to look at his client, he saw beads of sweat on Harker's florid face.

"Well then," the senator said, opening one of the folders on his table. "Let's get started, shall we? I'd like to begin by asking Walter Harker, Sheriff of Broward County, a few questions. Bailiff, will you swear the sheriff in, please?"

*** 

The senator's questions turned out to be more than a few, beginning after the sheriff swore to "Tell the truth, and nothing but the truth, so help me, God."

"Would you please state your name," the senator asked. "For the record, please?"

"And here I thought we all knew one another," the sheriff replied in his best down-home voice, which generated a few chuckles in the court room "But just for the record, as you say, my name is Walter Francis Harker—the Francis being my Mama's first name and of course, Walter being my daddy's. He wanted to make me a Walter, Jr., but Mama said she didn't want no son of hers to be a junior. Damned if I know why, but that was just how mama was. Daddy, being a wise man, knew better than to argue with her, too, I'm here to tell you."

The courtroom thought this was funny, as well, to the sheriff's delight, who went to add more to his little homily, but the senator cut him off.

"Your date, and place, of birth, please?"

"Certainly, Senator. January 21ˢᵗ, 1905, on the banks of Lake Worth, Florida, in what was then Dade County, but has since become Broward County."

"Thank you, Sheriff," the senator said. "Now, if you would, how long have you been sheriff of Broward County?"

"Well sir, off and on, more 'on' I might add, since 1935. The fine folks of Broward must think I'm doing a good job for them"

"Yes, I'm sure." The senator turned the page in the folder he was holding in his left hand before looking up at the sheriff. "Let's talk about that 'off' time if you would. You were suspended from office in 1943 by the governor, I see. Is that correct?"

"Yes sir."

"And why was that, Sheriff?"

"The Governor and I had a little misunderstanding."

"A misunderstanding?"

"Yes sir."

"One that involved your connection to off-site gambling at the Pompano harness track? Gambling that was—and still is—illegal at the time?"

The courtroom went silent, it being suddenly obvious to everyone in attendance that the polite banter between the sheriff and the senator had come to an end.

"Now listen here, Senator," Harker said, "And I mean no disrespect, but all of that was just malarkey." Raines noticed a bit of red of creeping up his client's neck, just above his shirt collar. "Malarkey, I might add, put out by Fred Moore in that newspaper of his." Harker turned to glare at the "Sentinel" reporter in the back row of the courtroom "None of it was true. Not a bit of it. Just political nonsense put out by Moore in an election year. Instead of standing up to the pressure, and the truth, like a man, the Governor suspended me. To save his sorry ass, if you ask me, excuse my French. Not only that, and as I'm sure it's noted in those papers of yours, my constituents in Broward County didn't believe it, either. Seeing as how they re-elected me two years later.

"Yes indeed, Sheriff Harker," Kefauver said, putting that folder down and taking up another one from his table. "The details of your suspension in 1943 are duly noted, as you mentioned. But let's turn to a new topic, shall we?"

"It's your dog and pony show, Senator."

Raines wished his client hadn't said this, but it was too late. The judge at his bench didn't seem to like it, either this touch of contempt from the witness. He was just lifting up his gavel to warn the sheriff when the senator interrupted him

"What do you know about prostitution in your county?"

"You mean whores?" Harker tried to look dumb but no one in the courtroom, least of all the senator, seemed to be buying it. "I suppose there might be some of them over to colored town. But there sure as hell ain't any no white man would go to. Not any respectable white man."

"Do you happen to know one Florence Willis? A white woman, I might add."

"Heard of her." Raines had heard of her, too—through Tom Ryan, of course, who knew everything. "I believe she owns a restaurant and lounge out towards the end of Griffin Road. That who you're talking about?"

"I have witnesses, if needed, who have testified in sworn deposition, that they have eaten with you at Miss Willis' Red Bamboo Lounge on numerous occasions. These same witnesses have also testified that Miss Willis' restaurant is more than just that—have testified it is a brothel, in fact. A brothel whose customers are indeed respectable white men of your community."

"I don't know nothing about any of that," Harker said, fidgeting a little in his chair. "I might have eaten out there, but I never met this Miss Willis. And if what you say about her is true, then I don't ever want to meet her."

"Hmm …" the Senator let his voice trail off a moment. "I want to remind you Sheriff that you're under oath. But no matter. We can let this issue go for now. Though I will tell you that witness depositions disagree with what you have said here concerning Miss Willis and her establishment."

Harker went to get up out of his chair but Raines' hand on his shoulder stopped him

"What about bolita?" The senator asked. He was facing the judge when he asked this, but then turned to the sheriff again. "What do you know about this in your county?"

"Some kind of game, I've been told," Harker said, pulling out his handkerchief to wipe his face. "Like whores, it's something the niggers do."

"A game that people bet on—is that correct?"

"I guess they do. Niggers, like I said. Why I don't pay much attention to it." He turned to the spectators and reporters behind him, that shy little smile on his face. "'Cept in election year of course. When every little bit helps."

The laughter Harker had expected came. But it didn't last long, the senator putting an end to it quickly with his next question.

"While we're discussing games, as you put it, what can you tell me about the Progresso Novelty & Games Company? To be more specific, what is your involvement with this company?"

A flustered look suddenly on his face, Harker went to get to his feet again—and again, Raines' hand on his shoulder stopped him After whispering something in Harker's ear, it was Raines who stood up to face the senator.

"Your Honor, and Senator Kefauver, I will respond for my client to this question. My client will respectively avail himself of the protections afforded to him by the Fifth Amendment to the Constitution of the United States."

"He means to plead the Fifth?"

Both the judge, and the senator, asked this question at the same time.

"Yes, Your Honor."

An uproar of shouts and questions from the reporters in the back rows of the courtroom erupted, the judge's banging of his gavel on the bench, while threatening to clear the room if it continued, finally putting an end to it.

"All right, Senator," the judge said when order had been restored. "You may ask your next question."

"Thank you, Your Honor." Turning the page in his folder, Kefauver looked at Harker. "Do you know an individual by the name of Jacob Meyers, Sheriff Harker?"

Raines, who had sat down, was on his feet again. "Your Honor—" but was stopped by the judge.

"The sheriff is pleading the Fifth, I take it, Counselor?"

"Yes, Your Honor."

"Duly noted, then." Raines went to sit down but again the judge stopped him "I have a feeling the Senator has more questions to ask of your client, Counselor. You might want to remain standing."

Raines did so—and remained that way for the next hour until lunch recess was called. When the afternoon session was brought to order and Kefauver began again, Raines was back on his feet.

***

It was quiet between the two in Raines' Buick after the hearing was over. Harker had wanted to go straight away to the bar across from the courthouse. But Raines said no, claiming he wanted to be closer to home before they started drinking. Instead, he bought them coffee at a diner a block down from the courthouse, the two of them nursing the hot brew in silence as Raines drove them north up US1 to Fort Lauderdale.

What Raines hadn't told the sheriff was that he needed some time— and a clear head—to put the events of the day in order before alcohol and his client could muddy the waters.

The hot coffee, the quiet in his car as he drove, the evening coming on with the day ending, helped. When he pulled into the parking lot of Brownie's Bar & Grill, once back in Lauderdale, and they had found a booth in the back where they wouldn't be overheard, ordered double bourbons on the rocks, Raines felt that he was ready.

"Well, Walter," Raines said after finishing his drink and signaling to the bartender for two more. "It was certainly an interesting day."

"You can say that again." They were the first words the sheriff had said since protesting Raines' decision to forego drinks and opt for coffee instead. "But tell me the truth, John. You think that Kefauver sonofabitch really has anything on me?"

Raines had to stop himself from laughing, the answer to this question being so obvious.

"That Meyers stuff the senator referred to sounds pretty damning. But until we get him on the stand in a trial it's still his word against yours."

"I never did like that Hebe," Harker said. Between the coffee, the quiet ride, and now the bourbon, Harker's features seemed back to their normal state—that confident look of amusement he strutted around the courthouse at home. "Never trusted him, either. But my brother swore by him. Told me the boys up north said he was the best bookkeeper in the business. It was Don's show, so I just kept quiet and went along with it.

"So it's true, then? What the senator said about you and your brother being partners in Progresso Novelty and running slot machines all over the county?"

"Not on any paper, it isn't." A look of defiant denial swept over Harker's face. "Least ways not on any paper I know of. And if there is such a paper I damn sure didn't put my name to it!"

Raines hoped this was true, as he broke his normal practice and signaled to the bartender for a third round of drinks. It had been that sort of day, after all.

"That's good then. Will be very important, actually, if it comes down to a trial."

"You think it will?"

"It could. If Kefauver turns over whatever evidence he has to the State Attorney, and the State Attorney convenes a grand jury to go over it, well yes, there could be a trial. We'll just have to wait and see."

"All right then," Harker said. "Here, let me get these drinks, counselor. You done a fine job by me today and it's the least I can do."

Mulling over the day that night at home before going to bed, Raines didn't see how there wouldn't be a trial. Not with all that evidence Kefauver and his aides had gathered up and presented in the hearing on the charts, and graphs pinned up on the easel they had brought into the room before the hearing began. Evidence, that with pointer and his easy-going way, Kefauver had referred to time and time again as he asked the questions that Raines—on the behalf of his client—had refused to answer under the protections afforded to his client by the Constitution of the United States.

No trial? Maybe. Hell might freeze over, too. Though it wasn't likely.

***

The hearings went on for two more days. The second day centered on Harker's brother, Don, chief deputy to the sheriff, and his involvement in illegal activities in Broward. The third day focused on the sheriff of Dade County and his ties to organized crime in that county. At the end of the three days of hearings, Senator Kefauver folded up shop, though not before taking the time to address the reporters gathered on the steps of the Dade County courthouse.

After quieting the questions reporters shouted at him, and with flash bulbs winking on and off, Kefauver said that he was very satisfied with what the hearings had accomplished in such a short length of time. His next stop was Washington, D.C. where he was to address the full senate on what he had found. Before leaving, though, he was going to turn over his findings to the State Attorney's offices, both in Dade and Broward counties. Where the State Attorneys went from there was up to them. He had done his job and it was time to move on.

And that was that—for the time being, Raines felt.

Two events of importance occurred after the hearings were over, both of them serving to break up the monotony of the daily business of Raines' law practice—civil suits, divorce proceedings, and the like—while he waited to see what the State Attorney's office was going to do with the evidence Kefauver had provided them

The first, in mid-August, was a slow-moving hurricane that made its way across the ocean from Cuba, and the Bahamas before coming to a complete stop over South Florida. The winds were never much over 75mph, but the steady rain seemed to never end. By the time the storm moved on up the state to finally die in South Georgia, it had dumped over twenty inches of rain on ground already saturated to the breaking point by the normal summertime thunderstorm activity the state was accustomed to. The dairy and produce farms west of Fort Lauderdale, and Miami, were severely flooded, halting their daily operations, while the growers could only watch helplessly as their crops were destroyed, the rains washing away a year's livelihood.

The canal behind Raines' house flooded over the seawall and came almost up to the house before stopping. Raines and his neighbor had packed sandbags around the doors of their houses just in case, but they weren't needed. Pine trees had blown over throughout the neighborhoods, knocking down power lines with them, and the lack of electricity for over a week added to the soggy misery of the residents and the businesses downtown. But the flooding was the worst of it, causing upset and aggravation for everyone in the city — other than the children. They took great delight in having to miss school, playing instead with inner tubes and rowboats in the flooded streets.

The local papers took much delight in the aftermath of the storm, as well. For several days, the headlines magnified the damage done. The papers published photographs of local businessmen in their flooded offices, pants rolled up to their knees as they did their best to carry on with business as usual.

The second incident, a phone call from Raines' daughter, happened on the third day of September, just as Raines and Sadie were sitting down to dinner.

"Hello, Dad," Marilyn said when he picked up the phone ringing in the hallway. "I'm not catching you and Mom at a bad time, am I?"

"Never a bad time to hear from you, sweetheart," his stomach suddenly tightening at the sound of her voice. "How are you?"

"Oh, Dad, I'm wonderful. Just wonderful! Did I tell you how wonderful everything is?"

Her words came rushing over the line, the hint of shrillness in her tone alerting him to the fact that she must be in her "excited" frame of mind, one of the two moods she had alternated between since becoming a teenager. The other mood was a deep, all-encompassing sadness, wrapping its way over his daughter as suddenly as the other state of overflowing happiness and excitement did — and never a clue to when either of the two were about to make their presence known. Worried at the change, in what up until then had been a very even-keeled child, Raines and Sadie took her to see the family doctor.

After a complete checkup, while the two parents waited nervously in the reception room, the doctor explained to them that he had no idea what was going on with their daughter—other than, "It's most likely just a phase she's going through. She's a teenager, after all. A female one at that." His amused smile did nothing to alleviate Raines' and Sadie's concerns. "I'm sure she'll grow out of it. Certain of it, actually."

Not much help, Raines had thought then, as he took his daughter home that afternoon. But now, before he could ask Marilyn why she was so "wonderful," she told him, "We're back together, Dad. Tom and I. Isn't that the absolute greatest? We're a family again!"

A grown woman, Raines told himself. Twenty-five years old in a couple of weeks. And yet she sounds like the shrill, excited, teenage girl they had taken to the doctor's office ten years before.

"That is very good news, darling," Raines said—not that he could see how it could be. "When did this happen?"

"Two months ago. He finally answered one of the letters I sent him. His reply came special delivery. Doesn't that just tell you how much he wanted me back? Special delivery, Dad!"

When Raines didn't say anything, Marilyn rushed on with her story. "Tommy and I had been staying with a nice lady we met in Albuquerque. She was a customer at the grocery store where I worked, and oh so nice. Took to me and Tommy right away, invited us to come stay at her house and everything. Oh, Dad, there's so much I have to tell you."

"So, I take it you're both in New York, now?" Raines cut her off, knowing if he didn't, she'd go on and on about this woman in Albuquerque.

"Yes, just the three of us, Dad. Isn't it wonderful?"

"If you're happy, sweetheart, then yes, it is." The words tasted awful to him, but he continued anyway. "How's young Tom doing?"

"Really great, Dad, he's so happy to be back with his father and the three of us a family again. He starts first grade, right there at the PS down the street from us, on Monday."

"Good for him"

"You didn't think my plan would work, did you Dad?" Before he could say yes, she said, "You don't have to answer that because I know you didn't. Know how you feel about him but you're wrong, Dad. I knew that if I gave him time away from us like I did he would come to his senses. I just knew it. And he did."

"Well, darling, I'm glad for you and the boy it worked out. Really glad. Would you like to talk to your mother?"

"Of course, I do! I have to tell her everything. Love you, Dad."

"Love you too, sweetheart."

His head hurt and he had lost his appetite, even though the roast pork dinner Sadie had made, and sat going cold on the kitchen table, smelled delicious. He sat in the big armchair in the living room, trying to read the newspaper while Sadie talked on the phone in the hallway. Her voice, even though muted by the wall between them, sounded almost as excited as his daughter's had.

Raines hoped Marilyn's newfound "wonderful" life with her husband and child would last. He hated the thought of her being hurt again. Knowing Thomas Morgan as he did, he didn't see how it could be prevented. That wasn't true, exactly. There was a way it could be prevented. She could move home with Tommy. It would be rough at first, but they were family, flesh and blood. Together they could make it work. Morgan was no good for her. Raines had known it from the minute he met him, a tall, bright-eyed, handsome young man in his Navy uniform ready to go off and fight for his country. Sometimes you just know how a man is, he thought, from the first minute you meet them. And Raines had been right about Morgan. Everything that had transpired in the eight years since their first meeting proved it so.

The Raines ate a cold dinner that night. It being late when they were finished, both of them worn out by the phone call, they skipped after dinner brandy on the porch and went to bed. The next morning, at 8 a.m. sharp, Walter Harker called to let Raines know the state's Attorney's office had convened grand juries in both Dade and Broward counties to go over the Kefauver Committee findings.

"What'll we do now, John?" Harker asked, none of the defiant confidence on display in the courtroom during the hearings in the words he spoke over the phone that morning.

"We wait and see if they issue a true bill," Raines told his client. "Then take it from there."

\*\*\*

They didn't have to wait long. The grand jury in Broward brought back a true bill after three days. Two days after that Sheriff Walter Harker was indicted by the State of Florida on charges of aiding and abetting illegal gambling. The day after this indictment was unsealed, the sheriff, along with his attorney surrendered at the courthouse. At his arraignment later that afternoon, a trial date was set for October 25th, to take place in Courtroom A, at said courthouse, and to be presided over by Judge James Harrigan. Despite a furious argument against it by Robert Ross, the state attorney for the South Florida area, the sheriff was then released on his own recognizance

Raines couldn't help but be amused by that despite Harker's earlier worries, the trial was to be held in Broward County after all. A change of venue hadn't been necessary, and Harker had fired his first attorney over nothing. Was Raines a better lawyer than Joe Whittaker? He supposed there were arguments both for, and against, this. But it wasn't for Raines to say and he knew that.

Besides, it certainly didn't matter now. Harker had hired him, and now it was up to Raines to provide the best defense he could for his client. Raines was willing to bet, though, that if Whittaker were made privy to the evidence against Harker, he'd breathe a sigh of relief that Harker had fired him

"At least the charges against you relate only to bolita and slot machines," Raines told Harker the day after he was released, and they were sitting in Raines' office going over the indictment. "There's nothing in here about narcotics or prostitution. That's very good for us, as it narrows the scope somewhat."

"Like I told you before, John," Harker said, leaning back in his chair, as he wiped his forehead with a handkerchief. Harker seemed to sweat all the time now, but Raines had chalked it up to the illness he was fighting. "And just like I told the Senator that day—I don't know anything about whores and dope. Don't want to know, either. That's nasty business all the way around."

"Yes, it is, Walter, no doubt about it."

It was a Tuesday morning, and the sheriff was in full uniform—this reminded Raines of something, and he said so.

"I don't want you coming to trial in your work duds, Walter. I mean that. This is serious business we're up against, and you need to look—and act—like you know that."

"Being a sheriff is serious business, counselor."

"Yes, it is. But you need to appear as a concerned citizen, charged unfairly with crimes you didn't commit. That Cowboy Sheriff persona won't sit well with Judge Harrigan, either. Not when you're a defendant in his courtroom"

"I know the judge pretty well. Been a witness for the prosecution many a time in his courtroom and dressed just like I am today."

"Exactly," Raines said, as he straightened up the indictment papers on his desk and put them aside for his secretary to file. "You were in Judge Harrigan's courtroom as a witness. Being a defendant is a whole different matter."

"If you say so."

"I do say so. Trust me."

"I do trust you, John." Harker said, that down-home, country boy, smile of his spread out all over his face. "Wouldn't have hired you if I didn't."

"Good." Raines stood up, indicating that the meeting was over. He didn't bother to say that he trusted Harker as well. He had made it a point over the years never to lie to a client—saw no reason to change that rule now.

*\*\**

October 25th, a Monday and the first day of the trial, was crisp and pleasant, the wet heat of the summer in the past, the sort of day that Raines liked the best. The sky was as blue as blue could be, marked only by a trace of wispy clouds here and there. The mornings had come on cool the last week or so but had warmed up quickly into the mid to high seventies—the kind of weather, Raines thought comfortable enough for a man to do just about any pleasant thing that came to mind.

Sitting in Judge Harrigan's courtroom trying to save a man from his own bad behavior was not one of those pleasant things, in Raines' opinion. Not by a long shot. Not when quail season was set to open the following week and he was eager to spend some time in the woods with his dogs and gun. Beyond that, Raines had finally come to a decision over something Sadie and he had been discussing for close to a year. It was time to close up shop. Take his shingle down from his law office, sell the house, the two other properties he owned in the area, and move permanently to their ranch west of Jupiter. With the children gone — the one forever — the only thing keeping the Raines in Lauderdale was work and the few friends they had. Raines wouldn't miss the work. The ranch would provide more than enough of that to keep him busy. As for their friends? Jupiter was only an hour's drive north. They were welcome to come visit him and Sadie. If they chose not to do so, well then, that was on them

Meanwhile, Walter Harker's trial stood in the way. How long the trial would last was anyone's guess. If he were to go by the list of witnesses for the prosecution, as turned over to him per the discovery process, it wouldn't be long. Only three names were on this list: two of these were men who owned establishments in the county where slot machines had been placed — according to their depositions at least — by employees of the Progresso Novelty & Games Company. The third name on the witness list was an alleged bolita operator who claimed he had paid the sheriff's office for protection in order to run his racket.

Strangely enough, nowhere on the prosecution's list was the name Jacob Meyers. The man, according to Kefauver, who did the books for Progresso Novelty& Games. Raines didn't know if he should be happy about this or worried.

The first day of the trail went pretty much as Raines expected it would. Most of it was spent on selecting a jury out of the fifty potential jurors called to duty for the event. There was a slight twist at the beginning—one Raines didn't see coming—when the prosecution filed a motion for a change of venue.

"Your Honor," but the judge cut Raines off.

"Not to worry, Mr. Raines. There will be no change of venue approved today."

"I have to protest this decision, Judge Harrigan," Bob Ross, the State's attorney said. "Vigorously protest I might add."

"Don't waste your breath, or my time, Mr. Ross."

Judge Harrigan was a tough Irishman in his late forties, red-haired, short and stocky in build, and nature, and known to put up with no foolishness in his courtroom. Raines had tried cases before him in the past, and by doing so had come to respect the man very much. From Boston originally, the judge had married a girl from Fort Lauderdale he met while stationed at the Naval Air base west of town during the war. Unable to say no to her pleas to stay in Fort Lauderdale, where her family and friends were, Harrigan had started a law practice in town when he returned at war's end. Through a fluke of circumstance, one of the judges on the circuit court had taken sick and died, and via a recommendation from—who else—Tom Ryan, Harrigan had been chosen to replace him

"I have all the faith in the world, Mr. Ross," Judge Harrigan continued, "that through voir dire, the two of you will be able to select a jury composed of Mr. Harker's peers who will be able to judge the case impartially."

"But Your Honor."

"Sit down Mr. Ross. Motion denied."

The sheriff nudged Raines and with a wink, whispered, "Don't look like ol' Bob Ross is off to a good start with Judge Harrigan."

"I'm surprised, actually," Raines whispered back. "If I were the judge, I would have approved of the motion."

"Good thing for me you ain't the judge, then."

"Yes," Raines said, and with more reasons than he felt necessary to explain right then.

Once it began, jury selection went quickly and by noon recess they had seated six out of the necessary twelve. Raines used only two of his strikes, while the prosecutor used only one of his.

Raines strikes were both used on women. The Florida Statutes had been amended in the last session of the legislature to allow women to serve on juries. The current trial would be the first one since the statues had been changed where women were in the jury pool. While Raines was sorely tempted to be a participant in such an historical first, the two women called just wouldn't do—both of them being staunch churchgoers, morally opposed to gambling and other sins of the flesh, as their answers to Raines questions showed.

"Well ladies, "Judge Harrigan said, after excusing the second woman from jury duty. "I was sorta hoping at least one of you would be picked, but it didn't happen. Better luck next time and thank you for your service. You ladies are excused."

The prosecutor's one strike that morning was used on the lone Negro in the jury pool. When Judge Harrigan raised his eyebrows at this, Ross answered simply enough.

"Your Honor, this man is a member of the community where much of the alleged activities take place. I don't see how he can't help but be prejudiced in this matter before the court."

"But you haven't even asked him the first question," the judge replied, eyebrows still raised.

"Yes, Your Honor, but my strike still stands."

"So be it, then," and the black man was excused, with a thanks for his service as well.

When court reconvened after the noon recess, the remaining six jurors were quickly seated. The twelve chosen were all men, white, all of whom said they did not know the sheriff personally, or had any official contact with him, or his department. To a man they swore they were able to listen to the evidence presented in a non-partial light, and when time to do so, render a verdict based solely on said evidence, and according to the rule of law. That being determined, the bailiff swore them in, and the trial began.

But it was getting on in the day, and Judge Harrigan, seeing as how it was too late to begin opening statements, said perhaps it would be good to address the issue of whether or not to sequester the jury. The prosecutor was all for it but seeing the look on the faces of the jurors, Raines said he was opposed. The evidence—as Raines knew from the Kefauver hearing—against his client was pretty damning. Having a sympathetic jury might mitigate some of that. Not that he said this out loud. Instead, he argued that the jurors were all honorable men. They had just sworn to abide by the evidence presented during the trial, and only that. In light of this he saw no reason to burden them with the stress of being sequestered and away from their families.

"I tend to agree with Mr. Raines," the judge said after listening to both arguments. "Being a juror is hard enough without depriving them of the comforts of home at the end of the day. We will not be sequestering the jury."

The prosecutor rose to object, Judge Harrigan gave him a hard look, banged the gavel down, and court for that day was adjourned.

"Another one for our side, eh counselor?" Harker said as they were exiting the courtroom and before they were mobbed by the reporter's looking to get a comment on the day's proceedings.

"Yes, indeed," Raines replied. "Hopefully, we will get more of these little victories as the trial goes on." He grabbed Harker's arm to steer him away from the reporters. "You've got nothing to say to those boys. Not today."

"You're right—probably for the best I keep my trap shut for the time being."

"Damn straight I'm right. Let Bob Ross talk to them He's good at it. You're not."

Harker laughed, went to walk away, but turned. "You know, John, as for those little victories?"

"What about them?"

"I believe there's a few out there still to come our way. Yes sir, I do."

The look on Harker's face after he said this bothered Raines— bothered him for the rest of the night. Over dinner at home and cocktails with Sadie on the back porch afterwards, it was still with him as he turned the light off on the bedside stand and tried to sleep.

\*\*\*

Next day Raines arrived at the courthouse at 9.30 and found Harker in front of Courtroom A talking to the reporters waiting for the trial to begin. He didn't reprimand the sheriff, just hustled him inside to the defense table and readied himself for what was to come. The prosecution led off with their opening statement, the State's Attorney rambling on for over an hour about the heinous nature of the crimes alleged against the defendant. Crimes perpetuated against the good citizens of Broward County, who, by God, had suffered long enough under these crimes. Furthermore, he was certain that after hearing the witness testimony, as well as after a careful review of the documents entered into evidence, and despite the defendant's attorney's efforts to muddy that evidence, the jury would have no choice but to enter a verdict of guilty on all charges. And by doing so, rid Broward County of the grievous stain on its honor perpetuated over the years by the defendant and his cohorts.

It was a serious opening statement, the grim expression on the State's Attorney's face as he delivered this statement, plainly calculated to add weight to his words. A serious statement delivered by a man with serious ambitions. After all, Bob Ross was in his prime, had a lengthy record of convictions behind him, was well dressed, good looking, tall and of a solid build, with thick black hair and dark eyes. The word among those in the know was that Ross would be Governor one day. Prevailing in the case against the sheriff would be a fine feather in Bob Ross' cap—one that could go a long way toward getting him into the Governor's mansion.

Ah well, Raines thought as he rose to deliver his opening statement. They all had their job to do today in the courtroom: Bob Ross, Judge Harrigan, the jury, Harker, and even the spectators. Now it was time for Raines to get started on his for the day.

"Your Honor," he began, looking at the judge up on the bench before turning to the jury box. "Gentlemen of the jury, and the good citizens of this county—as my colleague, Mr. Ross, alluded to." Polite laughter rippled through the courtroom, Raines ending it quickly when he spoke above it. "Mr. Ross, the State's Attorney for our area, is a fine man, a good lawyer, and very proficient in his work. In the course of that work, it has become his job to lodge serious allegations against my client, Sheriff Walter Harker, who is also a fine man and a good sheriff, and proficient in his work as well. Now these serious allegations of the State's Attorney's office would be very damning ones indeed—if they were true! And that, gentlemen of the jury, is not the case here. Not at all."

Raines went on for less than a half hour, not wanting to bore the jury any more than he had to but needing to put forth his take on the matter at hand.

"I have no doubt that the crimes of gambling, slot machines, bolita, and the like, take place in our county. I can't imagine that anyone in this courtroom today—including my client, who should know, seeing as he is the man responsible for enforcing the laws prohibiting these crimes—could be so naive as to think these sorts of crimes do not take place in our community. What I also do not doubt, is the fact that my client is innocent of being involved in these crimes."

He went on to say how flimsy the prosecution's case was, "Why, he only has three witnesses to call to the stand." He said that he had known Walter Harker for over twenty-five years, and in all that time, had never known him to be anything but an honest, upright citizen, as well as a law enforcement officer beyond reproach. It was a good opening statement, Raines felt when he was finished—and it didn't matter one bit that he didn't believe any of what he had said.

"Mighty fine job there, Mr. Raines," Harker whispered when Raines sat down at the end of his statement.

"It's early yet, Walter."

"Maybe. But hells bells, man, I don't see how any man jack of those fellows sitting there in the jury box could deliver a guilty verdict against me. Not after that speech you just gave. No sir."

"Like I said, it's early."

"Call your first witness, Mr. Ross," the judge said, Raines grateful for the excuse to turn away from the smile on his client's face.

This first witness was a man named Ralph Willis, owner of a grocery store on the west side of town. The store also had a bar in the back that served beer and wine.

"Quite an operation you have there Mr. Willis," Ross said when this was brought up during the prosecutor's direct examination.

"Is there a question in there," Raines said, more to rattle Ross a little than for any serious objection—which the judge picked up on right away.

"Now, now, Mr. Raines. Are silly shenanigans going to be a part of your defense strategy? If so, I will warn you in advance to forget about it."

"No sir, Judge," Raines replied. "I was just curious is all."

"Carry on Mr. Ross."

"As I was saying, that is quite the operation you have going in your store, Mr. Willis."

"Yes, sir and thank you." Willis was a small man with sharp features, most of them hidden behind the thick glasses he wore. "It's taken the Missus and me some time to get her where she is today. But we like it."

"Yes, I'm sure you do. I'm curious, though—much like Mr. Raines," and Ross turned to smile at the defense table. "For different reasons of course. But why the bar in the back of the store? You don't usually see that in grocery stores. Leastwise, not the ones I've been in."

"That was my wife's idea. She said people coming in might be thirsty and looking for something a little stronger than a soda pop when their shopping was done." He looked down for a minute at his hands clasped together in front of him before adding, "I like a cold beer on occasion my own self, so she didn't have to twist my arm much."

When the laughter died down—laughter the judge joined in with—Ross asked his next question.

"You have slot machines in the back of your store, Mr. Willis?"

"Yes sir, I do."

"Are you aware that slot machines are prohibited in the State of Florida?"

"I am. But the man who came around asking me if I was interested in setting up a couple of them, told me—when I said, aren't they illegal—he said, why yes, they were, but nobody cared much about that law and it would be all right."

"Who provided you with the machines?"

"A fellow from Progresso Novelty& Games."

"Progresso Novelty & Games, you say?"

"Yes sir."

"The same outfit owned by the defendant, Walter Harker, and his brother?"

"That's what you told me."

This time Judge Harrigan had to bang his gavel several times before he was able to quell the laughter in the courtroom

Raines had only two questions for Ralph Willis.

"Is my client the individual who approached you in the first place about setting up slot machines in your grocery store, Mr. Willis?"

"No sir."

"Is the individual who did approach you that first time, and who subsequently installed those machines and maintained them for you — is he in the courtroom?"

"No sir, he is not."

"Thank you, Mr. Willis," Raines said, and then turning to the judge, added, "That's all I have for this witness, Your Honor."

The prosecution's next witness, a nondescript looking man in his mid-to-late fifties owned a bar on US1 just outside of the port. During questioning by Bob Ross this man, too, said he had rented slot machines from Progresso Novelty& Gaines. Again, during Raines' cross examination, the man had to admit that the individual who he dealt with regarding the slot machines was not in the courtroom

The prosecution's third witness for the day was a different matter altogether. Lucas Jones, a Negro, and according to him, sixty years of age, was the manager of a bar and small restaurant on Sistrunk Boulevard, an area of Fort Lauderdale known as Colored Town, at least to the white residents of the city in polite conversation.

During questioning by the State's Attorney, Jones admitted to running a bolita operation out of the back of the bar. It was further established that Sheriff Harker had known about this operation. And that because of this knowledge the sheriff and his deputies had raided the place just two months before, arresting both Jones and his wife, Leila.

"Is this true?" Raines whispered to his client, while Mr. Jones was still on the stand.

"Sure it is. I had to do something to take the heat off of me after that hearing down in Miami."

"Right now, it doesn't appear to have worked," Raines said.

"We'll see."

"And were you surprised by this raid on your business, Mr. Jones?" Ross asked.

"Sure I was."

"And why is that?"

"Well sir, I been paying the sheriff good money for years to keep him from doing such a thing. Him and his boys busting in like that just didn't seem right. Not to me it didn't."

"What didn't seem right, Mr. Jones? Paying the money? Or the raid?"

"Why now, both of them, if you was to ask me."

During cross examination, once again Raines asked the witness if the man he had been paying protection money to over the years was in the courtroom

"No sir, he ain't."

"Is it true that the State's Attorney's office offered to drop all charges against you in exchange for your testimony here today?"

"Yes, sir that is a fact. I didn't see how I could say no to that."

"I'm finished with this witness, Your Honor," Raines said and returned to the defense table.

When Bob Ross called his next witness, Raines supposed he should be surprised but was not.

"Your Honor, the prosecution calls Mr. Jacob Meyers to the stand."

"I object!" Raines was on his feet, the prosecution's witness list in his hand. "This witness is nowhere on the list provided me by the prosecution."

Before Judge Harrigan could say anything, Ross was on his feet as well. "Judge, I apologize for omitting Mr. Meyers from our witness list. But I was hoping I would not need to call him today." Ross flashed a sheepish smile towards Raines, and the judge, "But in light of how the proceedings have gone so far today, I see that I do."

Raines didn't believe the first part of what Ross had claimed, though the rest of it was certainly true.

"I request a mistrial, Your Honor." Raines didn't believe for a second Judge Harrigan would grant such a motion, but it was worth a try.

"There will be no mistrial declared today, Mr. Raines." Glaring at the State's Attorney, Harrigan added, "At least not yet, there won't be. But this is highly irregular, Mr. Ross. What do you have to say for yourself?"

"It was an honest error on my part, Your Honor, and will not happen again."

Once more, Raines didn't believe the first part of that statement, but was certain the last would hold true.

"How about you, Mr. Raines? Anything to say?"

"Well judge, if you decide to allow the prosecution's witness to take the stand, I'll offer no objection—as long as you order Mr. Ross to turn over to the defense what he has concerning Mr. Meyers, and his potential testimony. And then allow the defense ample time to do discovery on what the prosecution gives us."

"Exactly what I was thinking, Mr. Raines," the judge said, before glaring at Bob Ross again. "You're right this *honest error* of yours Mr. Ross won't happen again. Not in my courtroom it won't. Any objection to what both myself and Mr. Raines have suggested."

"None, Your Honor."

"Good. I so order the prosecution to turn over to the defense all documents pertaining to Jacob Meyers and his potential testimony regarding these proceedings. They are to be delivered to Mr. Raines' office by the end of the day. Court will be adjourned until next Monday, 9 a.m. sharp. That work for you Mr. Raines?"

"Yes sir, it does."

"All right then. Court is adjourned," Judge Harrigan's gavel emphasizing his decision as everyone in the room rose and turned for the exit. Raines and his client, along with Ross and his assistant were the last to leave the courthouse, Ross stopping to talk to the reporters waiting outside. Harker paused, but Raines' pressure on his arm kept him walking.

"Another dog and pony show, yes counselor?" Harker said when they reached the corner across from his office on the other side of the street.

"You could say that." Raines was in no mood for idle chat with his client, tired as he was from the long day and the surprise turn—not that it was really a surprise, he reminded himself—the proceedings had taken. "We'll see what happens once we see what Meyers is going to testify to."

"Well now, I don't think there'll be much to worry about." And there was that confidant smile on the sheriff's face that bothered Raines so much. "Not on that score, I don't think."

"What do you mean by that?"

"Nothing. Nothing at all."

"Then I'll see you in my office at ten o'clock tomorrow morning so we can go over what Ross' office gives me."

"You bet, Johnny. See you then."

The sheriff crossed the street, ducked into his office on the other side, and was gone, leaving Raines with that casual, "Johnny." Raines didn't know which irritated him more—the Johnny' or that grin on Harker's face.

\*\*\*

The crisp clean early fall weather they had been experiencing the last two weeks of that October, was gone come Monday morning when the State of Florida v. Walter Harker reconvened. A late season tropical storm had passed over the state to the north of them over the weekend. Fort Lauderdale hadn't suffered the full effects of the wind and the rain the storm produced, but the dry, cool, cool air of before the storm had been replaced by a dreary, overcast sky, and a blanket of wet heat.

An ominous start to the delayed proceedings? This was one of the thoughts coursing through Raines' mind as he met Harker outside the courtroom, where again, he steered his client away from the eager reporters surrounding him, and inside to their seats at the defense table.

"We got lucky with that storm, now, didn't we John," Harker said as he placed his white Stetson on the table in front of him. "Those poor bastards up in Delray got flooded out again." He gave a dry chuckle. "Not that there was anything left of their truck farms to worry about. Not after that hurricane in August and all that flooding it brought with it, there wasn't."

"Excuse me?" Raines said. "I didn't catch what you were saying."

And he hadn't, upset instead at the fact that despite his instructions to the contrary, today Harker had come to court in his official uniform of Sheriff of Broward County.

"Aw, it don't matter John. Best focus on what's coming our way this morning, I suppose."

"Yes."

And then, what was "coming their way" began when the door of the judge's chambers opened and the bailiff sang out, "All rise."

"Good morning, learned counsel," Judge Harrigan said, beaming a smile to the crowded courtroom "And good morning to the gentlemen of the jury. Now then, Mr. Ross, is the prosecution ready to proceed?" Turning to the defense table before Ross could answer, the judge added, "I hope the defense has no objections that during the somewhat lengthy delay you were able to prepare yourself, Mr. Raines."

"No objection, Your Honor."

"Good. Call your witness, Mr. Ross, and let's get this show on the road."

"Your Honor," Ross said, rising to his feet, a grim look on his face. "I beg the court's pardon, but my witness has not arrived yet."

"Excuse me?" the judge said, over the muttering in the courtroom

"There seems to be a delay of some sorts," Ross continued. "But I'm sure he'll be here any minute. A deputy was sent to bring Mr. Meyers to court this morning. They must be hung up in traffic."

"It is Monday morning," Judge Harrigan said, his fingers crossed in a steeple on the bench. "I'll allow fifteen minutes. Hopefully, your witness will have arrived by then. Ah, perhaps he is here now," the judge added as the doors in the back of the courtroom opened.

Expecting the prosecution to call the lately arrived witness to the stand, everyone there had turned to look to see who was coming into the courtroom. Instead of Jacob Meyers, though, it was a uniformed deputy who walked hurriedly up to the prosecution's table. Raines and Harker, at their table, were close enough, not to hear, but to see the deputy say something to Ross—to see Ross take a step back, his mouth slightly open, his eyes wide, as he shook his head slowly.

Taking a deep breath, Ross turned to the bench, his voice strained as he said, "Your Honor, the deputy has just informed me that there has been an accident. One that involves my witness, sad to say."

"An accident, Mr. Ross?" Judge Harrigan had unlaced his fingers as he leaned over the bench. "Are you trying to tell me the prosecution needs more than the fifteen minutes the court has allowed?"

"Judge, I honestly don't know what I am trying to tell you."

Raines had seen unexpected setbacks in trials before, some involving him—but the look on Bob Ross, his lips tight and features drained of color, suggested this was no mere setback.

"The accident, Your Honor," Ross finally continued after taking several deep breaths, "has been a fatal one. Both Mr. Meyers and Deputy Sharp, the driver, did not survive."

The clamor that erupted in the courtroom took a long time to settle, the repeated banging of Judge Harrigan's gavel on the bench finally enough to put an end to the shouted questions from the reporters in the back, and the stunned comments racing through the rows of spectators.

"Mr. Ross," Judge Harrigan said when it was quiet again, "This is a most unfortunate turn of events. In light of what has happened the court is willing to grant a delay for the prosecution until you are ready to proceed again."

"The prosecution thanks you for that, Your Honor, but I have no other witnesses to present."

"Are you prepared to rest your case, then?"

It was stone silent in the courtroom after this question, the flimsiness of the case the prosecution had presented being so obvious, Raines figured—even to the casual spectators who had come every day for the entertainment of it—that to rest now could only have one outcome: a not guilty verdict.

"No sir," Ross finally said. "I am not prepared to do that."

"I'm all ears, Mr. Ross," the judge said.

"The prosecution would like to enter into evidence the sworn deposition of Jacob Meyers, Your Honor. Either myself, or my assistant attorney, Mr. Proctor, can read this deposition out loud, and when he is done the prosecution will rest, and turn the proceedings over to Mr. Raines."

Judge Harrigan burst out laughing. "Well now, Mr. Ross, I appreciate a good joke—even in my courtroom."

"I wasn't joking, Your Honor."

"And neither am I, Mr. Ross."

The judge looked long and hard at the prosecutor; Raines glad he wasn't the one suffering under that glare. He almost felt bad for Bob Ross—until he glanced over at his client and saw the smile on Harker's lips.

"I like to think, Mr. Ross, that attorneys who come before me in my courtroom are familiar with Constitution of the United States. But I am also aware that sometimes a man might let a sizable amount of time pass before he bothers to brush up on his Constitutional law. That apparently being the case here, Mr. Ross, then let me help you out. A defendant has the right to face his accuser. Has the right to ask questions of said accuser. A piece of paper read out to the courtroom does not meet that standard, Mr. Ross. Are we agreed on that, Mr. Ross?"

"Your Honor, I just thought—"

"Mr. Ross," Judge Harrigan cut him off. "Save your breath. And the court's time. Your proposal will not fly in my courtroom Not today. Not ever. Now, as I asked earlier: are you prepared to rest your case?"

"No, Your Honor, the prosecution is not prepared to rest." Ross looked over at the defense table, shrugged, and then turned to face the bench again. "The prosecution requests—in light of the disturbing events of this morning—a delay until we can gather more evidence to present in the proper manner before this court."

Harker leaned forward in his seat, nudging Raines in the side as he did so, his face gone well beyond that tight confident smile he had been wearing all morning, into a downright gloating grin.

"I am going to deny that request, Mr. Ross," the judge said. Turning his glare on the defense table—though more truthfully, at Harker, the judge continued. "At this time, the court has no choice but to dismiss the charges against Walter Harker."

"No, Your Honor!" Both Bob Ross and Proctor, his assistant attorney, were on their feet.

"Do not interrupt me again, Mr. Ross, or I will hold you in contempt of court."

"Yes sir."

"Now, where was I? Oh yes, the court is going to dismiss the charges—without prejudice—leaving the State the opportunity to bring this case back to trial. Sheriff Harker," and the look Judge Harrigan gave Harker, made Raines squirm some in his seat, "as much as it galls me to say this, I have no other recourse but to tell you that you are free to go."

The ensuing uproar would never be solved by Judge Harrigan and his gavel, though he tried, and if one listened hard enough over the noise, as Raines did, they may have heard the judge say, "This court is adjourned!" Even though Raines *did* hear the judge, he doubted anyone else in the maelstrom did—or cared to.

It wasn't quiet again until Raines and his client were standing on the corner outside of the courthouse across the street from the Sheriff's office. What Harker had said to the reporters outside of the courtroom—"Boys, all I can tell you is that I am one lucky man!"—still rang in Raines' head. The sun had come out while they had been inside, burning off the overcast, the brightness of it, sending wet heat up from the sidewalk and the roads.

How quickly things could change, Raines thought. Just like that, his client was a free man. Just like that the gray sky had disappeared, the sun come out, and even though it was sticky hot, a trace of wind was rising in the east, and probably, maybe the matter of only a few days, cooler air from the north would blow through again, and the days would be comfortable once more. The sort of days that came with that time of year, in the fall, when, as he had thought just last week before the trial started, when it was comfortable enough for a man to do just about anything he pleased.

"Well, Mr. Raines," Harker said, interrupting Raines' chain of good thought. "Looks like that's it."

Not John. Or Johnny. But Mr. Raines. They were back where they had started in the early days of summer. When a different Walter Harker had come to Raines' office, dressed in a business suit, the effects of his illness showing, to ask for Raines' help. But Harker was wrong about something and Raines told him

"You're not out of the woods just yet, Sheriff," Raines said. If his client wanted to be formal that was fine with him. "Harrigan dismissed the charges, true, but without prejudice. The State's Attorney can re-charge you and we'll be right back where we were."

"Oh, I don't know about that. Seems to me anything they might have had on me went out the window with Meyers kicking the bucket like that. Now, I'm sure sorry about Deputy Sharp, let me tell you. He was a good deputy and a fine man. But that Jake Meyers? No sir. Not a good man at all. If you ask me, counselor, he got just what was coming to him"

Raines started to say something, stopped, took a step back, and turned to look hard at his client. That word. Counselor. The way it had been spoken to him just then. By a man with a brash smile on his face who was on top of it all again.

So that suddenly, Raines was not where he was—on a street corner in front of the courthouse in downtown Fort Lauderdale. Instead, he was on a rickety wooden bridge crossing a nighttime river some twenty-five years back. Lying at his feet were the bodies of four men. And a man standing over those bodies, with a smile on his face, confident and brash.

A sheriff. Not Walter Harker. Though he had been there, too, but only a deputy at the time. No, a different sheriff. Who, as Raines looked up from the dead men, said to him, "Well counselor, you have anything to say about this?"

Raines had said something then to that sheriff—something flippant, even as his insides were going away from him. But that time—on the bridge—was long gone. There was nothing he could say now. And he didn't. He simply turned away from his client and walked away, aware of the Sheriff calling out to him as he did. But it didn't matter.

Did not matter at all.

# PART SIX

The morning, even at first light, was warm and humid. It was to be expected that time of year. Another month, October, the long heavy heat of the Florida summer would be gone, and fall would have arrived in South Florida. For now, John Raines was comfortable beneath the paddle fan on the screened porch of the house, coffee, and the morning edition of *The Miami Herald* close at hand. As the sun came up so did the wind, blowing across the pine and palmetto scrub on the other side of the dirt two-track that ran past the front of the house. The steady wind soughed through the tops of the bamboo stand at the edge of the sand drive into the front yard, a stand a farmer long before John Raines time had planted to spruce up an otherwise barren and repetitious landscape. The sound of the wind through the bamboo tops had always been a comfort to Raines—for no other reason than the fact that it just sounded pleasant to him

Just past dawn, now, Raines, restless with what had to be done that day, had been up an hour already before any light. He was glad for the breeze—coming from the ocean ten miles to the east it added to the cool comfort of the porch. Because of harder gusts blowing periodically, instead of being able to lay the paper flat on the table in front of him, Raines had to hold the paper in both hands to read. A minor annoyance, really, one he could correct by going inside to the dining room table. But it was too nice a morning to waste—too nice on the porch as dawn grew into full morning. He didn't choose to leave it.

The news for that morning, Monday, September 4th, Labor Day of 1961 wasn't much different from any other day, and as he often did while reading the paper John Raines wondered why he subscribed in the first place. After all, he had to get up a half hour earlier than was normal when they lived in the city to make the drive down to the highway and the newspaper box standing off the road next to the mailbox. A drive made necessary by the fact that no matter how he had cajoled and plied his lawyerly wiles, the carrier refused to bring the paper the two miles up the dirt road to the Raines front door.

Not that Raines minded the drive. He had been doing it nearly every morning now, with no complaint, since the fall of 1951, when he and Sadie left Fort Lauderdale for good, the big house on the Isles sold, law practice closed, son dead, daughter gone. No. Wait. The morning was too fine to let bitterness creep in. There was no need for it, none at all, no matter the past.

It was gone, then, and he thought again how leaving all that town life had been one of the best decisions of his adult life. So, it was a trade-off: thirty minutes in the Willys every morning to get yesterday's mail and the morning paper, rumbling down the dirt road to the cattle guard spanning the ditch in front of Indiantown Road, watching the property come alive with the rising sun as he drove: coveys of quail whistling in the palmettos, cattle grazing in wiregrass fields, marsh birds calling out from the wetlands bordering the creek cutting through his property. It was easy to see he had made the right choice.

The news that morning was more of the same. The USSR had announced it would resume nuclear testing. Spanish troops were leaving Morocco. A Negro had been appointed judge of a U.S. District Court, the first time ever, an event of so little importance the editors of the paper consigned it to a sidebar column without including the Negro's name, or even the district court he'd been appointed to. In the sports section a feat of note was how Baltimore pitcher Jack Fisher had managed to walk twelve Los Angele's Angels batters in nine innings during yesterday's game, but the Orioles still won.

In local news *Africa U.S.A*, a wildlife theme park west of Boca Raton was closing its doors after eight years of being in business. The owner, one Jack Peterson, was quoted as saying it was very sad for him to see it go, for the last eight years had been the best of his life. The current economy was to blame and having been a businessman for many years, Peterson said as much as he hated doing so it was time to cut his losses. John Raines knew Jack Peterson. The man had been a client of his—there had been issues pertaining to the purchase and zoning of the property. Minor matters really, the three liens, though the far-reaching idea of one county commissioner that the site was perfect for an elementary school was a little more difficult to resolve. To Raines surprise, two briefs, two appearances at the Martin County monthly commission meeting, and these issues disappeared. If he suspected that money he hadn't known about had changed hands, he couldn't prove it. Besides, if he wasn't party to it then it was none of his concern. Raines had learned long ago from his brother RL in Fort Myers that real estate dealings and the law didn't always go hand in hand. Of course, as a result of learning this he had removed himself from RL's businesses. So that when the work for Jack Peterson was over and Mr. Peterson offered to put him on retainer, Raines declined.

The faraway hum of a light airplane suddenly intruded on the early morning and his thoughts.

The mosquito-like drone grew louder as the plane came in to land on the airstrip the Cubans had built out in the palmetto scrub between his house and Indiantown Road. Either a Piper, or a Cessna, John figured, one of the post-war models the Cubans had secured somewhere. They always came in the early mornings like that, didn't stay long, fifteen minutes, sometimes a little longer, and then took off again, the drone of the engines fading as they headed east out over the ocean. To where? From where? Though he pretended not to know the answers to that little riddle, he did. The pretense of ignorance had been the one part of the deal John insisted on when Tom Ryan had called and asked for his help.

"Why my place, Tom?" Raines asked when Ryan explained what he needed. "Why not yours?"

"Yours is closer to the coast, John."

This was true—Tom Ryan's acreage, though certainly big enough to accommodate an airfield such as the Cubans needed, lay outside of Okeechobee, Fifty miles further inland than the Raines place. Fifty miles didn't seem like much of a difference Raines thought at first. But in a light plane? Overloaded with men, maybe weapons? He supposed the extra miles could add up quickly.

A week after Ryan's phone call the two men got together over lunch, at the *Governors Club* on Las Olas Avenue in downtown Fort Lauderdale. The old three-story stucco hotel, though white and faded on the outside from time and the elements, was always immaculate on the inside. The cool and dark leathery interior of the Club afforded a comfortable intimacy while the rest of the city, visible through large rectangular windows spaced along the front wall, continued on outside. The hotel and downstairs club was a place where the truth, secret confidences, and outright lies could be revealed, explored, or simply tossed out for effect, the fine food and expensive liquor further facilitating the above. Raines, like most of the other businessmen and lawyers and judges who practiced and worked in Fort Lauderdale, had been a regular there for many years, utilizing the ambience of the establishment for both business and pleasure, sometimes to his advantage, sometimes not.

"Mr. Salas promises me his men will be so discreet you'll hardly know they're there," Tom Ryan continued. "Considering the nature of their business I'm sure they will be."

"I sure don't want to know 'the nature of their business,' Tom. That's all I ask. If it blows up in their faces, I'm looking to you to keep me out of it."

"That shouldn't be a problem." Ryan's lean, grizzled face broke into a slight grin, the dry chuckle following, spreading the grin further across his features. "The Attorney General owes me a few." Ryan chuckled again as he reached for his Scotch and soda and finished it off. "In the unlikely event we need him he'll be there."

Raines saw no reason to doubt it—he knew the Attorney General as well. Knew him to be a man rarely bothered by scruples if they threatened to get in his way. Much like Tom Ryan, who had none when it came to business, and only a few if one were his friend. Though they had better be a very good friend.

"Don't you think you're a little old for this kind of adventuring, Tom?" It had been on his mind ever since Tom brought up this Cuban business. "Look at us. You and I aren't young men anymore. Haven't been for quite a while."

The facts certainly seemed to bolster Raines opinion: they were both in their late sixties, hair, what little left of it, gone gray, skin burned dark by years in the sun, the hunting and fishing, and work that was his life on his ranch. As for Ryan, pale and weary looking in the dim light of the club, the Brooks Brothers suit he was accustomed to wearing, hung loosely on a frame much thinner from the years and the time spent in his office spinning the schemes and half-truths that were the nature of his business. Raines just couldn't see the sense in men of their age being involved with intrigues in foreign countries. Especially one as close to home as Cuba. *Especially* one like that.

"No, you're right, John. We aren't the men we once were."

And there was that dry chuckle, the little grin as he contemplated the drink on the table in front of him

"But I'm certainly not dead yet. Neither are you. And as much as I sometimes think it's time I hung up my spurs, so to speak, followed in your footsteps and retired to the simplicity of life at my place in 'Chobee, I can't get away from this nagging feeling I've had lately. That my work here isn't quite done. It's been eating at me long before Castro turned his coat down there. And snatched up my lands, yours, and those of other friends. When Mr. Salas approached me with his proposition everything suddenly seemed to fall into place."

Ryan picked up his Scotch & Soda and brought it to his lips, pausing in a dramatic fashion better suited to a lawyer in the courtroom ready to drive a point home—than two old friends in a quiet club downtown—before he drank.

"Besides, my involvement in this 'adventuring,' as you call it, won't be on any physical level. Other than what it takes to open my checkbook and write out a check."

This conversation had taken place the year before, towards the end of July. Given the go-ahead, the Cubans had moved quickly and in less than a month the airstrip was up and running. Judging by the coming and goings at the crude airfield, the Cubans stayed busy at their work. Yet, Fidel Castro was still in power, having survived the recent Bay of Pigs fiasco and neither Tom Ryan nor Mr. Salas had been able to return to Cuba and their holdings there. At least Tom Ryan hadn't.

But he didn't want to ponder over the Cubans this morning. It was too nice of one to waste on matters he couldn't affect in any way. Besides, thoughts of the Cubans inevitably led him to Tom Ryan, who was not the same man he had conversed with at the Governors Club the summer before. The stroke had seen to that. Now, a man who just a short time back had been eager to go after a house and lands improperly seized by a Communist dictator, lay abed in his home not a mile east of the old hotel, a rotting husk of what he once had been, shallow breathing and the blinking of his eyes the only evidence he was still alive.

Funny, but the Governors Club, a good fifteen years or more before his conversation with Tom Ryan, had been the site of another disaster in the making: the wedding reception for his daughter Marilyn.

And that man she married. That son-of-a-bitch Tom Morgan. Who did exactly what John Raines knew he would. And who after breaking Marilyn's heart left her in New York City to pick up the pieces the best she could. Not only that, but to take care of their six-year-old son, alone, with no help from him, her family fifteen hundred miles away and unaware of any of it. She had toughed it out as best she could until finally one night, three months after the bastard left, desperate, the electric turned off, the pantry bare, except for a few canned goods for the child, and with no one else to turn to, Marilyn picked up the phone and called home.

Now she was gone, too. Apparently not dead because they received the occasional card or brief letter from her. But gone. Sadie and he left to raise the boy. Thomas Morgan, Jr. Tommy. The only good thing to come from the union of John Raines daughter and that bastard. It certainly didn't take a genius to see that.

A good thing indeed—and leaving it on that note he turned again to the paper, and his coffee, wanting to finish both before the boy came to get him and they set out to do what they had planned for the day.

***

"Pop!"

He had heard the boy earlier, rousting out of bed at first light, the flushing of the toilet in the bathroom separating the two bedrooms, followed by the padded sound of bare feet on the hardwood floor as the boy moved around in his room getting dressed. Now the boy called out to his grandfather from the kitchen in the rear of the house. John Raines always thought of him as "the boy" but Tommy—or Tom, as he preferred to be called now—was really a young man. He was eighteen and off to university soon. Raines wondered if his friends still called him Tommy. He'd ask him today if he got the chance. Not that it mattered for much more than just one of those curious thoughts Raines got on occasion. Curious thoughts he got about a whole range of things and wondered why, at his age, he even bothered.

"I'll be getting the horses ready, Pop," the boy called out again "Did you hear me?"

"I did." Raines grabbed up the newspaper and empty coffee cup from the table and went inside the house. "I'm coming, boy." He had a brief, intense moment where he wanted to hug his grandson before he disappeared to the barn to saddle up the horses. "Just hold on a minute."

"Don't rush, Pop," the boy said, still unseen in the kitchen and as suddenly as it had come the longing in John Raines passed. "There's grub on the stove for you. Eat your breakfast and meet me out front when you're ready." Raines heard the sound of the back door closing shut behind the boy as he went out outside and then he was alone in the house.

A cast iron skillet sat on the stove filled with scrambled eggs and sausage bits. The eggs were still steaming warm when he ladled a big spoonful into one of the pewter plates he liked to use when Sadie wasn't around. That woman was a stickler for the china, he thought, as he sat down with his food at the rickety table in the corner of the kitchen. The pewter reminded him of his boyhood on his father's tobacco farm in Georgia. One of the few good memories. There were others he was certain, even if he mainly remembered the ones that weren't, a bad trait he seemed to have acquired not long after Hilton died.

Preference for china or not, Sadie Raines had certainly taught her grandson to be a fine cook and Raines wolfed the breakfast down, grateful his wife had passed along her kitchen skills to their grandson. He and the boy would've been on thin rations, otherwise, at times like this when Sadie was away. At the moment she was down in Fort Lauderdale for the week, visiting with their daughter-in-law and the other grandson. Emmitt. The one who looked so much like his father that John Raines still ached for a moment whenever he saw him.

Raines cooking skills were basic, to say the least. He could scramble eggs if he had to. Could fry them, too, though usually the yolks broke. He might even have added the sausage bits had he thought to. His forte, if you could call it that was boiled chicken, rabbit, or squirrel, a method of cooking prevalent on Lewis Raines farm after his wife passed away and he was left to feed his boys. He guessed his father had passed the taste for boiled meat along to his middle son. As it turned out, this stood John Raines in good stead when he entered the army and boiled meat seemed to be the only item on the menu.

Thankfully, Sadie was a wonder in the kitchen. She had certainly opened up Raines eyes, along with his taste buds, to the delights of other forms of cuisine. This, in turn, served him well when it came to wining and dining clients. She had taught him many other wonderful things, even if the best of them, and because of their age, they didn't enjoy much anymore.

Of course, cooking wasn't the only thing Sadie Raines taught her grandson. He wouldn't be entering the university in two weeks if that were the case. The mornings at the dining room table with the schoolbooks and tests she brought up from Lauderdale, had paid off. His grades on the entrance exam were above average and coupled with the fact the current president of the school had hunted on the Raines ranch over the years and was familiar with the boy, had secured Tommy his admission. So that in two weeks the boy would be off to school, Raines and Sadie left behind, alone on the ranch.

They had been alone before. Raines scraped the pewter plate clean and rinsed it in the sink, letting the warm water from the tap dissolve the left-over bits of egg. Alone all those nights at the big house on the Isle after Hilton was dead and Marilyn up in New York with her husband. Without Sadie, that time would have been even harder on him than it was. Of that there was no doubt in his mind. At night, together in bed, the sounds of boats moving on the New River not far from the house, drifting in through the open windows, they had known how to comfort one another, the two of them going to that place where, just for a little while, none of the rest mattered.

As before—when he had suddenly longed to hug his grandson—Raines missed his wife. Missed her badly. She'd be home that evening, though. He and the boy would have a good day together in the scrub counting stray head. When Sadie pulled the Cadillac into the yard the house would be all lit up, the two men waiting for her, and everything would be as it should be. Thinking of this the ache of missing his wife softened in John Raines guts.

The sound of creaking leather, the soft metal jangle of a bridle in a horse's mouth, came from outside. Looking through the window above the kitchen sink Raines caught a glimpse of the boy leading the big Arabian, Prince, around to the front of the house. To the hitching post and rails they had erected not long after the boy came to live with them. It could be a way of getting to know his grandson better, John thought at the time, this working together on a simple project, yet one that required the digging of holes, pouring of concrete, and the use of hammer and nails.

Though he was only eight years old at the time, Tommy turned out to be a pretty good worker. He did as he was instructed, did not get in the way, and managed to come away from the project with only a few minor scrapes and bruises. Standing back after the last coat of stain had been applied to the bare wood, the hitching post gleaming in the spring sunlight had been plenty enough reward for Raines. If the look on his face as he stood next to his grandfather was an indicator, then for the boy as well.

That look was on the boy's face every time they tied their horses up to the varnished rail. It faded only when he had grown older. After his life on the ranch had become established fact, the daily chores, the bedroom he slept in at night, his grandfather, grandmother, the horses, dogs, cattle, pine scrub, creeks, and lakes, that made up his life there. Not taken for granted necessarily but accepted for what they were.

Remembering how Tommy had slowly, but surely, changed from the nervous little boy on the doorstep that long ago night with his mother, Raines hadn't noticed the boy returning to the barn. Now, hearing again the creaking of leather and the soft plodding of horse hooves on the dirt, he looked up from his thoughts and saw the boy leading the other horse they would be using that day out of the barn.

Damn it all to hell. As always, the sight of Booger bothered him. The horse was a beautiful creature, no doubt, part quarter horse, part Tennessee walker, just shy of fifteen hands and possessing a coat deep burnt brown in color that set off nicely the four white stockings on his forelegs. A rich black mane and flashing dark eyes added to the intensity of the horse—intensity evident to Raines the first time he laid eyes on the animal. It was the end of the Labor Day Rodeo in Okeechobee three years back, and Booger, to the viewing delight of Raines and his grandson, was foiling the attempts of his owner to lead him into a horse trailer. Jack hammering his hooves in the dust of the corral the horse maintained a prancing, sideways gait that kept him just out of arm's reach whenever the old cowboy approached him to slip a metal hackamore over his head.

Now there's a horse that wants to run, John Raines thought. Not from any fear. But just for the pure sake of doing so.

"Goddammit Brownie, now hol' still for one minute, damn it," the cowboy said as he eased up to the horse again.

"That horse for sale?" John Raines called out and the cowboy stopped in his tracks. Why he didn't back away from what he'd just said Raines wondered about for the next three years. It was like he just couldn't stop himself. "By any chance?"

"Hell man, the way I'm feeling right now I'll give 'em to you. Thought I was getting the best of the hand with that fellow. Surely four eights had to be a winner. She-et. Guess I was the loser after all."

With a sheepish smile on his face the boy couldn't help but laugh.

"You think this is funny?" There was a fighting light in the cowboy's eyes, the frustration of dealing with the horse hadn't completely put out. "Some little act I like to put on come Sunday afternoons 'cause I got nothin' better to do?"

"No, not at all," John said, sorry he and the boy had offended the man, which had not been his intention at all. "But if that's how you feel about the horse then maybe I can put you back on top. Just give me a price."

"I'll sell you the horse, mister. I jes' hope you the sort who likes a little adventure."

"What sort of 'adventure' are we talking about?" Raines asked. "And how much for the horse?"

"A hunnert dollars will do jes' fine," the rancher. "Hell, if you only got fifty, I'll take that, too."

"No," Raines laughed. "I feel like I'm cheating you at one hundred."

"She-et. You ain' cheatin' me,'" the rancher said. "Yo're doing me a favor."

"What about that 'adventure' you spoke of," Raines persisted.

"I reckon you'll find out. But let me warn you: he's a real booger all right. Comes and go as he damn well please. An' usually 'bout a hunnert miles an hour if he gets the chance. When he stops, he stops, boy. Jes' like that. Last week my wife give him one more chance and he threw her right into the chicken pen. I wanted to shoot the sonofabitch then and there, but she wouldn't let me. Clipped nuts, or no, that horse is jes' plain wild. Pretty, maybe, but not worth a good tinker's dam. Not in my book, at any rate."

"He sounds like a firecracker, all right," John Raines said.

"Yessir. Don't say I didn' warn you."

The three of them were finally able to get the horse into the rancher's trailer with only one misstep, that being when the rancher came up behind the horse without thinking and received a kick in his shins that sent him backwards off the lowered ramp. Picking himself up from the ground and dusting his clothes with his straw Stetson, he gave Raines that sheepish grin again.

"See? Whut I tell you boys? That horse is a sonofabitch!"

The cowboy followed Raines and the boy from the rodeo grounds in Okeechobee all the way to the Raines property. Out of concern from the fact it was obvious the man had been drinking a good part of the day, that it would be full dark for his return trip on two-lane country roads that were dangerous enough under good conditions, Raines had argued against this. In the morning, he said, when they were both fresh, he'd come with his own trailer and pick up the horse. Really, there was no need for him to go out of his way like that, what with the night coming on and him tired and worn out from his long day at the rodeo. But the man insisted, hopping into the cab of his beat-up Ford pickup, tilting a bottle of dark whiskey to his lips before grinding the truck into first gear.

"Let' er rip, pardner," the rancher grinned from behind the steering wheel at John Raines and his grandson. "As the ol' poet said sumwheres: 'an' miles to go 'fore I sleep.' Or sumthin' like that. Let's go!"

The cowboy had called the horse, Brownie, a name neither Raines nor the boy particularly liked. Instead, they re-named him Booger, as the cowboy had referred to him the day Raines bought him Three years later John Raines detested the horse—didn't think he'd ever dislike an animal as much as he did Booger. In that time span the horse had tossed the boy a number of times, most of them with only minor injuries, the worst of them being two broken ribs. But the boy bore up under his injuries with admirable grace and still continued to ride the horse. The incident that turned Raines away from Booger completely was the day Sadie, at the boy's teasing, mounted Booger and rode him out of the yard.

The smile on his wife's face that spring morning was something Raines would never forget, her look of triumph as she trotted Booger up and down the dirt road in front of the house, gray hair streaming out from beneath a cowgirl hat perched jauntily atop her head, the boy and he cheering her on. He could remember thinking then that perhaps this was the key: Booger was a woman's horse. Just as he was remembering the rancher telling him how the final straw for him had been when Booger tossed his wife into the chicken pen, Booger broke into a full gallop, stopping as suddenly as he had begun, and with all four hooves in locked position, threw a screaming Sadie Raines over his head and into a fence post at the end of the drive.

While Raines and the boy helped Sadie to her feet, Booger trotted off a few paces, and then bowed his head to graze. Sadie received a dislocated collar bone for her troubles that took two months to heal and Raines swore that given just one more good reason to do so, he'd take the horse out and shoot him.

That had been a year ago and the only time the horse had been ridden since was when Cecil, the ranch foreman, on a whim asked if he could give him a go. It had worked out about the way Raines expected. Now the boy had gone and saddled Booger up and damned if Raines could figure why. Other than the fact that it was a beautiful late summer morning, and the boy would be leaving for school in a short while, and perhaps, like the challenge the university would be, the boy wanted to give Booger one more try.

Goddamn that horse, Raines thought as he rinsed his breakfast dishes in the sink. I should have sold that demon to Cecil last spring when I had the chance instead of letting the boy talk me out of it. Booger's not near the animal the Arabian is. Prince. A good name for that one. A gift for a princess. Raine's princess, in fact. Marilyn. His sweet daughter who he would have done anything for anytime she asked and did so. Sadly, the gift, the stallion, hadn't achieved the desired end, though. His little girl still left. Still married that damnable man, leaving Raines with the horse. A horse who by default became his own, the only one he ever rode.

With the Arabian's pale grey color, his long flowing pale mane, the two horses, Prince and Booger certainly made an odd match. The one tall and stately, even more dignified now that he was approaching his twentieth year. And the gelded, squirrely little devil of a quarter horse mix, burnt brown and eager to go. Yet, there you have it, Raines thought. A lot of his life had involved odd matches, man and beast alike, horses, children, hunting dogs, and friends. Some of which he may have wished to change or remove from the picture at times but hadn't been able to do so. The horse, Booger, a case in point.

But there was nothing to be done for it now. The boy had made his choice. John Raines went to get his boots, figuring to go ahead and make the best out of what he considered a poor decision. Pray for the best be more like it, he thought as he pulled on the last boot and headed out the screen porch, into the yard where his grandson and the two horses awaited.

***

"Pego off his feed this morning?"

Raines checked the cinch strap of Prince's saddle, giving it one hard, solid pull, pleased when he found no slack in the sturdy hemp strap. As usual, the boy had done a good job saddling the horses.

"Sir?"

"I'm just surprised you didn't saddle up the gelding." Raines, one hand on the rump of the big Arabian, came around behind the horse and placed a few strips of jerky in the boy's saddle bag. "Or Old Dan. 'Stead of this one."

"Pego, and Old Dan would have been suitable for today's ride, I imagine." The boy's grin was wide and bright in the sunlight beneath his straw-like hair. "I just thought Booger here might bring a little excitement to an otherwise routine day."

"I'm sure he's capable of it." Raines un-tethered the Arabian and backed him away from the hitching post. "You know how I feel about that horse."

"Yes sir, I do. And I think you've got him all wrong. He's high-spirited no doubt. But he means well. Besides, he could use some exercise. No one's ridden him since he tossed Cecil in the palmettos last spring."

"High spirited is one way of putting it, I suppose. Ride the devil if you must. It's your funeral."

The boy laughed as he swung up into the saddle. As effortlessly as his mother used to, Raines thought. She would've liked that little quarter-horse half-breed, too. Would've bedeviled me to ride him no matter how many times I said no.

"Too nice a day for talk of funerals, Pop. If you're nice to me, mebbe I'll let you ride this little firecracker."

The boy slapped the ends of the reins against Booger's rump and horse and boy bolted, out of the yard like a shot out of a cannon and leaving Raines behind. He had to give it to that horse. Unfortunately.

Booger was fast all right. Might have been a good horse, too. If he'd had a trainer other than a drunken fool, who after winning him in a game of five card stud in Okeechobee and possessing no idea at all of what to do with such a horse, set about ruining him for anyone else.

The boy yelled something that Raines couldn't catch over his shoulder as the galloping horse raced him up the dirt two-track, his white hooves kicking up a trail of dust in his wake. A breeze coming across the field held that dust in the air for what seemed a long time until the sunlight shattered Raines' momentary illusion, turning the cloud of fine dust invisible as he trotted Prince out onto the road after the boy.

"C'mon Pop," and now Raines could hear what his grandson was saying. He had managed to rein Booger up some two hundred yards down the road where he stopped to turn in his saddle to look back. The smile across his face might be barely visible in the distance that separated them, but Raines knew it was there just the same. "We're burnin' daylight, I tell you!"

The boy spurred Booger into a steady trot—trot and run being the only two speeds the horse was really comfortable with. Two can play that game, Raines decided. Leaning forward over the saddle horn he whispered in Prince's ear "Let's show 'em what we're still made of Big Feller."

Tapping the big stallion in the ribs twice with his boot heels, the yellow Arabian broke out into a full gallop, legs stretched out as Raines urged him on. A wild whoop of joy burst from his lungs and the loud thudding of hooves against the dry dirt of the road, keeping time with the pounding of his heart, they swept past his grandson and Booger. He heard the surprised laughter of the boy but didn't look back. Instead, Raines kept his head low over the stallion's neck until they reached the first bend in the road, Tommy and Booger hard on their heels. The whole of Raines existence seemed caught up in the thudding of hooves as they rounded the bend and into the straight stretch that ran for another quarter mile or so, the whooping Rebel Yell he couldn't seem to stop, the rush of air against his face, the horse beneath his thighs. It was the best he had felt in a long time. Since Tom Ryan's stroke, maybe.

Since the Cubans came and built the airstrip, intruding on his structured life.

It was a wild, good feeling and he was glad to share it with the boy. But they had a long day yet ahead of them, the horses would need all they had, and well before the next turn in the two-track where it turned to run north again. Raines decided it was time to end the race.

"Whoa boy." Raines pulled back on the reins with one hand, raising the other in a signal for the boy coming on behind to slow it down. The leather reins were dry and soft in his fingers as he used them to guide the horse into a steady trot. Not even damp, he thought. The big stallion hadn't even begun to lather even with the warm humid air of the September morning. As always, he marveled in the strength of the animal in its older years.

"That's not fair, Pop." The boy was laughing, his eyes and mouth wide and shining, as they came abreast of Raines. "Ol' Booger here was just getting his stride. We'd have beaten you to the turn easy."

"Perhaps." But Raines knew it wasn't so. If he had given Prince his head the little quarter-horse mix would never have caught them. Not even with all the speed he was bred to possess. "But we've more to do today than horse racing up and down these dusty roads."

"Still, you've got to promise me a rematch before I leave for Gainesville. And this one with no tricks!"

"We'll see," John said, adding, "Booger seems to be on his best behavior today."

"He's not so bad, I tell you.' In the boy's face Raines could see the conviction behind his words.

"We'll see," Raines said again.

The horses trotted along in matching stride, occasionally Booger breaking away in that prancing sideways step of his, that though it looked pretty, infuriated Raines. At the start of the northward bend in the road, where a lightening shattered pine lay across the drainage ditch running the west side, with no word passed between them, man and boy headed east, stepping off into the wiregrass prairie. By the time another hour had passed both men and horses were sweating. The sun seemed even hotter out on the wiregrass with no shade anywhere to break it. Other than the men on horseback, the only thing moving in the mid-morning sun was an occasional dragonfly or buzzard wheeling overhead in the hazy sky. Game and birds had finished with their foraging long before, holed up now in the brush up above the creek running east and west across the property to the north of where Raines and his grandson rode.

As the sun beat on his face, Raines could visualize how it might be in the shade of the creek bottom: squirrels chattering in the branches of the mossy oaks overhanging the slowly moving water. A bobcat, coming down to drink from the cool water of the creek and the rise of a bluegill on a spinner caught in the easy current. Right behind that bluegill, perhaps a bass seeking easy prey as well. Most likely, though, both bass and bluegill were not feeding, but lazing up in the shade offered by the oak trees, or swimming slowly in the currents of the deeper pockets of water in the middle of the creek.

On those days when he had nothing more pressing to do, Raines—with the boy most often, though sometimes Sadie came, too—he liked to take a coffee can full of fresh earthworms down to the creek and sit up on the wooden bridge crossing it, fishing for bass and whatever else took the wriggling, tempting bait. Hilton and TJ helped Raines build that bridge thirty years before shortly after Raines had acquired the property. The old one had rotted badly, badly enough that the north end of it lay collapsed in the creek bed. For a week, Raines, his son, and Raines' younger brother worked until the new pilings were up, the planks in place, and it was safe again to drive a vehicle across. The bridge was still there. Unlike two of the fragile humans who had worked to make it so.

"Hey," Tommy up ahead on Booger called out. Faced into the rising sun the light coming down through the hazy sky made the boy and horse shadows against the copse of green palmettos and pine trees Tommy pointed at. "Looks like one of 'em's holed up in there."

Two actually, a cow and her calf as it turned out, the first of the stray beeves they were riding east to the fence line to locate. The boy and horse circled the clump of palmettos, Tommy slapping against the sharp stalks of the gnarly bush with his reins until the two cows flushed out into the open prairie. In a little notebook he carried in his top pocket Raines marked the location and number of beeves, information he'd give to Cecil later. It would be up to Cecil, and his crew of rough and ready young cow hunters, to come out later and drive the strays back to the main herd for the fall branding. Raines and the boy had the easiest part of that hard work, and with the finding of these first two beeves Raines put aside his thoughts of bridge building and people no longer in his life.

\*\*\*

Booger threw Tommy a little past eleven o'clock that morning. They were busy trying to flush a young steer from a clump of scrub when Raines heard the faint droning of a plane lifting off from the Cuban's airstrip to the west. A few minutes later the plane passed overhead, white against the hazy sky, the late morning sun glinting off its silvery fuselage and wings. As the plane banked southeast toward Cuba, heading out of sight, Raines heard Booger snorting loud and anxiously.

The rest of it happened so fast Raines barely had time to register it as he wheeled Prince around to see what Booger's commotion was about. Booger, reared up on his hind legs, was flailing wildly at the sky with his front hooves as the boy held desperately to the saddle horn. The straw Stetson Raines had insisted the boy wear seemed suspended above boy and horse in mid-air. In another moment Booger had all four legs down on the ground and the straw hat was nowhere in sight. Booger didn't stay grounded for long, rearing up again in a hard jerking motion that was more your standard rodeo bucking than anything else.

If the boy hadn't let his guard down just then to push the hair back out of his eyes, he might have stayed in the saddle. But his momentary lack of caution, along with Booger's sudden rodeo bucking act, sent the boy flying off the horse, much like the straw hat had flown from his head just seconds before.

"Well Goddamn," John Raines shouted as he dismounted. He let the reins drop from his hand, leaving the big Arabian to graze as he ran across the field to his fallen grandson. Meanwhile, Booger, just as he had the day he tossed Sadie Raines into the fence post, sauntered away to graze, as if nothing violent, or out of place, had just occurred.

"Damn it," John Raines shouted again as he reached his grandson and took him in his arms. Bending over the boy Raines forgot his anger for the moment as he asked, "Jesus, boy, are you all right."

"I'm okay." The boy struggled out of his grandfather's tight grasp; the arms wrapped across his chest as he tried to catch his breath. "C'mon, Pop. Let me go. I'm not some baby you have to hug and rock when they fall down."

"Yes, I'm aware you're not a baby anymore."

"What happened?"

"Your favorite horse threw you, that's what happened. Here, grab my hand and let me help you up. If you're not too grown up, that is, to accept a man's offer of assistance?"

"No sir, I guess I'm not."

Raines pulled the boy to his feet, brushed loose grass and sand off his clothes and arms while Tommy rearranged his T-shirt and jeans that had gotten twisted up in the fall. Raines found the straw hat lying on the ground a few feet away and retrieved it, handing it to the boy as they walked over to Booger, who in his grazing had ended up with Prince.

"Wonder what spooked him to make him do such a thing," the boy said, grabbing up the horse's reins trailing on the ground.

"I doubt anything spooked him," John Raines said. "Other than his own natural desire to be contrary. It was only a question of time before he acted up this morning."

"Aw, I bet it was the plane coming out of nowhere like that."

But it was a weak defense for the horse—the boy knew it, and so did John.

"He's heard airplanes before."

"Yeah, I guess."

"That's what I thought."

The boy went to mount up, but Raines stopped him

"Hold on a minute, Tom. Let me ride that little troublemaker for a bit. Maybe it's time I gave Mr. Booger here a lesson in manners. God knows, he's been begging hard enough for one."

"Sir?"

"You heard me. Just sit here a spell with ol' Prince."

Raines stomach growled, reminding him it was getting on towards noon and lunchtime. Ignoring his stomach, he placed his left foot in the stirrup and holding onto the saddle horn and reins swung up into the saddle. Have to wait a little longer yet for that, he thought. One thing yet to do this morning and then we can eat. The horse jerked back a half step when Raines settled into the saddle, the horse nervous with the different weight on his back. Raines pulled hard on the reins, pulling the metal bit deep against the horse's soft under-jaw to put a stop to the nervous pacing. It was different for Raines, as well, being in the saddle atop Booger. For a long time, he had known only the height and feel of the Arabian beneath him when he rode. Now, he was atop this little horse, who, judging by the quivering of his flanks beneath Raines' thighs, was itching to burst into action.

"So, you want to get going, do you? Then let's see what you can do."

He kicked the horse hard in both sides with his heels as he slapped Booger's rump with the tail ends of the leather reins.

"Giddap!"

The word vanished from his hearing as suddenly as he had said it, lost in the pounding of Booger's hooves into the dry wiregrass.

There was no getting past it: the quickness of the little horse was a surprise. They shot across the open field as Raines continued to goad the horse on with his heels and the leather reins, and there simply seemed no end to how the fast the horse could run, or for how long. Caught up in it with the horse Raines yelled out again. "C'mon and run."

But as suddenly as he had spurred the little horse into galloping across the field Raines yanked back hard on the reins. Booger reared up, front legs clawing at the empty air as he danced back and forth on the two legs remaining on the ground. Leaning forward in the saddle Raines held on to the saddle horn and urged the horse's front hooves back down.

"Easy does it, you little devil," he whispered into Booger's ear. "You won't get rid of me that easily."

The horse brought his hooves down and stood quiet for a moment, panting heavily, and wondering—Raines hoped—what would come next. He didn't make Booger wait long to find out. Kicking the horse's sides with his heels again they set off once more at a full gallop, towards a slough running along the far edge of the field. Raines kept his eyes on the slough as Booger carried him pell-mell over the wiregrass. It was empty now from the dry summer that year. In wetter times, though, the slough turned into a shallow, running, creek, not wide or deep enough to sustain fish, but the water drinkable and the cattle and other creatures of the scrub did so. If one rode far enough north along its bed they would wind up eventually on the banks of the Loxahatchee River. Raines had no intention of going that far this morning, though. Just before the edge of the slough he yanked Booger's head hard to the right, so that they were racing parallel along the slough in the other direction. Booger was beginning to lather now, flecks of white foam spraying from his wide-open mouth that hit Raines on the sleeve covering his left arm. He would run him a little bit longer. Not enough to wind him. Not yet. But when they stopped it would be on his terms. Not Boogers. No sir. Raines wasn't going to allow that. Not today.

And just like that he jerked the horse's head again, this time to the left, wheeling him around full circle, forcing him to slow down, lest man and animal go over sideways in a dusty heap. The slough had come to an end, a dried-up rivulet more dirt than anything else, the only evidence moisture ever was a part of its course being two gnarled cypress trees growing along its sandy edge. The horse tried to run again but Raines pulled the metal bit deep into its mouth.

"Whoa, you sonofabitch. I said whoa! We'll run again when I say it's time to run."

As before, when Raines dug the metal bit all the way into the soft part of its jaws, Booger reared up. For the boy's benefit, more than anything else, this time Raines held the saddle horn with just one hand. With the other he waved his hat in the air like any cowboy at the rodeos in Okeechobee did when they were atop a bucking bronc.

"You're getting the idea, now," John said when Booger had all four hooves on the ground again. The horse's eyes were wild, and his breath came in angry snorts. "Oh yes, I know you're mad. You don't like finding out who's the boss, do you? That's just too damn, bad, though. Now get!"

He ran the horse hard, back across the field toward where the boy waited patiently with Prince beneath the shade of some live oaks growing close together up from the wiregrass. Maybe an eighth of a mile out Raines pulled the horse up and trotted him in the rest of the way, the horse snorting and blowing from its exertions, both man and horse hot and tired. Two buzzards circled lazily in the sky over the field, looking for carrion that wasn't there, while a lone hawk sat in the very top branches of a scraggly pine tree not far from where the boy waited with the other horse. It was high noon and tired and sweating and not sure if he had accomplished what he had wanted to, or not, still, Raines felt much as those three birds did.

"I'm hungry, boy," he said as he reined up beside his grandson. "Let's find a place where we can sit quietly in the shade and eat."

"Has he learned his lesson, Pop?"

The boy pointed at Booger with his free hand. Father's irritating smile, or not, it was contagious, at least this one time, and Raines smiled along with him

"Maybe," he said. "Not that I would bet money on it."

"You sure gave him hell." The boy lifted up into the saddle atop Prince and fell in beside his grandfather as he trotted off across the field. "I'll say that much."

"He'll be good for a while I imagine. I doubt it'll stick, though. He's way too spirited for his own good, I'm afraid."

"Like the man riding him?"

The boy's smile lifted John up away from the sweat-soaked weariness he had known for the last few minutes atop the little quarter-horse mix—when the excitement of racing across the open field had faded and what he was doing was just another job, plain and simple.

"Here's hoping you're right," Raines said. About the man at any rate."

"Oh, I am, Pop. I'm surely right about that."

***

Less than a mile from the slough, up against the barbed wire fence marking the northeast boundary of the property, stood a crude lean-to.

Raines and the boy made for it. It was Raines' intention to let the two horses graze on the sparse grass surrounding the building while they ate their lunch in the shade offered up by this shack.

There were two of these lean-tos on the property, rough line shacks built by Cecil, the foreman, and his cow hunters, this one on the northeast boundary and the other on the southwest fence line. It was a ramshackle affair, to say the least, and from experience Raines knew the one to the south wasn't much different. Three walls made of plywood, with small windows cut into each wall screened to keep the bugs out. A screen front with a canvas tarp pull-down if rain was coming from the southwest, and a tin roof, comprised the affair. The wooden walls, from lack of paint or varnish, stood warped and stained in the sunlight, the tin roof, when seen from a distance, laced with rust blotches. It wouldn't have surprised Raines to come up on it one day and find it just blown away. Yet, it had been there for a long while, warped walls and rusted roof a crude refuge for the cow hunters if inclement weather blew up and they were close enough to take advantage of the shelter the shack provided.

The outside amenities consisted of a stone fire pit, containing charred pieces of a shattered whiskey bottle and other burnt leavings from the not-so-distant past. A few paces away from the pit, Cecil and his boys had dug an artesian well, the brass pump handle shining dully in the noonday sun. Raines and the boy took turns washing their faces and hands at the pump, the Sulphur-smelling water, good and cold from deep underground, washing away the heat, dust, and grime from the work of the morning. The boy laughed as he watched his grandfather at his ablutions—the cool water, along with the laughter, helped to restore the good feelings Raines had known as they rode.

The cow hunters had placed a fold-out card table in the center of the shack, and while the boy took a seat on one of the two wooden benches built into the walls, Raines placed the old fishing creel he had brought along from the house, on the table. The creel contained their lunch: thick sandwiches made of cured Virginia ham on sourdough bread, topped with slices of Vidalia onions and covered with brown mustard. A Golden Delicious apple each for dessert rounded off the meal. To keep the lunch cool and fresh he had wrapped the sandwiches in wax paper and then covered them with damp cloths. Along with the sandwiches, he had packed bottles of mineral water. The strong water was not only good for quenching their thirst, but along with washing the food down, would rinse away any remaining grime in their mouths. Except for the lowing of a cow somewhere off in the scrub and the sounds of the humans eating, it was silent inside the shack as they ate.

"Mighty fine lunch, Pop," the boy said when he was finished. "You have a real skill with sandwiches." Resting his shoulders against the wall he stretched his legs out to the side of the card table; dust motes created by the shifting of his legs drifted up in the sunlight streaming through the windows and screen front of the shack. "It feels good to get off that horse for a bit, too, come to think of it."

"I guess you're not the only one who can whip up a meal when your grandmother's not around. And yes, it's good to get off the horses and stretch out."

"I miss Grandma. Glad she'll be home today."

"Me, too, son. Me, too."

It was quiet again and, in the silence, Raines studied the boy's features, wondering—and not for the first time—why only the father's and none of the mother's were present. For a weak sonofabitch that Tom Morgan had some strong genes. Not wanting the bitterness to sneak up on him again, wanting only to enjoy what was left of the day with his grandson, he closed his eyes and tried to think of other things.

"I hope I do okay in college," the boy said. "I really do."

The uncommon concern on the boy's face startled Raines and he was glad his wife, who doted on the boy, wasn't there to witness it.

"You'll do your best," he said. "That's all you can do. All anyone can expect. Certainly, that's all your grandmother and I expect from you."

He took the fishing creel on the rickety card table and put the wax paper that held the sandwiches and his empty water bottle in it, feeling a sudden need to do something.

"Have you put any thoughts into what you might study?"

"I imagine the law," the boy said. "I figure you kept that dusty set of "Blackstone's" around for a reason."

Raines insides lurched at the mention of the set of old law books and his possible 'reason' for keeping them in the bookshelves in the living room, not taken down, that he knew of, by anyone in a very long time, and the reason for keeping them, of course, his son, dead now for thirteen years.

"Well, don't go into law just because I did."

"Good!" The smile spreading across the boy's face seemed to light up the shadows playing across the walls of the shack "In that case I'll just stay here. Ask Cecil to find me a place in the bunkhouse with the rest of the boys."

"You and I both know that's not what you want to do with your life."

"That's the problem, Pop. I have no idea what I want to do. Seems like it'd just be easier to stay on for a while. To work for Cecil, learning more about the cattle ranching business, who knows? Maybe I'd end up being a gentleman rancher such as you."

"Then you're serious about this?"

"I don't know. Like I said. That's the problem"

"Cecil Bronson's a good man, and if I didn't raise any objection, I'm sure he'd take you on."

Raines tried to picture the boy as just one of Cecil's bunch — knowing how much his grandson loved everything about where he lived and grew up, it wasn't hard to do. Besides, who was he to tell someone how they should live their life? Hadn't his own father wanted him to stay on and take over the tobacco farm for him and he had refused? At a younger age even than the boy was now? Had insisted on going his own way and done so?

"The problem is, son, that I would object. For your own good. Hell, I've known Cecil for a long time. Longer than you, actually."

He smiled to himself for a moment, thinking about the burly, rough-hewn man who was his ranch foreman.

"He's a hard worker. No one can say he isn't. Works his boys hard, too. And is proud of making an honest living. Not that that was always the case."

"No?"

He had piqued the boy's attention, now, who had turned away when told Raines would object to his staying on.

"That's how I met Cecil in the first place. Over a slight difference of opinion between him and the federal government as to how the tax codes concerning the making and sale of alcoholic beverages should be applied."

"Cecil was a moonshiner?"

"That he was. Fortunately for Cecil, I was able to make Judge Grenner over at the Federal Courthouse in West Palm see how it was all just a big misunderstanding."

He remembered well that day at the courthouse in West Palm. Hilton had been gone a little over two years by then and Raines was in the process of moving what was left of his family from Fort Lauderdale to the ranch. He was practicing law in name only, had not taken on a client since his son's suicide. When the Legal Aid Society in Palm Beach contacted him about doing some pro bono work for them his first instinct had been to say he wasn't interested. Instead — and he suspected now that boredom settling in had played a part in his decision — he said yes to the lady on the telephone.

It rained the February morning he drove up to West Palm for the trial, that cold, and steady, drizzling sort of rain that came in the early winter, blowing in from the ocean and staying, before moving further inland to die out over Lake Okeechobee and the sugarcane fields. But when he pulled up to the courthouse the rains stopped, the sun came out, and for the first time in a long while Raines had the sudden thought that something good was going to happen.

Parking the car, he walked around to the front of the stern red brick building where a tall, heavy-set man with a long gray mustache, sideburns, and hair the same color hidden under a big Stetson, stood on the steps. The man's dress-up cowboy shirt was cleaned and pressed for the court, boots freshly polished as well, and Raines met Cecil Bronson for the first time.

Cecil's handshake was firm — stronger, as it turned out, than the prosecutor's case against him, and it didn't take much on Raines part to convince the judge that the hundred-pound bag of sugar in Cecil's trunk was for his livestock. Certainly not for an illegal whiskey still as the prosecutor contended. The charge was dismissed, Cecil walked free, and that was how John Raines last case came to an end. A year later he ran into Cecil at the feed store in Jupiter and when Raines mentioned he was looking for a foreman and a crew of cow hunters for a beef operation he was starting up, Cecil said he knew just the man.

"Was Cecil really guilty?"

"Hell yes!"

The roar of his sudden laughter in the small space surprised Raines, too, and it was a while before he and the boy were able to stop and he could continue.

"Cecil had been making and running whiskey for years out there in Indiantown and everybody knew it. The Feds could never get enough dope on him, though. No sir, that bunch in Indiantown knew how to keep a tight lip. The night the Revenue agents pulled Cecil over outside of Palm Beach and found that sugar in his trunk was only dumb luck on their part. The fact they didn't have anything else is what destroyed their case. That," and he smiled at the boy, "and my brilliant lawyering."

"I bet, Pop. You know? When you tell me stories like that, I can see how law could be a good choice for me."

"Well, not to take too hard on Cecil or his boy's stock in life, but they aren't ever going to be any more than what they are now: cow hunters. One or two of them may get lucky and wind up owning their own spread someday. But knowing that bunch down there it's unlikely. Law, or whatever else you choose, is fine with me. But not cow hunting. Or," and Raines chuckled, "moonshining."

"No. I don't see it for myself either, Pop." The boy tilted the bottle of mineral water to his lips and finished what was left of it. "What about those fellows over at the airstrip? Maybe I'll take up with them and help them bring down Castro."

"Why would you do such a thing?"

"Why did you allow them to build the air strip?"

The quickness and sharpness of the retort startled Raines.

"Because a very good friend asked me to. That was enough for me."

It was silent between them in the shack again and Raines was just starting to get up from the bench, having decided it was time to head back, when the boy spoke up.

"Pop?"

"Yes?"

"You ever think about my mother?"

"Yes, I do."

"I don't. I hate her."

It had been a long time since the boy had asked about his mother and never with the look on his face that was there now.

"How could you say such a thing?" Raines asked, though God knows he figured the boy had reason and then some.

"Because I do."

There had been another boy who hated his mother. After Thanksgiving it had been. 1948? '49? A lawyer's son to boot and like Raines grandson with plenty good reason to be angry with his mother. Raines hadn't known that boy very well. But he knew this one. The one sitting there in front of him Whose mother, half-drunk one January night ten years before, had left him with her parents, saying only that she had to do this for the good of the boy. That she had to find the husband who left her. That she could never rest easy again until she had gotten an answer from him as to why he had done so.

A mother, a daughter, who neither the boy nor John Raines had seen since that time, the only contact from her being the occasional letter, cards at Christmas, and the boy's birthdays, and the ever rarer drunken phone call late at night where she proclaimed over and over her sorrow at what she had done and that could not be undone now.

How untrue that was, Raines thought as he looked at his grandson in the shadowing light of the shack. Anything could be undone if the parties to the action were still alive. Yes, if they were still alive and willing to do so.

"My father told me something once that has stayed with me," Raines said. "I was asking him about the war, what he had done, what he had seen. I suppose I was a little younger than you. Well now, I had to be because by the time I was your age now I'd been gone from the farm four years. Come to think of it, RL was there—he was slopping the hogs while my father and I talked because even then RL didn't have much use for our dad. TJ hadn't been born yet. My brothers," and he looked now at the boy sitting across the rickety table from him in the line shack. "Of course, you never knew your great-uncles, both of them being dead long before you were born."

Raines stopped for a moment to catch his breath. The small space of the shack suddenly crowded with the memories of his brothers. Of his father, who he had last seen alive in the tobacco rows of their farm outside Pendleton on a hot July afternoon when he had just knocked Lewis Raines down for the first and last time.

"My father, that morning, was telling me about the last day at Gettysburg. How, when Pickett's men set out across the field that afternoon, he saw through his spyglass how the South's artillery barrage hadn't achieved its goals and he tried to send word to stop the charge. But it was too late and instead he watched Pickett's men get shot to ribbons and he didn't think he'd ever forget the sick feeling that came over him then. And of course, me being young and brash and full of envy for our Southern heroes I blurted out, 'Those Goddamn Yankees! I hate 'em all!'"

Now, as soon as I'd said this, I realized what I'd done, the using the Lord's name in vain. Not that my father was a religious man. But my mother certainly was, and he was honor bound to uphold her feelings towards that, so I was expecting immediate repercussions, if you will. Instead, he just looked at me with that half grin of his that came over him the few times I can recall him ever really looking at me. And he told me how these days he tried mightily to live as a man without hate. Said in a world such as ours he realized it was a hard task. But that he tried. Even though he failed mightily at times.

"That's what he told me, son, back then, one of the few things he ever said that stayed with me because he didn't let on to us children, or his wife even, any of who Lewis Raines really was. But that stayed with me."

What Raines didn't speak of was how that was the last conversation of any substance between him and his father. They didn't speak of how that winter his mother, shortly after giving birth to TJ, took a chill, came down with a fever and died of pneumonia. They didn't speak of how from that time on Lewis Raines, other than what had to be done to feed himself and his sons, and to deal briefly with the outside world, buried whatever was left of him deep inside.

"Do you think he succeeded, Pop? At not hating anyone?"

"Like he told me, Tom, he tried. Mostly he seemed bitter, though. So, I think, to answer your question, no, he did not. It's still good advice, though."

"How about you, Pop? Have you been able to live that way?"

"Like him, maybe, on some days. Hell, most days, really. But hopefully you'll have better luck with it than me or my father. And be able to live like that all the time."

"I doubt it. Not when it comes to my mother. For sure not today."

Raines saw in his grandson's face how that was very true. Tired of the past and where the present might be going and thinking how very much he wanted to see his wife, he jumped to his feet.

"Well, today won't last forever. But c'mon. Let's work our way back. I'd like to be home when your grandmother gets there."

"Sounds good to me."

Outside, with the afternoon sunlight harsh on his eyes from being in the shack too long, Raines whistled up his horse, a desire so strong inside of him suddenly that he could almost taste it, of wanting to be home—wanted this day, that had been so back and forth with good things and some that were not, to be done.

***

But Raines changed his mind, about one thing, at least, and said as they were starting to mount up, "Hold on there, son."

The boy had his foot in the stirrup and both reins clutched in the hand grasping the saddle horn when his grandfather stopped him

"Sir?"

"If you don't mind, I'd like to ride that little devil in. Make sure his recent 'lesson' stays fresh. If it hasn't sunk in, then I'll be there to remind him again how it goes."

"I don't mind at all, Pop."

Raines wasn't sure why he decided to change horses, to ride Booger home—other than it was simply one of those sudden whims that when he said it aloud made perfect sense. It was certainly all right with the boy, whose smile spread even wider across his face, if that were possible, with the idea of riding a horse that no one but his grandfather was ever allowed to.

And my daughter, Raines thought. And just like that, with one sudden bitter thought of the past, the good feeling the idea of being home soon had washed over him, was torn away.

The bitterness was enough that the boy had noticed.

"You sure about this, Pop?"

"Now, now, there's nothing to be afraid of, Tom," Raines said. "I rode the meanness out of Prince a long time ago."

"That's not what I was worried about."

Raines knew that was certainly true—knew for a fact a horse didn't exist the boy wouldn't attempt to ride, if given the chance.

"You looked sick for a minute."

"I'm fine," Raines said. "Let's go."

The matter was dropped, and they rode away from the line shack, the quick, nervous gait of the little quarter horse mix beneath him a good distraction for Raines. Enough, he found, to keep his mind away from the other. To the west dark clouds had begun to build and the air in front of the looming storm hung wet and hot on the open prairie. Raines hoped they made it in before the skies opened—hoped they could have the horses put away, be washed up, and in clean clothes before the storm broke. It would be nice, after a day such as this, to sit back with a Manhattan on the front porch and savor the coolness that would come in the aftermath of the storm. If he were really lucky Sadie would be home, as well, and they could enjoy the remainder of the afternoon, he with his drink, and she with one of those weak martinis she favored on the occasions she joined him for an afternoon drink.

It was a selfish thought, he supposed. To have it that easy. But hadn't he done enough for one day? For an old man? Between culling and counting stray beeves in the palmetto scrub, the lesson he had taught Booger, the conversation over lunch with the boy and where that had taken him, he was worn out. Ready for a nap, that refuge of the young, the old, and the sick. Though of the three to the best of his knowledge he was only old.

But just as he went to kick Booger up into a canter, an easy gait, and one sufficient to get him and the boy on Prince, back to the house with time to spare before the storm, two unrelated events occurred.

The first was a jagged slash of lightning, followed by a slow, rolling clap of thunder, in the distant sky to the west. The storm was moving faster than he originally thought. In the quiet after the lightning and thunder had faded away, the air hung deathly still, the ocean breezes blowing hard in their faces all morning gone. Also gone, as Raines saw now, any chance of arriving home high and dry.

The second event concerned a new sound—that of a small plane coming in off the ocean. Something sounded wrong, though. As Raines strained to hear more clearly, he realized that instead of the healthy, steady vibrations of a motor in good working condition, this one sputtered and broke up, the sound of it rising and falling in the quiet hanging over the prairie. He turned in his saddle just as the plane came into view, a dot way above the horizon growing bigger and bigger before disappearing into a fluffy cloud bank above the ocean, only to reappear after another long second, the silvery fusillade obscured by dark smoke blowing out from the engine cowling drifting up to be lost in the cloud bank.

"Pop!" The boy, turned in the saddle like Raines was, pointed at the plane coming closer and closer.

"I see it, son."

"That plane's in trouble!"

"It most certainly is."

Easy enough for him to say, from the safety of being on the ground, perhaps. But it was undeniable, and unlike the courtrooms and judges and juries Raines had practiced his craft before reasonable doubt would play no part in the plane's fate. The airstrip, and a safe landing, were too far away—that much was obvious. Worse, Raines could think of no suitable alternative where the pilot might put down. It was all pine and palmetto and broken field everywhere he looked, none of it clear enough for a plane to land.

"We'd better hold up here for a bit, Tom," Raines said, keeping the reins tight on the little horse, which had gone skittish with the sudden uncertainty around him "We'll see where he puts down. When he does, he'll need our help."

The wind had shifted a little to the northeast, enough maybe, to hold the thunderstorm at bay. For a little while, at any rate. With a little luck that pilot might land the plane in one piece and they would all get home high and dry. When the excitement of it all had died down, maybe even share a joke or two over a strong drink about the seriousness of their recent experience.

But when the plane came in overhead the straining engine blew. Not so much in a violent, ear-shattering explosion, Raines was surprised to find, but just a gentle popping sound, followed by flames and thick clouds of dark smoke billowing out behind it. The next thing he knew the plane simply turned nose down and dove straight into the ground. What did they say in books and the movies? It all happened so fast. Exactly, was Raines last thought, before the plane crashed in a fireball of flame rising up from the open field.

It was too much for Booger. He whinnied once, a high, almost feminine wail, when the shockwaves of the crash and resulting fireball washed over him and his rider. Raines, looking back to see where, and what the boy was doing, noticed the difference in the horse's manner but didn't have time to react. Booger, unattended, did what came naturally to him He reared up on his hind legs, front hooves clawing at the empty air before them, the back ones scrabbling nervously in the grass for purchase. Instead of loosening his grip on the reins and leaning forward in the saddle to urge the horse down, Raines held tight on the leather straps—and by doing so, pulled the horse all the way over.

He was conscious then of going over backward, still in the saddle, one hand clutching the saddle horn; was conscious of how very strange it was to be staring up at the sky from beneath the horse like that. When his back hit the ground and the full weight of the little quarter-horse mix followed on top of him, driving the hard leather stub of the saddle horn deep into his stomach, like the little plane before that had suddenly fallen out of the sky, everything inside of Raines seemed to explode.

He was aware of Tommy leaning over him,

"C'mon, Pop. Wake up."

The urgency in the boy's voice bothered him even more than the fact he had passed out. For how long, he wondered? It couldn't have been long, for he didn't even know he had. A searing wave of liquid pain ripped across his lower stomach where the weight of the horse and saddle were still centered. Caught up in the intensity of it, and unable to stop himself, he groaned.

"C'mon Pop," the boy said again, his voice high and thin sounding above the flames starting to crackle from the plane. "I've got to get you out of here."

Sitting down by Booger's haunches and resting his hands palm down on the ground for support, he pushed with his boots against the horse's quivering flanks. Booger, it appeared, was only too happy for the boy's help. Snorting and whinnying all the while the horse managed to twist his body over to one side and scramble up once more on his legs. The struggling movements from the horse served to grind the pain even deeper into Raines' guts, who up until then hadn't thought it could hurt any worse.

Funnier still, if he could call it funny, was how when the horse, and saddle horn digging into him, were lifted, the pain was still there, something he hadn't believed would be the case until he tried to sit up.

"Oh dear God in Heaven," Raines groaned, letting his head and shoulders fall back on the ground, and wondering that he could hurt so bad and still be alive.

The crackling of the plane on fire less than a hundred yards from where he lay filtered into his attention. With the horse falling on him, and the pain that followed, he had forgotten the plane. The sound, and smell of it burning brought it back to him, if only for a moment. Enough to know if the storm to the west of them didn't come on soon, they stood a good chance of burning to death. A sobering thought, he supposed — to desire a soggy end in fresh grass out in the middle of nowhere with the earth clean and damp after a good summer storm unlike the poor bastard in the plane.

With any luck it was the crash that killed him and not the flames. Either way, the result was the same. But one didn't survive the sort of pain coursing through Raines' insides. Everything in there was crushed, a liquid mess he could feel oozing out of him. He lifted his head and looked down the length of his body, grateful by what he saw that Sadie wasn't there with him He wished the boy hadn't seen, either but he had. They had both seen the rusty red puddle soaking into the grass beneath John Raines groin.

"We've got to go," the boy said, twisting his head away from the sight. At least, Raines thought, he sounded calmer now and maybe because by getting the horse off of his grandfather he had done something useful. The boy would be okay. Would know what had to be done. "Let's get you up on Prince and go home."

The idea of being back on the big Arabian was a good one. Even if Raines knew it wasn't going to happen. But it brought back those memories of other days riding that horse, sometimes with Sadie on Old Dan, or the boy on the gelding, Pego, and sometimes the three of them together.

What Raines had liked best were the all-day trips to the ocean. He thought of how good Sadie always looked in her riding habit. The faded blue jeans, worn leather boots, and light blue Lady Western shirt she favored when they rode together. Oh my God yes, but she looked so fine then with her black hair streaming out behind her as they cantered east across open fields toward the ocean, land that was still wild then, as was his wife. Before the weight of Hilton's death fell on her—before the added weight of Marilyn's running off.

Yes, she was still pretty, and wild, and free when no one was looking. When it was just her, him, and the horses, and the ocean lying on the other side of the sand dunes. When on a hot summer's day, sweating after the long ride, the breezes cooling them off. The ocean and the beach and running wide and long in both directions—no one else there, just Sadie, and he atop the line of dunes stretching north and south.

The boy was saying again how they needed to get out of there and Raines groaned and said, no. And said, "Let me lie here a minute, son and collect my wits before you try to get me up on that horse."

He was only stalling for time, he knew. Time for what? The boy wasn't buying into it.

"We've got to go now, Pop. You can collect your wits once I've got you up on Prince and we're away from here."

"The pilot," Raines started to say but the boy cut him off.

"There's nothing to be done for him. But you're still alive. I plan to keep it that way."

There was merit to what the boy said, if only a little. Raines wished the pilot of the plane were still alive, that the boy might be able to help him instead of wasting his time on a lost cause such as his. Not that that were possible. Just then the metal of the plane, the braces and struts that once held it all together, gave off some kind of screeching, wrenching, metal sound and no one could have survived that. He turned away and looking up at the sky closed his eyes, almost drifting off with the pain into sleep and hopefully, relief, when he felt the boy kneeling down beside him and cradling his head in his hands.

"Please, Pop. Please, let me help you."

"In a minute, son. In a minute you can help me all you want."

He was a good boy. No, a good man, and it wasn't his fault he looked so much like his father. Thank God for the difference, though. If not in appearance, then certainly in spirit. The boy wasn't going to run. Not like Thomas Morgan had when faced with a sorry situation. No matter how it was going to be, how unpleasant it might turn for the boy, he was going to stay.

They had managed to teach the boy well, Sadie and he. What was that about small favors? Taught him like they had taught Hilton, who if the war hadn't struck him down might be with them yet. Like Marilyn, who God love her, hadn't really run away, but ran toward what she thought important. And who knows? Perhaps she was right, though Raines couldn't see it.

"Pop, you've got to listen to me," the boy said. "It's either going to come down a bad storm or this field's going to catch on fire, and we'll burn to death out here."

"Okay, Tom Like I said, in a minute. Just let me die here and then you can take me home and let Sadie take care of the rest."

"You're not going to die."

"Yes. I am."

The words came with more difficulty now and he knew what he had just said was true and was surprised with how easy he was with that fact. The reward of a good and fruitful life. Though certainly not how he would have liked it to come. Yet, there it was. He thought then of Tom Ryan lying in his bed in Fort Lauderdale where the stroke had taken him, unable to play any part in his own death. Able only to lie there, all the power gone, and simply wait, unknowing, for what was to come. And here was another surprise—his own was a position he would not trade with his long-time friend.

And he said, "I sure would like to see old Tom and I'd damn sure like to see my wife. One more time."

The truth of this was too much and groaning as he felt another surge of blood and pain flow out of him, he closed his eyes.

"Goddammit, Pop," the boy shouted. "This isn't right."

The movement of his grandson standing up and leaving opened Raines eyes. Turning his body as carefully as he could against the pain, he watched as the boy ran in a sprint across the field to Prince, where reaching up with one hand he grabbed something from the saddle. Raines knew what it was before the boy turned back around and he saw it in his grandson's hand: the old Army .45 Raines carried in a holster strapped to the saddle horn. In case of contingencies such as dangerous snakes and other varmints and that was rarely used. For just a second he thought perhaps the boy planned to put him out of his misery. But in the next instant he realized the boy's intentions. Not wanting that to happen he tried to sit up, fell back down, and said as loud as he could, "No, Tommy. No."

Did he say it loud enough to do any good? And saw that he had not—that the boy would not be stopped.

"Goddamn you horse!" the boy shouted as he ran toward Booger, who in his usual manner after something terrible of his own doing had just occurred, was grazing peacefully on the edge of the field. "Goddamn you!"

The horse lifted his head at the sudden commotion so close at hand. But the boy was on him by then and just as Booger went to shy away, to run, to escape an unnecessary fate, the boy shot him, twice, in rapid succession, both times in the head, the horse crumpling on all fours to his knees before falling over on his side as the crack of the two shots drifted away on the field, much like the thunder from the coming storm had before any of what had happened.

That was too bad. Raines couldn't maintain his sideways position any longer and rolled over so that he looked up into the cloudy skies. About the horse. Yes, that was too bad.

"Listen," Raines said, and thankfully the boy had heard him, was back at his side, one hand still clutching the .45, the blue of the barrel well oiled and gleaming in the light allowed through the gray clouds, his grandson's other hand cradling Raines head again as he bent to hear. "About my father."

"Not now, Pop," the boy hushed him. "I killed that sonofabitch and now I'm going to take you home."

"Listen to me, Tommy. It's important. What he told me that day. I want you to remember."

And though he knew that, yes, it was important, the pain had another idea. He could feel it rise up inside of him again, hard and strong and not to be denied. What he had to tell the boy would have to wait for one minute more. John Raines closed his eyes and let it take him it where it would.

# Epilogue

Forty years later to the day the boy, now a man, sat in a waterside bar down the street from where he lived, drinking a bourbon and water in honor of his grandfather as the sun set over the river in front of him

Thomas Morgan's life—since carrying his grandfather, tied across Prince's back, home—had not gone as he and John Raines had discussed that day. Law school had not happened. Nor had working as one of Cecil's cow hunters on the ranch.

And that was quite all right. From what his grandfather had told him more than once, his life hadn't always gone as he thought he would. Either way, Raines usually added when this topic was discussed, for better or worse it had been a good life. Full of joy, and tragedy, that eternal balance as most of God's creatures were prone to experience. If they were lucky.

If that were the case, Morgan thought that afternoon as he sipped carefully at his drink, then he had been lucky. For his life—stretching from the Florida scrub to the halls of the University of Florida, and from there, after an early exit, somehow to the redwood forests of northern California, where after marrying a woman he met one morning in a coffee house in San Francisco, his daughter was born—had been good. For a little while, at least. When he was a young man and it seemed everything lay in front of him

Though, he was to learn it would not always be good days. Not after that fatal move to the wilderness islands of the Gulf Coast of Florida. Where, in a series of random events he hadn't figured out to this day, he managed to lose both wife and daughter.

Still, all of those days had somehow led him to where he was now: sitting in a bar on a warm, humid afternoon, having a drink in honor of his grandfather as the river, where he made his living, flowed north, unmindful of the humans who made use of it. The past—when he bothered to think about it on the rare, lonely night when he sat in the quiet of his darkened house feeling sorry for himself—might have beaten him down at times but it had not broken him

For he was still alive. And if living—and again as his grandfather also liked to say—then there was a chance.

He heard someone shouting out on the docks behind the bar. Looking up from his drink Morgan saw a woman coming up the planks, yelling over her shoulder at a man on the deck of a boat tied up at one of the slips. Giving the man an angry wave over her head the woman stomped into the bar and sat down on a stool across from Morgan.

She wasn't bad looking, Morgan thought, as he ordered another drink. A little thin, maybe, but her long, sort of wild, blonde hair framing an aquiline face, made up for that. That, and vivid—made even more vivid perhaps by the anger in her—blue eyes. She was younger than him, by a good twenty years, that was plain to see. Which could mean something if he was interested. Which he wasn't.

Seeing him staring at her the woman said, "What the hell you looking at?"

"Damned if I know," Morgan told her.

He wondered, as he stood up with his drink in a plastic go cup and went to leave, if he would find out.

"What's your hurry?" the woman asked.

Being still alive, instead of leaving, Morgan took his drink and sat down next to the woman.

Yes, he was alive. Willing to find out what came next.

# About the Author

Gene Lee, has been writing fiction and poetry since he was a teenager. A third generation Florida native his fiction is derived from family history. His poems have been published in various anthologies and small literary quarterlies, such as *The Cathartic*, The *South Florida Poetry Review, The Kerouac Review* and others. His short stories have appeared in Sporting Classics magazine and Grays Sporting Journal. *Raines in the Day* is the second installment in the Raines Family trilogy. The first book in this trilogy, *Men Without Hate,* was published by All Things That Matter Press in September of 2018. Mr. Lee currently lives with his wife in Sebastian, FL. An avid sportsman he enjoys wing shooting and fly-fishing and has done so all over the country. At present he in the process of developing the further stories of the Raines family, and expects this to keep him busy for the next several years. His website can be reached at geneleeauthor.com.

**ALL THINGS THAT MATTER PRESS**


FOR MORE INFORMATION ON TITLES AVAILABLE FROM
ALL THINGS THAT MATTER PRESS, GO TO
http://allthingsthatmatterpress.com
or contact us at
allthingsthatmatterpress@gmail.com

**If you enjoyed this book, please post a review on Amazon.com and
your favorite social media sites.
Thank you!**